GRYPHON IN LIGHT

KELVREN'S SAGA
BOOK ONE

MERCEDES LACKEY AND
LARRY DIXON

DAW BOOKS
New York

Jacket illustration by Jody A. Lee

Jacket design by Adam Auerbach

Edited by Betsy Wollheim

DAW Book Collectors No. 1940

DAW Books
An imprint of Astra Publishing House
dawbooks.com
DAW Books and its logo are registered trademarks
of Astra Publishing House

Printed in the United States of America

Library of Congress Cataloging-in-Publication Data

Names: Lackey, Mercedes, author. | Dixon, Larry, 1966- author.
Title: Gryphon in light / Mercedes Lackey and Larry Dixon.
Description: First edition. | New York : DAW Books, 2023. |
Series: Kelvren's Saga ; book 1
Identifiers: LCCN 2023013185 (print) | LCCN 2023013186 (ebook) |
ISBN 9780756414481 (hardcover) | ISBN 9780756414498 (ebook)
Subjects: LCGFT: Fantasy fiction. | Novels.
Classification: LCC PS3562.A246 G79 2023 (print) |
LCC PS3562.A246 (ebook) | DDC 813/.54--dc23/eng/2030330
LC record available at https://lccn.loc.gov/2023013185
LC ebook record available at https://lccn.loc.gov/2023013186

First edition: July 2023
10 9 8 7 6 5 4 3 2 1

Dedication:
To Josh Starr, the unsung hero

PROLOGUE

Valdemar has weathered the Mage Storms, and all the nations and peoples of Velgarth work to stabilize in the aftermath. In the north of Valdemar, Darian and his compatriots have returned from their quest to find Darian's parents. Errold's Grove, Kelmskeep, and the newest Hawkbrothers Vale, k'Valdemar, forge ahead alongside the western refugees, while in the east, ancient Iftel has opened its borders for the first time, and to the east and south, Hardorn and Karse are no longer the threats they once were.

The trouble now, though, is from within. A trade baron named Farragur Elm and a coalition of major tradesmen, distributors, and warehousers have seized all resources in the vicinity of Deedun and created a putative secessionist movement, using the entire—stolen—livelihoods of the region's workers as leverage. The strong arm of the plan is a mercenary force, once under Haven's pay, hired over to Elm's side. The Crown has sent Heralds, Guard regulars, and Cavalry to test the situation. And k'Valdemar—sent gryphons. Or rather, *a* gryphon.

Kelvren. The Brave. Or at least, that is what he likes to call himself . . .

Second Guard Hallock Stavern fought toward consciousness, only to find that his eyes had been glued shut.

There was a feeling that he knew was pain, but it was of such magnitude that it was not a part of him—instead, he was just a bit of flotsam tossed around on its churning flow. Hallock felt only a sickening detachment. His awareness of his body extended as far as knowing he had limbs—two legs, yes, and arms—two of them. Breathing created a heaving pull of muscle that seemed to roll upward and never recede quite as much in return. Moving his hands was no more productive, because Hallock's body seemed to be restrained by a web of thick syrup. At least that was how it felt, insofar as he could feel anything with certainty. He couldn't move by his own volition, but as best he could tell he was moving. Carried—that must be it. He was being carried.

Hallock moved his head to the left and right, feeling wet webbing restricting the sway of his head and neck. The viscous glue that held his eyes shut cracked, apparently dry at the edges, but then returned to pool in his eyes, dimming what little he saw. His right eyelid reluctantly slit open enough for Hallock to perceive a lurching view of sky and trees. Vertigo made them spin around him.

That wholly unwelcome vision provided enough added disorientation that he gave up on consciousness as a place of residence. For an unknown amount of time, he would only be an occasional visitor there.

Hallock found awareness and memory returning in sporadic fits. There were recollections of the skirmish, the fallback, and the formation for retreat. Then, the peculiar memory of falling to the ground, watching an arrow fall with him. That much he remembered, as clear as remembering his last birthday or his daily sword drills. In memory, he was on a dapple-gray stallion named Dughan. Hallock had been yelling a break order to his company third, and then he found himself spinning sideways. He hadn't intended to. As the ground came up to meet his face, he remembered seeing a great war arrow dropping along with him. Its bladed tip was as long as his own sword hand, barbed in well-cut triangular serrations, and it was trailing a line of slow-falling blood. He struck the earth, left shoulder first, then rolled to his side and onto his back. He remembered seeing a riderless horse churning the earth to run away. His vision narrowed in from all sides and that was the end of the memory.

Then there was the vague memory of jostling and trees, and the unsettling vertigo, and being carried. Then—nothing for what could have been weeks.

When Hallock regained awareness of his own being, it was from feeling his eyes being prodded at. There was a voice, murmuring a reassurance in Valdemaran. It didn't register just yet what the specific words were. Even though that sensation of tremendous full-body disorientation was still present, he knew someone was messing about with his eyes, and that was truly annoying. He hazily realized that the clinging goo that had blocked his vision had been congealed blood, and plenty of it. He lifted his right hand to swat the offending "help" away, but his arm didn't respond as expected. There was a movement, to be sure, but his hand might have been waving a baton in front of the Company Chorus, as far as he could tell.

"Just stay still until I get you cleaned up, sir," the voice insisted, and Hallock felt his arm being put at his side. There, at last, was a point of reference. A nudge of his left hand against his hip confirmed that it was in a similar position. Left leg— kick. Not quite. More of a twitch.

"Sir, you aren't helping," the voice snapped, with clear exasperation.

"Is he giving you trouble, Birce?" another voice called out from afar.

"I've had worse," the voice responded close by Hallock's face. "I've had to patch up Heralds before. They think they're ready for action with two broken legs and a hangover. This one's just twitching right now because he had his bell rung, I think. Could you come over here for a look?"

There was still a surreal element in all of this. Reason told him that he was hurt and being attended by Healers, but to Hallock it felt like it was happening to someone else. He was aware he was alive and that things were not right. There was something where pain should have been, pain that somehow didn't hurt him as much as it filtered out anything in his mind that made normal sense. Fear, logic, or linear thought were immaterial. Time was just an unneeded detail, discarded in favor of a floaty haze.

Hallock sucked in a deep breath and had an inexplicable sensation that he couldn't exhale as much as he'd drawn in. His forehead felt the size of a horse regiment, and it throbbed like a regiment's hoofbeats with his pulse. The sensation of pressure was relentless, in his lungs and in his head. The Healer attending him held a glass vial to his crusted lips and poured a syrup into his mouth, which somehow absorbed into his tongue and throat and never got any fur—

Hallock surged upward in a cry of pain, very much awake. Full consciousness rushed in. To say that he suddenly "hurt" would be like saying that Lake Evendim was "damp." His eyes came open suddenly, and he found himself on a cot, looking up at stained and patched canvas strung with cords holding dozens of bright oil lamps. Clots of blood, still stuck to his eyelashes, blotted out most details. The dozens of slightly different shadows cast by the individual lamps complicated the view further, mixed with the dazzle from the pain. Hands pushed him back onto the cot even as he already felt himself falling backward, and the two healers in attendance were practically screaming at him to calm down. Hallock realized that they were screaming to be heard over his own howls of pain, and pulled himself together enough to lower his utterances down to a series of groans.

"Sir . . . sir, I'm going to give you something for your pain," the one apparently named Birce told him as he propped his head up from the cot. "Stavern, right? Second Officer Stavern? I had to get you awake and cleaned up first, I'm sorry. I know that was unpleasant. Things will be better. I'm Senior Healer Birce Bedrin. Drink this." *Birce. I know that name. Birce Bedrin.*

Birce Bedrin, heavyset but clearly strong, was not in the best of shape himself; his own neck and temple had small bandages, and several uncovered abrasions and bruises graced his businesslike midlands features. His accent was upper-class Haven, but this was obviously a man who was unafraid to be in the thick of mud and muck to do a job.

"Just—" Hallock began, then grimaced as a cupful of some cold, thick, and lumpy juice laced with something tasting of charred bark was all but poured down his throat. "Just get me an officer in here to report."

"Soon, sir. Sorry about the taste. Devon's going to get someone for you as soon as he can. Devon?" Birce looked around to find the only other man in the spacious tent. "Devon, the Second here needs an officer from his unit."

"Sixteenth Regiment, Third Company," Hallock murmured, and heard it repeated to the other man more loudly. Devon was thinner than Birce by half, with the swarthy skin of a far southerner, and hair as black as coal. Devon gave Birce a significant look, and the senior Healer excused himself, wiped his blood-caked hands on his Greens, and went to confer further at the tent entry. Devon nodded and left, flipping the tent flap aside with a hint of frustration.

What Hallock saw hanging from the tent flap filled his attention entirely, all pain and misery forgotten in a moment of dread. It was horrible to contemplate. And a wave of nausea swept him as he looked at it. Just a ribbon. Just a simple ribbon. But oh, not so simple after all. Just last week had found him walking with Genni under trees laden with fragrant white blossoms in the narrow presentation walk in front of the Guard house. Genni, with her lovely light brown eyes, and her dreams of the future and their children, had lovingly taunted him that they would grow old together as great-grandparents before he retired from the Guard.

He had known and trained with enough Healers to recognize what was tied to the tent's closure tab and what it meant. It was a loosely knotted yellow ribbon—one knot indicated "one patient."

And yellow, in Healer sorting code, meant "unlikely to survive."

A sullen-looking man in a Guard-blue undershirt and riding pants lurked around the tent's doorway as a light spattering of raindrops tapped at the stretched canvas of the tent. He wore a uniform cap with Support bars and looked as weary as if a horse had been riding him. He didn't give his name, but related a briefing from four respectful steps away that allowed Hallock to piece together the order of occurrences that had put him here in this isolated tent. The candlemark of steady medicinal fluids had made Hallock lucid enough to realize the impact of the past days' events.

Haven's Sixteenth Guard Regiment had been sent at point, with three companies of light horse and moderate support following a day behind, to reinforce Lord Breon's household troops after reports of a particularly nasty trade dispute. On the way there, the Herald who rode with the captain warned that the situation was bad enough that there was a possibility of encountering a full insurrection around Deedun. The word was that a former city magistrate named Farragur Elm had been propped up by twenty or more major trade barons and declared "Chancellor of Prosperity," a pompous title at best. He was reportedly already making declarations about a fledgling nation claiming independence from Haven, in the northwest of Valdemar. Secession was not forbidden in Valdemar, but this coup was apparently being built upon goods seized from honest tradesmen, expressly for the purpose of staging the secession. The illegality of that was clear, but what was clearer—and had brought the troops out—was news from Kelmskeep that entire villages had found their expected income cut out from under them. Entire taxpaying villages of loyal citizens, to be more specific.

When a Herald returned with word from Deedun that a mercenary force under contract to the Crown had been hired out from under Valdemar by this Chancellor, the Guard mobilized. When it was realized that the Herald was a circuit rider evicted from Deedun at swordpoint, the response from Haven took on an entirely different feel. This wasn't a trade dispute, it was an insurrection.

The problem with Hallock Stavern and his fellow Guards being dispatched to assist Lord Breon, though, was that Deedun was between Haven and Lord Breon's hold of Kelmskeep. The Terilee River ran as strong as ever on the eastern side of Deedun, and the only main route was the trade road north from Haven. This was, he'd suspected at the time, a testing mission to get a feel for the resolve of the insurrectionists' hired swords when they saw troops of some kind on the move toward them.

The Sixteenth Guard Regiment advanced to the brink of Pawta's Wood and found a double picket of professional mixed cavalry and three lines of war archers barring the road. The flurry of arrows that rained into the Valdemaran ranks confirmed that battlefield diplomacy was not an option. The closing assault that followed left no doubts about the resolve, or skill, of the mercenaries.

Hallock had gotten the retreat call from his captain and had been shouting out fallback orders to his Third when the first arrow from the initial volley had creased him across the forehead. That was the memory of the falling arrow.

A second arrow had pierced his left side between the belly muscles and his intestines. His Third had pulled him up onto his horse and led the rest of the company back toward Haven. The Sixteenth's relaying retreat was only barely quicker than the mercenaries chose to disrupt. As soon as a rout was apparent, the mercs held their attacks and went defensive in posture, finally pulling back to what their employers had evidently declared was their border. Mercifully for the Sixteenth, the mercs sent no clean-up units to finish off stragglers. Hallock and the other wounded were relegated to travois and stretchers for the remainder of the fallback. Individual Guard units had been scattered into the countryside and regrouped on the roadside south of the attack, some of them riding candlemarks to get there. Even now, they continued to straggle in to this improvised camp around a riverside mill town.

The clerk rubbed his eyes and begged off for some sleep. The patter of raindrops had increased in frequency, and it was plain even to Hallock that he wanted to get to his rack before getting soaked. Hallock was clearer of thought, but hadn't even realized his time perception was so badly altered by the juice he had been fed until he had been asked for dismissal three times. The Healer Birce guided the clerk out once Hallock had grunted an assent, then returned to answer a few questions before another draught. The explanations didn't make him feel any better.

"Healer Birce, isn't it? Mmm. Let me guess. Gut wound. Bleeder."

Birce nodded gently. "Yes, sir. You don't seem like the kind of patient who wants me to make it sound any better than it is."

"I'm a veteran, son. I know what a yellow ribbon is in Healer code. What's keeping me from being fixed?"

Birce rubbed his right hand, hard, and picked at his dark-stained nail beds. He paid a great deal of attention to his hands while finding adequate words. "It isn't that I am not skilled, sir. It's that I'm not Gifted, nor is anyone here. You've just had some wounds of a type that we don't have the ability to cure under the very best of circumstances. You were hit when you were already down, by another arrow, after the first one had creased your forehead and unhorsed you. In your belly, a couple of fingers' width below your stomach. It wasn't incurable, then, I don't think, because it was mostly in the belly muscle. But when you were dragged off the battlefield, the arrow was still pierced inside you. While you were carried, the serrations of the war point sawed away until . . . well . . . things degraded pretty quickly."

Birce held his hands apart, letting his explanation end there. "I'm an herb-and-knife Healer. I've sent word with the dispatch rider that a magical Healer is needed, someone with a Gift or spell or maybe some kind of obscure knowledge I just don't have. But whether Haven responds with anyone, or quickly enough, I cannot say." He folded his hands, wringing them twice before letting them be still. "In the meantime, I have drugs that can keep your pain down, your mind in the here-and-now, and keep you asleep when it's best for you."

As optimistic as the Healer tried to be, Hallock knew better than to think he had much of a chance of seeing Haven again. Or Genni. Or even too many more sunrises.

It was one of the worst thoughts to have as the last one before a helpless sleep. So he tried to chase it away with his next words to the Healer.

Hallock had much more to return to than just Haven, a point he tried to stress to Birce as he drank his medicine. When Birce turned his back to put the cup away, Hallock mustered up his voice of command. Midway through, he was all too aware of how it weakened and cracked.

"Healer, listen to me. I have a wife. We're going to have a family. I know you probably can't get me well enough for active duty again. I can accept that." Hallock paused for a breath, and there his stoic demeanor broke. "But at least keep me alive for her. At least keep me alive long enough to get back to Haven for Genni. She needs me."

Birce pursed his lips so tightly they turned pale. He resumed picking at his nails and then exhaled gustily. "Sleep now," was his answer. "I should know by the time you wake up how things will go. All right?"

Clearly Birce was not prepared to give him anything but blunt truth or silence. At least he was honest. There were worse things than honesty, especially on a battlefield, or the aftermath of a battle. Hallock couldn't find fault with the Healer, although in some ways he wished he could. What he wanted was to find something, someone, to blame, to rail at, to storm at, and of course there wasn't anyone.

It wasn't all right, but that was how it was. The oil lamps faded, and Hallock was in oblivion by the time Birce had even left the tent. His dreams were confused, but full of regret. Strange that there was no fear. Only regret.

———————————

Hallock heard a commotion outside, but it was as if it was far distant, and heard through a tube of parchment. Peaceful rest was hopeless. His sleep was a storm of memories of rain, uniforms, sunlight, brown eyes, smiles, horsemanship classes, weapons drills, war, falling, Genni, the arrows, spinning trees, and Haven. He wanted to stay in the initial oblivion the Healer's draught had put him in, and couldn't, but the drugs he had been given wouldn't let him be as awake as he wanted, either. Now some bastards outside were making more noise than a free beer festival full of cadets. Shouts and hoofbeats passed around his tent, followed by a group that must have been twice as many and the sound of wagon wheels.

The din was split by an inhuman and impossibly loud shriek, answered by expletives and sounds of breaking wood and bodies falling. He was shocked fully awake, sucking in a deep breath. He couldn't sit up, due to the bindings and stitching of his belly wound, but he did manage to edge up on his elbows little by little, only making the tent spin mildly in his vision. He tried to see through the slight gap in the tent flaps.

Birce's voice was raised in exasperation and anger, shouting as he passed outside the tent, "No! He cannot be moved to another tent, I strictly forbid it! You, come with me now . . ." and nothing more of that command was discernible to Hallock's thrumming ears.

More lucidity helped him take control of his limbs. He had been warned not to try to use his belly muscles for anything at all, but it was much easier said than done. Funny how you never noticed the way you used some muscles until they were hurt, and then it seemed as if you used them for everything.

Because, well, that was the way the universe went. Some of the gods, at least, must have a perverse sense of humor.

He knew that kind of shriek—a piercing, raspy blast from a strained, capacious throat driven by huge lungs. He recognized it—from Haven. From the Collegium.

Hallock heard Birce's voice calling for supplies and lamps, and then there was another bestial shriek that fell away into a rasping gurgle, then silence. A candlemark could have passed, or two, or half of one. It was impossible for Hallock to tell, but when the tent flaps were pulled back, he was still up on his elbows with his chin against his ribs. A throng of Guard regulars burst into the tent, and several of them stared at him for one surprised moment before dashing out, yelling for the Healer in charge. The ones remaining in the tent stammered apologies, apparently not realizing they had mud and fresh blood spattered across their uniforms, making them look as bad as the bedridden officer they stood before.

Devon pushed past them to get to Hallock and blurted, "Sir, there's something here, it's one of the—" then turned back to yell, "I'm asking him now!" to someone outside. "Sir, there's—"

A minor Guard officer appeared at the tent entry to interrupt the Healer and jabbered something to Devon quicker than the Healer could follow. Surprisingly, Devon smacked the soldier with an open palm on the cheek, and screamed, "Pull yourself together! Healer's orders!"

There were two heartbeats of absolute stunned silence from everyone except Devon, who just said, "Tell the Second what happened." The soldier composed himself and explained more slowly, and with significantly less vigor.

"What I was told was, the patrol found merc outriders, an' got spotted, an' the mercs chased 'em down. An' the patrol turned to make a stand, 'cause the mercs was faster. An' when th' mercs was closin' in, this thing jus' came screamin' out o'the sky an' tore inta th'mercs—killed'em, killed'em all! Th' mercs kept stabbin' an' hackin' at it an' it just wouldn't fall! An' when th' patrol came out from hidin', there was heads bit off, an' arms an' legs strewn 'round by th' bodies an' all! An' the thing spoke—spoke Valdemaran! Said it was an ally to the Crown an' then keeled over. Been delirious th' whole way—they jus' got it dragged back here on some farmer's wagon." He turned angry and jabbed a finger at Devon's chest. "Look! It's as may be that it's some weird ally, but I jus' saw the thing tear up the earth like a whirlwind an' slash at people what was tryin' ta help it.

Yer Healer Birce wants ta fix it up, that's his say, but I'm tellin' ya! You put the thing where ya' want but nowhere near me an' my Company!"

Annoyed, Hallock raised his voice. "Healer! Attend now!"

Devon blinked, stopping with his mouth open in his reply to the regular, and turned toward Hallock.

"You have a gryphon."

Devon nodded earnestly. "Yes, sir. And he's hurt pretty badly. Birce is trying to stabilize him, but he can't do it in the rain. We need somewhere to put him and it looks like we don't have anywhere but in here. Would you—"

"I've been around gryphons before. Permission granted," he replied, before the spinning of his vision grew to be too much for him. He drifted again.

Lucidity became intermittent after that, but he was aware of much talking and activity. His cot was moved against the wall of the tent by at least four people, he could tell, and the susurration of rain against canvas lulled him into true sleep.

Hallock awoke to an awful throbbing in his head again, and a burning ache in his gut. He groaned and clutched at his belly. It seemed as if the wind from last night's rainstorm had moved into the tent with him, slowly but rhythmically changing in magnitude. Strange, acrid, and earthy smells struck his nose. When he opened his eyes, Birce was leaning over him. The Healer was dressed in a green tunic far cleaner than the last one, except for what looked like parallel rips and brush-strokes of dark paint all down the front and sleeves. He was wiping his hands with a rag as he looked Hallock over. "Good morning, sir," he said gently. "Sir, just keep looking right at me. There was something that you said last night that I need to confirm with you. I need to be sure that it was not because of the influence of your medicine. You gave permission to share your tent with someone."

Hallock grunted the confirmation Birce wanted. The Healer nodded and remarked, "Not many people are brave enough to share their tent with a wounded gryphon." He laid his rag aside and offered his patient a cup of the dreadful but familiar drugged juice. "No one else wanted anything to do with him. Devon said you'd served with one before. In Haven."

Haven. Where Genni was, even now, not knowing at all that her husband had fallen. Genni with her bright smile and milky gauze scarves, always ready to help anyone she met—probably going about the market stalls hunting up a good length of dyed cloth for those crinkle-skirts she loved to make.

Hallock blinked himself free of his wife's memory and grunted once. "Haven. Collegium Guard. During the Storms, I was Master Levy's escort. There were two gryphons at Haven, with two of their young. They helped the Crown. Helped the Crown save us all. When Levy went to confer with them, I went along. Met them. They were like royalty. Dignified." After a pause to luxuriate in the melting away of his worst pain, he added, "They aren't animals. I'm not afraid of them."

"Candidly, sir, everyone else is. No surprise. Devon and I wound up closing an even dozen lacerations and a pretty serious puncture just among the crew that unloaded him from the wagon."

Hallock rolled his head sideways to get a look past the Healer. What he saw was huge, as large as a horse, but in sorry shape. Flattened against the oiled canvas floor of the tent was what might have been a gryphon of the same species as the nobles at Valdemar's Court, but precious little looked intact. Stains, smears, and pools of unnamed dark substances showed all around his trembling body, even after the Healers' meticulous cleaning regimen. Broad patches of feathers were sheared away, revealing whipstitched gashes and a bulging, packed wound in the gryphon's shoulder, with an exit wound in his upper back. Hemp rope was cut and knotted in clearly improvised splinting made from tent poles and greenwood, interrupted by clumps of broken and skewed chestnut feathers down the length of the right wing, which stretched to fill the rest of the tent. The gryphon's eyes were covered with towels, and more rope to hold them in place. His body heaved in a wheezing but labored rise and fall as he breathed.

Birce frowned, gazing at his bizarre patient. "He's been shot up, hacked at, lanced once, and I think he's been poisoned," the unhappy Healer continued, pausing to lick his lips, ". . . and . . . he won't be flying again. At least as far as I know. That right wing of his was turned all the way around, with bone showing, when I got him in here. I've tried irrigating, filling him up with nutrients and keeping him warm, but beyond that I am lost. His blood's alien to me. I don't know his anatomy. I couldn't do anything to help him except bind and stitch his more obvious wounds. He didn't offer any useful help when he was conscious. He's coming in and out, sometimes delirious or twitchy, other times wide awake. He claimed to be a leader of some kind, ally to Valdemar. I don't know much more than that except his name. Kelvren."

The gryphon muttered something unintelligible and the Healer left. There was quiet in the tent for a moment, but then the gryphon roused a little and spoke again. It didn't sound as if he was aware that there was someone else with him, more as if he was talking to himself.

"Fffirrresssong. He may be a peacock . . . but he can fixsss anything."

"Herrraldsss! Mussst know. Tell Herrraldsss . . . ssshow k'Valdemarrr I live."

"Hurrrtsss . . . Ssskandrranon would not crrry . . . ."

"Why issss it ssso darrrrk . . . ."

The candlemark after the Healer left on his rounds was punctuated by fitful starts, groans and growls from the stricken gryphon, as well as scores of cryptic declarations. Hallock made it a practice to occupy his mind by piecing the rantings together, but could make little of it. The name "Firesong" he knew; that was the white-haired shaych Adept that he had escorted Master Levy to see numerous times, and "peacock" was accurate enough. If a Herald was anywhere to be found, they'd be told every word, but Hallock had yet to see any white cloth that wasn't a bloodstained rag.

If only he had just a little more information, if only he had the ear of a Herald right now! Small wonder the two of them were together now. Both dying, both helpless to stop it.

The gryphon stank, and the insects were finding their way inside to him, despite the repelling quality of the lamp oil. It offended Hallock, but he mused that it spoke well of the pain-killer Birce had him on, if something so minor was even an issue.

All the time that Hallock's mind was not on the meandering speech of the gryphon he shared the tent with, it was on Genni and her little habits. He could see her at his side now, bringing him medicines and sitting with her palm on his forehead, singing popular songs or telling stories of the neighborhood children. He could see her curly brown hair falling down her cheek and neck, catching the sunlight through their dormer window. He could see her curling a few strands of hair around her fingers as she spoke of her sewing circle and the ceramics her sister had presented to the captain, hoping to catch the bachelor's eye.

Then the gryphon clacked his beak loudly and said with surprising clarity, "Am I prrrisssonerrr?"

Hallock blinked and glanced side to side without moving his head. The blinded gryphon flexed a foreleg, the uninjured right one, and popping sounds of torn floor canvas punctuated the question.

"No. You're a patient," Hallock ventured, and saw the gryphon's ears prick forward as far as the improvised hood would allow. "You're in Valdemar, in a Healer's tent. They say you were hurt defending the Crown's soldiers, and when you fell they dragged you here."

"Hurrrrh. Feel morrre like badly drrrresssed game than patient," the gryphon hissed, not commenting on the rescue story. "Can barrrely think. Need Healerrr. Trrrondi'irrrn. Darrr'ian needs to know I am herrre, and Brrreon and k'Valdemarrr . . . wherrre isss Herrrald?" He raised his head and whimpered, dropping down again as the strain unsettled the lance wound, repeating, "Wherrre isss Herrrald?" A good question that Hallock would very much have liked to have an answer to himself.

A question that almost broke his heart.

"I'm sorry. We don't have one. No one knows when a Herald will arrive here, or a better Healer." Hallock winced at his own choice of words. "Another Healer. The ones here are doing their best, but it would take the Gift to save us." That choice of words was no better.

"Sssave usss," the gryphon hissed, apparently clear of mind enough to read the implications in the Guard's ill-advised comment. "Ssso you are asss clossse to death asss I. Hurrrh. I could Heal . . . ssstudied long at the Vale. But I am ssso exhaussssted . . . ssso much pain, makess it harrrd to think." The gryphon unstuck his foreclaws from the flooring canvas and tested his range of movement. Another whimper of pain and labored breathing revealed he could at least raise his head with evident effort. "Can block sssome of the pain . . . ssssimple charrrm. You sssoldierrr?"

"Hallock Stavern. Guard officer, Haven, Second of Sixteenth Regiment. I serve under the captain," he explained, in case the gryphon didn't understand their command structure.

"And the captain enjoysss you therrre, I am sssurrre," the gryphon wheezed, apparently trying to make a joke, but falling flat in the delivery. "I am Kelvrrren, of k'Valdemarrr. Wingleaderrr . . . of all the grrryphons of the Vale." A spark of pride lit in his voice when proclaiming his title, but was snuffed out when he went on. "Sssscouting forrr Brrreon. I mussst rrreport beforrre it isss too late. Therrre isss no one elssse herrre to tell. You arrre a ssseniorrr offisssscerrr—you have a good memorrry? Or wrrrite?"

"Yes, but—you can't see. I could be an enemy soldier pretending so I can find out what you know."

The gryphon tucked his head down against his filthy and blood-encrusted breast-feathers, to pick with his talons at the eye-blocking towels and ropes that were evidently annoying him. "You arrre Hallock Ssstaverrrn. I can tell you ssspeak trrrue. Lisssten and rrrememberrr. Frrrom the forrrk of the white ssstrrream therrre is sssupply line, and camp of prrri-sonerrrs to the eassst of the ssstand of black oak. Sssixty-two trrroops have built an arrrow-nesssst therrre—but arrrc of firrre isss blocked by fallen oak to the norrrthwessst . . . ."

Kelvren's report was exhaustive and, apparently, exhausting. Winces of pain and pauses for deep, sucking breaths stopped the gryphon's forced speech every minute or two. Half a candlemark or more passed before he summoned up the last of his strength to finish the report. It was, indeed, crucial information, giving a literal overview of the insurgents' military might, ranges of influence and deployment, and unwatched vulnerabilities.

Hallock had always been an honest man, and now was no time to start lying. These reports the gryphon spoke of were important to Kelvren, and Hallock could not bear the thought of lying to the broken flier. His pain was building up again, and the throbbing of his lacerated forehead ramped up steadily the more they talked. "It may not matter, Kelvren. I am dying. Gut wound killing me. They have me on strong medicine. No one can Heal a gut wound without serious magic. I'm isolated in here because they don't think I'll recover, and it's a bad idea to put the dying with the savable."

The gryphon snorted in obvious derision. "Valdemarrransss arrre ssso ssstrrange. We would put all the wounded togetherrr ssso they would heal each otherrr'sss painsss. If not of the body, then of the sssoul. Pain sssharred isss pain halved."

"It isn't that . . . it isn't my own pain I fear. It's that I won't see Haven again. Or Genni . . . ."

"Genni. Yourrr mate . . . ?"

"Mate, yes. Wife. We call a mate a wife. We were going to have a family . . . a big family. Genni . . . so beautiful. I wish you could see her, the way I see her . . ."

"Ssso tell me . . . I have hearrd of Haven, wherrre the Great Ones arrre. Grrreatessst explorrrerrs of ourrr time, Adept mag-esss, herrroesss. We sssurrrvive thisss, we ssshould see them togetherrr, yesss, Hallock Ssstaverrrn? They ssstay at the Palassce, in their own prrrivate Vale. And you can ssshow me Haven'sss bessst decadenccccesss." The gryphon wheezed a chuckle, surprisingly humanlike. "Tell me what you love therrre. Tell me of yourrr mate. Yourrr wife."

Hallock smiled. The tragically, perhaps mortally wounded gryphon was so much in his humor like the two he had encountered in Haven. "Genni. She is so . . . so sweet. I don't know how to describe her, but I can tell you stories about her. I can tell you about why she makes me smile."

"Tell me, then. Ssshow me in wordsss . . . keep my mind on sssomething that won't hurrrt. Hurrrh, whoever put thisss on me will pay dearrrrly!"

"Birce probably thought you were like a falcon, that if you were in the dark, you'd be calmer. He meant well." The gryphon replied with a growl but seemed at least a little mollified. "Haven, with Genni. There was a day off, just last month, before autumn had set in. Autumn in Haven is cool and breezy, and even though winter is coming, everything smells like newness. Late summer is when the hedges in the Collegium come into second bloom. Color is everywhere in little splashes, and the vines flower over every archway."

Hallock found himself smiling as he spoke, staring up at the canvas as it rippled lightly in the breezes outside. "Genni can make everything you do every day seem new, too. There was a carter who served the Guard houses, with meat pies and breads. I ate what he brought almost every day, when on duty; we all did. Not great food but not bad either, but it kept us filled. Well. Genni and I were out, and I was carrying bags for her, because we were going to walk all the markets in Haven together. She makes these skirts and shawls, you see, with ribbons on the edges. Really complex interlaces that make checkers, then fall in these long fringes." Hallock warmed to the subject, putting in details that on some level he knew the gryphon couldn't possibly care about—but he was talking about Genni. Nothing was unimportant about Genni. "Maybe out of habit, because she would stop in and visit me while I was on duty, we swung toward the Guard house. The carter was on his rounds, as usual, and Genni said, "Let's get something to eat!" I must have looked like a toad spitting up a bug, the way she laughed! But she took my hand and pulled me there anyway."

"Genni walked right up and said, "I want today's special," and the fellow went behind the cart, opened up an oven, and handed her a basket. A whole basket! With a wink, just like that, no money or anything. She had set me up, my Genni! I remember looking back at the carter, who was laughing so hard as to raise the dead, while Genni led me off. The Guards at the Collegium gates waved us through, and she took me there right into the grounds, through those flowering arches. Birds were all around, singing and swooping around. Skeins of geese flew overhead, one after another, going south through that wide blue sky. She led me in to one of the side gardens next to the Bards' auditoriums, by the practice rooms. No one there but the groundsman. Then, the groundsman angled off toward us. Brought something to Genni in a brown cloth bundle that was just dripping wet. Genni hid it from me, just giggling away. Well, see, I pulled the groundsman aside then, while she looked at whatever her prize was. Worked a deal with him, and off he went."

"Genni sat down in the grass, just like that, and opened up the basket. There was crockery inside, from our own cupboard! She'd planned this long in advance! There were no dried-out pasties and cornbread in there, oh no. She laid out hot plates and roast duck, steamed carrots and sweet potatoes in honey glaze. She had sweet breads and salted butter, and when she unwrapped the bundle from the groundsman, I almost cried right there. A cold bottle of wine, from who knows what cellar, oh I can taste it now. And then, right then . . ."

Hallock sniffled, and tears ran down his temples as he lay there. "And then, in the practice rooms, the chorus started. Bards' chorale, practicing together . . . forty voices, if there was one of them, singing 'Light of Freedom's Majesty' in the old style. Genni poured the wine and the groundsman arrived then, with what I'd arranged . . . a bouquet of lilies, daisies, and bluebells from Companion's Field. And he said, 'I'll make sure you aren't disturbed,' and went away to the entry of the garden, to work. Genni . . . oh, Genni. We drank the wine and ate, and listened to the singing of the chorus echo off the walls of the Collegium and surround us. We traded jokes, and we kissed, and fed each other sweet breads. We were young and new again. It was a perfect day. A perfect day . . ."

Hallock couldn't say any more. His medicine had almost fully burned off. There was no rain outside, but a dull roar filled Hallock's perceptions like a storm was raging. Before long, the sound of the gryphon's breathing, growls, and wheezing grunts as he worried at the improvised hood were drowned out by the rush of Hallock's pounding heartbeat in his ears. He looked imploringly toward the gryphon and made eye contact with the raptorial gaze at the moment the shreds of the hood were pulled free. He flinched when he heard the gryphon shriek—a word. A Valdemaran word, Hallock realized, before another wave of agony shattered his senses.

"Healerrrr!" the gryphon shrieked.

The gryphon swung his head sideways and called the word again, extremely loudly. The huge predator's keening was impossibly loud. It made Hallock's head hurt so badly that a mace to the skull would have been a mercy to him. Pounding heartbeats passed beyond counting, and coherence left Hallock completely. This could be death, he thought. But wasn't death supposed to be peaceful?

Motes of orange starlight swam in the Guard's vision. A shadowy shape and disconcerting sounds of tortured crying and tearing cloth burst in on the crackle of red lightning taking over his vision and the pounding noise in his ears. Hallock closed his eyes, but they sprang open again of their own volition. The tent and lamps were spinning all around him, but seemed so distant as the sensation of falling manifested into tunnel vision. Spikes of pain wrenched him from oblivion. Something huge was pressing down on his belly, and his gut screamed agony anew. His head felt split open from so much pain, and yet strangely, warmth was spreading into him from his gut and forehead. There was the distant silhouette of a raptor's beak against shuddering, dancing lamplight—his last vision before dying?

To die in Valdemar, in service of his nation, would be a good death. For Crown and Country, he would die as a hero, who had fallen defending his own. His name would be cast in bronze and added to the Honor Columns of the Guard house. A good death, if it was indeed his time.

He numbly realized there was a presence beside him, as the sunlike, spreading oblivion engulfed him, pushing out the darkness. It could be an angel of the divine, or a spirit to guide him to the Havens above.

But no matter who or what it might be, he wished with all his heart that it was Genni at his side.

Hallock couldn't see anything, but like the last time he had found himself in this circumstance, the fact that he could think at all was proof that he was alive.

"The gryphon's resuscitated, Healer," he heard a woman say. "Soft tissue's mostly knitted, bone fractures are fused, overpressures are alleviated. What a mess. He looked like he fell hard on a sword factory."

Devon's voice chimed in from nearby. "Should have seen him when they brought him in."

The woman snorted and continued. "He won't be flying for a long time. Wings and those other weird organs of his will take specialty work I can't do. I sure couldn't do any more today anyway. The lance hit and the slashes weren't so bad, but the blood poisoning and bruising took a lot out of me. You lot owe me more than a few dinners and some especially good desserts! I'm glad we got here when we did."

Devon replied, "We're lucky the Skybolts came north as quickly as they did. I'll be honest with you—we were not at all prepared for what hit us. We all feel a lot better knowing mages, Heralds, and Gifted Healers are with us."

The woman yawned, agreeing. "Yeah. Lucky break all around. You did fine, though, and you were probably wise not to risk drugs with his metabolism. I can't imagine the agony he must have been in, just to move an inch, much less use spells. Glad I'm not an Empath or you'd be hauling me out of here in a bucket." There was a pause. "Listen, I have a concern. I'm going to check with our mages about it. The gryphon has no magic left in him that I can find."

Birce's voice replied to the unseen woman, from very near. "When I got here, he'd dragged himself to Stavern's side. I had to pull his claw off of Stavern's belly. I think he used all the magic he had left on whatever Healing spell he had."

"Could be. I know the tracework. The more precise a Healing spell, the less energy it needs, but that takes a lot of medical knowledge. A broad-use spell takes fifty times the energy as it tries all kinds of things to set a bad situation right. For all I know, he used a Summoning and got whatever spirit he brought here to Heal up your Guard."

There was a long pause in which no one said a word, as they mulled over the implications of that. In those moments, Hallock could hear the deep breathing of a gryphon somewhere nearby, steady and reliable. The woman finally said, "They live on magic—use it to fly—practically breathe it, so far as I've heard. I don't know what a total depletion will do for his long-term health, but for now, I think he'll pull through."

The blurry image of a concerned Birce suddenly loomed in Hallock's vision as the cold compress that covered his eyes was lifted away. The senior Healer was at his side and for once was in a clean uniform. "Sir? You're going to be all right. You've received Healing by magic, for all your conditions. We'll feed you as soon as we can and move you to another tent."

"No," Hallock croaked. "Thanks, but—no. Get me two company clerks and prop me up. I stay here. You just change the ribbon. I stay with Kelvren."

"Kelvren," he heard the woman say as she left the tent, still unseen. "Huh. Well. That explains it."

———

Candlemarks passed, during which Hallock got a bland but filling meal into him, got cleaned up and into fresh bedclothes, and made complete reports for the Herald on station to peruse. Despite the weariness he felt, he still could not get to sleep, and his sleep medicine sat untouched at his bedside. Finally he levered himself out of bed, stretching muscles that felt like they hadn't been used in years. Hunching down, then going to his knees beside the great beast's head, he spoke to the sleeping gryphon.

"Kelvren? Can you hear me?" He tried touching the feathered brow. It was the first time since Treyvan had brushed against him in Haven that he'd put palm to feathers on one of them.

A low growl came from the feathered hulk on the floor. "Rrrrh. Hussssh. You talk too much."

Hallock grinned, then sobered as he tried to find good enough words. He finally settled for the simplest.

"Kelvren . . . I owe you my life."

There was a long pause, and then the gryphon heaved a gusty sigh.

"Hurrrh. Had to be sssurrre . . . my rrreporrrt . . . got thrrrough."

Hallock responded gravely, "You could have used your Healing on your own wounds, then reported it yourself. You could have killed yourself just getting to me."

Kelvren lifted his head up with obvious effort and fixed his gaze on the human before him. His beak swayed, and his eyes dilated, then focused again. They seemed somehow darker than before, but Hallock knew with a certainty deep inside that the risk of death had passed this noble soul by for now.

"Perrrhapsss. But yourrr life . . . would have ended. You have yourrr Genni. And in a life . . . no one ssshould be alone . . . and no one ssshould have . . ."

The gryphon laid his head down and dozed contentedly, after murmuring four more words— ". . . only one . . . perfect day."

Darkwind k'Treva handed over a strip of paper. "Here's trouble."

Elspeth turned away from the Lord Marshal and read the paper's battlefield shorthand aloud. "Gryphon, male. Defended First Company Sixteenth. Wounded. Recovered from field. Initial aid bad. Disposition: gryphon near death, from attempt to heal Guard officer by spellwork. Healers unable to aid further." She frowned as she put that dispatch aside from the rest, and tapped her command baton thoughtfully on her chin. "We'd better tell Treyvan and Hydona."

"Mmm. You know how they are. Protective," Darkwind observed. He leaned forward against the most massive of the many strategic planning tables in the Haven palace. It held charts far more detailed than the great map inlaid on the wall in the main court room. "They'll be concerned. You remember those parental instincts of theirs from when we first met. With Jerven and Lytha getting older, they treat every other gryphon as clueless little fledglings to be herded about and taught not to fall into wells." He murmured to a page, who nodded and left immediately.

Less than half a candlemark passed before results.

"Unbarrr the way," a deep voice boomed from behind the double doors as palace guards hastily tried to open them. An imposing male gryphon shouldered into the room, causing the guards to stumble back as the heavy doors swung against them. Truth be told, Darkwind suspected he liked the feeling of people trying to get out of his way. And no wonder people did, considering both of the resident gryphons' reputations and relative power—and sheer presence. Treyvan had a wicked beak and formidable talons that were, at the moment, sheathed in wood and leather coverings to protect the Palace's floors. He was golden-brown, with shadings of pure metallic gold and darker sable, and golden eyes the size of fists. Completely aside from being a predator the size of a horse, Hydona alone could wither a tree just by staring at it, should the mood strike her, or restore it to life. Treyvan was smaller, just as powerful magically, but faster, stronger, and more direct in action. Together they put forth a presence in Haven felt in more ways than just the body heat they radiated. Treyvan's crested head flicked side to side, then homed in on the main table and its dozen or so planners and pages. "Who isss it?" he demanded, with no preamble.

Elspeth retrieved the dispatch slip and looked it over for any new clues she might have missed in the dozens of lines of code. She finally shrugged, holding the paper up. "It doesn't say. Dispatches can be annoyingly vague, I'm sorry. It's just how they are," she offered.

"And consscerrrned about all grrryphonsss isss how I am. No morrre than that?" Any excuses about field vagueness clearly did not placate the beast that stalked toward the largest planning table. Respected friend of the Crown or not, Treyvan had long ago established that he wasn't someone to obstruct, for any reason. Lesser commanders, analysts, and staff alike parted to make room. Elspeth handed over the dispatch, and Treyvan accepted it delicately with the tips of his talons.

"It might be from one of the Vales due west of there, but that would be more than a hundred miles. It wouldn't have any good reason to be in this region, would it? Maybe it got lost," a lieutenant suggested, but that only gained him a loud click of

Treyvan's beak snapping a warning. "He," Treyvan said sternly. "The grrryphon isss a 'he,' not an 'it,' sssoldierrr. Flesssh, bone, blood, beak," and he clacked his own for emphasis, making a sound like branches snapping, "talonsss," and he flicked up thumb and forefingers of his right "hand," causing subtle magical sparks to split off, "and mind asss sssharrrp asss any herrre." A nearby sergeant visibly winced, and tapped the lieutenant's shoulder. They made themselves scarce, each giving a weak salute to Elspeth before fleeing.

Darkwind snorted a barely suppressed laugh. "Another stellar triumph for inter-species diplomacy, Treyvan. Good work."

The gryphon Adept ground his beak and clicked it softly. "He ssstrrruck sssomething that annoyed me. I cannot abide usss being thought of asss lesss than yourrr equalsss. Hissstorrry ssshowsss that—" He growled.

Darkwind interrupted. "Maybe he thought of you all as something *more* than equals. You don't call an Avatar or sacred vision 'he' or 'she.' Unless you're very good friends. I'm sure he was just overwhelmed by the dazzling thought of—"

Elspeth rolled her eyes and sighed, giving a wave of reassurance to the staff as they backed off. The Lord Marshal raised a brow, then drifted to another table, shaking his head. A few adjuncts stayed. Elspeth snapped her fingers. "You two. Featherheads. Come visit my world," she said, and loudly tapped her baton on the map.

Treyvan loomed beside Darkwind and studied the map, twitching his massive wings a few times. "K'Valdemar Vale," Darkwind surmised, and tapped a fingertip on the map symbol. "He might be from there. Firesong's new roost. They're near Kelmskeep, they've got a wing of gryphons, and they're threatened by the land grab. Assuming Kelmskeep and k'Valdemar are on good terms, they may have gotten gryphons to fly scout. Bondbirds can only do so much. Range and stamina would all be bested by a healthy gryphon."

Elspeth folded her arms. "Yes. Well. It sounds like all aid available's been given to *him*—" she eyeballed Treyvan, "—and it's failing. We only have so many Heralds and Healers, and they're more concerned about the hundreds of troops digging in. I don't much like the news from the north." She reached out and tapped her baton against the largest of the table maps. "It's more delicate than you might first think. For reasons we still don't understand, these insurgent leaders feel justified in seizing power and using force. But if we go in and squash that dissent—militarily—we send a poor message to the rest of Valdemar."

"And allies, and rival states," Darkwind pointed out. "The famed free country of Valdemar, open to refugees and the oppressed—its population pounded into submission." He leafed through other dispatches, laying them out to approximately match their places of origin on the map. "But we have heard the Bell ring twice since this began. This situation cannot stand, but handling it poorly could do great long-term damage socially." If anyone was aware of things in the long term, it would be one of the Hawkbrothers.

"Socially, yes, but our agents report the situation began economically. We've just sent the Skybolts and what regulars we can spare. Turning in on ourselves, after so many outside threats—it doesn't feel right. The timing of it. I don't think we know enough about action at the front . . ." She trailed off, seeing Treyvan—pacing. His raptorial eyes, crystal-sharp, appeared to be focused on nothing in particular. "What is it?" she asked of him, while a clerk handed her a new stack of notes to be signed.

The gryphon turned his attention back to the others by the table, explaining for the adjuncts' benefit. "Therrre arrre many waysss forrr a grrryphon to die," he began, rolling his Rs and hissing the sibillants in the accent all gryphons bore when speaking Valdemaran. "Assside frrrom the usssual overrrcasssting risssksss, frrrom headachesss to unwanted combussstion, overrrworrrk of magerrry can lead to deadly maladiesss in grrryphonsss. It isss why we take sssuch carrre. The more unsssskilled the casssterrr, the morrre enerrrgy isss usssed forrr a ssspell. The ssspell purrrpossse—itsss dirrrective ssstrrructurrre—trrriesss many posssible sssolutionsss to compensssate forrr the lack of prrrecssisssion. Each attempt usssessss powerrr, and then demandsss morrre forrr the next attempt to begin. Without knowledge of the ssspecif—"

"The point?" Darkwind asked, cutting off what might have become one of Treyvan's infamous lectures on magic theory.

Treyvan shot Darkwind an indignant glance. "You humansss have lesss rrrisssk in magerrry becaussse you can live without it. We live by magic powerrr morrre than food and drrrink. It isss one of hundrrredsss of rrreasssonsss why even sscenturrriesss afterrr ourrr crrreation, we rrrequirrre trondi'irn forrr conssstant help jussst to sssurrrvive. We arrre sssusstained by the converrrsion of magical enerrrgy jussst to live, brrreathe, and move. If a grrryphon pushesss too farrr, vital sssystemsss will ceassse theirrr functionsss. Even looosssing too many featherrrsss can kill a grrryphon, becaussse we mussst collect the frrree-field, orrr asss Massssterrr Levy callsss it, parrrticulate magical enerrrgy thrrrough them into the featherrr corrresss, sssocketsss, and frrrom therrre into the interrrlassced sssysssstemsss of . . ."

"That point you were getting to, Treyvan?" Darkwind prompted again.

"Hurrrhhh. Frrree-field enerrrgy isss denssserrr sssincsse the Ssstorrrmsss, and ssso, easierrr to sssift frrrom the airrr. A grrryphon ssspellworrrkerrr, asss the dissspatch indicatesss thisss one isss, could heal himsssself, if he could heal anotherrr. But the changesss sssinssce the Ssstorrrmsss have made mossst of Valdemarrr—hazzzy. Like a fog, magically. And any . . . dozzzen . . . thingsss could be wrrrong, jussst frrrom indisssscrrriminate ssspellworrrk alone."

Darkwind nodded. "*Indi'ta kusk*, for example. *Tcha'ki'situsk*. In k'Leshyan, gryphon heavy injuries translate to 'ruins.' Most deep injuries cascade into worse bodily failures, and are ultimately lethal. If it is, say, a nullment ruin, *hirs'ka'usk*, then even what we consider 'normal' organs will falter as a result of the magic conversion organs waning."

"Small wonder our Healers are lost. Magical *organs*? Converters? More unpronounceable words?" Elspeth could only shrug. "We don't know who the gryphon is or what the injuries are, and we have a thousand other problems right now. What are we going to do about it?" Elspeth and Darkwind both glanced meaningfully at the gryphon Adept while stacks of fresh dispatches were handed over.

The gryphon narrowed his eyes. "If you don't do sssomething, I will."

"You probably should, sheyna," Darkwind answered bluntly, sensing an opportunity and taking it. "Consider yourself assigned. We're in deep right here. All of our heavy magic work is going to be stopping a very un-civil war. And if there are no objections, if you can go north, I want you to take writ of authority and your badges of rank with you, and help out up there. At least establish a teleson link if you get the chance. We are only getting so much back by Herald and courier. I'd like your eyes, and your power, up there. Your gryphon's your priority, but the rest—best discretion."

Treyvan nodded firmly, and let his hackles smooth down as he turned to exit. The two door guards he'd bullied through before flung open the doors as the gryphon closed in on them. Treyvan eyed each of them and paused—then rumbled, "Sssorrry about earlierrr," and stalked briskly down the hall.

In a word, Kelvren was miserable. The rain persisted, and the too-small tent he'd been allocated had long since fallen down over him. The tent poles had slanted forward to begin with, and when the wind picked up they'd fallen all the way. It left his rump and tail out in the rain, and the canvas of the tent draped over his head like a very soggy, ill-designed cloak's hood.

He'd managed to inch his hindquarters up enough that they weren't as badly in the rain, but that was it. The trouble was, he felt so heavy. Not lethargic, like he'd been drowsing in the sun. That was different. This was simply the feeling that his wings weighed too much, and that his muscles weren't up to the task of moving him. If he still had his teleson set he could call for help. He could have called for help before he was even wounded—but it was long lost back where his skirmish had taken place and was probably since crushed under horse hooves. Kelvren was a weak Mindspeaker to begin with. The teleson amplified what he was able to muster, and without it, he probably couldn't Mindspeak past his tail.

The Healer who had tended to him after he'd saved Hallock Stavern's life had long since departed to the front—and she hadn't known even the basics of gryphon anatomy. She'd confessed to Birce that she'd used draft-animal Healing techniques on him, in fact. The indignity of it! She'd better not tell *that* to anyone else or she'd have Silver Gryphon Kelvren to answer to. And she didn't want *that*, he told himself.

His secret bravado was fading away with every minute of this storm. He feared some sort of awful infection from his wounds was causing his inertia. The day seemed hopeless, and tomorrow he'd be weaker still. He could feel it. *This is no way for a hero to end.* He thought again about a famed tapestry picture he'd admired as a youth, back at the city of White Gryphon. It was many centuries old, of Skandranon, the Black Gryphon, wings spread, standing majestically atop Urtho's Tower with all the people of the Kaled'a'in looking up at him adoringly. The moon and stars shone behind the hero and made a halo around his body.

That, young Kelvren Skothkar had beamed, just days before joining the Silver Gryphons for training. *I want to be like that. I want to be a legend.*

It had seemed like it might work, too. He trained hard, and emulated the ancient hero in every way that he could—superb flier, vicious fighter, fine strategist, *stupendously* skilled lover— well, at least *he* thought so—and when the choice was to be bold or prudent, he went with bold. And reputation was vital— everyone knew who Skandranon Rashkae was in ancient times, even the dreaded enemies Ma'ar and the *makaar*. Kelvren didn't precisely boast, but he always made certain everyone knew who he was, and knew every deed. He knew he'd be a hero if he tried hard enough. A glorious legend!

Instead, he was like *this*. Mud splattered up onto his chin and breast-feathers from the constant rain splashing the soil in front of the tent. Miserable. There was constant, throbbing agony from his wounds. The whipstitching felt like a line of fire. No one was coming to help him, either. His friends at Kelmskeep and k'Valdemar had to be searching for him—but he was weak, and without a teleson he couldn't tell them where he was—and there were none with the soldiers, not a mage or a Herald or even a hedge-wizard, who could Mindspeak or send word. He was angry, and anger was turning into one of the things that kept him going. They didn't bring him enough food, for one thing. There was no one to come clean him, no one to see to his needs. No one to groom him. No one to *admire* him. All the basics of gryphon well-being were absent.

And he was stuck on the ground.

Murky as the sky was, he couldn't help but gaze up at it. A Tayledras proverb said, "When once you have tasted flight, you forever after walk the earth with your eyes turned skyward, for there you have been, and there you will ever long to return." Never before had it been so heartbreakingly true. If he had bothered to count the number of times he'd twitched his heavy wings, gathered up his shaky haunches to leap, and almost surged forward to flight—but stopped, knowing he couldn't—he would probably feel even worse.

He'd been on his feet earlier in the day, when the downpour ceased for a while. He'd shambled around through the underbrush and high grasses of the hillock they'd put him on. Well away from the troops, the townspeople, their homes, their goods, and their horses.

As if I'd eat the horses, anyway. Of course I wouldn't. Unless they were offered.

Someone down there had probably seen him eyeing the corral, too. He felt like someone was always looking his way. He saw no smiles when he caught the locals at it, either. It definitely did not fulfill the ever-so-vital requirement a gryphon had, to be admired. This was more like—well, it was what it was—being kept purposely at a distance. Twice today he'd felt an overwhelming emotional wave, like a sour crop forcing its way up, that he simply wasn't *wanted* here. He'd swayed on his feet then and sat down abruptly, cracking the bushes underneath him. It just didn't feel right to be like this. They had to know what he'd done for Hallock, and what he'd done for Valdemar—didn't they? Didn't that count for anything?

It counted for something. He just hadn't realized, when he was walked to the tent and given an uncooked pork haunch, just how true what they'd said was.

It's the least we can do.

Apparently, it was.

He'd been put out here, with pleasantries about having free space to roam around and no crowding. How diplomatic a way to tell him he'd been literally put out to pasture. It took an effort to even heave a sigh when he thought about it. He had belly cramps. He attributed them to the food, to the weather, and to his discontent. And, he *itched*. He felt like he was getting parasites under his feathers, and didn't have the spare strength to gnaw and scratch at them. And now, here he was—the brave skydancer—soaked, stuck, under a tarp, having a thoroughly unwanted mudbath.

It just couldn't get much worse, he thought, *except there is a Tayledras saying that thinking those words is the first sign that it will definitely get worse.*

There was so much noise from the rain and thunder that he didn't hear someone approach until they were close enough to startle him. He felt suddenly furious at himself that instead of lurching to his feet ready for a threat, he only flinched. His eyes must have looked especially intense as a result, because the boy who came toward him immediately backpedaled. The boy had on loose, heavily patched pants and over-large boots, and the rain sluiced off of his wide-brimmed—and also quite patched—sun hat. Right now the hat only seemed to serve as a way of directing rain down his back. He carried a sack in both hands that for all the world appeared to contain—and be completely covered in—mud. He looked about as gaunt as Kelvren felt, and his untanned skin had irregular patches of very dark brown, like the hide of a wild horse or domestic cow. It wasn't like anything Kel had seen before on a human. Then again, like seemingly everything else in this part of the world, the dark splotches could have just been caked mud.

"Sir Gryphon, sir? 'S time for your feeding. Is that all right, sir? You hungry?" The boy's voice was strained with fear, and the words were obviously forced out between nearly clenched teeth. In fact, those teeth chattered a little from the rain as the wind picked up. "Come to feed you? Sir?"

"Hurrrh, yesss, come. Clossserrr. I won't eat you. What did you brrring?" The insult the boy delivered was galling. Come to *feed* him, like he was some animal in a pen? Did they have any idea who he was? What he was? He tried to stand, but instead just felt pinned by the soaked canvas. "Thessse polesss fell down. Come help with them firrrssst."

The boy looked around for a dry place to put his load, and since there was none, he settled on a thick clump of tallgrass to cradle the sack. It was still in the rain, but out of the immediate muddy water. Hitching up his pants, he clumped through the sludge to the edge of the canvas, pulled it up, and met Kelvren's eyes full on. Up this close to a gryphon for apparently the first time, the boy looked like a squirrel who just that moment realized that the pretty shadow closing in on him was an owl. Ten heartbeats passed before the boy moved another inch.

At that precise moment between ten and eleven heartbeats, the canvas weakly arched over Kelvren's head collapsed completely from the weight of the rain on it, leaving only the curve of a muddy beak sticking out.

Kelvren closed his eyes and sighed. *From the miserable to the absurd. I did wonder*, the gryphon thought, *and now I know. It does get worse.*

Treyvan walked to the recital chamber Hydona was using as a classroom. The sunlight from the dormers glinted on seven knife blades and illuminated the swirls of dust from feathers and age stirred up by the belt-fed brass overhead fans and the wings of the three gryphons already in the room. Sixteen people, a few in Herald's Whites, were in a loose semicircle strewn with books, folios, and large multicolored drawings. They all seemed comfortable, propped up on dozens of mismatched pillows, and Hydona looked most comfortable of all, lying on her belly on a short stage. Behind her, the two gryphlets, Jerven and Lytha, were doing their best to hover without flapping their wings. The lift that gave gryphons their ability to fly was in their bones, and it was a discipline to try to hover solely by mental control without moving any air with wings. Lytha looked to be a prodigy, almost a yard from the floor, with all four feet dangling down as if she was held in midair like a boneless cat. Jerven only managed to get his forelegs and wings to stay up without too much effort. He held himself in place and cried out, "Rrrampant!" then used his new position as an opportunity to bat at his sister's tail more easily.

Treyvan swept in and told Jerven, "Leave yourrr sssisssterrr alone orrr I'll feed you to the Companionsss," reached out, and bumped Jerven with a wingtip. The gryphlet's wings snapped out straight from his sides, changing his center of balance in his partial levitation. He fell over backward, whistling high-pitched laughter, while his sister joined in—but she sounded smug.

"Tyrrrant," Hydona trilled as her mate approached. "Come to conquerrr?" she teased as Treyvan tapped beaks with her and then turned his head upside-down to accept an ear nibble. "You sssee, ssstudentss, you mussst be prrreparrred to maintain yourrr worrrk durrring any dissstrrraction." The seven knives she held suspended point-down in midair between the stage and the students didn't waver. In fact, it appeared that she paid no attention to the knives at all. "Thisss isss why you esssstablish sssolid anchorrr pointsss when beginning worrrk. Rrrelative posssitionsss mean rrrelative forrrssce. When you know the posssitionsss well, you can then consscentrrrate on what might affect thossse posssitionsss. Contrrrol isss in how you sssenssse the changesss in thossse posssitionsss and compensssate. Thisss isss why ssso many trrraditionsss ussse diagrrramsss and patterrrnsss in magic; they arrre waysss of trrracking posssitionsss asss powerrr isss moved and changed. In thisss way you can ussse finessse, and lesss powerrr, by accurrrate persssception. Morrre awarrrenesss meansss using lesss brrrute forssce."

"Unlesss you like brrrute forssce," Treyvan teased.

"Unlesss you have a mate that interrruptsss you conssstantly durrring yourrr prrractissce. Then brrrute forssce isss authorrrized, and you may ussse the knivesss on him," she replied in the same tone. Gryphlets cackled from behind her, and most of the students laughed outright.

"You wound me," Treyvan complained.

"I wisssh," Hydona replied, and chewed on his other ear. "But I need you arrround ssso I don't torrrment the ssstudentsss asss much. What isss wrrrong?" Her tone changed from mocking to concerned as she sat up on her haunches.

"An unknown grrryphon'sss been grrrounded, up norrrth,"

Treyvan admitted. "He isss at one of the sssupply line villag-esss but therrre isssn't anyone who knowsss what'sss wrrrong with him. Rrreportsss sssay he isss without magic, and not doing well."

"You ssshould go," Hydona answered immediately. Gryphlet heads popped up from behind the stage. "I'll sssee to yourrr ssstudentsss and herrrd thossse two without you forrr a while."

"Hurrrh. Arrre you sssurrre you want me away?" Treyvan prompted.

"You can go away asss long asss you need to, loverrr," Hy-dona purred, "becaussse I know who you'rrre coming back to."

The rain had finally let up to just a haze and the boy had gotten the tent back up while Kelvren wobbled away through the field to relieve himself. He limped back, wings dragging in the tall-grass, and crawled into the tent. The gryphon bumped a wing and dislodged one of the four poles doing so, but the boy quickly sloshed around to prop it back up. Kelvren was almost turned completely over onto his stronger side, trying to get to some of his worst itches with his beak or talons, when the boy said, "I'll get your food, sir. Just wait right there."

Kelvren openly growled.

"I'll be herrre. Why would I want to leave thisss palace?" The gryphon snorted. "All the sssilk tapessstrrriesss and dancss-ing girrrlsss arrre rrreason enough to ssstay."

"It's not so bad, sir, just depends what you compare it to. That's what I always tell myself." He returned with the sack and plopped it on the slightly less muddy tent floor.

"Not ssso bad? I am sssoaked to the bone. I can barrrely walk, I look terrrible, and I have beetlesss and twigsss underrr my wingsss. Do you underrrssstand? *Beetlesss and twigsss.*"

"Ticks, too, probably." The boy shrugged. He undid the knots on the sack and left it open like a feedbag in front of the gry-phon. "We get a lot of ticks around here. When it rains they climb as high as they can up on the grass." The boy took his hat off and shook it toward the outside—an exercise in futility if there ever was one, since the hat had so many open patches in the weave, he may as well have been wearing an angler's net on his head.

Kelvren itched all over again, thinking about the ticks. "Thanksss," he growled, but the boy must have thought he was referring to the food.

"Y'welcome sir. I have to wait for the sack when you're done, so please don't tear it up much. I don't have too many."

Kelvren nosed into the bag and tasted at it with an extended tongue. He hadn't expected prime cuts, but it looked and tasted as if he was getting the least wanted body parts from whatever animals they'd already butchered. There were a couple of knuckle joints and what looked like some backstrap from a—well, he wasn't sure. Could be pork. Could be horse. Could be deer. Could be tax collector. He hoped for horse. A short leg here, a few feet of entrails, six chicken feet, and a hoof. Well, that part was identifiable at least.

It might be best just to eat it all, without looking too closely.

The boy was as far back against the side of the tent as he could manage, knees folded up to his chest and hands holding the hat in front of him. He stared at the gryphon.

Kelvren pulled his face out of the sack and regarded the boy. "Don't be afrrraid," he said, blood dripping continuously off his beak.

"Yes, sir. No, sir. Not afraid, sir."

"Hurrrh," Kelvren growled, and got another few pounds of the stuff down his gullet. "Ssso. Why sssend you up herrre? What did you do wrrrong?" the gryphon asked. He was only half joking.

"Lot of the town figures you're really dangerous, sir. And they need all able bodies down there, but I don't really count so much, and some of the folk, they want to stay with what stock they've got left to 'em in case you went down there, you know, on a rampage or somethin'. Monsters always rampage, they said."

Kelvren narrowed his eyes and peered out of the tent, letting his mood smolder for a long while. "Alwaysss," he growled.

"That's what I'm told, sir."

"Ssso. I am a rrrampage-to-be, and they sssend a boy to brrring me food? You mussst be verrry brrrave."

"Not so brave, sir. I get the work no one else wants, and I go with it. Gets my mum and me a little coin. Privy needs cleared out, fence strung through swamp, cleanup after calving, I'm who they get. Like I say, isn't so bad depending what you compare it to. There's folk out there losin' limbs and eyes and all. I figure I'm doin' all right. An' if somethin' happened to me, they said they'd just get someone else, so it's all proper."

"You'rrre herrre becaussse they can do without you if I ate you, and you'rrre—content with that?"

The boy shrugged and smiled. "Not like I want to get eaten, sir, but if I did get all killed, I'd still have had a life. Been told I shouldn't have, enough times, I figure I'm lucky havin' even a short one." He pinched the edges of his hat, staring at the water drips that fell from it while Kelvren finished the remains in the bag. "It might not be such a bad thing, anyway. They say you go to a really nice place when you die, where everything's warm and pretty. It's supposed to be a place where folk really like you no matter what. You probably know how it is, bein' a monster and all. No one can really be welcome everywhere."

Kelvren nudged the bag a few inches sideways toward the boy. "Ssso I am learrrning."

The boy picked up the bag and knotted the cords. "An' anyhow, I have my mum, an' she's good to me no matter what, even now that all's this happened. She said we were just about to get rich, too, which woulda been nice. Still, all the army trouble can't go on forever." He wiped his bloodied hands on his trousers. "Uh—thanks for not tearing up the bag or eating me," he said cheerfully, and put his soggy hat back on.

"Any time," Kelvren replied, still mystified by the boy's logic.

The boy smiled and waved as he tromped out through the muddy field toward his town.

3

"This haze is . . . intolerable," Treyvan growled in Kaled'a'in, lashing his tail in anger. "I can't do any better with my distance viewing, and that Herald with that Farseeing Gift just left for the Deedun front. The Storms haven't so much made things unreliable as they've made them . . . hurrh . . . unfamiliar. This all would have worked five years ago and now it is giving us nothing. All we know is where the target is. And just a glimpse."

"Did the glimpse show you anything useful?" a small voice crooned from below Treyvan. The gryphon turned his hawk-like gaze down past his magic instruments to the hertasi in the vast room with him. The little lizard creature looked up at the gryphon with a wide-eyed but unafraid expression.

"Rrrhhh. A Change-Circle nearby a Valdemaran Guard camp. A gryphon body in a tent. Head down, wings flat." Treyvan pondered. "Signs of heavy injuries but tended to. Looked like far westerner, but he was no gryphon I know. I couldn't read an identifying radiant—" Treyvan snapped his head up suddenly. "No radiant aura, Pena. No distinctive life glow to mage-sight. No wonder it was so hard to find him. He wasn't shielded, there was just nothing there to shield. I was looking

39

for gryphon aura traits, but I must have passed him by a dozen times since he only came across as a common animal from such a search."

The hertasi looked alarmed. She obviously knew what that meant. "*Hirs'ka'usk* you think? He'll be dead soon," was all she could think of to say.

"We'll see about that," Treyvan growled, with an undertone of determination, and stalked to a massive cabinet. He reared up onto his haunches, laid both claws flat on the upper corners, and dug his thumb talons into the sockets in the trimwork. He twisted them and spoke, "*Hiskusk*," and the sound of long metal rods shifting and clanging into place sounded from inside. The cabinet unfolded. Mage-lights inside gleamed off of teleson sets, a massive leather and brass harness, steel fighting claws, a narrow breastplate, and more. Treyvan pulled out and shouldered on one side of the harness, while the hertasi rushed in to clip and buckle the other side of it. More hertasi rushed in after three sharp whistles from the gryphon, and preparations for a flight gained momentum quickly. Three telesons were wrapped and packed into a flat case, and at a nod from the gryphon, the fighting claws were packed as well. Treyvan called out instructions about what must be brought, and side pouches were stuffed with arcane materials and clipped to the harness. Before long, a swarm of the little lizards were readying him for flight and unlacing his talon sheaths. When Treyvan reached the outdoors, he shook his wings and tested the harness for fit. A pair of hertasi affixed his ornamental breastplate and cinched it tight, while another one added several more pouches to his flight harness. "Pena. That downed gryphon is going to need a trondi'irn. Get Whitebird ready for travel right now. Tell Hydona I am going north."

Pena, the senior hertasi, turned to her charges still inside. "Get Whitebird ready for travel right now. Tell Hydona that Treyvan and I are going north."

Treyvan gave Pena a look of disbelief, even as she turned to clamber into heavy insulated clothing. He opened his beak but was stopped short by the senior hertasi poking a stubby finger up at him. "You know how this works, Treyvan. If you need supplies, you can't stop mid-spell to go fetch them. You get caught up in your magic and you know it. You don't get fed enough, you get cranky. And if *you* got hurt, yourself, who would see to you?" Pena nodded firmly, slapped her tail once on the pavestones for emphasis, and pulled her hood and glass goggles on as they were handed to her by another hertasi scampering by. "Now just pay attention to where you fly and give me a smooth ride, understand?"

Hallock Stavern, leaning on a greenwood stick that was either a too-short crutch or a too-long cane, glared at the clerk in the tent with him, and stabbed a finger on the papers and palimpsests heaped on a table that was obviously once a door. It still had the handle and hinges. "Now, you listen to me. I want answers, son, and I want them now. Is help coming from anywhere for the gryphon? Anyone, anywhere? I've got the rank to push you into Karse in your shorts if you so much as—"

The clerk held up a hand, looked up at the officer, and snapped completely. "No, you listen to me, you overbearing bastard. The dispatches were sent and there is nothing new from Haven. Nothing. *Nothing.* You understand? Look at this." He slammed his ink-stained hands on the stacks of documents. "This is what I have to deal with. Every bleeding soul in this camp, and three other camps, want messages, and they're all demanding them of me. Send me to Karse *naked* if you want. Please! It will get me out of here. But until you get twenty more clerks to replace me, you will damned well wait like everyone else! Sir!"

Hallock rocked back slowly. He narrowed his eyes and crossed his arms, as the clerk sat down. After a long moment he replied, "I should damn well promote you for talking to me like that, son."

"There's no need to wish a curse on me, sir," the clerk replied. "I know what the gryphon did for you. We all do. But no news is no news. When I know something, there'll be a runner sent for you."

Hallock frowned but had to accept it. "I'll be making the rounds of wounded, then. But I'll come back. Good luck."

The clerk didn't even look up as he resumed scrawling notes on teetering piles of papers. "Same to you, sir."

Hallock caught himself rubbing at the wide scar on his forehead, then hobbled his way out into the mess of the encampment. Woods had been cleared on either side of the main trade road, which had become the main thoroughfare of a tent city— well, a city designed by a drunken mob, maybe. There were no straight lines to get anywhere, and tents clustered around every tree that was too heavy to clear cut. Ropework between those trees appeared to have been created by myopic giant spiders during fits of seizures, and anything from canvas to blankets had been strung up as shelter. The poor tinder gained from the smaller felled trees made the cookfires underneath the canopies smoke and struggle for life. The main local source for firewood was a nondescript sort of scrubby, scrawny bush with annoying short thorns. It grew all over for miles, except for a former Change-Circle at the edge of the camp. No one wanted to even set foot in that circle, though it was set perfectly atop a circular mound that probably had the best drainage, and view, of any of this mud-ridden swamp.

The most orderly part of the whole encampment was on either side of the wide road to the river's edge, where the grain mill was. The miller had moved in with family in town and volunteered his home as a command post. Most of the officer corps had settled into the mill tower, which was the tallest building for many miles around. The rooms above the grindstones served as operation planning rooms for security reasons. In truth, it was mainly because the rooms were warm, dry, and had fireplaces—some comfort despite the incessant grind of the millstones.

Hallock should technically be in there now, but the drone of the mill gave him a headache. So did the thick concentration of junior officers arguing tactics, where they tried to justify staying inside where they were "needed." *Most of the staff at the mill mean well, but they don't seem to understand: an army cannot be administrated—it must be led.* After the southern border wars, the turmoil of the Storms, and the strife the Change-Circles had brought, one leader after another had retired from service. Few command veterans had stayed in field service after all of that. Stavern's First, his commander of the Sixteenth Regiment, had been the most experienced field commander the Guard could send northward at the time. Hallock knew the protocols, as the woman's subordinate, but he hadn't known her well. She'd fallen when Hallock had. The morning that he'd been cut loose from the Healer's tent and the yellow ribbon removed from it, he'd heard the horns sounding the mourning notes. She had been buried already.

And here he was.

A new stripe tacked on the sleeve.

A new ribbon under the badge.

Brevet promotion. First of the Sixteenth, Captain Hallock Stavern.

A senior officer, maybe, but still one of the regulars in his heart.

Filthy and unpleasant as the cantonment was, at least here he was with the Guard. He hadn't gained his previous rank by nepotism or bribery, he'd gained it by genuinely believing in what the Guard could be, and his soldiers knew. Just the fact that he was in the muck, waving off occasional offers for help, and took his time checking in on the units didn't go unnoticed. If he had to plod along on a crutch to see to the soldiers' well-being, rather than pass by in a driven carriage, then that's how it would be done, and the mill be damned.

He stopped in at one of the larger tents, an open-front, thirty-pole affair where cots and poorly strung hammocks were every one filled with the wounded. The most open section of the ill-set compound tent held a score of uniformed women and men with boiling pots of water, sorting rough buckets of more or less straight wood. Six of the ones in the hammocks were unconscious, but two were snoring, so that was a good sign. The ones awake were, healthily, complaining of officers and strategies. These twenty-some souls were the barely ambulatory Guard soldiers who were left over from most of the northern clashes. As was the Valdemaran tradition, if they weren't fit to ride or march, they had been put to work. Those that still had full use of their hands were engaged in basic fletching. All

Guards that were rated for field combat knew how to make arrows, bolts and spears of several types, of whatever native materials could be scrounged.

Supply trains were on the way from the south, and a wagon or two arrived every few candlemarks during the day. Proper, larger tents were being unloaded even now by a mix of the Guard and the local, but now largely unemployed, populace. Harvest crews would never come, so the large households that depended on them for their crops now faced hardship. The stalks and rushes from the grain harvests wouldn't be collected, and peddlers who sold the baskets and other wares made from them would have no goods, and so on down the line.

The locals were being compensated for their goods and work, but a government chit didn't change the fact that so soon after the terrors of the Storms, when hope was building up again, their livelihoods had been smashed.

Still, where there is life there is hope, he thought as he looked around the convalescents' tent. *And here I am alive to see it. And I'll see Haven again and walk its streets again with Genni.*

"First. Sir." The senior officer of the tent gave him a salute with her one unbandaged hand. Even that was unexpected; most decorum went out with the slop in places like this. "Good t'see y'back with us," she said, and it didn't take a genius to read the subtext.

"Thanks, Corporal. You being seen to well here?"

The obvious answer came right on cue. "Well as can be expected, sir." A couple of others chuckled—no matter what region you were from or what Valdemaran dialect you spoke, some answers are utterly predictable. Things sobered up quickly as she spoke her mind. "Whole thing's been a bit of a toss, honestly. It's not a proper deployment, we say, 'cause we're moving against, well. Our own really. Ain't a one of us feels right bein' here 'cause of moving on fellow Valdemarans. We ought not be fightin' our own. Sir." The senior enlisted man nearby coughed, trying to discreetly wave the corporal down from making some kind of blunder. She gave him a rude gesture with a few fingers. "'Ey, it's true. We talked 'bout it an' that's how we all lean. First's got the right t'know how we feel, even if we are stuck as gimps." She looked back to Hallock.

"Might be a black mark on m'record to say all that, sir, but just the same, I'd as soon not get promoted in the Guard over fightin' my own countrymen."

Hallock leaned a little less on his stick and eyed everyone there who'd meet his gaze. "It's not exactly treasonous to say this kind of thing, but it bends some regs. Someone with less ribbon than me might bust down hard on you over what you just said. So why tell *me* this, of all people?"

Hallock felt himself unexpectedly moved by the words that followed. Right here were all of his country's virtues summed up in a few minutes of hesitant confession. The corporal spoke up first.

"Because you're here, sir. I mean, we coulda writ it up, an' sent it all official. Or could've gotten a clerk t'pass it 'round in rumor-mail. But fact is, sir—" She hesitated, but then saw others nodding. "Fact is, sir, we get put off duty roster, there ain't much use for us. 'Cept as idle hands an' cot-warmers—but we ain't got idle minds, an' we're still Guard even if we get stuck off t'bleed-in-place." Another soldier grunted at that particularly derogatory term for convalescents.

"We told you, 'cause you came here to us. Not us to you. An' that means a bunch to us gimps."

Murmurs of agreement came from around the tent. A junior enlisted footman added, "You bein' so close to bein' one yerself, sir, we figured you'd understand better than the mill." The group nodded to that as well. "Isn't everyone gets magic-saved by a—" and he looked around for suggestions. "By one of those. Gods and spirits got t'have plans for you, sir. That kind of thing just doesn't happen to regular folk like us. We figure y'gotta be somethin' amazing for that t'happen."

Hallock steadied himself on his staff again, and licked his lips. "There is something amazing, at that, but I'll tell you what," he began. "We were under orders and got hit hard. A gryphon none of us had ever met struck out of the sky like a thunderbolt and near laid down his life to help Valdemaran soldiers just like me and you. Then he near killed himself just so I could get home to see my wife." He looked to each of them, completely holding their attention. "Every one of you here lost blood, bone, or tooth defending your fellow soldiers. You didn't even know their names, but you bled for 'em just the same, so they could get home to *their* families." He shook his head and leaned on his walking stick more heavily. "You're lookin' the wrong way here. You think *I'm* special because a fury shot out of the sky and fought to save Guard? To save *me*? Hell no." He paused for a few breaths, looking at each of them again. "*You're* all amazing because you're like *him*."

———————

Kelvren slept far longer than he'd intended, and it was a sleep with unsteady dreams. These dreams were more like sharp images that struck and faded like the pluck of a bowstring, leaving afterimages and the memories that spun off from them. The worst were ones of his body coming apart, splitting open from each of the wounds he'd suffered until he floundered, drowning, in a deep pool of all his blood. The other dreams were less grisly—there was sky in most of them, in the deep blue of chasing dawn, or the dazzling blaze of white only seen when emerging from one cloud toward another in the bright day. There was the view of the Londell River, and Lake Evendim, and the descent into Errold's Grove. Some memories were sexual—which was no unusual thing for a gryphon, especially him. He'd been on quite a few backs over the years. Skydancing, solicitous crooning, laughter, and intimate nibbling were well recalled. Then they'd fade away until another of those bowstring images shocked into his mind. His friends at k'Valdemar—Darian and Snowfire, and Steelmind and that insufferably enigmatic Firesong. And his trondi'irn, who made him feel so good and got him prepared so finely for his assignations—and then it was back to the sex dreams again.

"Sir? Time for your feeding, sir." The boy with the mottled skin was back, looking under the flap of the tent.

Kelvren rolled onto his belly, startled. He immediately regretted it, as he crushed his sheath. He yelped and then kept his eyes closed a while, seeing only dazzle.

"Sir? You all right? You made a funny noise."

Kelvren coughed twice and answered, "Funny forrr you.

Not ssso funny forrr me." He winced and slowly opened his eyes. "I may have brrroken sssomething I'll need laterrr. Urrrh. Food?" he asked, ears flicking forward. "Or isss it what you brrrought lassst time?"

"Uhm. It's not the, ah, exact same as last time. Some of it's new colors. And I brought some bread that didn't turn out right, but they didn't want me to tell you that. They figured, if you didn't know it was burned, you'd maybe think it was a treat."

Kelvren's eyes went to slits and he stood up on all fours, but kept his head down as he exited the tent. As he came out into full sun, despite the haze left from the heavy rain before, he swung his head to bear dead on the village.

"A trrreat. I am wearrry of thisss disssrrresspect. You. Boy. What isss yourrr name?"

"Boy. I mean, that's what most people say to call me, is Boy. My full name's Jefti Roald Dunwythie. The Roald part's named after the king, o'course. No relation. But like I say, most everyone here knows me as Boy. So I'll answer to that if you want."

"Hurrrh. Do you like being called Boy?" Kel asked.

"It's not as if I have to like it, sir. Boy's what they call me, so." At the gryphon's unblinking gaze, he finally admitted, "No, I don't much like it. My mum gave me a proper name, and if it's good enough for her, it should be good enough for anyone else. If things was right. But things ain't so perfect in this life. They are as they are."

Kelvren turned away. Half a minute passed before he returned his gaze to the young man. "Jefti Rrroald Dunwythie, if you learrrn nothing elssse frrrom me, I wisssh it to be thisss. Hold it clossse to yourrr hearrrt and never forrrget it. *It doesss not matterrr what otherrrsss call you, asss much asss it matterrrsss what you anssswerrr to.*" The gryphon limped away heavily, and stamped some tallgrass down on the other side of the tent for several minutes. He shook out his feathers, feeling renewed strength despite his restless innards. His anger and pain were transitioning into resolve, and a Plan. "And asss sssoon asss I am done making rrroom, we arrre going down therrre to get my next meal. If they *expect* a rrrampaging monssssterrr, they'll find out I am *not* that. They've ssseen me hurrrt and delirrriousss, but I ssswearrr to you—they'll neverrr forrrget what I am like when I am hungrrry, annoyed, and *deterrrmined*."

Kelvren set into the first part of his Plan. *Principles of magic*, he thought, *learned early on. Transmutation. Turn what is useless into what is usable.* He hobbled toward, and then past, his companion. *If I cannot preen for beauty, then I will preen for effect.* He laboriously groomed—badly—wincing several times from the persistent agony of his wounds. He took a few deep breaths and stared up at the sky when he was done. *If I am going out of this life,* he thought, *I am not going as a disrespected animal shoved away to rot. If I die, I am damned well going to do it with a full belly and the satisfaction of knowing I ruined some idiot's day.*

The gryphon limped around to face the young man. Bandages askew, feathers at all angles, and his stitches exposed, he looked to be in poor shape to anyone's eyes.

"Brrring yourr sssack, Jefti. Time forrr fun." Jefti did just that, crashing along through the tallgrass and brush to catch up. "Why arrre you ssso disssresspected that they give you the worrrssst jobsss?"

"It's my face, I think. I'm not any different from the other younglings here, 'cept my face."

"What isss wrrrong with yourrr fassce?" Kel asked, pausing ostensibly for Jefti to close in on him, but in reality, it was because he was having trouble moving well. His right-side haunch folded up on him and jarred his lanced shoulder badly, eliciting a short whine. "It looksss fine to me. You have good marrrkingsss."

"That's just it there, sir, these, uh, markings," he confirmed as he stopped beside the gryphon, pointing at the splotches that randomly covered his face. "People think my face is really ugly. They say it's 'cause my mum married a far southerner, and he had bad blood in him, an' so I came out like this, all ugly from both sides they say. And there's nothin' can be done about it, so I just do what I do." He hoisted the heavy bag up again.

"And yourrr fatherrr?"

"He died. He was one of the traveling harvesters, an' when

he was away up northwest, got crushed by one of those big carts, they said. Mum still hasn't gotten better after that. Anyway. He's in a better place now."

Kelvren levered himself up gingerly, mulling that over, then snorted at the flies pestering his wounds and resumed his trek. "I am . . . sssorrry you—hurrh!—have—*kah! sketi!*—lossst yourrr fatherrr," he said breathily, tripping on brush. "I have not ssseen mine in fifteen yearrrsss. We sssend messsagesss but—ah. It isss not the sssame as sssharrring sssky with him."

"Sky's prob'ly where my father is," Jefti smiled. "We always did like talking about birds, me and him, so's maybe he's a bird now. He'd like that a lot, 'cept I guess he couldn't get stew an' scrapings as a bird."

Kelvren could see that soldiers and villagers were taking notice of them as they closed the distance to the encampment. Kel angled toward a recently cut tree stump and suddenly fell against it.

"Sir? Master Kelvren, sir? What's wrong?" Jefti dropped the bag and crashed toward the gryphon. "You're bleedin' again, sir, an' that, uh, sewin' they did on you's torn up some. Sir?" He waved at the flies, to little effect, and then Kel could feel the boy's hand on his eartufts. "Sir? You hear me? Can I help? Sir?" He was sounding desperate.

Slowly Kelvren opened an eye toward Jefti. "Hurrrh. It isss— all forrr effect," he wheezed, and smiled as best he could. "Ssso brrrave. You rrrun towarrrd me when the rrressst of yourrr village would rrrun away."

"Well—I was scared, too!" he blurted, and then confessed, "I mean, if you—I—I'd be in a lot of trouble. Mayor said you were my problem now, an' I bet they'd whup me if you died." He pulled back his hand and wiped it on both of his eyes, under the brim of the sun hat. "It—I just don't want you t'die, all right? An', an', if y'need a healer, or somethin', I'll run an' get you a healer—" Jefti looked all around and saw a dozen Guard soldiers were headed their way at a brisk walk. "I, uh—I think maybe help's coming, sir?"

Kelvren rumbled softly. "Yesss. Ssso they arrre. Heh." He closed his eyes, to rest. "Let the gamesss begin."

Hallock heard a commotion from toward the town while walking around the last of the convalescents' tents. In a Guard encampment, it wasn't unusual to hear occasional incidents ranging from fist brawls to dirty-song competitions, or some poor soldier getting dressed down at top volume. This was the first one Hallock had heard, though, that began with shouting and running, and finally, laughter—and not all of it human. There was just that one loud, descending, burbling voice that mixed in with the rest, but it put Hallock into motion. Quickwalking with the stick in his hand, he rounded the mill road and followed it toward the sounds—which came from the main mess tents.

He saw a mix of backs in Guard uniforms and locals' work clothing, and then a flick of a large feathery wing above them. Then there was another ripple of laughter. He pushed his way forward, finally collaring a lieutenant to help him reach the center of it all.

There he found someone who appeared to be a town official, judging by his necklace. He was getting up off his knees, where apparently he'd been vomiting into a large sack—though on second thought, yes, it appeared he had been vomiting because his head had been *in* the sack. Now the man was coughing furiously into a handkerchief and attempting to wipe his face down. Some of his attendants were trying to calm down a few Sixteenth and Guard regulars who were still shouting and provoking the man.

Kelvren sagged sideways against a trestle table, with one wing slack on the ground and his bandages askew and seeping. The platter on the table was filling up. Soldiers brought their own bowls over to pinch off a bit of meat or bread and set it down on the platter. When they spoke something to Kelvren, the gryphon nodded or smiled—but even from this far away, Hallock could tell that the creature was exhausted. Kelvren reached for a bowl and some of the food on the platter, but his taloned hands shook too much to keep hold of the bowl. A strange-looking boy stuck close to the gryphon, and was there in an instant to catch the bowl and load it up with food.

"First!" someone called out, and the air filled with a mix of expletives, intakes of breath, and "Sir!" aimed nowhere in particular. All Firsts were captain in rank. Over a hundred Guard soldiers instantly *Weren't Involved And Were Doing Something Else When It Happened.* Whatever "it" might have been. Some soldiers saluted and then swiveled around in the mud to find who they were supposed to be directing their salutes at. "It's Stavern!" someone else called out, and then a small cheer followed. "Welcome back, sir!" called a junior rider, who jostled around the retreating official to reach Hallock. He saluted again, apparently just to make sure he'd been seen saluting at all, but he was also grinning. "Your gryphon friend there, well, we've just been taking care of him, sir. He wasn't getting treated too well, so, we just helped him out some." The rider shooed people out of the way to get Hallock over to Kelvren's side.

The gryphon swayed a little, and his eyes pinned and dilated several times as he recognized Hallock. "Ah! My fine frrriend Hallock Ssstaverrrn," he purred. "How isss the belly?"

"Feels tight."

"Hurrrh. Mine too. Thessse arrre good people, thessse sssoldierrss of yourrrsss. Know the value of a good meal." A couple of dozen chuckles from all around told Hallock that he was missing something.

"Kel, you look—"

"I know how I look," the gryphon growled threateningly, then mellowed the next moment.

"Then I hope you don't feel like you look."

Kelvren swallowed, twitching his ears and keeping his eyes closed as a bowlful of food went down his gullet. He sighed loudly and opened his eyes again to lock onto Hallock's own. "Well-known fact. Feeding a grrryphon isss good luck." He sighed. "Thisss *sssketi*-chunk therrre, the . . . what isss it called. Offissce warrrmerrr. That—" He indicated the retreating official and his staff, with his beak. "Ssseems he left orrrderrrs that I wasss to be given a sssack full a day of the ssscrrrapsss unfit forrr the ssstewpot. I took insssult." He swung his head around to indicate the soldiers in the mess tent with him, several of whom were still coming by to drop bits of their ration into what had become the gryphon's food tray. "Ssso in the ssspirrrit of equality between alliesss, I came herrre and sharrred the sssack with him. He looked well-fed, and ssso in the ssame ssspirit, added sssomething to the sssack himssself beforrre leaving, I think."

A couple more soldiers laughed outright, then stifled themselves at Hallock's withering look. The rider turned Hallock aside and whispered confidentially, "He was in awful shape when he came limping down, sir. An' we knew what he'd done for you, o'course. So when he asked so polite for help, well, we couldn't refuse. We brought 'im here to get 'im fed, an' sent word for the—well, anyway, things just went as they went. Some of the regulars, well, they crowded the mayor there and—"

"Mayor? That was the mayor?" Hallock sighed. He put up a hand to halt the explanation. "So some of you pulled the sack of—scrap—over the mayor's head."

"And pulled the ssstrrring," Kelvren finished with a hint of triumph. "Polisscy change wasss enacted immediately upon esscape from the feed bag."

Hallock frowned and asked, "Wait. Why would the mayor have anything to do with whether you got fed, anyway?"

The rider interrupted. "I know that one, sir. Guard feeds Guard, and buys meat and grain from whoever's nearest. The gryphon's a foreigner, so's when the accounting's done, the 'ospitality comes from the local senior diplomat. That's the mayor. I figure he thought the gryphon was gonna die soon anyhow, so why use the good meat he can sell to the Guard instead?"

Hallock nodded, and unhappily took in Kelvren's disheveled appearance. "I see. So. You. It was regulars that did it all, right?" The rider nodded. "You. There. Regular. It was horse that did it all, right?" The woman nodded. "All right, then. Clearly, there were no witnesses, and no laws or regulations provably broken." He waved a hand around loosely to dismiss the whole affair. "As you were." He angled in close by Kelvren, who reached up with a shaky taloned hand and pulled him close in against his head. Hallock was pressed against the gryphon's warm, feathered neck, cheek, and jaw.

"It wasssn't too much, Hallock Ssstaverrrn. I jussst—wanted

the sssame rrressspect of any Valdemarrran warrriorrr. Not . . .
hurrh, what would Darrrian sssay . . . the firrrst sssalt frrrom
the table." His stoic demeanor faltered. "Therrre'sss nobody
forrr me herrre."

Hallock squeezed a few of the neck feathers, each wider than
his spread hand. "I'm here, Kelvren. And believe me, there
are many here who admire you for what you've done for me."
Hallock saw that where the gryphon's feathers had been cut
away in clumps along his side and flanks, bandages had fallen
away, and seeping wounds glistened. "You have wounds coming open again, Kel, we need to get you out of here. You look
like you are in terrible pain."

Kel held him there for a few more heartbeats, then patted the
man's back before pulling back to meet eyes again. "A good
meal helpsss, and the goodwill of otherrrsss. And ssseeing
you, my good frrriend. What would Genni think of thisss day,
mmm?" The gryphon shifted his weight, flinched, and let the
wing he was trying to move lie where it was. "I do hurrrt, yesss.
And I need a plassce to ssstay. And to get clean."

The gryphon lowered his head to the table and let its weight
rest on the curve of his beak while he kept his eyes closed.
He sagged a little more with each breath. Hallock held out his
hand and rubbed the gryphon's mud-crusted brow ridge. "I
know somewhere you can stay, my friend. We'll take you there."

Kelvren lifted his head and looked sidelong at Hallock, with
a slight grin. "You know what I sssaid beforrre. Pain sharrred
isss . . . pain halved. I sharrred half of my pain with the
mayorrr . . . and I feel much betterrr now."

———————

Hallock gathered up a squad and they helped Kelvren trudge
from the mess tent through the cantonment, a pair under each
wing and one at each shoulder. Soldiers came out from almost every tent and watched the slow progression. Some came
over to ask if they could help—everyone seemed to know who
the creature was, or at least what he'd done. Jefti followed along,
looking worried each time the gryphon slipped or groaned.

When they passed one of the corrals, several horses pressed in closer to see what this curiosity was. "Why aren't they terrified?" one of the soldiers wondered. "He's a huge predator, shouldn't they be bolting?"

"We do not . . . ssscarrre mossst crrreaturrresss . . . unlesss we intend to. It isss . . . a peculiarrrity of usss," Kelvren wheezed. His exhaustion was showing, and he stopped to rest.

"You have a lot of those," Hallock teased. "Hoy, look. That dapple gray, that's Dughan, my mount when my forehead got redecorated."

Kel made an effort to look over, but still his head hung low.

Hallock tried to keep the gryphon's mood light. "I'm ordering that you be fed well. Some of the men were suggesting we make up a fake squad, to allocate the food for you. It's an idea with some merit—but I think I carry enough weight now to have you cared for outright." He spoke instructions to a runner and then sent her on her way ahead of them. When they arrived near the convalescents' tent Hallock had visited earlier, the sorting barrels had been pushed to the back and several cots had been folded and pushed aside. Nearly everyone was awake, and every eye was wide. Enlisted men spread out a canvas tarpaulin on the cleared space, and the squad gingerly guided the gryphon in. Kel all but collapsed on the spot and sprawled sideways onto his good—or rather, less injured—side, panting. An unhappy private, nearly pinned by the gryphon's fall, crawled out from under that side's wing.

"Healer Birce will be here soon," Hallock reassured Kelvren, kneeling down beside him. "Devon too, on his usual rounds. They'll fix up those plasters for you when they check everyone else." He waved over a folding stool and set it in front of Kel's beak, patting the canvas. "Here . . . a place for your head." He grunted, and lifted Kel's head to rest flatly upon it.

After a candlemark of reassuring talk and gawkers coming to see the beast that saved the captain, the Healers arrived to tend to all the self-named "gimps." In the hours that passed, a couple of dozen soldiers asked the captain if they could touch Kelvren, and after the first one scratched at his brow ridges for half an hour, Kel consented to all.

The cloud cover broke and Treyvan and Pena found themselves in searing sunlight. They'd made a short Gating to shorten their flight time, but then found themselves with a strong tailwind, and Treyvan calculated it'd be quicker to fly directly for as long as that lasted. Despite the desperate circumstances, Treyvan found himself feeling good about it. He hadn't been on a truly long flight since the return to Haven from the Plains. Now, feeling the sun on his back, the magic tingling through his feathers, watching the terrain roll on below, he exulted in the glory of flight.

:Pena,: he Mindspoke. *:You don't need a rest soon, do you? I have good thermals ahead.:*

:Oh no, you go on ahead. I'm thinking about new tunnels around the Collegium and the embassies, and where to tap a new hot spring. And where to set in a new baking oven.: Treyvan felt the hertasi pat his back. *:An idle mind is my workshop. But, Treyvan. Aren't we due to try another Gate attempt?:*

:Soon,: he replied. *:If I recall my maps right, we should be in range of a clean Gating within the candlemark. I'll try to anchor high up to correct for any targeting drift. We can fly the difference from there. I'll find us a good landmark by the main road, mark it with a lasting mage-light, and send word to Whitebird by teleson. We'll set an arrival time. When she gets there, I'll try another Gate to bring her in to where the gryphon is.:*

:Aren't you the clever one!: Pena chuckled in his mind.

:Just trying to keep up with you,: Treyvan answered, and laughed out loud as he soared higher.

Kelvren dozed off and on, as best his wounds would let him. The humans were given drugged drinks to reduce their pain, but Birce was not willing to risk mixing such stuff with a gryphon's unknown anatomy. It was very hard to get good rest when parts of your body were simply screaming at you and throbbed with every breath. Still—the attention, the full belly, and the company gave him new strength. When he was able to, he answered questions and shared scores of stories about his exploits and his people with dozens of eager listeners. He related the story of Hallock's Healing, but felt a pang of wistfulness when Hallock's wife Genni was brought up, because Kelvren was acutely aware he had no mate to go back to should he survive this. And by his age, he *should*.

The night swallowed up the sky, and he lost all track of time between naps. Most of the rest of the convalescents were asleep, their night dosages in full effect. He raised his head, looking up to the starry sky, seeded by sparks from the camp's fires. He whimpered softly.

This wasn't what Skandranon was like—he would never have been laid up with such injuries, wasting away. And they have to be looking for me—Darian and Firesong and the others, they must be able to send me help or bring me back. I know that great legends usually involve great funerals—but I don't want to die.

"Sir? Y'there, sir? You awake?" He heard Jefti's voice at his side and turned an eye that way without lifting his head. "Oh, good, you're awake. Sir, I, uh, my mum wanted to see you. I fetched her here." The young man waved someone in. A woman in trews and blouse carrying a large basket knelt beside him, and licked her lips.

"My lord gryphon," she said in a voice gentled down as if talking to a scared child, "Jefti's talked so much about you, I wanted to see you myself. You—" and she glanced at where Jefti stood back by Kel's flank, "—you've treated him well, better than most people ever have. I—wanted you to know it is appreciated. He's never really had many friends, and even then they didn't consider him an equal. But then here you are, this—wonder dropped into our lives—and you talk to him as a *person*. Not as a servant. You've done us a great honor."

Kel listened to every word and raised his chin up, then laid his head sideways. "The honorrr isss mine, Lady. . . ."

"Ammari. Not a Lady though, my lord gryphon. I am just a seamstress and artisan." She looked down at her hands when she said this. There was something in her tone that was deeply sad for a moment.

"Hurrrh. Jefti isss a brrrave—" and he paused, "I won't sssay 'boy.' But he isss brrrave. Sssmarrrt." He brought his head up and shifted his weight from his sideways slouch, which sent lightning-shots through his body from each stitch and scab. "Urrrh. Ssso. Welcome to my palassce."

Ammari pulled back the cloth cover from the basket and hesitantly pulled out a scrub brush. "Jefti said that—that you didn't look—uhm, that you needed some cleaning up. And he knew you were in pain. When he gets hurt he comes to me, so he thought if you were in pain—I should come to find *you*." She asked, apprehensively, "You won't bite me if I do this badly, will you?"

Kel smiled but took his time to answer. "Haven't the ssstrrrength to bite, Ammarrri. You have no fearrrsss frrrom me. But. You arrre herrre forrr morrre than tending to my filth." He glanced back to where Jefti was pinching and toying with the tattered feathertip of one of his primaries. "And it isss not jussst about him, isss it?"

Ammari swallowed and nodded to Kel. "It's—about both of us. I've never been like this before—I feel so lost, anymore. My husband—" She caught Kel's eye. He nodded. "You know, then? Jefti must have told you. I've been all alone with Jefti all this time, and we work so hard, but—when all of this happened, it just—it's just been too much for us. I've been trying to find work here at the camp—honorable work, I mean. But it's so hard." She reached out to Kelvren's face, but let her touch fall instead along his neck. His hackles looked black in the dim light. Flakes of dirt crumbled away off of feathers. "I'm sorry—words don't come easily about this. I feel selfish being here, when you're so badly hurt. But, with what happened—you're magic. And—magic does bad and good in this life, and you—you're good magic. Everyone talks about what you could do. What you did do. I don't know where else to turn, and Jefti thinks so much of you." Ammari pulled her hand back and wiped her eyes, where tears had welled up. "I just—is there any work I could do for you—is there anything you can do to help us?"

Kelvren let out a long, descending sigh and rested his head again. "Sssoldierrrsss have been coming herrre all day. My flessh isss brrroken, but my earrrsss arrre sssharrrp. They come to sssee the oddity—the thing that sssaved sssome of them. Sssome come in, want to touch featherrrsss orrr talonsss. They want to have sssome luck rrrub off on them. Hurrrh. Foolisssh—they want luck frrrom sssomeone who had all of *thisss* happen to him?" He snorted.

"Lord gryphon, *any* of those injuries would have killed a man. You survived how many? A dozen? Two? Cut, shot, stabbed, lanced through even? And still you can speak? Even walk?"

"Hurrrh. I am ssstill dying," Kelvren replied distastefully.

"Lord gryphon, we are *all* dying. But if you'll forgive me for being so bold, sir, until you are dead, you are still living."

Kelvren stayed silent for a while, and Ammari started brushing out feathers while Jefti picked away at the larger clumps of dirt around Kel's hindlegs. "You know, my husband would have loved to have been here with you. He loved birds and kept feathers when he found them out on his travels. Yours would be a prize, if you dropped one."

Kel looked sidelong at the woman.

"Jefti sssaid that you werrre about to be rrrich. What of that? Isssn't money what sssoothesss illsss in Valdemarrr?"

Ammari smiled a little—a flicker of pride, then the sadness again. "When the Change-Circle came—we—had just lost my husband. I was inconsolable. I ran into the circle in my grief. I just—clawed at the ground, crying out for someone to bring him back. Somehow. I knew there was magic there—else how could it have appeared?—but by morning, there was still no help. I clawed at the ground while I cried—I cried so much." She paused in her work. "When daylight came, I saw that my hands were—different. There was something in that soil that made my hands glimmer in the light." She resumed brushing. "My man was not back. But maybe he provided for us in his own way. I found a way to sift this from the soil and bind it, so that it would adhere to cloth and leather. No one but Jefti and I would go into the circle—so it remained ours alone. Almost all the money I had, I spent to buy the land the circle was in. I made jars and jars of my solution. And there it sits." She sighed. "Before all of this strife, traders were going to carry some to Haven, and Deedun, and—well, you understand. I staked all I had on a luxury item, and now no one wants it and no traders will come for it."

Kelvren rumbled a little and then asked, "Thisss—sssubssstanssce of yourrrss. Do you have any to ssshow me?" The glint of speculation was in his eyes.

Ammari set the brush down and brought out a kerchief from her blouse. Even in the meager light, it shone with an irridescence like oil on water in bright sunlight. Jefti beamed when he saw it. "My mum's special. She's smart. An' I helped with the makin' of the stuff."

Kel admired the cloth as Ammari twisted and turned it around, showing its shimmer. "And thisss—ssubssstanssce. Isss it expensssive? Doesss it poissson, or ssstink, or come off easssily? Doesss anyone elssse know of it?" He added, with a hint of shrewdness, "And doesss it bind to featherrrsss?"

4

By noon of the second day, Kelvren's plan was in motion. Through Hallock, he arranged the purchase of several jars of Ammari's mixture. It positively blazed in the full light of day. Small wonder she knew it would make her wealthy! With his guidance, several of the convalescents trimmed away particular stray and partial feathers from around his wounds, painted them with the bright substance, and set them aside to dry.

Transmutation, he thought. *Though I fade, I still have resources.* When he had time to rest, the pain actually sharpened his thoughts—it was only when he moved that it overwhelmed him completely. *I can turn what little we have into something important, whether I can fly—or even walk—again.* He *had* to be of use—he couldn't bear to slide off into oblivion meekly. So, then, what was there to do? Assuming he couldn't move, he had to somehow use what he was rather than what he could do. He was unique in the camp—an oddity. He had a reputation here, even a growing mystique.

The elements were there: the soldiers' superstitions about how he was good luck. A tent full of invalids making arrows.

And to bring it all together, Ammari's secret, beautiful mixture, that shone like—

Magic.

The history was told lovingly, in the way only someone who loved tales, and had actually experienced a part of them, could tell a story.

Far off to the west, there was a city made of hope and light. It was made to honor its people's savior, and named for him. White Gryphon was built of terraces and sweeping walkways carved from a white cliffside overlooking a perfect bay. In the centuries since its founding, its wings had gradually spread out around the bay, enfolding it as a loving protective bird would cover its nestlings from cold or rain. Its wings, in fact, truly did appear to be wings—canopies and promenades swept in complex curves on a massive scale, to outline individual feathers when seen from the sea and barrier islands. The city center was a huge complex of overlapping towers making the hackles, breast-feathers, and lower mandible. The highest and widest complex crested the whole of the city in a stylized beak, with its eyes and ears facing north. In summer, the sunrise cast the shadow of a raptor across the bay waters, and at noon the eyes of the beast were completely concealed by shadow. At sunset the water reflections shimmered upon the creation, and the sun's colors blazed upon it while the thousands of small lights and fires came up one by one to greet the stars for the oncoming night.

To the immediate east was the more conventional side of the city, which had sprawled out as more housing, workshops, and trade centers were needed—but past that, the terrain became terrible indeed. Forest that became impassable. Trees as broad as eighty men thrust up to canopy three hundred feet tall, above tree-falls and hidden rivers as deep as oceans. Deadly ravines lurked under simple ground cover, and nightmarish beasts hunted anything that ventured in.

Past that came hundreds of miles of marshlands and desert, two entirely different kinds of forest, and then mountain ranges

*and a jungle. Then grassland, and finally, after all of that, the
other great forest. The Pelagirs.*

*Gryphons need the help of trondi'irn, though like me, some-
times gryphons learn some healing along with other powers.
Yet, one pair endured the venture for over six years, alone,
blazing a trail eastward from White Gryphon, until they found
their city's long-lost brethren.*

"... That pairrr was Trrreyvan and Hydona. When I call them
the Grrreat Onesss, it isss becaussse they arrre the brrravessst
explorerrrsss of ourrr time. And they arrre herrre, in Valdemarrr. They helped everrryone sssurvive the Ssstormsss. And
Hallock Ssstaverrrn *knows them*. Essscorrrted them around
Haven—perrrrsssonally!"

Jefti looked up at Kelvren in amazement, having utterly forgotten the bow-wrapping he'd been tasked with, tangled between his fingers. The few other locals and Guard in attendance
and all of the convalescing soldiers had similar expressions. It
wasn't just that they had a six-hundred-pound, taloned killing
fury telling them fireside stories, it was that these stories were
uplifting. His tales fired the imagination in ways no one had
expected. Most of the soldiers would probably never see active
duty again, but instead of being stuck with the wasting-away
grousing of lousy encampment and the same old blather, this
creature they'd first thought would be an intrusion had become
needed—because *all* of his tales were new.

"And you got here because of that trail they found?" one of
the horsemen asked. Kelvren nodded. "An' so did all these
strange allies that came with th' Hawkbrothers?" Kel nodded
again. "An' these trondi-urn people could fix you up?"

There was a collective holding of breath as that question
halted the mood.

"Yesss. But that isssn't to be. Ssso. Let usss sssee just
how tough I rrreally am, mmm?" The gryphon tried to play it
off. "We ssspend time togetherrr herrre. It isss a good exchange.
You learrrn about farrr-away landsss and amazing culturesss. I
learrrn about mud and sssmoke." People laughed. "And fletching. I finally get to sssee some arrrowsss that arrren't going *into*
me." There were a few chuckles at that, and someone in the

back cracked, "Oy, I never really *aimed* at you, y'know!" The jovial mood was returning.

"Hah! You asssume you *could*!" he retorted. "I *have* dodged arrrows, you know. Jussst not enough of them. The one the city was named for, Ssskandrranon, talesss sssay he could fly thrrrough whole brrrigadesss of archerrrsss and emerrrge unssscathed."

"You ever notice that the older a story gets, the more invulnerable the heroes are?" one of the enlisted women snickered.

Kelvren answered in complete seriousness, "Oh, no. No, thisss isss trrrue. Thessse thingsss . . . they arrre important for usss. Grrryphonsss—we *need* to be known. Trrreyvan and Hydona, Kuarrrtess and Ussstecca, and Tusssak Kael the Elderrr. Zzzhaneel the Ssswift and Aubrrri the Ssstalwart, and Kecharrra—herrr name came to mean 'beloved' in ourrr language. They have meant asss much to usss in legend asss they did in life, and accomplisssh asss much by legend asss by deed. Ssskandrrranon Rrrasssshkae isss known to all of usss becausssse he *wasss* that amazing. And now—he isss known to you."

Kel's facial feathers fluffed and he held his head high for a few moments. With his stories, he had done his part to make his heroes immortal.

Above the mill, midday, there was suddenly a bright flash. What appeared to be a hole in the sky, rimmed by an ever-changing glimmery edge, showed through to a landscape of low grass beside a wide roadway. The light came from a column of mage-light the height of two men on the other side of the hole, bright enough to be noticed by people below. A hulking shadow eclipsed the light, and observers below shouted and pointed up. The shadow burst through the hole, and huge wings snapped outward to stop its arcing fall. It flapped ponderously to level its flight before circling over the encampment. Whatever it was, it wanted its outline to be clearly seen before it landed.

Treyvan spied the Command flag at the mill, circled the Guard camp four times, and glided to land in the road between the rows of carriages. The door guards readied pikes and called for reinforcements, and a junior officer went pale when he popped his head out. Treyvan stood with his wings up, then sat on his haunches to be received. Pena stayed on his back, as yet unseen, and appeared to simply be another bundle of cargo.

Then a familiar figure stepped into the road from the mill's entry. Hallock closed on the gryphon and hailed. "Ambassador Treyvan! This is unexpected! It has been too long since I saw you last." He gestured for the door guard to go back to vigil, and waved off questions from junior officers, still walking forward with the aid of his walking stick.

"Welcome. Are you here about Kelvren? He's in a bad way. Because of me, I fear—I was the one he Healed."

"Kelvrrren, you sssay? The wingleaderrr frrrom k'Valdemarrr?" Treyvan's knowledge of gryphons was encyclopedic. He could recite the names and positions of hundreds. "Hurrrh. Wherrre isss he? Frrriend of Firrresssong'sss. A badly wounded grrryphon isss harrrd to find by ssspell. If Firrresssong hasss not aided Kelvrrren, the sssituation mussst be grrrave indeed." Treyvan turned to accompany Hallock, and paused for Pena to dismount. She peeled off her helmet and goggles and tucked them under an arm while she walked alongside the others. Hallock filled in the senior gryphon on what he knew of Kelvren's condition, talking continuously until they neared the convalescents' tent.

They heard *singing*. Not just from inside, but from the eighteen soldiers standing outside, lacquering sheaves of arrows. In the middle of the song, a gryphon voice—thin and strained— nonetheless boomed a line, and made the others grin. The soldiers outside halted singing one by one, and moved backward as one as Treyvan, Pena, and the captain approached. Only a few remembered to salute. They had come to know Kelvren, a terribly wounded gryphon—but *this* was a fully healthy gryphon stalking toward them, bedecked in regalia of rank, all but dwarfing the captain beside him, with a little lizard creature padding along beside them.

:*I can hear you*,: Treyvan Mindspoke toward the gryphon he heard. :*I have come to help you. And a trondi'irn is on the way*.:

Inside the convalescents' tent, the singing went quiet voice by voice. Kelvren turned his head side to side, and upward, as if searching for something. Something was about to happen, and everyone in the tent could sense it. Kelvren cut short a whimper of pain as he rolled himself over to his belly. "I hearrrd—" Kelvren croaked, and then his eyes fixed outside, locked onto an approaching shadow. A *large* shadow.

Captain Stavern stepped around the edge of the tent, nodded behind him, and then came someone Kelvren had thought he would never see in his lifetime.

The breastplate adorned by the badges and bars of rank, the impeccably tooled harness, and the teleson headpiece around the feather-perfect gryphon's brow ridges and fore-crest, crafted to be as much a crown as anything—it could be no one else.

Completely against his will, Kelvren shuddered all over. Breath seized in his throat. He blinked his eyes out of their stare and lowered his head. The fletchers and attendants dropped their work completely or set their tools aside, all eyes on what—*who*—had just walked across the threshold of the tent's oiled-canvas floor. Then everyone who stood or sat went down to one knee and bowed their heads in recognition when Kelvren spoke the words—

"My Lorrrd Trrreyvan."

The power of the senior gryphon's arrival could be felt radiating into the tent, like sunlight sinks into the skin on a summer day.

"Rrrissse, all," Treyvan said. Kelvren's head felt light, as if he was about to pass out. Treyvan stepped to within arm's reach of the stricken gryphon, and then bowed his own head in turn. "Wingleaderrr Kelvrrren Ssskothkarrr of k'Valdemarrr. The Crrrown hasss sssent me to sssee to yourrr wellbeing."

What Treyvan said next made Kelvren certain he was hallucinating.

"You arrre the firrrssst grrryphon on sssite in thisss engagement. I name you Wingleaderrr of thisss forssce asss sssoon asss you arrre fit forrr duty."

Motes of light swam in Kelvren's vision. This must be a fever

dream. It was Silver Gryphon standing practice that whoever was on scene first was automatically the senior of that
engagement—"Incident Command"—the reasoning being that
they knew the situation, by being there first, better than any
who followed. It held, regardless of rank, until there was a
formal exchange of power. It meant that *he* was now empow-
ered *to command Treyvan*. One of the *Great Ones*! It was
mind-boggling.

Enough that Kelvren passed out on the spot.

Much happened while Kel was adrift. The supply tent across
the mud-path from the convalescents' tent was emptied out so
Treyvan could always be near Kelvren.

Treyvan used several spells—though relatively minor, they
were impressive to watch, because to enhance his precision
he used simple light effects to burn off any excess energy. He
used mage-sight and sweeps of power to discover what of Kelvren's magic-conversion organs were still alive and responsive,
and several probes to test the state of the still-unconscious Kelvren's injuries. Jefti stood by his gryphon friend's side and
asked—very possessively—exactly what Treyvan was doing.
Treyvan explained that he was taking away Kel's pain and
deepening his sleep, to help him regain strength—and to keep
him from trying to move and making his wounds worse.

Jefti wasn't the only one who acted proprietary about Kelvren. To the inhabitants of the convalescents' tent, this was
their gryphon.

Hallock Stavern called a muster on the main road, and each
company stood in formation while he introduced Treyvan
and Pena. He made it very clear that unless it directly contra-
vened "high end" regulations, the gryphon was to be treated as
captain—"or better." He held up the proof that the Crown wished
it so, and added that the little lizard with him was Treyvan's
personal assistant. Treyvan made a formal pass by each company. He nodded to each company's senior officer and gave
them polite greetings—but it was also calculated so they got a
very clear view of his rank markings by being close up to him.

Birce and Devon stood humbly while Treyvan thanked them personally for their good work, and astonished them when he suggested to Hallock that they be listed for commendation.

Treyvan explained to the mill officers how a teleson worked, and contacted Haven with one to report on Kelvren. The overworked clerk that Hallock had needled before was set in front of the device, and thanks to the link he might actually have had some sleep possible in his near future.

Pena was well on her way to becoming the most popular creature in the camp. Once word had been spread that any fast-moving lizards in camp weren't to be shot at, she'd become a blur. Not only did she tend to Kelvren's needs and bring materials to Treyvan, her abilities as a chef transformed the dull meals the convalescents ate into events to be savored. She bolted into the woods and returned with foraged materials half a candlemark later that by the end of the day made a basic stew bear delightfully complex tastes. The condition for off-duty soldiers eating any of her dishes, though, was that time must be spent assisting the convalescents and Treyvan. They never wanted for help.

Ammari spent more of her waking hours in the tent with the "gimps," as they'd now laughingly begun referring to themselves. One of the southerners pointed out—wisely—that a word is only truly an insult if you take it as such. Making it a joke, instead of a derogatory term, takes the power out of it, and makes it your power instead.

It reached its zenith when one of the fletchers asked Jefti to bring another basket of arrow shafts, and Ammari heard her son answer back, "That's *Boy* Jefti to you, gimp!" The whole group fell about laughing.

That laughter was what awoke Kelvren. He blinked a dozen times, cleared his mind, and found the pain that had been his constant, unwanted companion had dulled its screaming to barely a whisper. He still felt unbearably heavy, but lifted his head, and found Treyvan was there, and real.

Treyvan spoke to him with respect. "Wingleaderrr Kelvrrren. You have sssurrrvived woundsss that would kill thrrree grrryphonsss. I am imprrresssed by yourrr willpowerrr—and yourrr durrrability. And yourrr compasssionate sssacrrrifissce."

Kel smiled a little at that. Praise from Treyvan! "Wasss it not what ssshould be done? Hallock Ssstaverrrn had hisss Genni to rrreturrrn to. Hisss mate. I have no mate, but I have wissshed it ssso. I would not let him looossse hisss, if it cossst my own life forrr it. He lived the drrream I have. It ssshould not perr-risssh. You—you have Hydona, can you underrrssstand?"

Treyvan nodded gravely. "I would claw out the hearrrt of the sssun if it meant keeping herrr sssafe. And my young—the sssame forrr them."

Kelvren looked into the middle distance, as if caught in daydream. "It would be good to have sssuch perrrfect dayss as Hallock Ssstaverrrn and you have had. And young, yesss."

"In time, Kelvrrren. In time. Yourrr legend grrrowsss."

"Legend?" Kel looked bemused. "Legend."

"Yesss. I know that I will tell of you. And you ssshall rrre-coverrr. Whitebirrrd—ourrr *trrrondi'irrrn* frrrom Haven—isss on herrr way. In the meantime, if yourrr mind isss clearrr enough, I would like to know yourrr wissshesss."

Kelvren choked out a chuckle. "I want nothing morrre than to give insscident command overrr to you!"

Treyvan smiled reassuringly. "Verrry well, but I name you my rrresssident advisssorrr. I am currriousss—what arrre thessse people doing with yourrr cassst-off featherrrsss? They trrreat them with—rrreverensssce."

Kelvren rumblechuckled. "Ssstorrriesss, my Lorrrd Trrreyvan. Belief, and ssstorrriesss." He sobered and continued. "I told everrryone in thisss camp who would lisssten about ourrr people, ourrr herrroesss, and the deedsss we have accomplisssshed. I wasss all but sscerrrtain I would die sssoon. I *had* to tell ourrr ssstorrriesss. Yourrr tale wasss one I told. My Lorrrd Trrreyvan, you arrre one of the Grrreat Onesss. When you arrrived I thought I wasss feverrred. When you deferrred to me, I thought I wasss mad. Beforrre you arrrived, I knew my end russshed to-warrrdsss me. I knew that I had to end making a differrrenssce." He paused to rest for a few moments, then after several deep breaths, resumed. "The sssoldierrrsss trrruly believe that to ss-some degrrree, I am invinsscible. They sssaw I sssurrrvived thessse woundsss, and knew I prrrotected theirrr own. They believe that what I am—what I do—isss magic of a mossst potent kind. Ammarrri and Jefti—they paint thessse featherrrsss of mine in Ammarrri'sss liquid light. The fletcherrrsss—they sssnip thessse parrrtsss of my ssshed featherrrsss and bind them in with the norrrmal featherrrsss. And they shine—to thessse peoplesss' eyesss, they *look* magical. And the sssoldier-rrsss who ressceive thessse arrrowsss believe they arrre now gifted with sssome of my powerrr."

Understanding dawned on Treyvan, and he sat up straight.

"If thessse sssoldierrrsss go into battle with thessse arr-rowsss, they will feel morrre confident. It will rrreinforssce theirrr brrraverrry. It could be enough to help them win, if it comesss to that." He glanced around the parts of the camp he could see, and spoke more softly. "My lorrrd Trrreyvan. I will confide my beliefsss. We arrre not like otherrr crrreaturrresss, who wonderrr if a deity even carrresss if they exissst," Kelvren continued. "We grrryphonsss werrre not crrreated by godsss, we werrre crrreated by a man. We werrre made forrr a *purrr-posse*. We werrre not crrreated to fight warrrsss, though we have. We werrre not made to rrressscue, to thwarrrt, to chassse, or kill. I believe we werrre made to *insssspirrre*. With all my bonesss and hearrrt I feel that to *insssspirrre* isss the ultimate of what Urrrtho wanted of usss."

Treyvan cocked his head, his attention completely absorbed by what Kelvren told him.

"*This* isss what I wasss made forrr. When I sssaw ssso much missserrry herre—felt it frrrom them, felt my own life fading—I had to combine the worrrsssst sscircumssstansscess in sssome ssspecial way—I needed to trrransssmute ssso many bad thingsss into good thingsss. It became clearrr to me when I came down frrrom that hill jussst to eat. Sssoldierrrsss wanted to sssharrre theirrr food with me. They wanted to sssup-porrrt me, touch me forrr luck. I rrrealized what bound it all togetherrr wasss *wonderrr*. They believed in sssomething grrr-reaterrr than they had the day beforrre, jussst becaussse I wasss herre. And ssso." He gestured with a few taloned fingers toward the industrious fletchers. "I put sssimple plansss into motion, and theirrr belief imbued the motion with powerrr, and it moved on itsss own."

"Without a sssingle ssspell left to you," Treyvan murmured, incredulous.

Kelvren closed his eyes and, with some effort, pushed himself up to a sitting position, wings still flat on the floor. "Thessse people arrre watching usss. What they sssee rrright now will matterrr to them the rrressst of theirrr livesss, and they will tell theirrr children and the hissstorrry will sssprrread. It may be—a minorrr legasscy—but I hope that even if I fall, it will be in the tale that I *trrried. Even if I die, I will not have not failed, becaussse to the lassst I did not give up*. I am sssomething extrrraorrrdinarrry to them, and ssso. Therrre arrre no enchantmentsss on the arrrowsss, but the arrrowsss arrre not falssse. They *arrre* magic becaussse the sssoldierrrsss believe in them."

The arranged time for Whitebird to arrive was nearing. Treyvan sent word to the mill that, to bring in his trondi'irn, he would open a Gate to connect partway to Haven, and that anything they needed to send through in half a minute could pass through after his specialist from the other side arrived. He caught Hallock biting his lower lip as he sat by the slumbering Kelvren.

"What trrroublesss you, Firrrssst?"

"It's the Gate. A doorway to just step through to be closer to Haven."

"Clossserrr to yourrr Genni," Treyvan shrewdly noted.

Hallock nodded. "Closer to my Genni. I miss her so much, it's impossible not to think of being with her every moment. And returning to her is precisely what Kelvren diced his life on. I could just resign my command and step through a door to be a few days' ride from her. But I can't do it." He looked Treyvan in the eyes. "I do have a command here, and I owe it to my troops. But as much as that—I have to be at Kelvren's side."

Treyvan was silent for several minutes, finally saying delicately, "You mussst rrrealizzze he isss unlikely to sssurrrvive thisss."

Hallock held a fist in his hand. "I'm not knotting a yellow ribbon for him yet." He gestured out toward the rest of the camp. "And I have my soldiers to take care of. They just lost their First and I've replaced her. It would be too much for me to leave now. I can't risk them getting someone with no field experience in my place."

"You arrre a good leaderrr, Hallock Ssstaverrrn. The grr-reatessst of leaderrrsss arrre at the forrrefrrront of battle, wherrre the powerrr of theirrr prrresenssce can be felt by thossse they command. He isss a parrrt of hisss forssce, not ssseparrrate frrrom them. The Haighlei sssay that a wissse chief isss a man who sssaysss, 'I was beaten,' not 'My men werrre beaten.' You sssee the rrreality of battle widely, immerrrssse yourrrsssself in it, and ssset yourrrsssself apart frrrom thossse who debate it asss theorrry frrrom afarrr."

"This may be so," he agreed, "and thank you for the compliment. But just the same, I have to admit, there's a lot of me that wants to go through that Gate of yours." He turned toward Kelvren. "But I'm not leaving him."

Three light wagons laden with injured troops, and a courier on back of a pony were lined up, two horselengths behind Treyvan. The gryphon mage sat in front of a rope laid out on the road, which had been laid there to mark where the Gate aperture would be. He stared toward it, but not at it—as if he looked past it deep into the earth. He spread his wings and flapped them slowly, drawing his arms up and tracing talons through several motions, culminating with a wide gesture of two halves of a circle.

A short crack of thunder came from in front of the gryphon and made everyone flinch. The horses looked none too happy but didn't run. Then the air simply opened up. Forest, grass, and another road were brightly lit by a column of light on the other side of the Gate and rippled while the edges of the Gate stabilized. Foreclaws still up, Treyvan sidestepped to its right and called out, "Now!"

The light was eclipsed by three horses running toward the

hole, and then they were there in the camp, swerving off to the side at a gallop. "Go!" Treyvan called, and the horses pulling the line of wagons churned hooves toward the Gate and went through. The courier on the pony surged through the hole last, and then the Gate was allowed to collapse. Treyvan dropped back to all fours, swaying and panting.

Two of the horses bore trondi'irn Whitebird, her assistant, and a heavy load of supplies. Whitebird's appearance was striking—she was dressed in a half dozen shades of blue, and her hair was past shoulder length and as snowy as the third "horse" that had come through. A swarthy man in a Herald's uniform was astride a mare Companion, and dismounted to speak earnestly with Captain Stavern. Treyvan walked briskly toward the convalescents' tent, and the trondi'irn fell in behind him.

Whitebird let her assistant take the horses as she walked the rest of the way to the tent. When she saw Kelvren dozing, she stared, mouth open. "Oh, you poor thing," she gasped.

She rushed to Kelvren's side, resting her hands on his shoulder, his wing, and down his flank. She leaned in to smell him, taking in his scent from beak to rump. A minute later, her assistant came in, laden with cases and pouches. They extracted instruments and vials from them and took samples from the wounds, judged the colors they turned, and set them aside on a complex anatomical chart. Kelvren roused from slumber—barely—and rolled a glassy eye sideways to view the two new people.

"Oh, good," he murmured, and then drifted back to sleep.

Whitebird glanced at Treyvan with an unreadable expression, then stood to stand near him. She spoke in Kaled'a'in. "Trey—this looks very bad. He has such strong infections, I can smell them. I don't know how he's lasted this long, unless it's divine providence or pure willpower. We'll get to work on him immediately, but I'll be honest with you, it's definitely a ruin." She wiped down her hands with a wet cloth that smelled of vinegar. "Right now, it looks like *hirs'ka'usk*, and if you don't find a way to rejuvenate his magic, he'll be lost to us in days. I can give him medicine and prime his body for a rejuvenation, but if you can't infuse him with power, the best I can hope to do is stabilize him as he is. No strength, no flight—for a life of a few months." The elder gryphon rumbled and nodded, and Whitebird bent to her work on Kelvren. "I'll be here for four or five candlemarks."

"She's beautiful," one of the men behind her said. "I think I'm in love."

"Grow some wings and I'm yours," Whitebird answered without looking up. "Until then, get me some hot water."

Ammari, Birce, Hallock, and Whitebird's assistant Rivenstone sat on folding chairs, huddled with Treyvan in the tent across from where Whitebird still tended to Kelvren's wounds. Jefti stayed by her, fetching whatever Pena did not.

"Whitebirrrd and I have conferrred with Firrresssong and Hydona by telessson. What we attempt—we do not know what the rrresssult will be. If we take a longerrr terrrm path, therrre isss a ssslight chanssce he will rrrecoverrr, but find hisss flight limited orrr gone. If we attempt thisss—rrrejuvenation—he will jussst asss likely die frrrom it."

Ammari asked, "Why?"

Rivenstone answered her. "When his inner channels are opened up, it will be a surge through the feather roots—where gryphons collect their energy and begin its conversion. The sudden rush of power in to—by now—sensitized vessels might well boil out as heat. Or rather, boil in, and—ah—cook him. If we can keep the inrush to a steady flow, we may be able to draw it out of him before it becomes too much." He steepled his fingers, resting his elbows on his knees. "I must be honest with you all. No gryphon has *ever* been drained so completely as Kelvren has."

Treyvan rumbled, laid out a spread of pages from one of the trondi'irn's books. "We only have thisss frrrom the hissstorrries—an infusssion method unusssed sssince Ssskandrrranon'sss time. What effect it will have now, we can barrrely prrredict." He looked off to the northwest. "Firrresssong isss bessside himsssself—he wantsss ssso much to be herrre. He carrresss morrre about Kelvrrren than Kelvrrren prrrobably knowsss. He sssaysss everrryone frrrom Lorrrd Brrreon to the

Ghossst Cat Clan wantsss Kelvrrren back. He sssaysss the Clansss arrre holding rrritualsss and lighting firrresss to guide Kelvrrren home to them."

Everyone was silent for a moment.

"So," Hallock began. "The questions are, do we try this method, can it be done, what is required for it to be done, and what will we do if it fails or succeeds?"

"If it fails," Rivenstone answered, "he will be his own funereal pyre."

"But the firrrssst quessstion isss what the rrresssst hinge upon. I have ssspoken with him and Kelvrrren hasss rrresssolved that even if he diesss, he hasss done well. I doubt he would want to lingerrr in a living death. Ssso I sssuggesssst that we prossceed."

The others agreed. "We will need a sssite to prrreparrre," Treyvan stated. "And I confesss, it isss no sssmall rrrisssk to me. We need a plassce clossse by, but sssafe from casssual interrrferrenssce—becausssse in a matterrr of a day, I musssst consstrrruct a node."

There was an uncomfortable silence.

Finally Hallock asked, "What's a node?"

"A confluence of magical power," Rivenstone replied. "Like streams run to a lake, a node is where lines of force converge. But since the Storms, those lines have been largely dispersed. If Treyvan tried to use his personal power, he could wind up like Kelvren is, and Kelvren still wouldn't be healed. So he has to use an outside source of power—a node. There aren't any nodes around here, so we need a place to make one. Safely. Quickly."

Ammari raised her hand shyly. "Uhm. Will a Change-Circle do?"

Being gryphon through and through, Treyvan was very physical about his magic—but to human eyes he looked utterly mad while he worked. He had gotten volunteers to go into the Change-Circle and dig holes in specific places, with the deepest in the very center, a man's height in depth. He dropped particular stones in the holes and covered them up, and paced around the Change-Circle, muttered to himself, then did things his gathered audience found inexplicable. Many times he leapt ten feet in the air and suddenly dove down, thumbs locked, as if trying to push a stake into the ground with his forefeet; other times he would slink along the ground and turn his head side to side before jumping up to circle in the air over the site.

Shafts of light erupted from the ground periodically, equidistant around the circle. Treyvan walked around each one, then drew glowing lines in midair toward the center of the circle, and subdivided them. More shafts of light shone, higher this time, where those lines crossed, and then wavered. Treyvan growled and leapt on one that was brighter than the rest, and the others became evenly brighter.

He warned loudly that no one was to enter the Change-Circle for any reason, and took to the air, flew a circuit across the Change-Circle, and then arced back to the convalescents' tent, where Kelvren was awake after his trondi'irn's drug-enforced sleep. Treyvan murmured to Pena, who dashed off after something. Hallock intercepted Treyvan.

"Kel was just giving me his opinions about this political and military situation, in case the worst should happen," the captain said. "And I have to say, I'm impressed. You should hear this." He looked down at the notes he'd written. "'In this conflict the Guard is already beaten, because they do not want to fight their fellow Valdemarans. And this insurgent militia, brought to bear arms against the Guard and Heralds, are also beaten for the same reason. In their hearts—regardless of blades, arrows, and horse—they cancel each other out. Therefore the battle is between the mercenaries and the callous bastards who incited this, who owe no allegiance to this country and have no affection for it—and those mercenaries hired by the Crown, who do feel affection for this country, but hold no pressing regard to spare that militia or their hired counterparts. So to make this conflict collapse, the motives must be attacked, without swords and arrows piercing flesh, and thus make the mercenaries cancel each other out. Create a collapse within these insurgents' power structure, and the mercenaries fold up. Then may Valdemarans be brothers again, and meet in taverns to give thanks and apologize to each other, rather than soak their beloved soil in the blood of their brothers.'"

"Hurrrh. The Shin'a'in sssay, 'Therrre are only two power-rrsss in a warrr—the sssworrrd and the sssspirrrit, and the sspir-rit will alwaysss win out.' If Kelvrrren wasss a warrrlorrrd, we would all sssurrrely be in trrrouble," Treyvan said in all seri-ousness. "Hisss ability to find powerrr in the mossst minorrr of thingsss isss unnerrrving."

Hallock looked back toward Kelvren. "I think he really *needed* to tell me all of that. It seemed very important to him, even though it exhausted him to say it."

"He wantsss morrre than anything to feel effective," Trey-van observed. "But, I sssupposssse, ssso do we all." Pena arrived by his side and offered an unlatched case, which Treyvan deli-cately reached into. He pulled out a fist-sized sphere of glass, perfect in every dimension. With a calculating look he asked Hallock, "Do you know what a Heartstone is?"

It was dusk.

Whitebird set the last of the empty bottles and cups aside, then arose from her knees beside Kelvren. "Those should strengthen you," she said encouragingly, "and keep you going through what's to come. Everyone is ready."

Kelvren stood up on all fours for the first time in days. He shook all over from the muscle strain, but he did not buckle. Whitebird folded her arms, squeezing herself in worry. Ammari shuffled close from the back of the now-emptied tent. Kelvren pulled his shoulders back and raised his head to look her in the face. "Thisss isss a tale that tellsss itsssself," he rumbled wea-rily, forcing a raised-crest smile. "Pena hasss sssomething forr yourr ssson. If my ssstorry endsss this night—hisss ssshall go on. I have a favorr to assk of you, Ammarrri. Yourr—liquid light—sssparrre a few jarrrsss for Genni Ssstaverrn. Frrrom me." He lifted his head up to his shoulders' height, and Ammari cupped his lower jaw in her hands and rested his beak against her bosom. She tucked her chin down and kissed him on the curve of his beak. "You'll be all right, Kel—you will be."

His breath was hot against her body, and he trembled as he turned aside and took his first step toward the circle. "If I am not, I ssshall fly with yourrr husssband firrrssst of all."

Whitebird, Rivenstone, and Pena stepped in instantly to help him from the tent, but he warned them off. With wing tips dragging, Kelvren trudged to his fate on the hill.

Spectators had gathered, but guards kept them a hundred feet from the Change-Circle. They parted to let him through as he approached, and several murmured encouragements to him.

All of the "gimps" were there among them.

Treyvan awaited him several horselengths from the edge of the faintly glowing Change-Circle. "It is not too late to refuse this," he said to Kelvren in Kaled'a'in. "You may still live if we use the other method."

"Live. But not fly, or run even? Never climb a back again? I'd rather die." He chuckled weakly. "No—I must try this."

Treyvan shrewdly asked, "You already have plans for what you will do if this rejuvenation succeeds, don't you?"

Kelvren smiled slyly. "Oh, yes. A few. If you're in a fair fight, you didn't plan it properly. If this works, it will mean more than if I lingered on. It will be a glorious life—or a glorious death." He dipped his head solemnly. "Thank you for giving me the chance at either, my lord Treyvan."

Treyvan bowed his head, mirroring Kelvren's own motion. "The site has been prepared. You must go in alone, and lie down in the exact center. When I release the sequence, you must raise your wings if you can, and breathe deeply. In that instant, cast your self-healing spell. If you can stand, then stand. If you can—" He paused, obviously trying to hide something. "If you can fly, then fly. Straight up, as far as you can."

Kelvren said the obvious. "If I can't fly, then I burn."

Treyvan looked down. "Yes," he said softly.

Kelvren stared at the center of the circle. His heart beat harder as he stepped across the circle's edge, and more than a hundred people held their breath.

Pena stood at Treyvan's side, with a look of dismay and sorrow on her face. "He doesn't know it's a Heartstone—does he?" he asked Treyvan.

The gryphon mage looked down at her with a look of resignation. "No. He doesn't know."

Pena's eyes glittered from the reflected lights that were starting up from the ground as Kel approached the circle's center. "It is probably best that he doesn't."

Whitebird and Rivenstone walked up beside them. "Treyvan's made a minor node," Pena explained to Whitebird and Rivenstone, "but it's channeled into a Heartstone—a purposely fragile one. It's why Treyvan used glass. When the spell reaches its height, it will consume itself. Even a tiny Heartstone will release its power in a saturated burst."

Treyvan nodded. "I didn't tell him. I completed the node hours before I buried the glass sphere. And the control points I buried, around the rest of the circle, are not to draw the power in from outside. They are to contain the power and direct the burst upward from the center. If his system restarts—he will absorb it. If it does not—hurrrh. He will only feel pain for a few seconds."

Ammari and Jefti approached the four, who were speaking Kaled'a'in. "What're you all talkin' about?" Jefti asked.

"We arrre—wishing Kelvrrren luck." He stepped toward the circle and spread his wings widely as Kelvren neared the center. "It isss time."

Pena ushered the humans back to where the Herald and his Companion stood even with the soldiers, locals, and patients who came to see the fate of their gryphon. Dusk descended further, making the light from the circle even more apparent. Kelvren neared the center and walked around the packed earth there, until he faced the crowd.

He lay down on his belly, and carefully and deliberately folded his wings.

Treyvan stepped to the edge of the circle, sat on his haunches, and pulled his wings straight back behind him. Faint beams of light broke through the ground around the perimeter. The light of the nearer control points visibly pulled toward him as his wings swept slowly back. Treyvan spread his arms wide, curled his claws toward the sides of the circle, and swept his wings forward again. The light pushed back and caused the next nearer points to flare brighter.

Kelvren watched Treyvan—and then looked at every one of the gathered crowd. A sharp eye could see that tears ran from his eyes and dripped from the hook of his beak.

He laid his head down flat on the ground and his wings slumped.

The sixty control points around the perimeter blazed fully now, all of them matched columns of light tapering to a foot high. Treyvan went back to all fours and walked a horse-length further from the crowd, and stopped again at the edge of the Change-Circle. He sat up, raised his forearms higher than before, and swept his wings back, then forward again, harder. All the perimeter lights swayed inward and another ring of them blazed up from the ground in unison. Another massive flap of his wings, and a third ring shot up and steadied, encompassing Kelvren. Arcs of energy extended from one light to another, seemingly randomly, and then all at once they made a stable, steady pattern that looked like a stained-glass rosette.

Treyvan held his own breath for a moment, and said in Kaled'a'in, "Wind to thy wings, sheyna."

Treyvan snapped his wings open.

A boom of thunder struck the crowd.

Inside the circle, a rising ring of light closed in on Kelvren in the center.

And consumed him.

Daylight surged upward from the circle's center, and the briefest shadow of wings flickered in it before everyone watching was blinded by it. Treyvan's irises pinned to the width of a finger. He peered resolutely into the light.

There was movement.

There was the shape of a gryphon—getting to its feet. Standing. Its wings were unfolding, and rising up.

Except it was not a shadow against light.

It *was* light, and everything else was shadow compared to it.

Treyvan stepped back, one step. Two. The figure in the center rose up onto its hind feet. It was Kelvren, but he was radiating light like nothing Treyvan had ever seen before. His body color wisped away, replaced by a glow from inside the feather shafts themselves. The edges of every feather gleamed and rippled in a yellow-white radiance, like the edge of burning paper. His eyes more than glowed—they shone outward in tapered rays of light, wherever he looked.

Kelvren raised a hind foot, then the other, and stepped up into the air. Calmly, he shone there, suspended off the ground, watching everyone.

And with a single wingbeat, the gryphon of light shot up into the air as a streak, and was gone. He went up higher, until he was a bright speck in the sky amidst the stars.

No one could say a word.

The mote of light descended a minute later.

It shone even brighter than before and swept over the encampment, making shadows shift as if a new sun was lighting the night up. Kelvren's flight seemed effortless.

He backwinged once, and with the lightest of touches, settled atop the mill with his wings spread wide, and regarded everyone below.

Hallock, Pena, Ammari, Whitebird, Rivenstone, and Jefti staggered, stunned, to Treyvan's side. "What—just happened?" Ammari asked.

"I have no idea," Treyvan admitted.

"Just look at him," Whitebird gasped. "He's beautiful."

"That's the damndest thing I've ever seen," Hallock said.

"He looks just like that tapestry back at White Gryphon," Rivenstone gasped.

"That's my gryphon," Jefti said.

The gryphon of light stayed atop the mill for ten minutes, then he sprang up from the mill's roof and dove to alight in front of the crowd, banking in to brake and hang in midair without a single wingbeat. His eyes swept them, one by one, and murmurs of astonishment came from nearly everyone.

Kelvren spoke.

"I have become—sssomething morrre than I wasss beforrre—but my hearrrt and allegiansscesss arrre unchanged. Ssso hearrr me," his voice boomed. "I know what I musssst do. The forsscesss at Deedun know little of magic. Theirrr sssoldierrrsss arrre mosssst likely bewilderrred by magic; and by now, they know what a sssingle grrrryphon can do. I believe they will rrressspond to what they can sssee, and by that, even the sssimplessst of magic is made magnitudesss ssstrrrongerrr. He who isss afrrraid isss half beaten." He lifted up further from the ground and fanned his wings as he rose, suspended in mid-air. "I will ssstrrrike, and I will ssshed no blood. And I do it in the name of the Guarrrd, the Herrraldsss, and the Crrrown. Forrr all of you. Forrr all of usss. Forrr Valdemarrr!"

The crowd erupted into cheers and shouts.

The light from Kelvren's eyes flared brighter, and swept over to Treyvan. "You underrrsssstand," he said, his voice seeming distant. Kelvren gazed upon the rest, where they'd gathered with the convalescents. The illumination surrounded them all, sharpening the shadows. "My frrriends—I will neverrr forrrget you."

And with those last words, Kelvren rose, did a wing-over, dove down from four winglengths up, and slammed his claws down to the ground. The earth trembled, and loose earth momentarily heaved up to knee height. The resulting crater ignited into a white, scintillating brightness. When Kelvren leapt into the sky, the sunlike glow stayed. Then, with several massive wingbeats, the gryphon powered away from the crowd, driving up debris and dust, and with each downstroke his brilliant wings surged brighter. Below him, a jagged incandescent line two wings'-width wide crackled up from the shimmering focal point and split away from its origin. The shimmering swath on the ground directly followed his flightpath. He swept through his skies, leading the line of sunfire from the Change-Circle through the camp, to the great Trade Road. He followed the Trade Road precisely, and the brilliance followed him on the ground. With each wingbeat Kelvren absorbed more magical power from the air, and the swath trailed him as light, following every twist. He coursed faster with each wingbeat than any gryphon he had ever known of. He flew for hours, tracing the Trade Road below, leaving a trail of light all the way to Deedun.

And it did not fade.

Mercenaries and militia alike looked up in astonishment, uncertainty, or stark terror at the figure that shot past them by the time an arrow could be nocked.

Candlemarks passed, and the path of coruscating light etched into the road still did not fade.

Only when he reached Deedun did Kelvren backwing and hover in midair in front of the tallest of the High Keep's towers. He stared at it, and concentrated.

The citizens of Deedun saw, line by line, the crest of Valdemar, three stories high, burn itself into the wall of the keep's tower, and blaze like daylight across the city.

And like the wide line of light the length of the Trade Road, it too did not fade.

Kelvren turned his gaze across the city. Citizens, guards, militia, and mercenaries alike were coming out of buildings, all lit by the bright path that came from the far distance through the center of the city. Kelvren knew that with the sheer power he'd put into his mage-light spell, the crest of Valdemar would not fade away for a month or more.

He smiled.

Then the gryphon of light soared into the sky, becoming a bright star, and went home.

Captain Hallock Stavern and the Sixteenth Cavalry, three companies of Guard regulars, and Kerowyn's Firebolts advanced steadily along the Trade Road. The militia they met offered no noteworthy resistance, and laid down arms almost apologetically. The Herald with the Crown's forces adjudicated the conditions of surrender, town by town, and left the locals with their pride. The mercenary company hired by Farragur Elm and his cohorts all but disbanded, demoralized by the showy display of magic they could not possibly match.

Kerowyn held her Firebolts back from taking the city. She was of the opinion that it would be damned unseemly for a merc company to take over the city rather than the Crown's Guard regiments—especially since so much of the troubles had been caused by *other* mercs.

When the Guards rode in and liberated Deedun, "Chancellor of Prosperity" Farragur Elm and several of his insurrectionists barricaded themselves in the High Keep. Others guilty of the thefts that financed the power grab were, over time, discovered, arrested, and jailed. In time, Elm himself was dragged, screaming obscenities, from the very tower that Kelvren had marked.

Treyvan conferred with Whitebird and all the mages he knew, still amazed by what had happened. They finally deduced what Kelvren had done. When the power of the Heartstone dissolution surged upward into him, Kelvren Healed himself, but there was too much chaotic raw power, flooding in too quickly. Kelvren used the simplest, but most stable, spell that any mage knew—mage-light—and quelled the chaos of raw power into a tuned current. Instead of ending the spell, as mages normally did when they had enough light, he let it flow through him. The ordeal of having no magic in his body had left his channels and conversion organs needy, and the magic filled them to capacity, then flowed into his bones, then into the feathers themselves. Then with so much free-floating energy in the air, his every movement brought in more.

The road of light was far more than a psychological ploy. The rate he cast it matched the rate the power was absorbed as he flew, and it burned off enough energy for his system to stabilize.

Firesong reported by teleson that Kelvren returned to k'Valdemar the night after his rejuvenation, still as bright as a sunrise. He flew over the Clan fires, Kelmskeep, Errold's Grove, and the Vale purely for effect.

And so the mill was gradually emptied of officers, and the village was freed from the Guard camp, and trade was re-established along the great glowing Road. The light faded slowly over the fortnight after Kelvren's flight, but it wouldn't leave anyone's memory anytime soon.

Before long, it was time for Treyvan, Whitebird, Rivenstone, and Pena to go back to Haven. They said their goodbyes, and with a small bow, Pena gave an oilskin-wrapped package to Jefti.

Jefti opened it up, and inside were three gryphon feathers, bound with strips of leather, a folded scrap of paper, and a small leather pouch attached to them. Inside the pouch were six gold coins. His mother read the message.

"Jefti Roald Dunwythie. My friend. If you grow tired of being 'Boy,' with this you will be welcomed into Hawkbrother lands and accepted as our own. Your mother will be welcome also. So speaks Wingleader Kelvren Skothkar of k'Valdemar Vale, Ally of the Crown of Valdemar."

Ammari felt tears in her eyes, and she hugged her son as strongly as she ever had. They gazed up at the encompassing sky, and listened to the birds together.

———————

Darkwind handed over a paper slip to Elspeth. "Mmm. Oh, this is good. Repercussions from the Kelvren affair. Says here, some mayor demands reparations for gryphon's presence in his village. Cites him as a hazard, detrimental to the town's morale, and an insult to the dignity of his office."

Elspeth browsed the slip, shrugged, and handed it off to a passing clerk to be handled. "Sounds like a healthy gryphon to me. What's next?"

What a sight I must be! What an amazing sight! Kelvren thought as he approached k'Valdemar Vale. Two gryphons surged upward through the Veil when he was leagues away, and now they banked in behind him, level, one on each side in an escort formation. Gleefully, Kelvren called to them. Kelvren felt like he was in a scene from a story—a *legendary* story— returning triumphant, blazing with magic, magnificent and battle-proven, and handsome, with an honor guard!

He led the pair in a wide circle over the Vale, and Kelvren could see humans, hertasi, tervardi, even dyheli looking up at the spectacle. The Veil around the Vale distorted with the flyover, creating a rainbowed halo of light on its surface that followed him toward the Vale entrance. *Excellent!* Kelvren thought. *I didn't even plan that part. It must have looked great! I hope the artists were paying attention. And the songwriters. I could always do another flyby if they need it for reference.* Kelvren's escorts followed his lead, falling back further so the glide to the entry road would be unobstructed for the lead gryphon. Kelvren slowed and backwinged, creating dazzling flashes and shadows against the trees and decorations, despite the brightening sky. The hundreds of rods that surrounded the Vale, used here as posts for a burgeoning vineyard rather than buried or disguised, glowed when he coasted down to lightly touch the stonework. His flight was so effortless that he simply stepped down to the paving. The Vale's rods gave off the illusion of a glow, bending toward him, through the twining of grapevines.

That doesn't seem natural, but then again, neither am I right now. I am something new! Maybe they're bowing to me. Maybe someone's making them look like they're bowing, as some welcome-home gesture! That is adorable.

His escorts landed more firmly, carrying their momentum into a distance-closing stride. Kelvren didn't recognize either of them, but then again, he had been gone a long time and must have missed new gryphons' arrivals. "We will escort you further," the nearer of the two gryphons said as she approached. She was a breastplated and badged Silver Gryphon, umber and white with a narrow black crest. "The trondi'irn want to see you immediately, and the senior mages too." She sounded anxious—no—she was edgy. "I've been Wingleader in your absence. You should know that you can't resume command until you're cleared by them." She flicked her wings twice and raised her head, as if ready for an angry challenge. She added, "You've gone strange."

Kelvren looked at her and the other gryphon. They both had their fighting-claws strapped on, and Kelvren's glow glinted back at him from their razored curves, from the two gryphons' eyes, and from their badges. "I am still a senior Silver Gryphon. I am only different," Kelvren replied suspiciously. "I am still Kelvren Skothkar."

"*They'll* determine who and what you are now," the new Wingleader said flatly. "We will walk you in, or you can attempt to flee. If you try, the archers will drop you, and we'll finish you." For emphasis, she repositioned her forelegs a little wider apart, making the fighting-claws more obvious. She had absolutely *no* warmth in her voice. "Don't make this a sad day."

Kelvren opened his beak to reply, and tried to speak to her with Mindspeech, but found her utterly walled off. He then darted his gaze around, seeking other minds to speak to, but found no one talkative. His vision was disrupted by the glare from his own body, but even so he had no doubt that unseen Tayledras scouts were ready to fell him should he try to take flight. No opponent saw a Tayledras scout until they were ready to be seen, or they only knew a scout was nearby when they saw an arrow shaft sticking out of their gut. "I can't imagine what you'd think I could be—" he began, and was cut short.

"Neither can we," the new Wingleader snapped back. "There are things we can't imagine, so when a flier that appears to be our missing Wingleader arrives ablaze like a new sun, we want to know more before we trust anything. In you go."

Kelvren agreed with the logic of it, sure, but that didn't stop him from sulking. Huffily, he refolded his wings a few times and stalked toward the Vale's main entry and the intricately laid red stones that marked the Veil's boundary. The tall arch's usual complement of guards and greeters was gone—no festive celebration? He'd been heroic, and returned to . . . this? It wasn't fair. It wasn't *right*. *Wait*, he thought, *wait. This* isn't *right. There's no cheering crowd for me to be modest in front of. Did something happen to the Vale? Is this the real Vale? And this new "Wingleader"? I don't even know her, rank badges or not! I'd better be on my guard . . .*

The Vale smelled like it should: flowers and aromatic oils, flavorful smoke, scents of cooking, healthy gardens, and generally full of life. Yet, apart from bondbirds and the colorful flash of messenger birds, Kelvren saw nobody except for the two gryphons behind him after he passed under the Vale entry. His ears twitched in aggravation. He could hear voices aplenty, but aside from his surly escort, saw no one of any intelligent species, no matter where he looked. He paused to rise up on his hind legs and then a single foot, part-perching in the air as gryphons could, and saw some humans and gryphons in their daily lives thirty-some wingspans away behind the cover of archways and hedges, but no one closer. This only agitated his well-armed escort. The Wingleader snapped a sharp "Down!" at him, and Kel complied, with a grumpy hiss back at her. Another pair of Silver Gryphon–badged gryphons flew over, banked, and landed on the wide main path ahead of a four-way branch of paths. These two he knew well from before he'd left; in fact, he'd trained them in high-altitude search patterns. *Or did I?* he wondered. *They look the same, but if this is some kind of illusion or mental attack, or if the Vale has been replaced somehow . . . they might* only look *the same. They don't act happy to see me, and yet, they would surely have been among the searchers for me, when I went missing.* It wasn't hard to spot that they bore the fighting-claws and armored equipage of someone expecting a deadly fight, too—definitely not daily wear in a Vale, and not a polished honor guard to receive their heroic leader. Even gryphons had a dozen outfits, thanks to the hertasi. No, these four were herding him as if he were some high-ranking or high-powered prisoner. A mere three wing-spans from the second pair of gryphons, Kelvren said toward them, "What has happened here? Why aren't there throngs of people here happy to see me?"

Kurrundas, the gold-crested female on the left, answered guilelessly, "Because no one is happy to see you."

"That hurts," Kelvren replied, equally honestly. He stopped midway between the escorts. "And it doesn't make sense. Why wouldn't everyone be happy to see me? I am Kelvren! The Brave! Hero of the North, Finder of the Lost, and Ally of Valdemar! Best friend of the Owlknight!" He shot a very pointed look backward. "Wingleader of k'Valdemar!"

"Don't try me," the new Wingleader growled.

"Control your jealousy," Kelvren retorted, then looked back to Kurrundas. "Seriously, Kurry, what is going on? I've *never* been disliked here, especially by the gryphons."

Kurrundas shifted her weight foot to foot and ground her beak, and finally just replied, "I have been ordered to not talk with you." It was in a tone that actually said, *I want to tell you so much that we'd be here for a candlemark, but I don't dare.* Just the same, she did add, "Just go where we're guiding you, and they'll explain it."

Kelvren overdramatically flicked and swished his tail at

them all as he turned onto the rightmost sidepath. If there had been branches to "accidentally" snap back at his "new Wing-leader," he would have, purely to spite her. Kelvren knew k'Valdemar's layout to the smallest walkway, the highest tree, and the deepest pool, and before long he stepped into a council circle as expected, which was anything *but* unpopulated.

Kelvren's senses had only a moment to register the two dozen or more humans, gryphons, and hertasi before he was assaulted from multiple directions, by binding spells, mind-readings, paralyzation, and things he couldn't even identify. Rings and tendrils of colored mage-energy whipped around him and rebounded wildly, licking at some of the attendees, who dove for cover. Short thunder-cracks and sizzling sounds erupted from below him. Kelvren threw his body upward as if trying to escape, but was left with a single foot still firmly frozen in place on the paving, his wings up half-spread and back arched in, bound up immobile but for his harshened breathing and a single strangled cry.

He caught a side-glance through a tear-pooling eye at Tyr-sell, the king stag of the dyheli, and Kel understood the paralysis at least. No creature yet known could resist Tyrsell's body- and mind-control. Tyrsell's control over Kelvren was so complete that the king stag was utilizing the gryphon's internal lift to support him in a pose suited to a statue, without even tipping sideways. He felt his wings being spread fully, only they weren't being yanked at; his wings "wanted" to be wide open. Little wonder that when Tyrsell was not around, the Tayledras said he was probably the most powerful being alive. Sure, he could be attacked with a spell, but what good was that when Tyrsell could just make the mage's body impale itself on his horns while he kept calmly eating leaves?

Millions of motes of entoptic light swirled and pulsed with Kelvren's speeding heartbeat, obscuring his vision further. His head pounded and his hearing was disrupted, but he could hear voices, some in his mind.

:*He thinks he is Kelvren.*:

"Whoever he is, he's a mess inside. His pain's blocked almost completely. I mean, wide open, it's amazing he can even breathe the way he's pumped up. His intake's like nothing I've ever heard of."

:How did his bones not splinter with that kind of swelling?:

:They have, in three places I've found so far, and who knows how many fractures besides. This is too dangerous.:

"I can't recommend him staying in the Vale. In fact, I put forth that we exile him immediately, for everyone's safety. We can chain him to someplace neutral, and keep the rest of us out of danger from him."

"Are you just stupid? This is Kelvren. We owe him."

:Are we agreed it's Kelvren, now? Not some other monster?:

:Watch it.:

:You know what I mean.:

"This is Kelvren's home, regardless of what he did, or what happened to him. It is also the most stable and guarded place we could put him."

"So you want him to go unstable here in the center of our home, where things are the most controlled? Won't that, logically, do the most possible damage to everything?"

"We can shield him and stabilize him, and the best healing mages are here. We can watch the Veil to see his effects on it, like during that flyover."

:Again, are we all in agreement now that it really is Kelvren?:

:If it isn't, it's the most convincing copy ever made. I'll say yes.:

"Yes."

:Yes, I agree.:

"I can't win the argument that he be kept far away from your parlor, apparently. So, he'll roast the lot of you. Fine. I still want him under constant monitoring, and I mean by mages and more. And he still has to answer for what happened at Deedun."

"The Shin'a'in proverb states, 'The hero that can kill you should be admired from a safe distance.' Just because we love him doesn't mean he can't unintentionally destroy us."

"I'll take care of that as best I can. Just make him better."

:This is Kelvren, and he is a friend to the herd. Kelvren is to

have the best treatment from all *of you or I will be displeased.:* Oh, that was surely Tyrsell.

"Agreed that this is genuinely Kelvren. Tyrsell, let him down, with limited movement, would you? That's safer for everyone."

Kelvren's dizziness ebbed, and he found himself able to move as if weighted down and navigating a mud bog. His vision cleared somewhat and he tested his jaw movement before shrieking, "What is *wrong* with you all?"

Just two body-lengths away, his dearest friend Darian k'Valdemar stood with his hands folded in front of him, brightly lit both by Kelvren and by the seething field of his magical shields, normally invisible but now lit in thousands of short silvery tendrils pointed at the glowing gryphon. His hair was cut back more harshly than expected for a Vale resident, and he wore a lightweight pair of symbolic silver pauldrons. "I know this is a shock, Kel. The reports we got, and what we could learn as you came home, and now—how you look—it's surprised us."

"*You* feel surprised? Guess how I feel! I thought I'd return to a hero's welcome. Instead I was brought in by my *replacement* and ground-bound by my *friends!*" Kelvren growled, well past a reasonable tone.

"We *are* your friends," Darian offered. "That's why we're gathered. We wouldn't allow anyone to hurt you, and *as* your friends, we need you to calm down, so we can work on your internal injuries."

I'm convinced this is the real k'Valdemar, whatever is going on. I don't have the imagination to hallucinate in this kind of detail. If I was hallucinating, I'd have hallucinated twenty weeks of feasts, adoration, and exhausting sex, not this kick under the tail.

Nightwind, Kelvren's longtime friend and his trondi'irn, stepped up beside Darian. Nightwind's heavy gloves were folded through her smock's belt, her sleeves were rolled up, and she sweated profusely. Her husband Snowfire, in light scout leathers, stayed just a few armlengths away from her, and her sister Nightbird stood in a wing position to them both. Nightbird wore a silver-piped, shield-styled woven breastplate with her Silver Gryphon badge in the center. Nightbird's badge was the same size as her sister's, but placed in a more prominent position; Nightwind considered herself more caregiver than enforcer, and just kept *her* badge pinned out of the way on a sleeve.

Nightwind wiped at her brow, and confirmed what Darian said. "My first look inside you tells me that you can't feel pain right now, and that means you will injure yourself worse without knowing it, and starve yourself too." She opened her arms and slowly, deliberately closed them until she held the gryphon's head in her palms, causing Kelvren's vision to constantly adjust to her. "We have to work deep on you, Kel, and so I'm ordering you to surrender," she spoke clearly. "Keep your eyes on me, Kel, and let your defenses down. Concentrate on me, believe in me, surrender to me, and we will save you."

Kelvren let the throng in the council circle fade far away in his perception and drop out of focus, until the kind, concerned face of his trondi'irn thumb-brushing his cheek-feathers was the last thing he was aware of.

———————

Kelvren lost awareness of time, of place, and of his body. There were periods of unknown duration when he perceived a bewildering separation of his consciousness from his body, as if they'd been very precisely cut away from each other and set aside in the sun to bake. He honestly did not know that k'Valdemar had gathered so many trondi'irn until he'd undergone the most invasive examinations of his life. Tyrsell was present for many of the procedures and tests that Kelvren underwent, occasionally walking past Kel's field of view before shutting off Kelvren's consciousness as easily as flicking away a fly. Firesong was there a few times, in his Adept finery and mask one moment, and an eyeblink later it would be night, and Firesong would be standing up in a basic, single-layer garment while hertasi washed his hands for him and helped him back into his robes. Each time, Kelvren awoke without any grogginess. He wasn't ever really drugged, he was simply being shut off and on. Sometimes he'd notice he felt well-fed, another time he felt upside-down, and another time he was aware he stood fully on his hind legs. On occasion he would see piles of bloodied bandages and instruments, obviously from trondi'irn work, but he felt no pain. He couldn't remember speaking to anyone, nor anyone talking to him.

This time when he awoke, he did spot Tyrsell, Nightwind, the rump of another dyheli, two hertasi with a stack of scrolls with his name on them, a few unknown Hawkbrothers, and a kyree. They and a few trondi'irn he knew were tidying up the glade they were in now, and as they left, he saw that the two humans under a vine-wrapped awning were Nightwind and Darian. It was late afternoon, but of what day, he couldn't tell.

Nightwind, her eyes as gray as stormclouds and her knee-length hair dyed as black as a new moon night, shrugged on a fresh set of her trondi'irn working clothes, belt, scarf, and apron. Wearily, she approached where Kelvren lay perfectly symmetrically on a grassy spot amongst clover. The dyheli king stag Tyrsell simply turned and walked away out of sight, sending, :*Good fortune to you, friend of the herd, gentle slopes and tasty feeding*,: accompanied by faint mental images of just that, but they were full-sensory ones. It was a strange feeling indeed to have the subtleties of berries, grasses, and leaves on your tongue, and register the tastes, when you weren't even the same species as who put them there. Tyrsell was accompanied by another dyheli Kelvren had known since youth, Snowfire's usual mount Sifyra, and they walked through a curtain of vines under a stone arch where a coiled pair of brightly colored plump snakes dozed.

Kelvren flexed each pair of appendages in turn. Everything felt better than it had in months, and his full-body glow had lessened significantly. He asked the obligatory first question, the one that everybody asked when they regained awareness, regardless of their era, situation, or species.

"How long was I out?"

"Six days, and maybe ten candlemarks," Nightwind answered. "I know you've been hurt before, Kel, but this time, you were in a bad way like *nothing* we'd seen before. We learned a lot from you. A lot *about* you. You've had almost a hundred people looking you over or consulted by teleson, and there's nothing quite like this in any records. Kyree historians all the way back to White Gryphon were asked about it, and trondi'irn from two Vales were brought in. Everyone from Adept to handwaver in the Vale's been talking about you. We think this is unprecedented."

"I drew a crowd, at least," Kelvren commented, immediately sorting out the part that was important to a gryphon, while standing up and fanning his wings. They tingled when he did, and the tingle flowed into his chest and spine heartbeats later. "I remember arriving, being insulted, being assaulted, then surrendering to you. Some *sketi*-sack said I should be exiled!"

"We aren't proud of that," Darian conceded. "They only saw the surface problems. You know as well as any of us how tricky magical biology can be."

Kelvren returned to his self-absorption. "It was Treyvan that did this to me, did you know that? Treyvan himself! Whatever it was, he made it work, and he did it for me. This was done by the *best*."

"We know—we investigated you very deeply. We went into memories past what you think you know. Firesong said it was a brilliant solution, 'for a generalist like Treyvan.' What Treyvan did was very risky. He turned a known ruin into a new *kind* of ruin." Nightwind sighed and shook her head.

Darian took up the thread of conversation. "You survived long enough to make it here, but you're not just *in* trouble, you *are* trouble. In a few ways more than usual. We *think* you will live, but it may not be long, and it won't be the life you had."

Kelvren huffed at Nightwind and Darian, and walked in a wide circle around them. "Hurrh! I thought I taught you, Dar'ian, none of us live long and every new moment means the life we had is gone. So give me the details, what is such a ruin now? I feel good. Hungry but good." He said the last part loudly enough that any hertasi nearby would get the hint.

Nightwind took the answer up. "Without getting too technical, we rebroke your bones, set them, accelerated their healing, and repaired a significant amount of internal damage. Your *virtusgan*—the larger-bone linings—normally draw in magic energy at a steady rate and refuse the rest, but yours were dying off when Treyvan got to you. That meant your *virtutem* organ was essentially going dry, and your spleen tried to compensate. Your *indusvenarum* system had nothing to distribute, so it was shutting down. When Treyvan's gamble actually worked, the *virtusgan* feasted. In fact, it gorged and didn't self-limit. It became dangerously swollen, the *virtutem* had too much to handle, and you had *virtusgan* ruptures all through your body. You were so overwhelmed that what should have been agony from it was just washed away. You didn't have a clue how hurt you were. Just the opposite, in fact. You were euphoric."

"Of course I felt euphoric! Look what I had done!" Kelvren proclaimed. "I rallied a Valdemaran army! I lit their path to victory!"

"You—did do some impressive things," Darian said, tactfully.

Nightwind said, "And you came back. Your feathers were as dry as any I've ever seen. Without trondi'irn care you went un-oiled too long. You could have gone up like breezecotton if a campfire popped a spark near you."

Kelvren turned his head to look himself over. "I think I knew that somehow. When I felt that new energy surge up into me, I was scared. I thought I'd turn to ash. But then I thought, *to dump away the heat from too much magic power, use it for something*. The fastest, simplest thing I knew was Lightcasting. You should have seen it!"

"During your interrogations, I didn't just see it, I *felt* it," Nightwind replied. She was, after all, an accomplished Empath, which was a significant part of why she was a successful trondi'irn. Even when she did not know a creature's anatomy intimately, she could at least understand what they felt, and that informed her healing abilities. "Tyrsell and the stronger Mindspeakers linked us all. Believe me, now they know *far more* about gryphons and their needs than they likely *ever* wanted to."

Darian joked, "I think Greywinter wants a gryphon costume now. Much of what you like appeals to his tastes. He is newly, ah, invigorated."

Nightwind chuckled briefly, but returned to solemnity soon enough and rubbed at one of the gryphon's ears. "You went through so much, Kel. I have lost gryphons before. You were close to being my third. I have never worked on *anyone* like you. I am so sorry, you were pushed too far when you were interrogated—"

"I was *what*? Who was responsible for that?"

"We all were," she lied. Kelvren could usually tell when a human was lying, and he had known Nightwind so long it was very obvious she was covering something up. "We needed to know what you knew, so the search went deep into your mind. Too deep. Too far *back* into you, and it made you—well, it hurt you. In your mind. There were some arguments about what to do, and what was done made your breathing and your heart stop, and—the important thing is, we brought you back."

It's not difficult to imagine whose horns that "mistake" lay upon. Tyrsell was never spoken of as being gentle, and the king stag had all the subtlety of a horizon-wide thunderstorm over a wildfire. *It also explains the mental tone of that farewell. It was solemn and apologetic. What she's trying so hard to hide is probably that Tyrsell found me to be too much of a threat to the Vale and killed me, and the others beat away at reviving me.*

"Firesong and I fixed the trouble," Nightwind continued. "Together, and with help from k'Vala, we put things into a . . . kind of working order. It took a while."

"It is a wonder that you are making any noise at all, since you're putting so much work into not *saying* anything," Kel grumbled.

Darian spread his hands and pleaded, "It is just that we don't know what memory of the past few days you actually have, Kel. We're afraid that if we say the wrong thing, you might get angry."

Kelvren's building displeasure peaked. His eyes flashed, then pinned at them both, before he abruptly stood up and stalked out toward his home. "Angrier."

They deserve better than that from me, but right now, I just don't want to be near them, and I hate the idea of that damned dyheli laying every secret I've ever had out bare as a book page. We keep secrets for good reasons, but dyheli don't. They only know indifference, neutrality, invasiveness, and more invasiveness as their degrees of "secrecy." Now they all know who and what I actually am, not what I want them to know. It is infuriating!

Crows and ravens chased two falcons through the distant branches, disturbing a roosting vulture who loped through the air for someplace more peaceful. Kelvren shouldered through the arch's thick wall of trimmed vines to find the hertasi Ayshen and his mate Drusi, the dyheli stag Sifyra, and the human kestra'chern Silverfox.

Oh, here's a coincidence, the same dyheli stag Tyrsell was with. I'll lay odds he's Tyrsell's prize pupil. Probably here to paralyze me if he feels like it, or share my deepest thoughts if he feels bored. "Bring me a bowl of berries and I'll tell you Kelvren's deepest fears!" Won't that be fun? Just hilarious, you hoof-holes.

Sifyra twitched both ears forward and stared at Kelvren.

Silverfox did not exactly show age ungracefully, but although his hair matched Nightwind's in length, by now a full third of it was streaked in stripes of light gray. The two hertasi wore long, customized tool vests and tail cuffs with long fringe to match the vests, and each other. They were in a semicircle on the far side of the pathway junction, and Ayshen was showing Silverfox some decorative chains when Kel stepped right into the middle of them. The four of them were not blocking Kelvren's way, but it was clear that they'd been waiting there to be an escort.

:Greetings, Sky Warrior,: Sifyra Mindspoke to the group. *:We are here to assist.:*

"Assist who, exactly? Me, or those who near-killed me, after I was treated as an invader, and my mind was cut up like a feast of ribs?" Kelvren snapped back.

Ayshen and Drusi both went a bit wide-eyed. Ayshen dropped his chains, then swiftly picked them up and pocketed them.

Silverfox rocked back a little, then commented, "Ho. Ah. That punches the air out of our happy welcome-back." He raised his arms from his sides. "I think I understand why you're upset. Don't rage at us, Kel, we're your friends. You're no enemy of ours." He spread his hands wide and palms up, in a k'Leshyan display that translated to "I have no weapons, I bare no claws toward you." Silverfox then gestured down the path toward Kelvren's cliffside home, and the ekeles near there, far from the Heartstone. "We're here to walk with you. Firesong wants to see you."

Ayshen chimed in, "And that's where your meal awaits, with sweet-bread and the honeywater mix you like."

Drusi added, "Baked just for you. We have missed you so much. You're the talk of the halls."

Kelvren was placated by this and let his hackles drop somewhat. He became aware that he was illuminating the four as much as any of the mage-lights dotted around the walkway. He raised his head and looked around over the others' heads, and noticed something odd about the lights. The lights looked as if they pointed toward him. In fact, all of the mage-lights in sight were flaring toward him, as if they were candles and a breeze blew their flames in Kelvren's direction. Something here was very strange.

Silverfox had apparently noticed the phenomenon, too, and ventured, "Kel, there are some situations that are different now, and you have some changes ahead. No small number of things have happened that relate to you, and we need to explain what they are."

Without acknowledging Silverfox at all, Kelvren suddenly snapped his gaze to Sifyra and loudly said, "You called me *Sky Warrior*, not *Wingleader*. Ever since I have been Wingleader of k'Valdemar, you have called me by my rank."

:I call you as you are, with the respect due to you.:

Silverfox ushered Kelvren along, although the gryphon was reluctant to break his stare at the dyheli. "That is part of what we need to explain to you. We just don't want to do it out *here*. Let's get to the receiving room at our ekele, shall we?" Ayshen and Drusi vanished in a burst of hertasi speed, presumably going on ahead. Nightwind and Darian followed the irate gryphon through the vine-fall, and Darian said, soothingly, "You're probably just famished, Kel. You know how you get when you're hungry."

Grrr. I am not a gryphlet!

The dyheli stayed several bodylengths back, but always within sight.

Kelvren grumbled, "It isn't hunger that has me angry. It's the feeling that I am being handled because I'm as dangerous as a leaking oil-bomb. I feel like I have eyes upon me, and not in the way that hertasi are always watching. It feels like I have scouts ready to slay me with bowshot and mages ready to vaporize me. It is like I can hear the whispers of their thoughts with Mindspeech, and the whispers are all about how to be rid of me."

To his shock, Silverfox replied with disarming frankness, "That is fairly accurate."

Darian started, "Some of the—" and was cut short by an explosion.

The walkway mage-light nearest to Kelvren at that moment disintegrated with a loud crack, sending hot shards of glass all around, and a whip-crack of light the width of a human thumb lanced from the explosion into Kelvren's wing feathers. Everyone flinched, and when Kelvren recoiled from the explosion, the mage-light on the other side of the path did the same thing when he leapt near it. The mage-lights, made to last for decades of steady light, hadn't faded—they'd detonated.

Quite literally, the glowing gryphon's eyes blazed.

"Maybe you should stay toward the center of the path," Darian suggested.

Everyone agreed, and edged away from Kelvren.

The ekele of Firesong and Silverfox had expanded constantly since their arrival from Haven. Broad walkways now led to new levels, where decks large enough to host a half-dozen gryphons or thirty humans served as the roofs of tall gathering-rooms beneath. Silverfox led Kelvren into the largest of these rooms, laid out as a much more comfortable version of an enclosed council circle. The center of focus was a huge pile of lounge cushions with a graduated, curving stone perch nearby. Serving shelves and various amenities were placed artistically in every direction, mostly formed of sinuously curved blond wood. Two heavy tables were laden with slabs of beef and swine, one side cooked, the other raw. Heavy glass carafes of beer and honeywater were chilling off to the side, and a hertasi-sized bounty of baked goods made the layout complete. The floor was hard-tiled in sandy colors, but when Kelvren stepped in, he could feel that he stepped not only onto hard stone, but also through several layers of shields. He noticed one other thing immediately after seeing the meal laid out: aside from the carafes, the room had been cleared of anything easily breakable.

Firesong leaned by the only other exit, his arms folded, and commented, "You do know how to light up a room, don't you?"

Silverfox almost soundlessly joined Firesong, and guided him by one elbow to the nest of cushions. Darian and Night-wind followed Kelvren through the shields and inside, and the dyheli stayed outside. Kel was fine with that, and centered his gaze on the food he'd been promised.

Firesong gingerly removed the day's mask, and with it the mask's six long falls of braided hair and feathers that obscured his scarred ears. Kelvren knew that Firesong's appearance star-tled most people, Tayledras or not, but after years, most peo-ple had come to think of the masks as Firesong's actual face. Only in private, with close friends like Kelvren or Silverfox, would he let himself be seen unmasked, because neither of them cared what he looked like—for very different reasons, of course. For Silverfox, it was love. For Kelvren, it was indiffer-ence. Kelvren didn't care about what a horror Firesong's face was—Kelvren only cared about someone's "need to be hurt." If someone was beautiful but tyrannical, they needed to be hurt. If someone was ugly but kind, they didn't need to be hurt. Firesong was ugly to the nearly exposed bone, by human standards. Much of Firesong's face had been burned away by molten metal, but Kelvren only cared about his quality of character. Because of that, Firesong didn't "need to be hurt."

"I am here for two reasons, Firesong," Kelvren growled. "Food and courtesy."

"Food first," Firesong wisely replied. Kel needed no fur-ther invitation to dig into the meal—very literally. He immedi-ately sat down on his haunches, grasped a great chunk of meat with his talons, and hooked his beak in, pulling away deep gouges.

Firesong leaned into his mate's touch. Once his overmask was set aside, the thin, perforated leather undermask that matched his skin color was peeled away by Silverfox's gentle fingers. After Silverfox laid both masks across the perch, he retrieved cold water for both of them. Darian and Nightwind each sank back into heavily padded chairs.

"I want to talk to you about power," Firesong finally said.

"Still eating," Kelvren replied. Firesong sighed and waited. Darian cleaned out an ear with a finger. Nightwind took a boot off and emptied it of grit. Kel packed his gullet well, downing a carafe of beer to follow the first helpings of meats. The sounds were enough to make any prey animal flee.

"Are you ready to—" Firesong began.

"No," Kel replied.

Darian worked on the other ear now, and Nightwind rubbed at her foot. Firesong picked and scratched reflexively at some of the burn scars on his forehead and scalp, though they had been unchanged for years now. His expectedly dramatic presentation could not overcome the focus of a hungry and perturbed gryphon.

Silverfox lit some incense and waited Kelvren out. Finally sated, for the present, Kel lay down to face Firesong.

"I want to talk to you about power," Firesong began again.

"I want *you* to tell me what is happening in k'Valdemar. What madness has overtaken everyone? And what did all of you *do* to me?" Kelvren growled, despite his packed throat and crop.

"It isn't madness. It's all completely logical," Firesong replied.

"Most madnesses are *completely* logical, to those who are mad. I am *outside* this madness."

"You can judge the amount of madness for yourself, but we'll explain things as they are," Silverfox replied, seating himself on some of Firesong's cushions. Firesong took a deep breath, and started in.

"We need you to look at our history, Kel. Of White Gryphon, of the Far Flights, of k'Vala and k'Valdemar and the Storms. Think of what we have lived through, and what we have seen. Remember how many strange things, and awful things, we have experienced. Think of what you have experienced. You were trapped by a cold-drake once, yes? And you know how dyheli can control minds and bodies, and that some Adepts and Masters can do the same, yes?"

Kel nodded, thinking he knew where this was going. "Of late, I know that *very* well, and I don't like it. At all. *I don't like it.* But go on."

"There are creatures from *beyond*—that is the only way to describe it simply—and demons, and there are even shapechangers that are a part of our world. Now consider what has happened, from where we could understand it. You, k'Valdemar's Wingleader, vanished in a conflict inside Valdemar, in an area riddled with Change-Circles. Your teleson went silent. We searched for you, using probes of magic above and below our world, and could not find you. We despaired, and took risks of our own, and could not find you. We nearly risked invoking Kal'enal for you."

This mollified Kelvren just a little. *Calling upon Kal'enal always means a heavy price, if the call is answered at all. Velgarthian deities only help those who are out of other options or chances, and the further from hopeless someone is, the more it costs them. That they even seriously considered it for me means a lot.*

"Suddenly, there was a faint, faraway detection of a Gate, and not long after, a flare, of a new node. And then, after a pause, we narrowed it down to Deedun, something fast aimed directly for us and closing in," Silverfox added, while Firesong had a drink.

Firesong resumed the explanation. "In Oversight, you looked like nothing less than a fireball headed our way, or a major demon. Then the—whatever it was—you, it turned out, making a show of it, which I understand—scouted over all of our allies. You actually left a wake behind you that disturbed the lines at the time. You never knew this. Treyvan saved you by creating a node under you, and then before he had any chance to calm you—or the node's energy—down, you left. You made your now-famous flight and then aimed yourself for home. Only, to everyone at home, you looked like a possible attacker coming from the heart of Valdemar—again, a place full of Change-Circles, and no stranger to demon infiltration." He paused to let that sink in.

Darian leaned back and hooked his elbows over the chair's back. "While you were in flight, the Companions relayed a short form of what happened, though they knew very few details. It was only in the last candlemark before you landed that we recognized it was actually, possibly, you."

"So you asssumed I was a *threat*, not your Wingleader returning," Kelvren added up.

Darian just gestured in a way that conveyed "obviously." "Worse than that, there was a reasonable possibility that you were another creature trying to *look* like our missing Wingleader. We *wanted* it to be you, Kel, but wanting something against facts leads to ruin. Remember k'Sheyna. And if it was some creature using you, or the appearance of you, it probably knew all of our secrets and relationships. We had to be sure it was really you."

That explains why the new "Wingleader," as she claimed, was so caustic toward me. If I was an impostor, she wanted me to know they were aware of the possibility, and that they'd kill me before I even crossed the red line. She even goaded me to try something.

Kelvren mulled that over for around twenty seconds before deciding he had room for more beer. "Then I want to know this," he demanded between gulps. "You knew who I was quickly. So. Why have I not been greeted as a hero, and why are so few people coming near me?"

Firesong frowned, and answered, "Two main reasons. They treat you like you're diseased because you came back changed in a way that threatens all of us, Kel. I had to fight for you to stay in the Vale at all, and you aren't allowed anywhere closer than this to the Heartstone. Here is the ugly truth, Kel." Firesong leaned forward, with as deadly serious an expression as Kelvren had ever seen on him. "Every time you move, you draw in more energy. Ambient, anchored, focused, it is all affected, and you draw it toward you. It strains your body intensely, so you have to discard it. You used Lightcasting before, but at the same time, you were flying, which only drew in more energy. If you discard the energy in your sleep, it could be in a wild form, in any amount, in any direction. Gryphons gather the energy needed to live by movement—you learned that as a gryphlet; that's what gryphon wingbeats are for, as much as maneuvering. If you move, you gain energy. If you fly, you gain even more energy, which in turn keeps you flying. But now, if you move at all, you gain *too much* energy. And if you stop moving, you starve your new *need* for energy. If you don't use that energy, you burn."

Kelvren was very alarmed. *I know from my magecraft training how to ground and center, but that requires, well, ground. Is he saying I could fly and just erupt into flame because I couldn't ground? Or that I'd only fly if I were continually casting? This is awful . . .*

"And, if you move in areas with heavily structured spellwork, like k'Valdemar, you draw their energy toward you and disrupt the structure."

Skies above, it gets more awful.

"That explains why the mage-lights exploded," Nightwind offered.

Firesong glanced at the others. "Mage-lights exploded?"

Darian replied, "Ho, yes. From the stone core through the glass. Blazing hot, too. Their stored energy arced into him."

Firesong went deep into thought. "That bears out what we learned when we tried so much of, one could say, the usual things while Healing. You weren't there for all of that, Darian. It wasn't that the spells didn't work, it was that they lost cohesion before long." Firesong had done so much teaching over the past several years that he'd developed a habit of explaining things, even if it wasn't needed. It was a significant difference from the purposely enigmatic, brash flair of twenty years ago. "The manner wasn't just disruptive, it was disjunctive. Disruption would be like a loud noise drowning out a chant so it couldn't be heard. Disjunction would be breaking the chant into random, very loud noise."

Darian finished, "Which is what the Cataclysm was, eleven-hundred-some years ago. Two massive, radiating, cascading disjunctions. I remember my lessons, Firesong. So, again, you are proven right by insisting we keep Kel on isolated, evacuated paths. You can gloat about being right again."

"I've never stopped," Firesong absently replied, and pointed two fingers at Kelvren. "But it emphasizes that we can't allow you to fly, and we must keep you away from crafting circles and the like, because you could catastrophically harm even established spellwork just by being too near to it." Firesong sat back, cracking his spine and shoulders, adjusting to his new position. "Our Heartstone is robust, but we feed it by careful alignment of the lines we draw to it. Imagine what would happen if you got near the Heartstone during its daily tuning. It would be like dropping a boulder into a clear, steady stream."

"Sketi."

"Yes. *Sketi.*"

"I can't stay here!" Kelvren blurted, and jumped to his feet. "Why would you tell me this *here*, in the *Vale*? I should be far away from here!"

"You're safe enough for the moment, inside the protections in this room, Kel. So stay calm, and digest a while. No one is exploding just yet," Firesong reassured.

Yet, he says. Yet! I would be afraid enough if it was only I who could burn up, but this means I threaten everyone by even existing!

Silverfox said, "We may have thought of some things that can be done."

Kelvren looked up and around, twitching his ears in agitation, and paced in figure-eights. "You may have ideas, but you aren't the only clever ones. I remember Nightwind said I was *held*—" he nearly spat the word, "—for over six days. What has happened at Deedun?"

"Ah. That is another situation." Firesong looked to Silverfox, and it was clear that the next part would be bad news. They both looked to Darian, who got up to stand squarely before Kelvren. He spoke slowly and steadily, clearly trying to be as calming as he could be. "Kelvren, you—as we understand it all, and from what we learned in your mind—we know you did the right things. We know you were gryphon-fierce, and brave, noble, and heroic."

"As it should be," Kel replied.

"But—Valdemar is not doing well at the moment. The border wars, the attacks in Haven and on the Trade Roads, and the Storms, plus lesser-known troubles, have resulted in the Heralds, Guard, and no small amount of the Valdemaran population supporting them being far away from the center of the country. The Crown can only assist so much with the bad times deep inside their borders, and only spare so many Heralds. In short, the small keeps, holders, barons, trade leaders, and so on have fallen back upon their own troops, and tightened their local control. They are infighting, in the absence of the system that stabilized Valdemar before. It isn't just Deedun that is troublemaking. The trouble is all over."

Kel blinked blankly at Darian.

"This means that ambitious, greedy, or scared people are using rumors as weapons, to gather influence. And so, overwhelmingly, your noble actions on Valdemar's behalf have been interpreted by many as, ah . . . as the Crown bringing in monsters from the Pelagirs, and using the might of the terrifying Hawkbrothers against the small folk of Valdemar."

Kelvren screamed in rage, and by the way the others winced and fell back, it actually hurt them. "*That is untrue!* Untrue! *Wrong!* It is not how it is! I did what was right for an ally!"

Firesong yelled back, "We know! We know! But our truth is not what they see!"

Kelvren continued to rage. "Then they are liars, and they twist what happened! I defended the Crown and its troops! I was a good ally!"

Again, Firesong shouted, "We know! But that's bad too! Some of us argue that by acting as a full combatant and not a scout, you pulled us into Valdemar's internal struggles, and we can't afford that! K'Valdemar's position is precarious enough as it is!"

Kelvren fumed, beak shut, but his sides heaved in fast, deep breaths. His nares whistled with each inhalation. "Which ultimately means *what*, exactly?" he snapped at the four.

"Which means," Darian gasped as he rubbed at his temple, "diplomatically . . . it is a difficult dance, Kel, and we're doing the best we can with a new dance floor and new steps. What we came up with is, your actions have been claimed by Lord Breon and disavowed as an action of the Tayledras. He has claimed officially that you were under his orders to act on your own best judgment."

"But—I wasn't! I scouted for all of us, and we shared the information with Kelmskeep as a favor—"

"—but in the mess Valdemar is in, Breon's story is better," Darian countered.

"For who? For Breon, for Valdemar, for the Vale, for the Tayledras? No, I *hate it*! As Wingleader, I hate it! It makes gryphons sound—uncontrollable! It makes me sound impulsive and undisciplined!"

Firesong and Silverfox instantly met eyes with each other and held their breaths. Both shook their heads and exhaled a moment later.

"Silver Gryphon Chief Redhawk put forth the suggestion that until you are reliable, physically and mentally, you should not be Wingleader. Your responsibilities are, as the final say put it, suspended," Darian explained. "And that allows us to honestly say that your rank was taken from you if Valdemaran leaders take issue against Breon."

Kelvren slit his eyes, and his crest and hackles went up.

"Kel," Nightwind pleaded. "We don't know whether your condition will make you insane, or simply fall out of the sky suddenly. We don't know if you'll unknowingly walk past a Working in progress and suddenly incinerate yourself and half of the Vale. A Silver Gryphon has to be relied upon to execute justice, and a Wingleader must be sound enough to take gryphons into danger without question. As an *absolute*. Right now, Kel, you are one big, glowing question. You are still beloved, and still respected, but you can't actually be trusted to be Wingleader because of what you underwent in that Change-Circle. Hate it if you must, but you know it is reasonable."

"I do hate it! Diplomats, lords, and power-grabbers turned my virtue, then my pain, into a reason for my punishment?" Kelvren clawed at the tile, vaguely aware that he was drawing his talons side to side, sharpening them.

Darian drew his hands to his sides for fear that Kel would

snap at them. "It was my solution. Valdemaran culture is different from ours, Kel. They—they prefer to have someone to blame. They don't just act upon a circumstance like we do. They prefer to fill a target with arrows first, and then check if it was the cause of the problem. Breon's taking the arrows for you, so we have the time to fix your body if we can. We can fix your reputation later."

"I hate it," Kelvren growled, but gave the situation its due thought. *I sacrificed myself to save a Valdemaran and so Breon is making a sacrifice to save me. I can't disrespect that, but I don't have to like something to respect it. A gryphon's life is worth the story the gryphon leaves behind, and this is not where I wanted my story to go. I haven't even had gryphlets yet! Wait—how am I ever going to have any young? I could burst into flames on someone's back! I do not want to be remembered that way either!*

Darian said softly, "Rukayas is new to k'Valdemar, from k'Leshya by way of k'Vala, but is the oldest gryphon here now, and Redhawk appointed her as the new Wingleader."

"Rukayas. Her name is Rukayas. Hurrrh."

"And you're glowing brighter," Firesong added. "I'll draw you down. Just open up a bit, Kel, let me take some of that energy from you."

"Oh," Kelvren grumbled, "*now* you *ask* before taking something from me."

"Food and *courtesy*," Firesong chided, quoting the gryphon.

"I hate you *so much* right now," Kelvren growled back.

"Neither for the first nor the last time will you hate me," Firesong said while the room dimmed in response to his gestures. "You could only survive this in two ways that we know of. Three, really, but you wouldn't like the third."

"Oh? What is the third?"

"Leave forever so you aren't a problem to us."

"Like Skandranon's last flight."

"So some stories say."

Kelvren shook his head. "I do not want to be like him *that* way. And his acts of heroism brought him nothing like these lies and intrigues and hate from others."

Silverfox's composure vanished. He covered his face with both hands, in a bout of laughter. "Sorry, it's just—sorry. Please. Go ahead."

"What?" Kelvren demanded.

"Just that kestra'chern have stories from Amberdrake's side of history."

"To continue," Firesong picked up smoothly, "the other two ways I have considered work together. One, we can train you to be a mage much, much better at handling magic power, and more sensitive to feeling it around you. Two would be—" he hesitated.

Firesong opened his mouth to speak a couple of times, but it was half a minute before he finally continued. "Two would be to create a Heartstone for you. A very, very small one. Heavy, but not too heavy. Portable. This has been tried in the past and the concept is sound, but there were no—long-lasting successes. I am curious; in your flight, did it ever occur to you to tap a line or a node to Lightcast? Or did you only use your own power?"

"I did as felt right. I used what I had inside me, I used what I collected as I flew."

"Ah. Interesting. That deserves some further thought. You've partly answered an old theory about whether a living thing can be a node, with that. And a node can feed a Heartstone."

"*Sketi!*" Kelvren exclaimed, sitting down abruptly.

"Yes. Very big *sketi* if we can make it work. It is your life, Kelvren. I mean that sincerely. It is your life—you live or die by this. Right now, nobody wants to come near you because they think you're as likely to explode as talk to them, and you're politically toxic. That can change over time, but meanwhile, we just have to keep you alive."

"I hate this. This is not right," Kelvren repeated.

"It isn't right, but it is the way it is," Firesong answered.

Darian rested his hands on Kelvren's right alula. "I know this is a terrible situation, Kel, and I know you want someone to slash and bite. I say, don't even bother to blame anyone, because you have more important things to work on. Your survival must be ensured. It is like k'Sheyna. It is true that their Adepts did not think of what happened as being an attack from

Falconsbane, or anyone. They just dealt with the situations, and yes, that caused them much sorrow. But had they gone looking for enemies to blame at the time, instead of calming the disruptions, their situation would have been far worse. I say, don't fall prey to cursing others, and complaining about what you deserve and don't deserve. These people in Valdemar are much different from everyone you knew far west, and you are going to have to adapt yourself to them, because they are more numerous than our kind."

Darian smoothed Kelvren's feathers along the leading edge of his wing, and it did soothe him. Firesong and the others exchanged a pointed look, and they began to slip away, Firesong leaving first. Kel didn't really care—he was well-fed now, they weren't contributing anything to the conversation anyway, and more importantly, they certainly weren't giving him cozy feather-scratches. Besides, he was still especially irritated with Firesong, so, begone with them.

"Hurrrrr," he grumbled, lying down again. "I do not like it, and it is not fair, but the world does not move by what I like, and the world has never been fair. But listen to yourself, Dar'ian of Errold's Grove, referring to yourself as Tayledras, not Valdemaran!"

Darian sat down on the floor in front of him, cross-legged, and worked a hand into Kel's neck-feathers, scratching soothingly. "I've had to learn all this myself. You were there for it. And technically, yes, I was born in Valdemar."

"Dar'ian, my parents taught me, wherever you land is your home. But I feel that k'Valdemar is *most truly* my home. It is what I think of as *your* home. Your parents raised you to be a child, Errold's Grove raised you to be a boy, we raised you to be a man, and then you made yourself an adult. And alongside you, I went from someone to be cared *for* to someone who is cared *about*. I do not want to leave our home, Dar'ian. Or be chased away because of what happened. I was *good*, Dar'ian."

"Yes. Yes, you were," Darian murmured into Kelvren's brow-feathers. "You did the right things. You were there for me, you fought for me, and then you went out and did it again for people you didn't even know. You don't deserve all of this, but there's that world-isn't-fair thing, again, isn't it? But you know that I will always be thankful for you, and you'll always be with me somehow."

"For you I would be shot and slashed a hundred times," Kelvren rumbled, then added after a few moments, "But not all at once."

Darian chuckled and twisted around to rest his back against Kelvren's side, as they'd done dozens of times, basking in the sunlight. This time, though, the gryphon *was* the sun. "I don't know if it helps, but not everybody in Valdemar is afraid of us, or of you."

"They *should* be afraid of me. *Everything* should be afraid of me."

"We all are, we just hide it well. What I mean is, the Crown and most of Haven think of us as strong allies, and think of gryphons as wonders. I know right now you must think of all Valdemarans as a bunch of idiots, but try and walk on their paths for a moment. For most people in Valdemar, until the Storms, they tended crops, built roads, milled grain, and were ordinary soldiers at most. The ongoing border wars were distant. Magic was just something in old legends, not something that was in their lives every day, affecting them personally. And then came the Storms. Instead of being something *good*, something that made roads that never needed re-paving, or built walls so strong nothing could knock them down—something that helped and protected them—magic became something horrible that brought strange beasts and diseases, ripped their ordered lives up, and scattered the pieces. And then, the news—mostly rumors—came that the Crown's sudden allies were the Ghosts of the Deadly Forests. It would be like you flying a patrol, being blasted into the ground by twenty whirlwinds, then being helped up by people who only spoke by clapping hands, wore giant hats, and ate poisonous tree bark."

Kel thought about that for a moment. "It would be hard to relate to," he agreed. "I would not think much about why those people were that way, I would only think of my own pain and well-being, and that I was knocked out of the sky."

"Yes, and now *every* demonstration of magic is looked at as something to be feared until it can be *proved* it isn't going to hurt them. And there are a thousand minds like that, versus every one Valdemaran who understands." Darian sighed. "That is part of what I am doing as a Knight of Valdemar. It's a rank and title they all know and understand. I don't have to be highborn to hold it. In fact, at least half of the Knights are as much mongrels as I am. So ordinary people consider me one of them. But it *is* a title and a rank, and high enough that the highborn grudgingly allow that I belong with *them*, too."

"And so you cut your hair back, and wear your armor. You have to appear more Valdemaran to them," Kelvren replied, and twisted his head nearly upside down so his friend could reach deep inside the feather layers.

Darian sighed. "I even keep Kuari far away when I go into populated places in Valdemar now. And I ride a horse. Being a Knight is not the same as being a diplomat or envoy. I can deliver messages of peace, sure, but they're delivered in an armored fist. It's understood in Valdemaran culture that Heralds and Knights have our diplomacy backed up by pikemen and archers. So here, I am Dar'ian k'Valdemar, and there I am Knight Darian Firkin."

"You are like a gryphon now," Kel pointed out, feeling very proud he had thought of the analogy. "Not a bird and not a beast! Something better!"

Darian laughed ruefully. "Yes, I guess I am. But if I'm a gryphon, Kel, I am going to ask you to trust me with something more important to you than your life. I am going to ask you to trust me with your *reputation*."

"Mrrrph," Kel replied dubiously, and beak-nudged at Darian's shoulder and chest harder than was necessary.

"Kel, we have been friends for a very, very long time now," Darian pointed out earnestly, pushing back. "It's not going to be quick—and it probably won't be everything you want *or* deserve. But I'm going to stake *my* reputation alongside yours, as the Owl Knight, because you are that important to me. You have to leave your story to me for a while."

Kelvren huffed, "Because if I went to them, I would just be a magical war beast raging about injustice while brandishing my claws, yes? So you must speak about me, and for me. Hurrrh.

As much as it amuses me to frighten others, maybe it is best that I don't display myself for a time. It is the way of a Wingleader. We train in formations and combined attacks to multiply our force, and to defend each other should one of us become defenseless. We have to trust in our flight companions. There are some battles I cannot fight myself, so I suppose you will fight them for me."

Kelvren laid his head down flat on the floor, his beak-hook tucked between the edges of two tiles. He heaved a loud sigh, and the lighting shimmered around them.

Darian blinked rapidly, as if his eyes were stinging him, but he smiled. "And in the years to come, if I find myself in a battle in which claws and beaks are all that can save me, I shall depend upon you."

At that, Kel raised his head high. "My talons are at your service, now and evermore, Dar'ian Owlknight."

"Well, right now, I'd like you to trust us, and sleep," Darian told him. "Or your trondi'irn will probably skin me."

"I would not like you to be skinned, friend Dar'ian," Kel replied gravely. "You would be most uncomfortable without your skin. Perhaps she could settle for stripping your clothes off instead?"

Darian choked on a laugh and stood up. "I'll see you again, Kel," he replied, but then sighed while dusting himself off. "I have to ride overnight and leave from Kelmskeep at dawn. Val and I are taking thirty of Breon's loyals to garrison Millbridge, and then we're off with an envoy and a strongbox to make sure the Weavers stay allied. I wish I could stay here, but I know you would want me to go. Our friendships must often fall second to our duties, but a true friend knows that duty is part of what makes someone their friend." He stopped at the doorway and added, "I'm going to make what you did in Valdemar—*for* Valdemar—mean even more."

They both said nothing for a minute, as if trying to memorize each other's appearance and expression.

"You are my hero, Kel," Darian finally said.

"You are my hero, Dar'ian," Kelvren replied.

Then the Owlknight turned away, and departed into the dusk.

Kelvren had stuffed himself at breakfast, and sleep and food had gone a long way toward soothing his temper. So he was also ready to listen as Firesong spoke, or more properly, lectured. "An Adept is well-learned, but primarily, an Adept is a durable, fast-thinking problem-solver. This is one of the great truths of being a Tayledras Adept. It is not the high magic that makes an Adept, it is the clarity of mind to solve the problem of the moment. That moment could be all the time there is to act in, and the Adept must only let in other concerns when things are safe. Time taken to think about hate, love, blame, or justice could be an Adept's last thoughts. Adepts find dangers and traps all the time, but they are taken as the way of all life and the world, not as something done *to* them."

"We discussed this already," Kel growled. "None of you want me to think about blame and the wrong I am being done."

Firesong instantly replied, "It is so important, we repeat it. You are an emotional soul, Kelvren Skothkar, and while passion serves you well in life, it can be your death now. We are going to try to teach you Adept ways so you can control the ruin inside you. Let that sink into your feathered skull a while."

Kelvren did. *I doubt they expect me to become an actual Adept, but he did talk about a small Heartstone. A Heartstone is like a rain barrel that draws in and stores power to be drawn out as needed. But . . .*

"We should not do any of that here," Kelvren declared. "Not in the Vale. Not even *near* the Vale. I won't allow it. If my training strayed, I could tap the Heartstone of the Vale, or affect the flow into it. We need to be far away if we're going to attempt this. And not in Valdemar, nor near the Clans. If I fail, I don't want anyone to see it . . . and I know that you can shield anybody nearby if I did."

Despite today's mask, Firesong looked both impressed and smug. "So you want to travel again, so soon?"

"I want to keep k'Valdemar and our allies safe. Here is not the place."

Firesong nodded. "An expedition it will be, then. Because you're right. I was going to lead up to it, but you suggested it yourself." He did a little bow, and Aya sparked in a shower of light-dust on the stone perch. "Smart gryphon. A Healing Adept's way not only involves fast thinking, but also how to prevent harm in every direction and every level of repercussion while you're doing it." Firesong interlaced his fingers and leaned forward. "Magic at Adept level is something you can barely ever escape. It hums in your head, it brushes at you like a breeze or a scent. Magic can have surges, and crackle, and go awry. It can have flavors, and drop away when you need it only to reappear stronger an instant later. The larger swells appear in your mind like waves of life and lightning, as tall and wide as you can comprehend, but it may have a single flaw amongst its millions of threads that you must smooth away or it will twist something leagues from you into something hideous and deadly. Some power drops from the Over, right through ours, and into the Under. Out there, in the Pelagirs, an Adept with their senses wide open could feel changes like that with every step." Firesong stepped back then, having Kelvren's full attention. "So, when all that you can perceive has a potential for disaster, an Adept must live by, *how do I turn what I encounter into an advantage*? That is why I think you can save your own life, because it is how you already think, Kelvren. Believe me, I know. I was in your head. What you did in Valdemar was Adept-style thinking."

Kel considered this, and decided that he was flattered. "So. Let us look at this. How can my being a pariah become an advantage?"

"Ah. Because your admiration for Treyvan and Hydona and Skandranon can make you like them, if what I have in mind can be done," Firesong answered, with a sly look.

"How?"

"Because not being needed as Wingleader here means that you can leave here as you choose. Being claimed by Breon's statement means you do not have to be tried for justice in Valdemar," Firesong answered. "In short, because of what has happened, you are uniquely—*free*."

If these words came from anyone else but Firesong, I'd drop them in a lake. But—yes, he is right. Being Wingleader meant I was bound here to lead others. Now I am not only replaced, I

*am redundant. Dangerous, even to have around. And that is
their loss, too. And I can't go deep into Valdemar again because
I'm the best known, brightest target, so . . .*

Firesong stood up, whirling in an obviously practiced theat-
rical turn so his robes billowed out before draping, and concentrated for twenty heartbeats. He then gestured in two circles
and then a rectangle with his slender, tightly gloved hands,
and called up an image in midair of a very well-known map. It
distorted at first, pulled at by Kelvren's affliction, but Firesong
used his palm to pull the map image back into proportion. "The
Storms were caused by disruptive waves of harmfully structured magic power peaking and trenching in ripples between
the Over and Under realms. With the help of several wise and
lucky people, we determined that these were the results of the
'anti-spell' blast from the detonation of Urtho's Tower and
Ma'ar's Stronghold, traveling all the way around our world and
returning to their places of origin all these years later."

Kel nodded. He had heard this before. "As you have explained, a cascading disjuncture."

"Yes." Firesong nodded. "As they got closer, the waves became more concentrated and frequent. All indications were
that we could expect a new Cataclysm unless we did something
about it." The map showed these waves in motion like ripples from a stone, only flowing in toward the stone instead of
away. "During the Storms, we stopped one of the returning Cataclysm loci from expanding back outward from the remains of
Urtho's Tower by giving it a place to go, channeled away from
our world. But the question remains: what happened to the
other locus, from the point of Ma'ar's ancient stronghold?"

Kelvren listened intently. This was a good question, and it
sounded as if Firesong had been considering it for some time
now. And if *Firesong* was concentrating on something for
a good long while, it was probably worth thinking about. The
fact that Firesong was talking about it now meant it somehow
involved Kelvren.

Firesong continued. "The waves should have concentrated,
violently exploded outward. And while it would technically
have caused less devastation than the original Cataclysm, it
should still have leveled hills and forests, and killed untold

numbers. Exhausted as we were—we who were left alive, anyway—we braced for it." The glitter in Firesong's eyes reminded Kel that the Adept had very much put his own life at risk back then.

Firesong's map image increased in size until the shape of a well-known body of water with the sketches of a few very faint craggy islands near its shores filled Kelvren's vision. "The waves, with all their power, poured into the second location, as expected. And then they vanished. No mountain-powdering explosion, no disintegrating, rock-melting firestorms. Because of the haze caused by the Storms, no one has ever found out why. No one can Farsee or scry there, nor any creature's vision penetrate the haze. Prayers and spirit-realm queries go unanswered. The waters and weather are too treacherous for a ship exploration."

What was Firesong getting at? If no one could See there, and no one could go there, how was anyone supposed to find out what *was* there that had absorbed all that power? What did that have to do with him, for that matter?

"If you can learn what I can teach you, if we can create this new Heartstone, if you can control your ruin, and if a few dozen other factors fall into place as I have in mind," Firesong teased, "I ask you this, Kelvren the Bright." He let the map image stay in place, and faced the gryphon.

"Would you dare to explore what is at the center of Lake Evendim?"

Kel found himself waiting. Again. He had been under the impression that he and a couple of chosen companions—small "c"—would toss on some packs and head for Lake Evendim. If not that day, then the next, surely!

After that lecture on magic, Kel had been ready, eager, waiting for Ayshen and his packs . . . but Ayshen and the other hertasi just presented him with more food, and Firesong said nothing, just nodding in passing and leaving before Kel opened his beak.

He waited, luxuriating in the feeling of being dry and warm and groomed and pain free, and once his monumental breakfast had already worn off, he realized he was hungry again. There were those platters that Ayshen and the others brought in just waiting for him. And although he was greatly tempted to storm up and find wherever Firesong had taken himself, it would have been a crime to waste that good food, particularly when he recalled how the troops at Deedun were getting by on old goat and gruel sometimes. So he ate it to show his appreciation. And then, of course, he slept, eased by the warmth and lack of pain—and *perhaps* some incense that Silverfox set to burn in a corner might have had some soothing quality to it.

He woke to hear Silverfox somewhere above in the upper levels of the ekele playing a gittern and singing. It was fully night by now, perhaps two candlemarks before midnight, so his inner time sense told him. There were other sounds besides Silverfox singing, all the sounds of a healthy Vale that he had missed so much. And had *especially* missed when he'd first landed. Distant murmurs of voices, fluttering leaves, the far-off trickle of water, hints of music elsewhere that harmonized with Silverfox's voice. Kel just lay there for a moment, listening, since obviously no one was going anywhere tonight.

He has an excellent voice. Kel was no expert in human music, but Silverfox's deft playing and low, crooning song were both very soothing. Finally, he opened his eyes. It appeared that hertasi had replenished the scant remains of what he had eaten with more: this time not the heavy haunches and sides, but a deftly arranged platter of supremely thin-sliced, fat-riddled raw beef, thin-sliced heart and kidney, and more of the sweet breads he liked. Less than half a candlemark after he began snacking on what had been left for him, Ayshen turned up.

The hertasi made no attempt to be stealthy, announcing his arrival with clicks of his talons on the floor and a gentle swishing of his tail. He had changed his outfit, but that wasn't what caught Kel's attention, for he was laden with a bowl of tasty fresh brains, a bowl of liver, and even a small bowl of eyeballs!

"I want you to know," the little hertasi said, as he carefully put his three ceramic bowls down in front of Kel, "every gryphon in the Vale gave up their right to these tonight. For you. Just for you."

"Hurrrrr." He felt an emotion he couldn't exactly define waft through him, as if he had been brushed by a giant feather. It wasn't gratitude. It wasn't exactly pleasure, but it had some characteristics of pleasure. There was some relief in there too. Actually, it wasn't *a* single emotion at all, but a mix of them. He pondered how best to respond.

"Tell them . . . tell them I am grateful. That I am thankful. And that . . . that I understand why they did what they did." *I don't like it. But I understand it, and that's the truth.* "And I hope they understand why I did what I did."

"Nightwind has been your very vocal advocate," said Ayshen, as Kel lowered his beak to pick out an eyeball and tossed his head up to send it down his throat. The sweet-salty taste of it in the back of his throat, after days of the scraps no one else wanted in Deedun, made him realize several things in that moment.

That he really, really wanted to live. *Live,* not just exist. But on the other talon, life itself was exquisitely sweet, and if, when all of this was over, he didn't have the same kind of life he'd had before . . . well, he could accept that.

I will learn to appreciate what I have, as well as hope after things I do not have.

"You seem calmer," Ayshen remarked, as Kelvren finished the eyeballs and turned his attention to the brains. "If you will forgive my saying so, when you got here, you were acting, well, *drunk.* And when you first woke up, you were as moody as a sulky sixteen-year-old who has just been told they cannot attend a dance."

This morning, he might have jumped up and begun raving again. This time, he didn't. For one thing, it was Ayshen who was telling him this, and hertasi didn't waste time insulting people. For another . . .

He ate brains, and thought. Maybe eating brains would help him think. "I think I was drunk," he replied after a moment. "Or something like it. Fevered, still? Had I been given something that hadn't worn off? From . . . from what I remember, I remember being almost intoxicated, and then in something like a drunken rage. Didn't someone say I was shattered, yet unable to feel the pain?"

Ayshen relaxed and folded his legs under him to sit down beside the bowls. "Yes. They couldn't understand it. But I could. We hertasi have something like that happen when we are badly injured. It allows us to flee to somewhere safe before we collapse, or to stand our ground against an enemy to allow others to flee. It's as if someone opens our skulls and pours in every intoxicating thing you can think of. It hasn't happened to me, but it did to my father. He said he felt invincible, absolutely invincible, and if he hadn't known what was going on, he might have carried on with what he was doing. There was absolutely no pain, he said. And he said all his emotions were elevated as well. In his case, it was mostly anger as well."

That does sound like what happened to me. Complete with the feeling of utter euphoria and invincibility.

"Hurrr." He picked at the liver, savoring the rich, raw taste in his throat and on the back of his tongue. The other gryphons of the Vale had sacrificed their own pleasure to make amends, and it would be criminally bad manners not to show his appreciation by eating it. "That is very familiar. What was he doing?"

"Tunnel-digging. An unexpected rock-fall broke every rib in his chest," Ayshen said frankly. "He was angry at himself for not being more careful and about to try and free himself, but he stopped himself just in time when he remembered what that feeling of euphoria meant." Ayshen narrowed his eyes, and Kel suspected he was waiting for Kel's reactions.

Kel closed his eyes and cast his mind back. Yes, that did match what he had felt. He opened his eyes again and nodded. "Because if he had moved, all those broken bones would have turned his insides into a pincushion. Which, apparently, I was on the verge of becoming. For a second time."

But . . . surely that must have worn off by now. Or had it? He took an assessment of himself again and discovered something supremely unnerving.

Inside, his emotions were still a bubbling cauldron. He felt that if he let go, he'd find himself weeping, then laughing hysterically, then terrorized, then deeply depressed, then profoundly ashamed, then enraged, then . . . well, the list went on, every emotion rising to the surface of that stew, then vanishing into the depths again before he could do more than *feel* it. He gasped, and Ayshen tensed.

"What's . . . wrong with me?" he managed to get out. "I . . . there . . . too many feelings!"

Then, before Ayshen could answer that rather incoherent question, he managed to attain control over himself, and all the seething emotions faded again, until they were barely perceptible.

But not gone. They were all still there, waiting for a moment of inattention, when something—rage, probably, it seemed the strongest—would flare up like a fire in dry tinder, and he'd be—

—I'd be ranting like I did when I first awakened.

"Nightwind says," Ayshen said slowly and carefully, "that she was unable to balance something she called *humors*, by which I think she meant the . . . physical things in you that create emotions. That you'd have to learn to do that yourself. That she and Firesong could probably *help*, and that would be part of what he would teach you, because it is just an exaggerated version of what a Healing Adept already does. But that until you do balance all those things, you will have to do something else." He paused, and seemed to be searching for a diplomatic way to say something that Kel was *really* not going to like.

Less than I liked being controlled—ah. Ah.

"You are about to tell me that I am going to have to stop and think before I say or do *anything*, aren't you?" he suggested, trying not to sound resentful and failing utterly.

In the silence that followed, there were no sounds at all in the ekele, except their breathing. And that was when he noticed that all the lighting was supplied not by mage-lights, as was common, but by lanterns. And that someone must have gone around and replaced mage-lights with those lanterns, because while lovely, they were all mismatched.

Given what happened on the path . . . that was probably a good idea.

They gave a very different light from the mage-lights, softer, dimmer, and slightly wavering, as flames were inclined to do. Someone had added a subtle scent to the oil as well.

"Well . . . yes," Ayshen replied bluntly. "Now, we hertasi see gryphons as creatures of impulse and strong feelings, but you were . . . well, compared to even your former self, if your former self was a candle of emotion and impulse, what you were when you woke up was a bonfire. Not out of control . . . but we knew that only because we know you. Anyone outside our group of friendship would have looked at you and fled. And Nightwind says that *now* it's even more important that you stop and think and, well, I don't know, recite calming things to yourself, because this power you are barely controlling reacts to what you feel."

Bitter, bitter, this takes all the goodness of that lovely liver from my throat. But even as he thought that, he saw the light he was putting out become brighter, and he knew Ayshen was right. Nightwind was right. Firesong . . . was right.

"But don't suppress anything, dear friend," said Firesong behind him, from the stairs, making him start, and the light from from him flared and died again. He turned his head, and Firesong met his gaze before continuing his way down.

Firesong moved soundlessly down the treads, nothing hiding the scars of his face now; he was dressed, perhaps, for bed—or at least for lounging—in a tunic and breeches of some soft, fluid, unadorned material. "If you suppress your feelings, they'll only come exploding out at the worst possible time. No, you should feel them, and acknowledge them, and then transmute them into something useful."

"Like you have?" he bit off, not caring that his bitterness showed in the way he almost spat each word.

"Yes, actually," Firesong replied, and folded himself gracefully down in his favorite nest of cushions. "I'm not saying it will be easy, but transmutation seems to come instinctively to you. Being deliberate does not . . . but I know you are capable of anything you put your mind to."

"Hurr." *Was that actually a compliment?* "It will make me slow, thinking all the time."

"And what's wrong with that? Deliberation has its virtues." A hint of a smile was in Firesong's voice, if not on his face.

"But gryphons are *swift*!" he protested. "Skandranon—"

"Is in the past. You are in the present. All things change," Firesong pointed out. Then before Kelvren could reply, continued, "You are probably wondering when we leave."

"Yes!" The abrupt change of subject was at least to something welcome. "Tomorrow, surely!"

"You will have to learn patience," Firesong repeated. Kel felt himself flushing and was about to utter a scathing answer, when he saw Ayshen's sharp eyes on him and remembered what Ayshen and Firesong had both said about thinking before he answered.

I think . . . I am getting angry. And I think . . . it is for no good reason. Firesong knows better than I do how much of a danger to k'Valdemar I pose. He would not keep me here one moment longer than necessary. So there must be a reason. I think . . . I think there are going to be a very many things in my future that I do not like, but that will have good reasons I cannot argue with.

As he thought, the light that had flared up when Firesong had told him he must learn patience died down.

He snorted a very little, ate the last of the liver to soothe his spirits, and put his head down on the floor, eyes fixed on Firesong. "I am listening," he said.

It was easier to read Firesong's voice than his face. And the voice held warm tones of approval. "Silverfox and I have discussed this at length while you slept, along with several others here in k'Valdemar. Not Elders, because, to be frank, the way you get to be an Elder is to lose some of your taste for adventure."

Kel snorted laughter at that. It was true, and all the funnier for being so. "And you have not?" he asked.

Ayshen poured honeywater for Firesong and brought it to him. Firesong accepted with a nod of thanks. "Well," he temporized. "I am more wary of adventure than I was before. I don't rush blindly forward anymore. I adventure the way a cat would, if you will. With careful examination and taking plenty of time to look things over before walking, not rushing, into it. At any rate, we discussed this pretty thoroughly. Your injuries are still in the process of healing, and your energies are still unsettled; the latter is a good reason to be gone from here, but the former suggests that we should do so at a more temperate pace than we would if I were younger and you were in a less frangible state."

Wait, what? Did Firesong just say—he is old? He doesn't look old! He can't be old! Firesong had always seemed ageless to Kel. Like a tree, or maybe a rock. Was he saying that for effect?

All of Kelvren's senses sharpened—even more than usual— and then *much* more than usual! A gryphon's eyes were already sharper than an eagle's, but suddenly he was aware of the tiniest details. The herringbone weave of Firesong's tunic and breeches, the way one strand of hair kept separating from the rest and wafting out on a breeze only it could sense, the tiny, almost invisible lines at the outer corners of his eyelids, the—

"What are you doing, Kel?" Firesong asked, calmly, as Kel heard all of the over- and under-tones of his voice, saw the vibration at his throat as he spoke, even saw himself reflected as a self-illuminated image in Firesong's eyes—

"Watching you."

"Oh, you're doing quite a bit more than that," the Adept replied. "Keep your focus on me, but turn your attention inward. See what you are using your energies for."

Now, this was a whole new exercise, and the novelty of it kept him from doing anything but trying to figure out what Firesong meant. Focus on the Adept, but look inside *himself*? If a gryphon's eyes could have been crossed, his surely would be doing just that!

But his memory flung up an early image—how it had been to learn to use power to hold himself in the air, how that had been—*yes!*—looking inward and outward at the same time! And then everything snapped into place, and he continued to drink in the smallest details of his friend, from the elaborate silver rings on his hands that echoed the rings binding some of the locks of his hair, to the details of the subtle herringbone, which was not a single color, but two, very near, making a subtle difference that accounted for the shimmering of a fabric that was matte, and not shiny. But inside, inside himself he now was acutely aware of how some of that power he had tingling at the ends of his talons had moved to his eyes, creating, he somehow understood, a kind of lensing effect, with spectacular results. What if he could hear like—

Now the power moved to his ears, and he winced involuntarily at the result. *No, I don't like that!* And after a moment of internal struggle and a blip of panic, it all slowly subsided, slowly bent to his will, and the power moved away, leaving him with his normal—albeit acute by human standards—hearing.

I could bear to see less, too, he decided after a moment, as colors that had been muted in the shaded lights of this room of the ekele became saturated, and the heat-color coming from both Ayshen and Firesong became so bright that he would have thought it was the Adept and hertasi who were a danger to the Vale, not him.

He blinked, slowly, and with each blink, the power receded until his vision was normal again.

"Now imagine what could have happened if we were out in wilderness, something startled you, and your vision did what it just did," Firesong pointed out. "Suddenly and without warning, as it did just now." Ayshen said nothing, just listened, focusing on each of them as they spoke in turn.

Kel never had any notion that thinking could be so much work . . . but there it was. This was *hard*. Having to think about what he was doing inside while talking about what-might-be and analyzing what he said before he said it.

"It would have been a distraction," he agreed. "I could overreact, as if it was an enemy doing this, and not me doing it to myself. I think I am beginning to hate you less."

"And you love me still," teased Firesong.

"Yes, damn you," he growled. Then shook his head so that his ear-tufts rattled. "So, what you are saying is that instead of a handful of us making all speed to Lake Evendim, we should mount what you call an expedition and travel slowly. So if things get out of hand, the situation will be more controlled."

"Hopefully," Firesong amended. "But yes. That is exactly what I mean."

So there it was. A lightning-fast trip was not at all what Firesong intended, and Kel knew by now that once Firesong had made up his mind about something, there was no changing it. When he had said "expedition," that had been exactly what he meant.

Kel could just picture it now. A veritable parade. A full-scale expedition, with many creatures, and probably Tayledras floating barges, and a very great deal of organizing to do. K'Valdemar didn't have enough barges to spare, so other Vales would have to be asked, and then the barges would be sent through a Gate when the Vale didn't have anything better to do, and then the barges would have to be stocked with supplies.

We certainly are not going to be moving quietly or discreetly.

And just *who* was going to be along was yet another question. Kel had originally assumed it would be him, Ayshen, Nightwind . . . oh, Firesong would have to go, of course, if he was going to be training Kel on the way.

But now he realized that he wasn't the only one who needed tending. Firesong was as much in need of a trondi'irn as Kel was, and Silverfox would have to come as well . . . and a couple of dyheli for them to ride.

But once you started down that road, as Firesong said, you might as well just take your time and proceed deliberately, so their hertasi would have to come too, and . . . as Kel added up all the people who would need to come, although he had wanted to tell Firesong he could give over his luxuries and *just go,* it became very apparent that . . . well, that just wouldn't work.

But Firesong was a clever bastard. He must have known that Kel would rage again if he was told this would be more than a couple of comrades flying off to explore. So he had said nothing and allowed Kel to figure it out for himself.

"Hopefully," he echoed. "What else is it you intend for me to learn, now that the lessons have begun?"

The Adept's eyelids drooped a little in approval. "Well, this is going to be all new ground for both of us," he admitted. "Much as it pains me to say this, I don't know everything!"

Kel threw his head up and dropped his jaw, as if in shock. *"No!"* he gasped. "It cannot be!"

Firesong threw a cushion at him. Kelvren batted it out of the air with a flick of a wing.

Was it only days ago that I couldn't move that wing without wishing to die?

"This is going to be an exercise in patience for both of us, Kel," Firesong admitted. "Because the only way I can think to begin this is to observe *you,* and when you begin to move magic energies instinctively, remind you to look at what you are doing. The more you do that, *I think,* the better you will become at directing it, until you establish something *like* ley-lines within yourself, which will enable us to use your magic to create and empower a very small Heartstone. There are debates about what it should be made of; it is going to have to be very tough, but small. I favor an iron pyrite crystal myself, and I suspect the others will come to the same conclusion." The glitter in Firesong's eyes said, without words, *Because that's what I'm using whether they like it or not.*

That amused Kel. *He probably already has the one he wants in his magpie-stash. But he won't know where it is, so he's waiting until Silverfox unearths it for him. Ha!*

There was something comforting in knowing that Firesong had his flaws, and one of them was that he drifted through life scattering his belongings as if there was always a hertasi following along behind him, picking up after him. Of course . . . there always was, actually.

"So . . . I have to learn about how the power works in me now by observing it when something instinctive happens . . . and I have to be mindful of my reactions, because I can't count on instinct being *right*, now." He nodded and so did Firesong. "And if we set out to make the best possible time, there would be no time to do that. And given the amount of power siphoning into the Lake, that . . . would be a very bad idea."

"That's an understatement," Firesong agreed.

"So if we are going to have to not make best pace, it's your idea that we should travel so you have all the comforts of home." He couldn't resist that little jab.

Firesong only laughed, but it was a laugh tinged with sadness. "They aren't so much 'comforts' as necessities," he corrected.

Kel was about to fence back, when he realized that all this time, he'd assumed Firesong was in the same robust state of health as—as—well, as *he* had been before he'd joined the defense at Deedun.

Humans usually complain a lot about pain and discomfort. But maybe Firesong doesn't do that. Maybe he hides his problems . . . afraid others would think less of him? No, that can't be right. Wait . . .

Once again, memory came to his rescue, with a recollection of an exchange he'd overheard between Darian and Firesong. "Keisha is going to remove the skin of your back with her tongue when she finds out you've been hiding that from her,"

Darian had said. What "that" was wasn't apparent to Kel, and he still didn't know exactly what it was now. But Firesong's next words had at least narrowed things down.

"It's something time either will or will not mend," Firesong said. "If it does, good. If it does not, I will add it to everything else that creaks and hurts."

Creaks and hurts . . . I never even thought what that implied, then. Not once. Why didn't I think? I just assumed he had jammed a finger and generally had a headache from power manipulation. But, no, no, that was a very wrong assumption. What I overheard actually means Firesong is always in pain, and never shows it.

The memory carried on. "Yes, but—"

"There are no 'buts.' What can't be cured must be endured, and it's not as if any of us are immortal. Why should I make everyone around me irritated by constantly going on about my ills? The only time it's relevant is when it's something I physically cannot do anymore. *Then* I'll say something. This? This is a slip of a tattooing needle. A little nothing."

Kel hadn't heard the end of that conversation, but he knew at the time he had just glossed over it and taken it literally. He even remembered thinking, *Why would he want tattoos? Well, they don't have handsome feathers to decorate, so I suppose they must do what they can.*

"So . . . how many will we have on this journey?" he asked instead. He tried to keep himself from sounding . . . judgmental. It did help that he was spending a considerable amount of his attention on modulating his emotional reactions so as not to disturb things inside himself more than they already were.

As a result, his tone was flat, but either Firesong realized what he was doing, or didn't care. "I don't know yet. You, me, Nightwind, Ayshen, Silverfox, Snowfire, some fighters certainly. Ayshen will want other hertasi." He rubbed his thumb and middle finger across his closed eyes, ending in pinching the bridge of his nose between them. "After that . . . I don't know."

"Hurrr. I don't organize things. Things are organized around me."

"Kelvren holds still and the world revolves around him," Firesong teased, dropping his hand into his lap.

"Only when I am dizzy," Kel retorted, and looked over at the silent hertasi.

Ayshen snorted. "Of course I am organizing this!" he said. "As if I would let anyone else! I have some ideas. I think we should have some Valdemarans. Pity Shandi can't be spared, a Herald would be useful—"

"Not useful enough that we have any right to pull such an invaluable resource away from Valdemar at the time the country needs its Heralds the most," Firesong chided gently.

Ayshen looked unconvinced, but Kel nodded. "I feel bad taking Nightwind. Snowfire will come if Nightwind comes, and if it weren't that Keisha is here . . . but I need Nightwind."

"And not taking Keisha is why we are going to remind Darian that we know he needs to stay." Firesong blinked slowly. "See how taking time to consider everything can be beneficial?"

Kel reached for a beaker of honeywater. "I will admit this if you refrain from telling me *I told you so*."

Firesong just took a long drink from his glass.

"You just let me do this," Ayshen said, his tail moving back and forth on the wooden floor behind him, a sure sign that his mind was already spinning webs. "I have some ideas."

"And we look forward to seeing them executed. Meanwhile, what about the project I set you all on this morning?" Firesong prompted.

"Oh, that," Ayshen said, a little dismissively. "Already done."

"Ah, good. Come along, Kel, if you can move after all that food." Firesong stood up, went to the wall, and took one of his more "ordinary" masks down, slipping it over his head.

Curiosity now warring with sleepiness, Kel got to his feet and—carefully and gingerly—followed Firesong out into the Vale, taking great care to keep his emotions on an even keel, and to stay in the middle of the path.

Suddenly, he realized which path they were on. "This goes outside the Vale!" he said, stopping short.

"It does." Firesong stopped, turned, and folded his hands inside his sleeves, watching Kel carefully.

Kel took several long, deep breaths. "Why are we going outside the Vale?" he asked carefully.

"Because you were entirely correct when you were talking this morning. Yes, my hosting room in my ekele is very, very heavily shielded. But accidents happen, and you really should not be that near to the Heartstone. Plus, being forced to stay in one room for however long it takes us to prepare the expedition is going to make you restless and aggrieved."

"It will drive me insane," Kel admitted, though he grumbled it. He started walking again, and Firesong resumed his own leisurely pace.

"So, given the need to get you away from the k'Valdemar Heartstone and the need for you to be able to move about somewhat more freely, we thought it better to create a place for you to stay outside of the Vale and the Veil that protects it."

Kel flattened his ear-tufts. "Oh," he said, unable to keep the sarcasm out of his voice. "How nice. You're putting me in a tent. I don't have very good memories of being in tents."

To his surprise, Firesong actually laughed. "Oh, come now," he chided, looking back over his shoulder at Kel as they approached the edge of the Veil. "Ayshen took charge of this project. You should know better."

"But you haven't even had a day!" Kel objected, as Firesong made a sweeping motion with his arms and "made a hole" in the Veil large enough for both of them to pass through. Under other circumstances he wouldn't have needed to do that, but . . . Kel couldn't in the least object to him keeping the Veil and himself as far apart as feasible.

He shivered as they emerged into the damp spring air. After luxuriating in the warmth of the Vale, the unaltered world outside of it seemed very cold indeed. And it took a few moments for his eyes to adjust to the darkness.

But the path was broad and marked by stakes impregnated with something that made them glow in the dark. It wasn't bright enough to illuminate the path, but it was certainly bright enough to keep him from blundering into the bushes. *And there is no danger of these wooden stakes suddenly exploding.* What was more, Kel himself was providing enough illumination to see the path itself. *I could brighten more, I think, but I don't know what that would do. I've just managed to achieve a stable state; I'd better not risk that.*

But his ear-tufts perked back up again when warm light showed through the tree trunks up ahead. And as they drew nearer, he raised his head with interest. Because this was no mere "tent" that had been hastily pitched out in the woods.

I should have trusted Ayshen.

"What *is* this thing?" he asked, as they neared the round dwelling with its conical roof. Some light made the thing glow from within, but it wasn't a lot of light, and in fact, it was only just enough to make the structure a slightly brighter patch against the dark woods. Two bright lanterns marked the three wooden steps that led up to the entrance flaps.

"It's a variation on the tents our cousins of the Plains use," Firesong explained, holding aside one of the flaps so he could duck under and go inside. "It's quilted felt for the walls with a waxed canvas cover. The roof is made of the same stuff with an additional rain cover, and it's all over a latticed wooden frame."

And it was *not* on the cold hard ground. As Kel saw when he went up the three stairs, it had been built on a substantial wooden platform. He had to pause just inside to let his eyes adjust, as Firesong edged along his flank.

"What do you think?" Ayshen asked with pride. "Think this will suit you?"

Inside, the tent was furnished quite simply; the walls had been covered with cloth painted in soothing swirls of pale blue, yellow, and green. More oil lamps hanging from the wooden rafters supplied light, and there was a fine fireplace and chimney covered in green and blue tiles, sitting on a blue-tiled hearth square, making the place pleasantly warm. There were rugs on the oiled wooden floor, and short tables, and cushions of every size and shape, all different, all in the same color scheme as the walls. This tent was to the wretched slab of canvas he'd been left under in Deedun as a fine hunting lodge was to a hastily thrown-up shanty.

"How—did you do this in less than a day?" he asked. "It's amazing!" He tried to emphasize his admiration, because it occurred to him, now that he was trying to be slow and deliberate about things, that the hertasi had been working his talons to the bone for him since he'd landed. "Thank you!" he added, with emphasis. "This is perfect!"

Ayshen swished his tail on the floor with pleasure. "I had help," he pointed out. "And we'd been planning on building these things for visitors who were uneasy about living in the Vale for some time. The Shin'a'in call them *ker'ts* and they swear that they'll hold against the worst winter weather the Plains can dump on you." He looked around critically. "I wouldn't go *that* far; the walls are still fabric, after all. But you should be comfortable here until we leave."

"I was out here while you were asleep, putting up the same kinds of shields that are on my gathering room in my ekele," Firesong told him while selecting one pillow here, another there, to put himself a kind of throne together. "And I had help with that as well. There is plenty of room for us to work here in bad weather. In good weather, we can work out in the fresh air for a change if we don't need the heavy shielding." He folded himself down into his nest, as Kel snagged cushions with his talons and made a nest of his own.

Kel paid careful attention to the Healing Adept and how he moved as he made himself comfortable. Firesong moved with a deliberation that suggested he was moving *carefully*. More evidence that he was not nearly as robust in health as he liked people to believe.

But he wasn't going to ask Firesong about it while Ayshen was here.

Instead, he lay down, and sighed with the pleasure that came from *not hurting*. Although . . . now that Firesong had drawn his attention to the true state of his own health, he could tell that the sensation of being pain-free was at least partly false. There was pain somewhere under there, but he remembered what Firesong had said about how he now absorbed spell energy before the spell could do its work—so there was no point in trying to heal himself with a spell.

Or was there . . . ?

"Did you actually imply that I can learn to heal myself with a spell again?" he asked Firesong. "Or did I hallucinate that?"

Firesong took off his mask and pinched the bridge of his nose between thumb and forefinger again. "You're getting a bit ahead of yourself," he pointed out. "*First,* you have to learn how to control this new appetite for magic you've developed. Once you can control that, you can regulate how and when and how much magical energy you absorb, and *then* you can work Healing spells on yourself. Speaking of which—you haven't flown in days, and you're away from the Vale. How are you feeling? Drained? Draining? Weaker?"

The Kelvren-that-was would have immediately said that he felt absolutely fine. But after all of Firesong's lectures and those potent demonstrations of how hazardous he could be, Kel put his head down on the cushion between his forelegs, closed his eyes, and went back to some of his earliest lessons in magic: how to look inside one's self.

I haven't had to use this for years. I've always just done what gryphons always did: trusted my instincts. But now my instincts can't be trusted, and I really, really need to be able to analyze myself this way so it becomes as natural as breathing.

It was a struggle. Things kept going out of focus, and his focus shifted unpredictably. This was as hard as catching a fish in chin-deep water. Finally, he remembered his earliest lifting lesson and narrowed his concentration to just his left hind foot.

When it all snapped into place, he was astonished at what he Saw. Inside him, even in that single foot, power roiled chaotically. He had it under control, but barely. Still, barely was good enough for now.

He Saw thousands of hair-like strands of magic reaching out of him, questing, he assumed for more power. But there were no sources of magic in this room, and they pulsed and sought without connecting with anything.

But even as he noted these things, he also noted a slight ebb in the power within him, one that wasn't transitory. *So I am using magic to use mage-sight, and that is at a cost of power, and while I am still and quiet, there are no ways to replace the power I am expending, so I'm not dumping as much in light. Whatever it is that I am using to seek for power doesn't seem to have much range past a couple of arm-lengths. At least . . . I think . . . not while I am resting,* he amended. Because he really didn't want to test that theory right now.

Finally, he opened his eyes again and raised his head. Firesong watched him intently.

"I don't hurt," he said. "But that's because I've turned on

something—one of those *humors* that Nightwind talked to Ayshen about? I don't know. But it's like I've been given a pain-killing medicine, except that instead of making my mind foggy, it's got the potential to take away all my inhibitions and make me euphoric. Which is pleasant to experience, but not good for thinking. And very much *sketi* when it comes to acting on impulse." He sighed, but didn't add that it felt very strange and obscurely wrong not to just follow his instincts as he always had.

Firesong nodded. "Anything else?"

"When you use mage-sight, do you see millions of tiny, long hair-like things coming out of me and reaching for more magic energy?" he asked instead.

"Interesting. No. But that's probably because I haven't Looked at you in the right way." The Adept narrowed his eyes and stared at Kel in a way that, as a predator recognizing a predatory gaze, made Kelvren feel acutely uncomfortable.

So Kel looked away. *No shame in breaking gaze first,* he reasoned. And Firesong didn't need Kel to be looking at him in order for him to analyze what he was Seeing.

"Well, this is interesting," Firesong said after a moment. "We certainly have . . . altered things about you. The magic-collecting function of your feathers has taken on a kind of life of its own."

"Because of course it has." Kel sighed. "I suspect it thinks for itself too, at least in the same way that plants 'think' to seek the sun."

"That's not a bad analogy," Firesong admitted. He took a deep breath and let it out slowly. "I am tempted to see if we can get some control over this new development, but I am tired and Silverfox will give me *that look* if I return to our ekele looking like I have been Doing Things."

Ayshen nodded approval at that. It was the first time the hertasi had moved since he had sat down on a cushion after their arrival.

"It's late and you should go anyway," Kel pointed out. "I don't want Silverfox to give me that look. Combined with all this magic, I might burst into flames."

Ayshen cast Firesong a sharp look, but Firesong just shook

his head slightly. "It's all right to joke about it. I don't believe you are in danger of doing that as long as you are not moving too much."

"That's comforting," Kel said dryly, then checked himself again. "Not that it's your fault," he half-apologized.

"I will be honest with you, Kel. If you and I can unravel how all this works, we may be able to speed up our restoration of the ley-lines." Firesong stood up, his eyes glittering a little—in anticipation, Kel suspected, of a juicy puzzle to solve. Well, he'd probably be feeling the same thing if the puzzle wasn't *him.* "But mostly . . . mostly I want my friend whole again, and very much not in danger of bursting into flames or draining the Heartstone *then* bursting into flames." He looked as if he was about to say more, but stopped himself.

And Kel . . . thought.

"I am never going to be the same again, am I." He made a statement of it, rather than a question.

"No." Firesong cut straight to the truth without beating around the bush.

"As long . . . as long as life is good." He thought some more. "You can't stop change. You can't stop the years passing, or things from happening to you. So no matter what, if this hadn't happened to me, my life still would not be the same as it was yesterday, or the day before that." He paused, and Firesong waited. "It is a hard thing to accept, though. I will probably whine."

"As if I didn't hear whining from every resident of this Vale," Ayshen said scornfully. "Even hertasi! Everyone whines, everyone complains, and even if whining doesn't change anything, letting the frustration out doesn't hurt. And at least you're not whining *inside my head* like Tyrsell does."

That last startled a laugh out of him, and Firesong chuckled.

"On that note, I will take my leave. I will see you after you have eaten in the morning, and we can begin our explorations," Firesong said, touching his mask to make sure it was still in place. "Peaceful dreams, my friend."

"I'd say the same to you, but I don't think Silverfox is going to let you go to sleep. At least not immediately," Kel teased.

Firesong just tossed his hair and strolled gracefully out of the door, letting the flap down behind him.

But now Kel wondered: how much of that grace and apparent leisure was born out of moving carefully to avoid pain?

Before he could dwell on that thought for too long, Ayshen stood up, catching his attention. "In case one of us isn't here, look. Firewood *there*. This cabinet hides a gravity-flow supply of water from a reservoir above the roof of the tent. One of us refills it once a day. If you want a water-bath—"

"I'd rather have a nice grooming," Kel interjected. "It takes forever to dry."

"Well, then, here's your drinking water. There's a sand-pit outside the back door for—you know. We'll be bringing your food and drink out here and taking the remains away immediately. Otherwise this very nice tent will be ankle-deep in insects and rodents, and while I am sure you can snack on the rodents, the insects—"

"I had my fill of beetles in my feathers in Deedun, thank you," Kel said, shivering a little.

"And *here*, if you can't get warm enough with the fire, are gryphon-blankets. And last of all, see that chain that runs from the ceiling down to the floor?"

Kel nodded; it was not hard to see. It looked light, but strong, and he hadn't been able to figure out its function. It was much too light to suspend much, and very much too light to serve as an aid to get him to his feet, if that was what it was intended to be.

"That goes to a bell on the roof. If you start to feel sick—if you start to feel things changing about yourself—if you are worried about *anything*, pull it." He held up a taloned hand. "Now, I do intend to make sure there's someone here with you if that's what you want. But in case you want some silence and solitude . . . that's why the bell is there."

Kel had *thought* he'd had more than enough solitude in that wretched canvas excuse for a tent in Deedun, but as Firesong had drummed into him, instead of responding that he wanted someone right there at all times, he thought about it.

If it was Ayshen . . . but a hertasi I don't know? He knew Ayshen's breathing patterns, how he moved, and as quiet as hertasi were, they still made some sound when they moved.

Would the sounds of a stranger moving about the tent be disturbing? Startle him out of sleep?

And on the other talon . . . What if he had a nightmare? What if he *did something* with all this stored power out of sheer reflex?

"I don't want to be responsible for setting anything other than the tent on fire if I have a bad dream," he said aloud, and ducked his head a little. "It is a consideration."

"It is," Ayshen agreed. "Are you all right with sleeping unattended?"

"I think so." He nodded. "At least it's quiet."

"Then I'll leave you to it." Ayshen went around the tent and blew out all the oil lamps but one, and on that one, he shortened the wick. "Remember: sandpit to the rear, path to the front. Three steps down to the ground either way. Goodnight, Kel."

"Goodnight, Ayshen," he said to the tail just slipping through the door flap. He put his head down on the floor again, considered his position, adjusted it a little, and closed his eyes.

It was well after midnight, but not so late that Silverfox was quite ready to track Firesong down and herd him back to bed, when he heard his heartmate coming up the steps to the sleeping room. As always, he listened intently; there was a lot he could deduce from how those footsteps sounded.

As he waited for Firesong to make it up the stairs, he looked around the room and sighed. They'd just finished the expansion of their ekele. This chamber had been long in the planning, with many little secrets not obvious to anyone who might stumble in here. And it was quite luxurious: woven wicker walls to let the breeze through with drop-down quilted covers for privacy and sound-baffling, a bed big enough for four with a mattress he himself had designed with a firm pine-needle core and a thick down outer layer, specifically to cushion someone with aching joints and back. And pillows. Many, many pillows. The whole room had been done in warm shades of gold and golden brown. Mage-lights shaded with brown and gold-colored glass cast enough light to read by, but not so much that the eyes grew the least tired when reading.

He'd planned out this room in his mind the entire time they'd been traveling back from the Dhorisha Plains. He'd hoped they would never have to leave k'Valdemar Vale again.

Hopes dashed. But we can't abandon Kel. Still, he sighed. *Well, we'll just have to make the most of it until the expedition leaves.*

"Save your glare, I haven't been doing anything but talking and observing," Firesong said as he entered the bedroom. He turned, hung his mask on the wall, and slipped off his outer robe before reclining next to his partner. "Every time I start to think gryphons are simple creatures, Kel says or does something that makes me realize I'm the one that's simple, making broad assumptions like that."

"Sounds like it went well," he observed. "Which is not a given, with a gryphon. They are very passionate creatures."

He raised an eyebrow and Firesong answered the invitation by fitting himself into Silverfox's side, laying his head down on his partner's shoulder.

"It went better than I expected. I thought I would have to argue him out of making a fast trip of it, but he actually lay there and thought about it, and finally agreed with me." Firesong reached for a strand of Siverfox's hair with a narrow and graceful hand, and absently entwined it with one of his own. "It's the *lay there and thought about it* that is the surprising part. And he continued to do that the whole time we were talking. By the way, Ayshen was absolutely correct in sending him outside the Veil for now. I think he is likely to drain the magic out of any object that is a source of concentrated power that he gets too near."

"Well, that's not alarming *at all*," Silverfox said with mild sarcasm.

Firesong coughed. "Yes, well, I am sure Ayshen is not going to be backward in telling me *I told you so.* He enjoys being right much too much. At any rate, *kechara,* Kel actually listened to me when I told him he was going to have to think over every move he makes, and watch what is going on with the energies when he does do anything. He seems a great deal calmer, although I suspect that is a matter of deliberate control rather than actually *being* calm."

Silverfox shrugged slightly. "Does it matter which it is now? The more he practices calm, the less effort it will be."

"So pragmatic." Firesong yawned. "He seems safe enough for now, and I am mentally exhausted from trying to analyze him, but make no mistake, fixing him to a point where everything is functional and stable is going to be as much work as making a Heartstone. In fact—" he chuckled—"it's going to involve making a Heartstone."

Silverfox bit his lip. "Then I will have to consult with Ayshen about the arrangements," he replied, his tone one that said he was not going to take any arguments. "Because if you are going to be working with energies that powerful, you're going to need to be—"

"Yes, yes, I know. And I am tired *now,* and I will have to begin this work first thing in the morning." Firesong ran a finger along Silverfox's cheek to take any sting out of his words.

"Well, if you are *that* tired . . ." Silverfox let his voice trail off.

"Aren't you supposed to be keeping me at my peak?" Firesong teased.

"Always," the kestra'chern replied. And then he did not bother with words.

Hallock Stavern finished his rounds of the much-improved camp with his usual visit to the "gimp tent." From two wagon-lengths away he heard the soldiers in the tent, even over the sound of the rain, and not in a bad way. People were singing a work chant, and while it was not the sort of full-throated bellow it would have been if they were moving rocks or buckets of sand or water, the cheerful, slightly out-of-tune chorus lifted his spirits.

Inside the tent, the atmosphere could not have been more different than it had been before Kelvren the gryphon had joined them. The last of the "magical" gryphon feathers had long since been fletched into arrows, but you wouldn't have known it by the iridescent striping on the vanes of the newly finished ones stored head-down in racks by the tent-flap. Hallock had convinced the gimps that there was almost as much "magic" in Ammari's "paint" as there had been in the gryphon feathers—after all, it came from inside the same Change-Circle from which Kelvren had arisen, alight and rejuvenated!—therefore, it *must* be magical. The "paint" was in great demand now, and while Ammari was not exactly amassing a fortune from the tiny amounts

145

of it that ordinary folk could afford, she was no longer scrambling for every honest job of petty labor she could get, and was,
in fact, devoting all her time to making the paint.

*So that's three people who are better off since Kel landed
among us.* He counted himself among the three, of course.

"First in the tent!" someone barked as he lifted the flap. The
chantey stopped mid-word, and although most of the people in
this tent couldn't leap to their feet, they did sit up straight in
a posture as close to "standing at attention" as they could
manage.

"Be at ease," he said, as they had known he would; some of
them were already losing the stiff pose before he spoke the
words releasing them. Not that he blamed them. There was a lot
of pain in this tent, even with better and more drugs available
and Healers with the Gift, not just herb-and-knife Healers.

Not that I'm turning up my nose at any Healer. There were
plenty of things that the unGifted Healers did just as well as
those with a Gift.

"Have you heard anythin' at all about our gryphon?" was
the first thing called to him by a fellow who'd had to have a leg
sawn off below the knee. Hallock felt himself warmed by the
anxious gazes that met his; his "gimps" had taken Kel right
into their hearts, and properly so.

"Only that he scared the rebels witless, which you already
knew. Lord Breon has declared it was on his orders to do so,
and that he made it back to the Hawkbrothers. And that's
where what I know ends." Frowns met the second item on his
short list.

"But—" someone began.

Hallock held up his hand, silencing protests. "This is the tale
we will tell," he said firmly. "Orders from above. It's politics."

Groans and nods answered that statement. Everyone here
understood that when it came to "politics," the best policy was
for the grunts to keep their heads down and their mouths shut,
and say nothing that wasn't the official statement.

"Is our gryphon all right, though?" someone else persisted.

"No news is good news," Hallock replied, although he knew
very well that was cold comfort at best. "I'll be sure and let
you all know the very moment I find out myself. But I have

other news. We're not going home. Or rather, this is about to become our home."

Heads came up and jaws dropped. "That means we're being garrisoned here?" some bright spark asked immediately.

"We are." He nodded. "Full garrison. Which means, for those of you who still want to serve, there'll be places for you." That was the Valdemaran way; if someone wanted to stay in the Guard after suffering injury, there were always non-combat positions for them within the walls of a garrison. Clerks for the literate, cook's helpers, laundry, cleaning, weapon-crafting and repair—the Guard cared for their own.

"Lord Breon's looking at his properties for something that'll serve until the real garrison gets built," he continued. "I can guarantee four real walls and a roof; we might bivouac in some barns for a while, but it's spring, and by the time fall gets looking nasty, we'll be in our own quarters."

He didn't have to add *but if you want to go home, you'll be sent*, because that was a given with the wounded, and not out of the question for those whole and sound.

He waited until the conversation became general and didn't necessarily need him, then showed himself out. Going home *was* out of the question for him. He was First now. These were his Guards, and he had duties to them. Going back home right now—and going back to Genni—well, that was not an option, and it ached him much more than his healing wounds that such was the case.

You knew what you signed up for when you took the uniform, he reminded himself. Although it was a usual thing, it was not, and had never been, guaranteed that a man would serve somewhere near home. Rotations leaned toward at least one faraway posting in any Guard career, and compared to the border, this would not be terrible for him. Still.

I need to stop taking things for granted.

His rounds complete, he went back to his tent; the First he had served under hadn't brought much with her, and that little had been sent back to her people. Her body had been buried, along with the other casualties, even those from the "other side," in a plot donated by Lord Breon himself. Well, Hallock didn't have much more to his name than his First had had, and the tent was a pretty barren place, with little more than his pack and the cot, folding chair, and table all officers got as a matter of course. It had that musty-canvas smell all their tents did, after being out in the rain for so long, and having been packed away damp before they'd been sent out with the Guard to the North.

But there's no ribbon hung outside this tent, so I'm still ahead.

This was not the life he had imagined, when he'd signed up as soon as he was old enough to. He'd imagined riding against bandits, standing watch along the border with Karse, and maybe, if he was lucky, escorting someone important. Standing watch on the Palace walls had been the height of his ambition, and when he'd met and married Genni, life had seemed perfect. Everything had been turned upside down by the war with Hardorn and the Mage Storms.

He sat down on the cot, which creaked under his weight, but it was more comfortable to sit on than the little camp stool. Officially, he was always on duty, but in practicality, now that the Elm rebellion had been quelled (for now) and the mercs had slunk back across the border with their tails between their legs, there wasn't much for him to do except more rounds. And as a former grunt himself, he knew that there came a point when the rounds stopped seeming to be the work of an officer who cared, and started appearing as the work of an officer who wanted to manage every moment of every day of every one of his soldiers. So he sat, elbows on knees, hands dangling between them, restless, but unable to think of anything productive to do. There was too little time for a nap—a First's prerogative, and considered a positive sign rather than one of laziness. A First having a nap was interpreted as a mark of their competence, someone whose duties were fulfilled over long hours, and who was confident of their troops.

It was nearly suppertime. The mess tent was going to be full, and although as an officer he was entitled to go to the head of the line, this news about staying here-ish had killed his appetite. *They've surely told Genni. How is she taking this, I wonder?*

Knowing her, with a smile on her face and the determination

to keep her own feelings well under control. *She knew what she was getting into when she married into the Guard,* he reminded himself.

Still, he was going to take a few moments to himself to let his disappointment run its course. Like her, he'd go back to his people with a smile on his lips—or at least, *without* a frown—and keep his feelings to himself.

When he got up and walked to the mess tent, he found that not only were the new orders the main topic of conversation, they were the *only* topic of conversation. The huge canvas structure, full of trestle tables and benches, buzzed with gossip in which the word "garrison" cropped up every few moments.

He stood there a moment, taking in the space, listening to the tone rather than the words. The tone was positive, as far as he could tell. The word was generally pronounced with enthusiasm.

Of course it is, he realized after he thought about it. *A garrison means a real set of buildings. Walls, floors, ceiling, real rooms out of the weather.* Most of his people were unmarried, and one barracks was as good as another as long as the roof didn't leak. And those who had sweethearts back home, well . . . sometimes those relationships lasted, and sometimes they didn't, and the result probably would have been the same had this Company not been sent to this corner of Valdemar.

He made his way to the line of cooks standing over the benches laden with tonight's fare—although as he was nearly the last to be served, the kettles and stacks of bread were looking pretty depleted. As he held out his mess kit to be filled, one of the cooks gave him a wink, and instead of getting the scrapings from the bottom of the soup kettle, the cook reached under the table, pulled out a pitcher, and tilted out a bowl full of soup he must have saved when the kettle had first been brought in from the fire. "Garrison sounds like a fine thing to me, First," the cook said conversationally, topping off the kit with a round loaf of bread. "Real kitchen, real ovens."

"No ties back in Haven?" He couldn't resist asking the question.

"None to speak of. There'll be lads and lasses asking for transfers, no doubt, but plenty more at Haven wanting a touch of adventure and the promise of action." The cook shook his head, but didn't comment any further.

Hallock knew what he was thinking, old veteran that he was, and the cook was right. *Younglings think they are immortal.*

He spotted a few of his own people off in the near right-hand quarter of the tent and went to join them. Some officers preferred to eat alone in their tents, but there were enough like him that preferred to be with their people that he didn't stand out.

People quieted down as he took a seat, moving over on the bench so he could have the end. He nodded thanks and hello, then put his head down and concentrated on his food so conversation would start back up again.

And it did . . . but he realized, as he listened, that they weren't speaking as freely with him there as they would have without. Which was appropriate, after all; he was an officer. They weren't *supposed* to regard and treat him as one of them. On top of the realization that he wasn't going to see Genni for a good long while, this distancing made him feel melancholy.

So melancholy that it was several moments and a deepening silence before he realized that there was an orderly waiting politely at his elbow.

"Speak up, soldier," he said, straightening.

"Major wants to see you, First," the dark young woman said, all business, her uniform as immaculate as his was not. But this was his reserve uniform, so that was to be expected; the one he'd been wearing had been cut off him by the Healers, and hadn't been replaced.

"I'll see to your kit, First," Bennak Fenn volunteered. "Leave it clean in your tent."

"Thanks, Bennak," he said, and stood to go with the orderly.

It was a short walk to the major's tent, and Hallock reflected that things had vastly improved since Major Trask had been replaced by this new fellow. *Major Fisher.* Major Fisher had taken control of the situation between the Guard and the town, armed with warrants of every sort from the Crown that specified exactly how business was to be conducted down to the smallest detail. Not that Trask had been a bad leader; as a military man, he was highly competent. But the deviousness of politicians, and the chicanery of the politicians *here* in particular, had left him baffled and enraged, and he himself had petitioned to be replaced. The very first thing Fisher had done when he arrived was to march into the town hall with a squad, round up the mayor and every member of the Town Council, and present them with his warrants, which made it quite clear that Fisher had the backing of the Crown itself to enforce the provisions of those warrants.

They'd never dared have done to Kelvren what they did if Fisher'd been in charge.

The orderly rapped her knuckles on a tentpole, then held aside the flap for Hallock to pass through. "First Hallock Stavern, sir!" she said briskly.

The major, a handsome, dark-haired, dark-skinned, middle-aged man in an immaculate uniform that made Hallock twitch a little with envy, was standing at his table in his two-room tent, bending over a map. "Ah, Stavern," he said, and Hallock relaxed a little at the generally positive tone. "You may go, Liren," he said to the orderly, who saluted, dropped the tent flap, and went on about her business.

Hallock saluted. "Sir," he said.

"At ease, First," said the major, and took a seat on a camp stool. Hallock stood at ease, mentally going over everything that had been happening since Fisher took over from Trask, trying to figure out why Fisher needed to see him. The sounds of the camp settling down for the evening came through the tent walls completely unfiltered.

"Have you ever heard the old saying about marriage and the Guard, First?" Fisher asked, a hint of a smile on his lips.

Considering how he had *just* been thinking about Genni, he had to repress a start. *This is not going where I expected it to.*

"Can't say as I have, Major," Hallock replied honestly. "Though I expect it mostly boils down to, *don't.*"

The major chuckled. "Well the saying suggests that it is a very good thing indeed—mandatory, almost—for upper-level officers to marry, and lower-level ones are strongly discouraged from doing so."

Is this about Genni? But—

"I suspect whoever made up that saying never encountered your wife, First," the major continued, taking a folded document out of his tunic—one of the pieces of palimpsest that was used for messages from the teleson operator. "She makes a compelling argument for why she should join you here."

She—wait, what? Oh, of course he knew she was a Healer's Hand, one of the trained helpers that supplemented the Healers' work. And he knew she was a good one. But he had never pictured her as wanting to leave the civilized surroundings of Haven and Healer's Collegium for the rigors of a far-off garrison, much less a camp on a civil-war footing.

"Very compelling indeed. And if you were going to be staying with us, I would not have hesitated in authorizing her as a camp auxiliary. We can't have too many Healer's Hands out here, I suspect." He tapped his chin with the folded paper, as Hallock tried to get his mind wrapped around what his superior officer was saying. "And I would absolutely approve getting her here, no question at all. The problem is, you are *not* going to be staying. But since she could be equally useful where you might be heading, I am going to leave the decision up to you as to whether I have her sent through on the next Gate opening, or tell her that she can't go where you are going."

"Uh—sir?" Hallock said, feeling very much as if he was drunk or otherwise befuddled.

Fisher regarded him gravely. "Ripples and cracks, Hallock. That clever gryphon of yours did everything right, and still managed to stir up a bit of a hornet's nest. We are playing a complicated game on a four-level board, because some people are shortsighted and greedy, and will trample over their own mothers to gain far more than they could ever earn honestly in their lives. That's why I'm here, instead of Trask. That's why Lord Breon claimed he gave the gryphon orders to suppress the revolt and remind the insurgents that even though the Queen in Haven has her hands full, she has plenty of creatures ready, willing, and eager to act on her behalf. But people are still looking sideways at the Scary Monster acting on behest of the Crown, and wondering if this is some sort of long game by the equally scary Hawkbrothers. And that's why the gryphon needs to be . . . somewhere else, other than k'Valdemar Vale . . . for a while."

Hallock just blinked. He heard the words. They were in sentences. They just didn't make any sense, and mingled with his bewilderment was outrage. Kel was a hero! He had solved the conflict at Deedun with no further fighting! And obviously the Queen understood that perfectly, so why was Fisher saying Kel needed to be "somewhere else"? And where was "somewhere else"? And what did all this have to do with him, or Genni?

"Now, what this has to do with your wife and yourself is this," the major continued, uncannily, as if he was reading Hallock's mind. "The Hawkbrothers have told the Crown that they are going to mount an expedition to the northern end of Lake Evendim, led by a mage called Firesong and the gryphon. It has something to do with magic that I don't understand, but is evidently connected with the Mage Storms. They've requested that we send along a couple of representatives for Valdemar. They specifically requested Guard, and they specifically requested *you,* because you are someone Kelvren considers a friend, and as an officer, your presence makes things much more . . . official. It shows that what they are doing is investigating a mystery that has the same potential to wreak havoc across multiple lands that the Storms had, and that as a result this will be an expedition of allies. Does that make things clearer?"

Hallock gathered his scattered wits, managed to put it all together in his head in a way that made sense, and was able to answer. "I—that is a lot to take in, sir. Yes, sir. Am I to be thinking that you're in favor of this, and of Genni coming along?"

The major nodded slowly. "But I'm also loath to deprive you of an earned rank, and the time-in-rank that will let you rise further. I'm also loath to deprive your people of an officer they trust."

The silence that followed that statement suggested that the major wanted him to think about what he'd just said, and respond only after due deliberation.

Well, the first part was easy. "I'm not an ambitious man, Major," he said. "Rising in the ranks was never a great concern of mine." And since he was officially "at ease," he rubbed a neck stiff with anxiety before speaking again. "Truth to tell, I can give you the names of five people that would be better as the First of the Sixteenth than me."

"I'll ask you for those names later, if you decide you want to take these people up on their proposition," Major Fisher responded with a sage nod. "I can tell you that the Crown is strongly in favor of you going, and I don't want to tell them no. Gryphon Treyvan speaks very highly of you, I am told, and is the one who recommended you. But it's up to you—you, and Genni. Do you think you would both be willing to do this?"

"Does Genni still have a place here if I say I want to stay?" he temporized.

"We can use her, no doubt. I'll welcome her and put her on the payroll immediately. And I want you to entertain this idea. You don't have to act immediately. From what I am given to understand, this isn't going to be a quick dash across country, and there are no real roads out there. The going will be slow and they are taking their time about organizing this expedition. By my maps," and he gestured at the table, "to get to the Lake means going through the Pelagirs, and if it was bad before, I can't imagine what it's like after the Storms." The major looked at the dispatch in his hand. "I'll tell you what, don't give me any kind of answer now. I'll just give permission for her to come, and when she arrives, the two of you talk it over and tell me what you decide." He nodded. "Dismissed."

Hallock kept to himself that from what he knew of his Genni, she was already on the way. When she made up her mind about something, anything that stood between her and her goal was likely to find a Genni-shaped hole kicked through it. If she wanted to be here, neither hail, hellfire, nor Herald would stop her.

Instead, he saluted, and took his leave. And . . . he wished the gryphon was here. It would have been good to have a friend to talk this over with, and they'd shared something that made him feel close to Kelvren in ways that were hard to put words to.

Although . . . I know what he would say. "You cannot fly unless you take a leap first." Or something like that. Vague, inspiring, and clever. But this might be a leap in my small-clothes straight into a viper pit, hand in hand with Genni. I worry about her, but the truth is, if she was with me, she would make that leap feel easy.

The room in Firesong's ekele that served as an office was high up in the branches and featured panoramic windows that supplied a view of nothing but leaves and shimmers of dappled sunlight, to minimize distractions. Silverfox's new bondbird, Hesheth—a huge bearded vulture, of all things, probably the last kind of bird anyone would suspect for a gentle kestra'chern—lazed out there, occasionally buzzed by one of the ubiquitous messenger birds. Hesheth had a personality that had connected with Silverfox from the start: never in a hurry, never frightened, and with the deep inner contentment that vultures were known for. If one could stand his breath, he was also a great hugger, being three-quarters Silverfox's size. Mental contact with him was like a pain-numbing extract mixed with the maternal love of brooding under breast-feathers. Although the ever-present hum of Vale activity filtered up through the leaves from below, to Silverfox, the sound was no more than a soothing background peppered with bird calls.

Firesong tapped a wind chime just outside the door to the office to announce his presence and strolled in. There were doors in ekeles, but Silverfox never left his office door closed; it was a nice gesture on Firesong's part, but perhaps he recalled the time he had come up on his heartmate so quietly that he'd nearly startled Silverfox out of the window.

Firesong had several pieces of paper in his hand. *Someone has been busy.* Silverfox took the list that Firesong handed to him with a raised eyebrow and a repressed sigh, as he glanced at the first page. "We're *traveling*, my best beloved, not moving our household wholesale," he pointed out gently. "Surely when you and the Valdemarans made that clandestine journey into Hardorn, you weren't bringing enough baggage to require an entire pack train. And I know for an actual fact that you didn't take this much to the Dhorisha Plains."

"I'm older, I'm creakier, and I'm going to be no good to anyone if I wake up too stiff to move every morning," Firesong countered, carefully folding his legs under himself as he dropped down into a saucer-shaped chair. "I am fine with getting old. It's the looking scrawny, wandering mind, and being tired all the time that I dislike. My plans specifically included being young and handsome forever."

"You, too?" Silverfox sighed. Ayshen had put him personally in charge of keeping Firesong from turning the expedition into a royal progression, on the basis that he was the only person Firesong would listen to. He hadn't argued; he knew his heartmate all too well, and this list just proved that Ayshen had been right to delegate this particular task.

"Look," Silverfox said, picking up the first two pages of the five. "Everything on these two pages is completely unnecessary. Nice, but unnecessary." He handed Firesong the top two pages. Firesong frowned.

"But—!" he protested, holding up his hand. Silverfox cut him off with a look.

"You won't need a tent. We're getting a floating barge from each of three Vales: k'Vala, k'Onwen, and k'Treva. Everyone knows that you, more than anyone else who is going, *needs* to be able to sleep without pain and have secure, warm shelter if there's wretched weather. K'Onwen's barge has a bedchamber in the rear that we'll fit out for just us two when it gets here. So you also won't need everything else on those pages." The tent in question, of course, had been a four-chambered affair the size of a common cottage, and Firesong's list would have packed it so full of bedding, cushions, and furniture that it would have taken half the evening to set up and half the morning to take down and pack up again.

Not to mention it would have occupied half a barge, as opposed to the chamber Silverfox intended to set up, which took up perhaps a sixth of a barge.

We'd have managed about four candlemarks' travel a day at best. We intend to travel slowly, but not at the pace of a turtle.

Whereas the chamber in the rear of the barge was going to be a cozy little nest, and required no time for assembly and disassembly.

"All right. But . . ."

"I have been tending to your comfort for a very long time now, *kechara*. You should trust me when it comes to seeing that you'll be properly cared for." Silverfox put a little—a very little—admonishment in his voice. "Now, if there are things you think you have any possibility of needing for spellcasting, then I definitely want that list. But when it comes to simple living? Ayshen and I will care for you, as we always do. Trust us, and let us do our jobs."

Firesong stood there holding the list that Silverfox had given back to him, as if he didn't quite know what to do with it. For once, the Adept had been taken aback by something he had not planned on—his heartmate's interference in what he considered necessary to his comfort. Firesong, generally a force of confidence and self-determination, actually felt hurt, if his body language was a true indicator of his emotions. He was weighing arguments for how best to assert himself.

It isn't a good sign that he made a list at all, much less pages full, Silverfox thought. *He's a Great Healing Adept, and choosing pillows is beneath his notice, so this is a symptom. He never has completely reconciled the presence of the Unknown in his life. In Firesong's life right now, he's facing decrepitude and diminishment after a lifetime of amazing feats. Lake Evendim, Kel, the missing destruction, the political challenges between the peoples, all have no clear solutions he's confident he could pull off. Picking pillows is something small that he can feel in control of, and I just punched it in the nose.*

Being a kestra'chern was a life of ordered thought, but still, Silverfox could blunder. Insight too often came right after it actually would have helped.

With age comes dependency, and that dependency can sting when your self-believed reputation is that of an adored Adept who could do whatever he wanted, because he was always right. Even a small "no" can be a big affront, because of its clashing meaning—Firesong could compromise readily enough, but inside, he must feel like a small concession will only let bigger ones in later. And you know yourself, Silverfox. Truth told, they probably will.

"*Kechara* mine, this gives us the opportunity to embrace new delights that only come with traveling. We'll keep you comfortable, just in less bulky ways, and those things on the list you brought me will be all here in place, waiting at the Vale for your triumphant return," Silverfox maneuvered. "I'll come help prepare for the mysteries ahead. Say, isn't Kel due for another lesson about now?" Silverfox continued, to distract him.

The distraction worked. If there was one thing that Firesong adored, it was a meaty magical puzzle. And Kelvren was about the meatiest puzzle that Firesong had encountered since the Storms themselves. It was also much more personal—one of the best uses for ego was to make someone stay focused, and when something was personal to Firesong, the Adept would not settle for *just* a solved mystery; he'd discover every secret there was about it, or he wouldn't feel good about himself. Mysteries are jealous mistresses. *And if I wasn't looking for a way to distract him . . .* Kelvren had been the topic of conversation for long enough that Silverfox was just a little tired of hearing about the gryphon. But for the sake of getting Firesong off the idea of hauling the entire contents of the ekele, Silverfox was prepared to listen to magical gryphony neepery for a while.

Actually, this time, not about Kel himself. Just about the magic. From Silverfox's perspective, being nattered at about magic was not unlike being nattered at about the nuances of beers. He didn't know anything about beer except who liked it, and everything he knew about magic—being unGifted himself in that regard—he knew only because of basic education and Firesong. But one of the very many things that were required to be a highly-trained kestra'chern, the ability to listen—actually listen, not just pretend to listen—to things that bored one, was very high on the list.

"And then, once you can fake sincerity, you've got it made," the old kestra'chern joke went. *The Sacred Trust of the Benevolent Lie, a center of all kestra'chern traditions—analyzing the moral and ethical worthiness of engaging in deceit, in an instant. Sometimes, it is a matter of degree—like how interested*

I appear *to be. At the moment, though? I like hearing him talk. I'm happy when he's engaged rather than brooding.*

"Hmm. He doesn't have a lesson this morning, but I should go watch him anyway." The Adept's eyes took on a look of anticipation. "I should record some aura-paper stains as we go, come to think of it. There could be a pattern to them. It's been so long since I last took any, I just forgot. I wish that simply letting him follow instinct was less dangerous, because with time I believe he might work out a better answer than either Treyvan or I could. I had no idea that gryphons had such a visceral understanding of the art. It makes for some fascinating differences between how they handle power and how humans do. We're able to use magic, but we don't have any specialized organs for it. Gryphons, though, it's part of them. Blood and body, in ways I doubt we'll ever *completely* relate to, because our magic is forever outside us."

"Well, you know," the kestra'chern said, as an idea came to him, "Why don't you commandeer the time of one of the other gryphons, and use your mage-sight on them, in order to compare it to Kel later? You'll get a much better idea of how those channels and mysterious organs are supposed to work by direct observation than by listening to Nightwind try to explain it all in words."

"That—is an excellent idea." Firesong's eyes brightened further, and Silverfox smiled at him.

"Shoo," Silverfox said, making a motion with both hands to send him on his way. "Do that. Then, if you haven't gotten yourself a headache, go observe Kel. He'll complain about being under observation all the time, and when he does, just tell him what you told me. It sounds flattering."

"That's because it *is* flattering, at least in a way. I can't believe I never noticed it." Firesong got up to leave, shaking his head at his own obtuseness. "And I can't believe we didn't ask one of the others to stand by as an example of a healthy gryphon while we were working on him."

"You had a *lot* of other things to worry about at the time," his partner pointed out. "Now you don't. And since you'll be with him, I won't need to send someone to remind you to eat, because his hertasi will stuff both of you given half a chance."

Firesong actually chuckled and whisked out of the room, clearly eager to get back to his current most-favorite subject.

It's a good thing that gryphons are very pragmatic; a human might well take offense at being "studied." Kel just wants results that will end in him being more or less "normal" again, whatever that is for a gryphon.

Silverfox turned his attention back to his own lists. As a kestra'chern, he did a certain amount of Healing himself, and he was fairly certain that Nightwind, who was the closest thing to a Healer they were probably going to get on this trip, would not anticipate human needs until they cropped up. Not to say that she wasn't an expert human anatomist before her trondi'irn pursuits. Nightwind had had a knack for essential life-saving since childhood, even before studying anatomy and chemistry for her transition to female, and she was once a Silver Gryphon field medic. *Good thing too, being married to Snowfire. He could need intensive care at any moment.*

So Silverfox was using his own expertise to stock their journey's medicinal herbs, on the grounds that when there was a choice between magical or Gift Healing and herbs for the same result, it was wiser to use herbs. They took a little longer, but better to save the Healer's energy for emergencies when there was no time for concocting remedies. Come to think of it, it was possible there could be magical "dead areas" on the journey, and every bit of power could be vital to escape.

And bless that long-ago Healer Bear who came up with the idea of the standard kits for Valdemaran herb Healers. All he'd had to do was request one be sent with the latest Valdemaran personnel, and he got one. A big one. A *really* big one. Wardrobe-sized—the one sized for a village that was unlikely to get resupplied for a while. It felt bigger on the inside than on the outside, with crisp white and black lettering. It stuck out severely among ekele furnishings—a tall blue box with a handled, bifold door, amidst an alien environment of swooping curves and intricate textures.

The only real work Silverfox needed to do for this part of the job was order stocks of remedies specific to the Tayledras, and their dyheli, tervardi, and kyree allies—and those could all come from here and from the three Vales sending the barges.

Books to his right hand, and the list on the desk in front of him, he fancied he looked more like a scholar right now than a specialist in sensuality. He tucked a strand of hair behind his ear and smiled to himself. *This is enough of a novelty that I'm enjoying it. I wouldn't want to be doing this all the time, of that I am sure.*

Still, with the breeze coming in the windows, a comfortable chair, and the surety that with every item he added to his list he was making some progress, there was a lot of satisfaction to be had.

And Ayshen will double-check me. Of that, I am completely *sure.*

Kelvren paced around the outside perimeter of his tent, admiring the way the hertasi had created a broad, pea-gravel path that blended beautifully with the native vegetation. And how they had created the equivalent of a "bathroom" for him outside the rear of the structure. More pea-gravel over sand, which itself was over a layer of charcoal, which was over a layer of ash. He could eliminate there, and with a tug of a rope, a shower of water from an overhead barrel with a perforated bottom would wash everything out of sight. And if he chose, he could stand there and get a shower, himself.

He'd tried it out already, just for the pure unadulterated pleasure of knowing that finally, after that battle, after being taken to pieces and stitched back up again—in numerous ways—he was completely *clean.* Then, he'd had a good bask in the sun to dry his feathers properly. And if it wasn't for the fact that he didn't *dare* simply enjoy a walk without pain, that he had to monitor himself constantly, he'd have been pretty content.

Well, until I remember how I was booted from being Wingleader. And exiled from the Vale. And . . .

He caught himself before he lost emotional equilibrium. *That's the past. Work with the present. Plan the future. And figure out how not to burst into flames!*

Pacing helped, and pacing outside helped more. Ayshen must have known that; that was why there was this path. A path cleverly lit with stakes painted with something that—according to Ayshen—"ate" sunlight and then released it after dark. The hertasi had gone into a long and involved explanation about fireflies and glowing marsh fungus, and to be honest, Kel had let most of it flow over him without really listening.

Ayshen giddily enjoyed explaining things. And it wasn't often he had a captive gryphon audience.

I wish it could be just me and Ayshen and perhaps Night-wind on this investigation. Oh, Kel liked his comforts, no doubt, but he'd never had to travel with enough people and creatures to fill a small village, and he could think of all sorts of reasons why it was going to be a bad idea. Well, for one thing, it wouldn't be possible to move quietly, now, would it?

We'll be alerting everything in our path for leagues around. And attracting anything nasty to at least come and take a look and see if they want to take a piece out of us.

On the other talon . . . there *was* safety in numbers. A big enough group and it would take something formidable indeed to risk attacking.

Even though he was walking, not flying, he still sensed his body greedily drinking in every tiny particle of ambient magic, which he (automatically, at this point) turned into light, leaving him glowing brightly enough that he shone even in the sunlight.

This business of minding himself *inside* while he was doing something other than lying down was . . . disconcerting. It wasn't wrong, so much as it was keeping him ever so slightly off balance—he couldn't just *be.* He supposed he could get used to it, but he didn't like having to second-guess his gut. His gut had always known what to do, and he just did it without much direction. *I trust my gut. My gut has never steered me to a bad buffet.*

I think I had better go back inside and be quiet. I wonder if Ayshen left me any books.

He hadn't paid much attention last night to the smaller amenities of his new eyrie, and once he'd awakened, he'd first been immersed in enjoying every single beak-full of the breakfast a hertasi named Jylan brought him. And then, in basking in the admiration of said hertasi. She'd brought in food from a handcart she pulled herself, then stationed herself at his elbow, breathless and wide-eyed, waiting for him to speak. For the first few moments, his hunger prevented him from focusing on anything other than the haunch of lean venison in front of him. But after the first few chunks had gone down his gullet, he turned to the wide-eyed creature. Some hertasi, like Ayshen, liked wearing clothing. Some didn't. This was one of the latter; all the little lizard had was a belt full of pouches. Kel knew immediately that she was female by her muted coloring.

"Good morning," he said. "Thank you for bringing my breakfast."

"You're welcome, Kelvren, sir. My name is Jylan, sir," the hertasi said, eyes glittering with hero worship. "It's an *honor* to bring you breakfast, sir!"

Now, *this* was more like it! He bent his head modestly, but her open admiration did a bit to soothe the emotional wounds of his reception back at k'Valdemar.

"Is there anything more I can do for you, sir?" Jylan continued.

Now he was in a quandary. If he said "no," would she be disappointed? But he didn't want to say "no," because he wanted more of *this* kind of company. *Well, why not say as much?* "I would appreciate your company," he said, after another bite. "As long as you do not have other duties . . ."

"Oh! No, sir!" she exclaimed, hands clasped in front of her. "Ayshen said I was to make sure you have everything you need!"

Well, what I need *is more of those "sirs" and admiring looks,* he admitted to himself. "Then please, make yourself comfortable and stay for a bit."

Taking him at his word, Jylan sat down on the floor with her tail curled around her, and gazed at him while he ate. Her mere presence was like soothing unguent on his raw nerves. "Are you Ayshen's apprentice?" he asked, after the need to stuff himself became a little less urgent.

"Yes, sir!" she said. "He accepted me just two months ago!"

Hertasi usually apprentice in their early teens. Well! I'm glad the younglings think well of me! "Ayshen calls me Kel," he told her. "You should, too."

"Yes, s—I mean, yes, Kel." She was so excited she practically vibrated. "Oh, si—I mean, Kel! Is it true that—" and she was off, asking so many questions that he was hard-put to get in bites between answers.

All in all, he couldn't remember having had a better meal.

When he finished it, and she loaded up her handcart with the dishes and remains, he *almost* asked her to come back when she had delivered the detritus of the breakfast.

He didn't, but not just because he didn't want to keep her from whatever other duties Ayshen would assign to her today, but because it occurred to him that he should probably ration her admiration, since Firesong would, without a doubt, succeed in wounding his ego at least once before the day was over. And it would be nice to pull that bell rope and have little Jylan come around to pour out that balm again.

So instead, he stretched, and stretched, and then went for a pace around his tent, ending back where he started, and wondering when Firesong was going to show up. That was when he decided to take a closer look around the single room of the structure.

There's more here than I thought there was, he realized. Not that the furnishings weren't sparse, and mostly limited to rugs and cushions, because they were. But behind the cushions piled against the wall were other things. A couple of storage chests, some rolled-up blankets, extra firewood, and possibly other things, but he stopped when he came to four of the oversized, tough books that could hold up to gryphon talons. He pulled one out, tucked it under his right foreleg, and three-legged it to the center of the tent where the cushions were piled and the light was good. He propped it on a fat pillow slightly larger than the book was when open, and turned back the cover.

Somewhat to his surprise, it was a book by a trondi'irn about the magic-empowering system within gryphons. *Someone must have brought this from White Gryphon. The Tayledras would have had no need for such a book and had no* trondi'irn. The text was rather dry, but he had many, many compelling reasons to struggle his way through it right now.

But it did occur to him to wonder why it was sized and constructed for a gryphon to use, rather than a human.

He managed to get through about the first four pages before his head began to hurt. Not because he didn't understand what he was reading—he *did*—but because *thinking* about his insides, rather than simply going with what felt right, was a lot harder than he had expected.

He closed the book and looked up, blinking his eyes to refocus them. *Oh, that's part of the headache.* His eyes didn't like focusing on something that close for too long. They were made for distance viewing, like the raptors that the gryphons were based on. *Urtho probably never thought any of us would have time to read more than a single page of a message,* he reasoned.

Some of the headache ebbed, and he decided to spend some of the time waiting for Firesong to appear in trying to apply what he had just read about to himself. But it was hard to concentrate properly, when sunlight poured through the open flaps of the tent, and birdsong drifted in that sounded strange to his ears—because this was the sound of the birds native to here, unadulterated by the foreign twitters and chirps of the Tayledras messenger birds.

It begged for a nap. And even though part of him chafed at the notion that he should be *napping in the middle of the day*, another part of him cautioned that he was still recovering from not only grievous injuries, but still more injuries done to him in the name of fixing him.

Partly fixing me.

He yawned halfway through the thought.

That patch of sun is going to be in the doorway until sunset. He paced over to that very inviting slice of gold on the wooden floor, then dragged a nice rug and a cushion over to it. With a sigh, he dropped down on the floor and made himself comfortable. *I'll just put my head down and close my eyes,* he thought. *No harm in that, and a little tiny rest won't . . .*

"Still life with gryphon," Firesong's amused voice broke into what was not quite a dream.

"*Sketi!*" Kel yelped, jumping to his feet, and managed to damp down what was very nearly a flare of power into "just" a flare of light. Nevertheless, he flared so brightly that for a moment even *he* was blinded, and he blinked watering eyes until his vision came clear again, and he saw Firesong, dressed quite plainly for once, in leaf-patterned trews of dark green and a tunic of lighter green, with a mask to match the tunic. Firesong was nodding with satisfaction, much to his shock.

"Don't do that!" he snapped. "Don't *ever* startle me like that! I could have killed you!"

"I was shielded," Firesong retorted, "and you didn't. You got control: crude control, I grant you, but you got your reaction and your powers under control and you didn't harm anything. Not even the plants," he added, pointing to the plants on either side of the short path to the tent steps. "How do you feel—inside?"

The change in subject caught Kel off-guard, and he answered without thinking. "Like I just wrenched something, pulling a blow," he growled. "It's fading, though."

"That means you're on the right track." Firesong moved up the path and onto the steps, more or less forcing Kel to back up out of his warm patch of sun. Which was all right, at the moment; thanks to that pulled burst of power, Kel felt more than a little overheated. "And how are you liking that book?" Firesong waved at the abandoned book on the floor.

"Dry as bones a year old," Kel sighed, and went over to the cushions that someone—probably Jylan—had arranged into a pile while he dozed. He kicked a few over to Firesong, who accepted them and made himself a seat out of them, then piled up a few for himself.

"It isn't supposed to be a wonder-tale," Firesong pointed out. "But I do agree; both trondi'irn Jeika and Alach Abarenty, her gryphon charge, were rather . . . pedantic. That book is one of the few things Treyvan and Hydona brought with them from Silver Gryphon when they made their trek into the east. It is quite an artifact."

"Because if either of them had been sick or hurt, there were no trondi'irn where they were going, and the best they could hope for if they couldn't help themselves was to find a Healer or Adept who would try with the help of the book," Kel guessed out loud. He knew very little about gryphon Alach, and nothing at all about the gryphon's trondi'irn; they were very much before his time at White Gryphon.

Firesong's voice sounded pleased when he replied. "This is

the kind of planning we are going to have to do, Kel. We need to think about these things before we head out into the unknown. So that copy of the book I left with you will be going with us, and for exactly the same reason."

"And all the folderol and baggage you plan to take is doubtlessly going for the same reason," Kel grumped.

Firesong laughed, but with a touch of embarrassment. "Not . . . exactly. Silverfox already cut most of *my* planned amenities out. I suppose Ayshen put him up to it."

"Oh, your beloved is not going to put you through any hardship if he can help it," Kel shot back. "If you are looking for sympathy because you are not traveling like a king, do not look for it from me. I can—"

"No, you can't," Firesong cut him off. "Firstly, admit it, you are as fond of your creature comforts as I—"

"And I learned that I can be satisfied with a *great deal* less of those than I thought," Kel retorted, cutting him off in turn. "Try lying in the mud, in the rain, in a tent that won't stay up, and eating *literal* offal some time! Not drained, stripped, or cleaned, either!" Kelvren narrowed his eyes. "No. Condiments. Firesong."

Firesong threw up his hands. "You win! I surrender!"

Kel huffed, then subsided. "Well, what is my lesson this time?"

Firesong gestured to the book, still lying on its cushion. "Lessons for both of us. I confess I only glanced briefly through it when I was given my copy. I'll join you, and we shall valiantly suffer the dryness together."

"With many snacks," Kelvren finished. "We needn't do without just *yet*."

8

Genni arrived in the Valdemaran camp with the next wagon train of supplies, and, typically, did not go hunting for Hallock, but fended for herself—introduced herself to the right authorities, fed herself, found out where his tent was for herself, moved her baggage herself, and was waiting for him when he returned to the tent.

And if Hallock had not been warned by *several* people that "there's a wooman what says she's yer wife in yer tent, First," her arrival would have come as a bit of a shock. A pleasant shock, but a shock nevertheless.

There was an uncertain interval in which there was a lot of hugging, a lot of kissing, and a lot of murmurs about how much they had missed each other before they settled down and sat on the cot to talk. In low voices. Tents have notoriously thin walls, and he was not minded to share his conversation with his wife with anyone *but* his wife. In fact, he was more than a bit euphoric, and it took pure force of will not to just sit there gawping at her like a lovestruck ninny and actually speak real words formed into understandable sentences.

And even more strength of will to *not* suggest that they go stroll away from camp and enjoy the cool spring day, a day in which it was not raining, and most of the mud had dried up. *A perfect day in Valdemar with Genni, either way,* he thought. *But—tomorrow, maybe.* He was the First on duty, after all, and he could not go wandering off on a whim. *In fact, I may skip my usual rounds. They can send someone if they need me.*

As might have been expected, Hallock tried to gloss over how close he had come to death, and she was having none of it and insisted he show her his scars. There was quite a bit of explaining and some damp eyes (on his part) and crying (on hers). It was several candlemarks before they sorted themselves out, and the less said about that, the better.

Not a single moment of priority duty interrupted their reunion.

I think my unit's covering for me. That thought made him laugh out loud, and Genni joined in, and moments later they both escalated their affections, emboldened by the unexpectedly cozy feeling it gave them—to think others might be giving them their privacy.

Guard-change sounded from unexpectedly nearby trumpets, and in the First's tent, the pair took it as their cue to dress respectably and make their way together to the business of being here. It was their turn to "crank the handle"—that is, to go through the rings and ladders of registration, disposition, allowances, and more through Community Services. It split off from Guard clerks into a civilian business under hire of the Crown. "Being processed" was a derisive term for it, as in, "processed into sausage," but fortunately the camp was not at a high state of alert, so the task would be easier. When alerts were lower, everyone relaxed, and on occasion, some were surprised to find that they really liked their work. This was when the distinctive touches of a posting would form. *What do the people here think about, when not on active alert? Sports, contests, championships? Arts, performances, and training?* The Community Services had only been constituted twenty-two years ago, and their main mission, in short, was to manage negativity. Part of that included streamlining bureaucracy, which came along with a cadre of trained runners. Unsurprisingly, footraces were a mainstay of their sports programs, and locals were allowed to be part of several for talent-spotting. Those runners made for fast bureaucracy in collating the stamps and papers, leaving the petitioners free to get to their meetings.

The captain signed off to get Genni officially on the rolls—and by then it was suppertime—so off to the mess tent. Hallock knew that the "wooman in the First's tent" story was going to make the rounds, and it was best to cut off speculation before it had a chance to bloom. The captain kindly assigned her to the "gimp tent" for now. That would take some of the pressure off the Healers; a Hand could do just about anything a Healer could that didn't involve actual Healing. They could even dispense herbal medicines with the authorization of the Healer in charge.

As luck would have it, most of his people were in the mess tent, and those that weren't would soon get the proper story from the rest. He headed for the centermost of the tables, and at the sight of a strange female with him, the entire tent went silent.

"This is my wife, Genni," he said abruptly into the silence. "She's signed on as a Healer's Hand. Some of you might remember her from our posting back at the Palace."

Nods from those remaining of his people who had also been posted there. The rest, who had joined as replacements for the wounded and dead, took their cues from the old hands.

"With captain's permission, she'll be quartered with me." *No talking about the expedition, not until the two of us have a chance to discuss it.* "Otherwise, she'll be tending to the recovery tent."

More nods. And no smart comments about "officer's privilege." Well, he thought that he had instilled the proper mixture of respect and confidence in them, but it was heartening to see that he had been correct.

Of course, there was going to be a lot of jibber-jabber about it once he and Genni were out of sight. That was only to be expected. But it didn't look like any of them were going to make any kind of an issue about him having his wife here. He wasn't the only one in this camp to have a mate along, but none were there as prizes—*all* of them were working, some as laundresses, some as cooks, and there was at least one case of a married pair in the ranks, though that was . . . not encouraged.

Having established that this was nothing worth gossiping about, he and Genni got their stew—the cooks, of course, had heard all of this and took his word for it that the captain had put her on the rolls. "I'm sorry about the stew, ma'am," the head cook said while serving Genni. "Today is a Stew Day. It's just bad luck. Good food, but bad luck—I try. I truly do. It feels like the only thing you ever find at any camp or tavern is 'stew,' just stew, the same lumpy brown stew every time. And here, when you show up? New place, and sure enough—stew. But tomorrow? *Tomorrow* is fish fry, fried onions, soft-boiled taters, an' brown rolls. With *salted butter.* Then meat-on-a-stick with mixed veg an' peppers the day after, an' no stew again for another three days. Fruit when we've got it! But today . . ." The cook sighed, as a last drop fell from his ladle. "Today is just . . . stew."

The cook's assistant tugged the ladle from the man's grasp and took up the slack for others waiting. Someone dug out a discarded (clean) half-a-mess-kit from the racks and served them both. They exchanged a look once they got their food.

"'Today is a Stew Day.' That's going to haunt me," Hallock admitted. Genni maintained a frozen expression of happy neutrality as they threaded through the throng.

"Oh! Everyone is so polite," Genni commented, then in a lower register, added, "They're dying to talk about us," Genni whispered. "Let's take this to the tent."

So they left, and as soon as they got past the flaps of the mess tent, the hum of conversation tripled in volume. Hallock heard a strangled sound and glanced at Genni to see that she was stifling laughter.

That's my lady. His heart lifted, and with that came the certainty that she was going to fit in just fine. Maybe she'd never been in a Guard camp before, but she was going to fit in just fine.

They sat side by side on the cot to eat, with Hallock using the fork from his mess kit and Genni using the spoon. "I have a kit of my own somewhere in there," Genni said after the first few hungry bites, pointing with her chin at the three packs in the corner of the sleeping area. "We should return this to the cooks clean."

"Aye," Hallock replied. "It might cheer them up, after a . . .

Stew Day." He grinned, mouth full, just marveling in the fact that she was *here*, and *real*. And she was no gauzy hallucination, no—Genni was properly dressed for travel. None of her filmy scarves or flowing skirts for sensible Genni, not when such garments would have been a handicap. She had known to dress for hard travel, and for working, and he had no doubt that the clothing she'd packed was of the same nature. She was in her working clothes, and only one green apron short of her usual Hand garments. Curly brown hair escaping from the loose knot at the back of her neck, sensible long-sleeved brown linen tunic and equally sensible black canvas trews, sturdy, scuffed boots meant for long walking.

"I can't believe you're here," he finally said, warmly.

"You've said that at least two dozen times," she teased, brown eyes dancing with amusement. Then she sobered. "And if I'd known—"

"That doesn't matter," he told her. "It all came out right in the end, thanks to the Healers and Kelvren. And *that* is as good a place to start as any."

He told her everything that had happened after Kel had healed him, been healed himself, and shot out of the camp like a young sun to stop the fighting without the further loss of a single life. She listened intently, hands still, eyes on his. She'd probably heard some of this, back at Haven, but not the whole. She certainly would *not* have heard about how brave and how self-sacrificing Kelvren had been. Treyvan or Hydona would have told her, but she'd never been anywhere near the gryphonic ambassadors before he'd left, and it wasn't likely she'd have gone to *them* to find out about *him*. Genni's expressions changed rapidly on her face, from wonder to awe, abruptly to anger at how Kel had been treated after he'd Healed Hallock, to awe again as Hallock described to the best of his ability the sight of Kelvren rising into the sky like a beacon.

"So . . . of course some damn fools have to make political garbage out of an act of pure selflessness and bravery," he ended in tones of disgust, as she made vague, sympathetic noises. "Instead of talking about Kel like the hero he is, the captain tells me that poison tongues are nattering that he's some sort of monster in the service of the Hawkbrothers,

looming for some sinister takeover of the Crown or some such
horseshite. I mean, he should by all rights get a medal from the
Queen, and a parade through the streets of Haven! Instead,
there's nonsense about how he's a danger, and that the Queen
intends to use him to terrorize her own people. Can you believe it?" He didn't bother to hide his anger and indignation.
"Captain says that the boffins in Haven and among the Hawkbrothers have decided he needs to get right away from Valdemar
for a while, and that includes k'Valdemar Vale. So they're putting together an exploration trip to the north and west part of
Lake Evendim. The part that's not in Valdemar, and is still Pelagirs," he added for clarity.

She scrunched up her face. "Why?" she asked. "I mean, why,
leaving aside the fact that it's not in Valdemar."

He scratched his head. "I don't rightly know," he admitted.
"Something magical, like as not. But the thing is, the Crown
and the Hawkbrothers both want some Valdemarans along,
and Kel asked specifically for me, because we know and trust
each other, I reckon." He shrugged slightly. "Lots of times, Kel
doesn't think with his head, he thinks with his heart. Of course,
I have to be grateful for that, since it meant he practically killed
himself to Heal me." He paused to let her think about all of that
for a moment or two. "It's the Pelagirs, and I have no notion
of what they think they're going to do out there. So if we volunteer for it, that's going right into lands full of danger and
uncanny things. And the captain says he can use the both of
us right here . . ."

"But?" she prompted, when he trailed off.

He laughed awkwardly. "Well, this promotion feels like boots
that are too tight, and that's the honest truth. Now, maybe
time'd stretch the boots, but right now, it's damned uncomfortable. And I feel like I owe Kel just about everything. And . . ."
He sighed. "I wouldn't say this to anybody but you, Gen, but I'm
tired of the killing. And I'm tired of it being the Guard against
our own people, even if those people are full of crap and ought
to be behind bars. It doesn't feel right, and Kel said the same
thing, and that's why he did what he did. Still. It's the *complete* unknown against things we know, y'see. It's jumping off
a ledge and not knowing if the ground is an armlength down

there or it's a cliff. And it's taking you with me. Unless," he added hastily, "you'd rather stay here, while I go."

"Of course we're going," Genni said firmly. "If they'll have us both, that is. It's *their* expedition, and they have the right to pick who they take. I nearly lost you and never knew it, and never *would* have known it until it was too late. I don't want to be parted from you again. But if they won't have me, and you still want to go, then go, because I can see you're unhappy here and I won't stand in your way. I'll wait here and serve. But," she added, "I'll tell your captain I'm keeping your tent."

He had to laugh at that, and so did she, and for some reason neither of them could stop laughing until they were gasping for air. Maybe it was the relief at unburdening to each other. Maybe it was the relief at being together at last. Maybe it was laughing at the unknown they were about to hurl themselves into.

But all that really mattered for the moment was that they were of one mind, and they laughed themselves into each other's arms.

Kelvren's "tent" was assembled for him with a good view over a pleasant meadow—no doubt patrolled by hertasi cadres in the woods—which was split by a bushy erosion cut that fed a thickly tangled pond some twenty feet below. On either side of the cut, the actual pieces of the expedition were being put together right outside Kel's domed eyrie. Kelvren's sleep had been sound thanks to jugs of "specialty brew," so it had taken a lot to wake him. Chatter, clicks, calls, whistles, and shouts increased with the amount of sunlight, and he'd found the adoring Jylan and her cart just inside the privacy fly as he farted himself awake. He was barely into basic conversation and the first pounds of breakfast when he heard increasing volumes of hoofbeats and voices, and crushing branches.

"I still say we should just use horses," said someone whose voice he did not recognize.

:Horses are nervous, horses are prey, and horses are not weapons,: retorted what could only be a dyheli, though again,

he didn't recognize the Mind-voice. *:We are not nervous, we are not prey, and anything that seeks to prey on us will come to a pointed end.:*

"Sure, but we could *eat* a horse," someone else retorted, and the shouts and sounds of a scuffle started. At that, Kelvren left his breakfast and paced toward the entry, shoving it open with his beak.

There was a burst of activity outside. A sizable floating barge, guideroped by four Hawkbrothers, was towed by a single dyheli stag to a mooring in the meadow surrounded by building materials. The nearly comically undersized prime mover was a youngish dyheli, by the lack of rings on his horns, and judging by the coating of caked mud—not one to give up easily when there was worth to be proven. Just about the age when young male dyheli showed both restlessness and aggression, they were often asked to leave the main herd and join a bachelor herd for a few years. This barge had *until moments ago* apparently been towed by the same dyheli who was now whirling around chasing a Hawkbrother. The targeted Hawkbrother climbed their guiderope as quickly as they could, only to be thwarted by leaping dyheli headbutts until a truce was signaled.

As soon as Kelvren shoved his beak outside, everyone nearby turned his way, and chirps, hoots, and squawks sounded off from the rows of bondbirds atop the shelters. Kel still wasn't used to people shielding their eyes from him. Hawkbrothers in labor clothes were gathered under a score of weatherproofed tension structures, around trestle tables with scrolls and plans laid out upon them; another dome held banks of measuring tools, black wax crayons, and marked cords. Each table had its own hertasi, too, going down checklists. Non-Tayledras timberfolk and apparently fearless workers, probably from Kelmskeep, inspected saws and planes.

"Oh, pardon, Kelvren. Ayshen decided that since this is your expedition, and Firesong's, we might as well do the assembly where you can run your eye over everything," the young man, who Kel finally remembered was called Swiftbow, called aloud, and motioned him over.

Very diplomatic, Swiftbow, he thought, now a little irritated.

Who is here to keep an eye on whom? Not everyone was Firesong, and not everyone who knew Firesong trusted Firesong, so they might be here as much to monitor the Adept as anything. *A restless Healer makes a malady to cure,* the saying went. Maybe they weren't here just to build things . . . here next to Kelvren. *I'm sure "they" have other reasons for this . . .*

But on the other hand, Firesong *was* spending the greater part of his day here—sometimes in actual magic lessons, the kinds that humans, who didn't have the same instincts for handling magic energies that gryphons had, got. Sometimes just watching Kel. Sometimes both of them sharing that book about gryphon physiology and trying to work out how that applied to Kel.

So the bright gryphon paced down the shelter's ramp and moved closer to where the crew was maneuvering the barge. The not-actually-insulted dyheli bounded over the hertasi-trails toward Swiftbow, and shook himself off.

"Am I to understand that dyheli are coming along with us?" Kelvren asked, curious now. He said directly to the active dyheli, "Are you actually going to humiliate yourselves by putting yourselves in harness?"

The young stag threw up his head and snorted in the way that dyheli did when they laughed. *:Tyrsell volunteered the bachelor herd, but we don't mind. It's a chance to see new places, perhaps find territory for new herds of our own. And—:* the stag swiveled his head quickly around, as if looking for something, *:—and get out of Tyrsell's orbit for a while.:*

That surprised a laugh out of Kelvren, and the Hawkbrothers all chuckled. "We won't tell him you said that," Swiftbow said, as the mooring team cinched up the ground rings, anchoring the barge.

This "floating barge" was a strange craft to Kelvren's eyes. Its hull was like hammered armor, with bulges and ridges to break its way through obstacles. By the look of its creases and scrapes, it had done so for centuries. It hovered above the ground at about the height of the dyheli's horns. It was not made of wood, although the floating barges that Kel was familiar with from White Gryphon were. It was made of something extremely tough, something he did not recognize at all, and seemed to be made all of a single molded piece, somehow. It had a very shallow keel, so in theory, he supposed, it *could* be put in the water. This one had been painted very cleverly to blend in with forest undergrowth. Unlike flat-topped cargo barges, this had a sort of living quarters that rose above the deck with sides slanting inward toward each other, ending with a flat roof. The living quarters were where the windows were. The flat roof had a bit of a railing around it, so he supposed things could be tied down up there as long as weather wouldn't harm them.

Kel walked around it, as the Hawkbrothers untethered the dyheli from the barge, although they didn't take the harness off him. "So, you're coming?" he asked the stag.

:I am. I'm Ransem. And you're Kelvren.: The stag trotted out of the way while the Hawkbrothers secured the barge. *:We—the bachelor herd, that is—think that the way the Valdemaran humans are treating you is disgusting. They should have been giving you a procession and a medal! A hundred medals! A dozen hundred medals! One for every life you saved because you stopped the fighting! And prime grazing forever!:*

Kelvren was completely taken aback by this, and stood up a little straighter. "Well, thank you, Ransem. But . . . you know," he continued, because honesty prodded him to it, ". . . it's politics. I don't understand it either. But humans are strange."

Swiftbow looked as if he might say something for a moment, then thought better of the idea.

"So the whole dyheli bachelor herd is coming with us?" he continued, and thought about that as Ransem nodded. "Just how many is that?" he asked, finally, hoping his trepidation did not show. *Dozens? A hundred?* Tyrsell's herd was massive. As an extremely powerful Mind-mage, he attracted dyheli from all over and kept them in the herd with his leadership skills.

:Twelve,: said Ransem. *:Counting me. Two to tow each of the barges, while two more rest while grazing along the way.:*

Kel tried not to sigh. Not as bad as it could have been, but still . . . there was going to be no way to evade anything. Not with a procession of a herd of dyheli and three floating barges, and—

"Ah it's here!" Ayshen crowed, as he came around a turn in

the trail. "I particularly wanted this barge." The Hawkbrothers finished their tethering and greeted Ayshen with waves and nods. "Kel, do you see those things that look like bolsters along the top of the roof?"

He had, in fact, but had thought they were just there to help confine whatever was tied up there with something soft enough not to damage it. *Or perhaps to use as pillows for people sleeping up there.*

"Those are canvas flies that can be unrolled to provide a lot of rain shelter. With that, we won't need rigid tents for you and the others if there are storms." Kel tilted his head to the side. While he liked the idea that some provision was being made for him—obviously he wouldn't fit inside those living quarters—and he definitely had had enough of tents, it was "the others" that caught his attention the most.

"How many others?" he asked, warily.

"Four kyree and two tervardi, which Silverfox should be learning about soon. Plus the Hawkbrothers and I *think* that human you like, Hallock Stavern, is coming." Hallock! What a strange coincidence that of all the people who could—*wait, featherhead. How much of your life so far has been actual coincidence? Someone has to have arranged that.* Kel had assumed that once his Healing took, Hallock would recover just fine, but it was good to hear he might be fit enough for this undertaking. *Not undertaking in the dead-body sense, if we're lucky. The hertasi should have conditioned me to it by now, but it still feels odd to be the center of—how to put the feeling—benevolent conspiracies.* People cared about him in ways that made the shock and dismay in his life bearable. They nudged things toward his happiness, and he had to admit, at times it made him doubt his worthiness of *that* much good will. *We gryphons tend to act like we're superior and privileged, above others, but we know that's a joke. We would die sad, lonely, and ineffective without others. The best I can do is stay appreciative and keep succeeding, so they haven't wasted their heart on me. I couldn't bear that.*

I have to stay worth it for them.

"And the bondbirds, of course. But the tervardi will sleep in the barges, and so will the bondbirds in a storm. Plus, we're expanding the superstructure to basically add another deck. Then there is the well stowage, which can be kept comfortably dark. And the kyree, if there's room, can sleep in the well." Ayshen seemed very pleased. "Oh, and half a dozen hertasi, of course."

"How many people do these barges sleep?" This was sounding more and more like a circus to Kel, and less and less like the kind of lean, fast-traveling group he had hoped for.

"Eight each," Ayshen said brightly. "Maybe ten. Mostly hot-bunking. Plenty of room for everybody!"

"Ayshen. 'Plenty of room' may mean something very different to a compact, burrowing person like yourself. You sleep stacked on ledges." Also conspicuous by its absence in Ayshen's replay was *just how many* Hawkbrothers were coming. There would be Firesong and Silverfox, of course, and trondi'irn Nightwind, and Nightwind's partner Snowfire. That was four. Plus two tervardi. Plus Hallock. But how many more Hawkbrothers?

I have to resign myself. This is going to be a circus. And why are tervardi coming along? Kel didn't know much about tervardi; there weren't any at Silver Gryphon, and the only encounters he'd had with them at k'Valdemar Vale were when they'd sung for entertainment. Their music was highly valued among the Hawkbrothers. What they were supposed to do on this journey, he had no idea. The tervardi ancestors were songbirds; the tervardi themselves had lost their wings, and now the only signs of that ancestry were the feathers they sported instead of hair, a sort of beak in place of lips, and stubby, birdlike feet that were still useful for perching in trees. Like the gryphons, they had been created by Urtho, the Mage of Silence. Some said he had been looking for a non-raptorial version of a bondbird and had created the human-sized and human-smart tervardi by accident. Kel didn't believe that. *Urtho never created anything by accident.*

But tervardi were very fragile, and it didn't seem to Kel that they belonged on a trip that was likely to run into danger.

But he wasn't running this. Ayshen was. And after Ayshen,

Firesong. Which, realistically, meant Silverfox. *I am just so much possibly-will-explode baggage,* he grumped a little. It was very, very clear that even though the expedition was ostensibly because of him, he wasn't going to have any say in it.

"In good weather, you and the tervardi at least will probably want to sleep on the roofs," Ayshen went on, as if he hadn't noticed Kel's silence. "It should be rather nice. I can arrange for weatherproof cushions, or anything else you'd like. We'll probably set the barges down on the ground when we camp, just to conserve power. There should be more than enough space under the rain-flies for even you to avoid bumping your head."

Well, that was a generous assessment, seeing as his head would be a good bit higher than the roof-line of the barge on the ground. Still. It would be much, much better than that tent had been. And he'd have dyheli and probably kyree piled around him to keep him company.

Make the best of this, Kelvren, he told himself. *Maybe we'll be so big and strange a group that things will run away from us, rather than being attracted to us.*

He prowled around the barge, which, under the direction of a Hawkbrother mage named Sunstone, was slowly dropping into place on the ground. *Why tether it, then—oh, of course. So they don't have to tether and retether it when they want to raise it up.* If something caused a loaded barge to start moving, it could hurt someone before they got it stopped again. They'd want to do that at least to practice deploying those rain-flies. Probably they'd practice balancing the load as well. Kel prowled around it, but from a distance. He didn't want to suck the power out of it, and until it had completely settled down on the ground and everything was made "safe," there was a very real chance he would do just that if he got too close.

On closer inspection, this thing looked *old*. And whatever it was made of did not resemble anything in his experience except, perhaps, ceramic—but unladen, it was so light a single Hawkbrother could easily maneuver it around. "Where did these barges come from?" he asked, curiously.

It was Sunstone who answered him. "Would you believe, the

ancient Valdemarans? Our records say that they arrived at the Vale that we would turn over to them—a Vale that became the city of Haven—in a huge string of these barges. They didn't need the things after they arrived here, so we traded for some."

"But—" Kelvren was about to object that he had never, ever seen an object like this in Valdemar. Sunstone held up his free hand.

"The making of them was a specialty in Kordas Valdemar's duchy back in the Empire they escaped from," the Hawkbrother said. He finished pounding in the stake and attaching his tether, and straightened up, giving Kel a nod. "I build boats myself, so I was interested enough to research these barges in our archives. I wish they still made these things. The records say that the Valdemarans told them the hulls were made from some kind of fungus, and that their samples of it didn't survive the trip. A shame, really." He knocked his knuckles against the side of the barge; it made a much more "hollow" sound than the same boat made of wood would have. "Weighs almost nothing, takes incredible abuse, and I really hope that fellow that took over Hardorn brought the secret with him, because it would save a lot of time and trees."

"But wouldn't that mean that the Valdemarans brought . . . thousands of those barges?" Kel asked, trying to wrap his mind around the idea. "What happened to them all?"

Sunstone shrugged. "I know some were flipped over and used as shelters. At a guess, because they were common, no one took particular care of them. They were treasures to *us*, so we did."

"Well, really," drawled Redwind, another Hawkbrother Kel knew, as he came around from the other side of the barge where he had been setting tethers, "we haven't been any better about *our* archives. I think we've had whole centuries where all the records say is what happened when and where, not how it felt or anything personal about life there."

Firesong chose that moment to appear, today wearing a mask of sculpted grayish-blue leather, with leather ornaments on his robe to match. "This is the problem when people are busy trying to survive, you see," he opined. "They just don't write common things down. And by the time anyone thinks to wonder about those things, memories are altered or gone altogether." He folded his arms and surveyed the barge, giving it a nod of approval. "I like it. I suppose . . . it would be possible to use Pastseeing to discover how these things were made, but if it *is* a fungus, I don't know how we'd get a sample."

Kelvren shook his head. "Boring!" he proclaimed. "And isn't helping us *now*."

Sunstone shook his head and pursed his lips. "And this is why gryphons never become Artificers."

Kelvren did not ask what he meant by that, because, to be honest, he didn't care. How these things were made, and whether they could be replicated, was not going to help him with his magic, nor was it going to cut down on the number of beings it seemed were adding themselves to this expedition by the day. He just turned to Firesong and asked, "Are we going to try anything new, or are you just going to stare at me all day while I beat my beak against a wall like you've done the past two days?"

"You're not beating your beak against a wall, Kel," Firesong said in what were probably supposed to be reassuring tones. "You may not be able to tell it, but you are slowly getting better control over the energies you are collecting."

"It doesn't feel like it," Kel grumbled. "And I want to fly again!" He had to say it, even though he knew the answer already. He was gathering far too much energy just by walking; if he flew, well, there was that danger of going up in flames.

Firesong stopped, put his hand on Kel's beak, and turned his head so that Kel was looking into his eyes. "You're very close, Kel. That's why today we are going to walk *while* we work. Instead of just manipulating what power you have stored, I want you to *slowly* bring some in so you can have a try at using what I have taught you so far, as an ongoing process. Like breathing."

Kel stared into Firesong's eyes while pondering this. On the one talon, he *had* been getting exercise by walking, and he'd just dissipated the energy in light. On the other talon, he hadn't been using what Firesong was trying to teach him on those walks. On the third talon, there was the slight but measurable possibility that if he did this, he *would* catch fire. On the fourth talon, he was either brain-locked over the things Firesong and he were trying to make work, or he was bored out of his mind, and on the fifth talon—he was running out of talons!—Firesong was right here. If something went wrong, Firesong was the best possible Adept to catch it in time and *fix* it before he caught fire.

"All right," he agreed. "I just hope that you are correct about my being close to gaining control. I want the sky *so much* right now."

Firesong let go of his beak and patted his neck. "I know you do," he soothed. "But one step at a time. The smell of burning feathers is *horrible*."

That startled a bark of laughter out of Kel; he nodded and fluffed, and he and Firesong set off on what outwardly would look like a leisurely stroll away from the Vale—but inwardly, at least on Kel's part, was a struggle not unlike trying to wrestle with giant snakes.

"Question, Firesong. If I am too dangerous to be in the Vale because of what I do to magic, why are people using magic gathering around where I'm staying? Isn't that stacking oil barrels around a bonfire?"

Firesong gave a thoughtful grunt, and after a few moments answered, "Even the smartest of us do unwise things because of our feelings. Silverfox would say that sometimes when we need one kind of happiness, it's worth all the dangers just to feel like it *might* be attainable. Obviously, clustering around you is a bad idea, but they want to be near you to help you and to show support. I've been a symbol for a lot of people, for a long time, and that means being more than a person . . . people feel like if they let a symbol die, then what they're a symbol *of* dies. If things went very badly, when they could have helped, I think—nobody wants to feel like their neglect caused something good to fail, so there's an urge to feed the symbol as much as the person, if that makes sense. The meadow is a good place to work. The work needs to be done somewhere. Being near you feels like supporting their belief in what you represent." They strolled side by side onto the compacted road from k'Valdemar's outer fields toward Errold's Grove, surrounded by bird calls and the whirring of insects, leaving the increasing activity of the day behind them. "But, ultimately, there is really only one conclusion for certain. You are just too pretty to be away from for very long."

Kelvren bumped against Firesong's shoulder. Often the comfort gained from a joke lies in its familiarity, and some variation on this exchange had surely gone on between gryphons and their friends for centuries.

"That *must* be it," Kelvren agreed, and he raised his wings to shine.

Silverfox crossed a few more names off the list of people and creatures who had volunteered for this quest. Both he and Ayshen had been surprised at the number who *had*, to tell the truth. So many that he had an embarrassment of riches, and rather than hoping he had someone who had at least dabbled in something, he found he had at least three beings who were experienced in just about anything he and Ayshen could think of that might be needed.

It seemed as if half of the experienced fighters of Ghost Cat Clan wanted to come; he'd finally narrowed that list down to four. All of them had experience in combat against humans and against non-human creatures. All of them were also skilled hunters and trackers. None of them were older than thirty or younger than eighteen. None of them had romantic partners.

Though that might change on the trip. The crew would be a mixed group, all alone in the wilderness, and things were bound to happen. It would be his job as a kestra'chern to poke his nose into their private business and make sure whatever happened would not negatively affect the group as a whole.

By manipulation, if he had to.

A thankless job, but a necessary one. Hopefully, everyone would understand that on a mission, some social manipulation was necessary to maintain focus. If he did his job well, they wouldn't mind, either.

As Ayshen's job was to take care of the transportation and

supplies, his was to take care of the—well, call it "staffing." This involved a fatiguing number of interviews and a great deal of diplomacy.

Strangely, it had been the Ghost Cat warriors who had proven to be the least of his worries. He had traveled to their camp and set up next to the central fire, in order to talk to the ones who wanted to go. It had been an education, in all the best ways. They politely came to the fireside to sit down while everyone else stayed away, and he found they were quite practical. The last of them, Tutack son of Kagen, had finally explained to him *why* they had been so cooperative and so accepting of rejection.

"The Bright Gryphon Kelvren, our friend, must have the best," Tutack had said, with immense dignity. "But also, he must have those who will be a *clan*. We know who among us is best, but only you can find who will fit among those you have already chosen. To not be chosen is not a badge of dishonor. It is merely a sign that if you picked such and such a one, among those you have already chosen, there would be—" Tutack struggled for a moment before finding the word. "—what happens when you spin the firestick."

"Friction," Silverfox had supplied.

"Aye," said Tutack. "And with friction comes flame."

It had actually been that which cemented in Firesong's mind that Tutack would be in the party.

If only this were something like a first-year Bardic student Episodic Tale, where a group of people unknown to one another meet in a tavern, immediately hit it off, and form a seamless whole.

With friction comes flame, indeed.

Silverfox could very easily define what he needed from those he selected. The ability to encounter an adversarial situation, and instead of denying it, confronting it, or blowing up at it, saying, "Well, what can *we* do, what is different, and how can that fix things?"

And I am quite good at finding out if they have that characteristic, thank you.

The only set of creatures he had not bothered to run through his interview was the bachelor pack of kyree. There was no point; they were already a pack. Five of them, to be precise, though one of them, the pack leader, was a kyree neuter with a taste for adventure rather than staying with the home pack and pursuing a less hazardous life.

The dyheli, on the other hand . . .

To say that Tyrsell had been displeased when Silverfox had insisted on interviewing—and rejecting some!—of the dyheli that the king stag had proposed was an understatement. He'd been furious. And he had assaulted Silverfox with a mental tirade that had only ceased when it became apparent to even Tyrsell that the kestra'chern was impervious to it. Then, for a moment, there had been blessed mental silence.

"You," Silverfox had said, with all the stern demeanor of a teacher who has waited out a toddler's tantrum, "have not heard the word *no* nearly enough."

Tyrsell had pulled back in indignation at that. But as he gathered himself to resume his tirade, he stopped, turned his head to the side so he could get a better look at the kestra'chern, and took in Silverfox's posture. Back erect, arms crossed over his chest, toe tapping with impatience.

"You are certainly the most formidable wielder of Mind-magic that I know," Silverfox had said into the sudden silence. "But that doesn't mean that you know *anything* about group synergy."

:I!: began Tyrsell.

"You don't know anything about it, *because* of your powers," Silverfox interrupted him—something that simply didn't happen to the dyheli, and so it knocked him off balance mentally. As Silverfox had intended. Tyrsell might be the mental master of all he surveyed, but a kestra'chern was generally Adept-level at verbal martial arts.

"When you *need* the herd to do something, you compel them," Silverfox continued. "You don't ask, you just do it. And it's the understood agreement among all dyheli that this is the right of the king stag. Humans don't work that way, nor do tervardi or hertasi or kyree. Attempts to try will result in resentment at best, rebellion at worst, and rejection the moment you turn your subjects loose. Well, look at how Kel feels about what you did to him!"

:I did what was best.:

"But was it what was *right*?" Silverfox had countered. "Was there a better way, a way that wouldn't have resulted in anger and resentment on Kel's part?"

He did not add, *Because now Kel is never going to trust you again,* because Tyrsell simply wouldn't understand that. *Trust* was not a thing dyheli thought about most of the time. So he put it in terms of Kel's emotional response, and the question of right or wrong.

:He will adapt. He is respectable.:

Silverfox knew that Tyrsell would never admit that he had been in the wrong in the way he had treated Kelvren, so he just moved on to the matter of the dyheli who would be going along. "We need twelve dyheli who are not going to object to being in harness," he continued. "Four for each of the three barges."

Tyrsell had snorted. *:Just take the whole bachelor herd, then,:* he'd replied, in tones that suggested he'd probably welcome the young bucks' absence. *:We can make more. It's not as if you are going to have to worry about entertaining them.:*

Just to be sure, Silverfox *had* interviewed the entire herd, and it was immediately obvious that the bachelor herd, like the kyree pack, was exactly what they would need for the known terrain. The young stags were all quite independent-minded, but in the dyheli way—once a direction was chosen, all of them pulled together. Literally so—youthful dyheli loved tests of strength. If Silverfox was any judge of these things, the young stags were all very likely to have their own herds one day, rather than being satisfied to follow Tyrsell and take the one or two mates that he would allow them.

Best of all, they were, one and all, great admirers of Kel, and quietly indignant about the way the gryphon had been treated. *Kel could do with a good dose of that admiration right now,* Silverfox had judged, and so the herd of sixteen joined the expedition.

But strangest of all were the pair of tervardi.

When Urtho created tervardi, he had probably begun with birds, but they had come farther from that ancestry than the hertasi had come from lizards. Flightless, but covered with feathers no bigger than a baby's fingernail, they tended to wear loose clothing that would not pull those feathers with movement. They had abbreviated crests and curious mouths with horny lips, something like a cross between a mouth and a beak. Fortunately, they did not need lips to be able to speak perfectly well.

K'Valdemar Vale played host to several of the secretive creatures, but all Silverfox really knew about them was that their singing was exquisite, and that, like gryphons, tervardi were created by Urtho. Unlike gryphons, Ma'ar had not made any counterpart to tervardi.

Perhaps he wasn't a music lover, was all Silverfox had thought at the time.

But then the pair of tervardi had turned up at the ekele after Firesong had gone out for his lessons with Kel. Silverfox knew immediately that they were a bonded pair by their body language; they mirrored each other constantly, adjusting their poses so that, if you ignored the male's brighter feathers, they looked like identical bookends, or a single tervardi and its reflection.

"We wish to accompany the Bright Gryphon and your questors, that we may witness and assist the challenges you face," said the male, when they had perched themselves on the stools in his office, feet on the seat cushions. That speaking voice was rich and resonant, with flanging builds and falls that added yet another layer of emotive subtlety behind the cadence of the words themselves, as if they were accompanied by a melody.

That took him completely by surprise. The tervardi had always seemed shy, fragile, and historically disinclined to stray out of the Vale and its safety. "Why?" he asked bluntly.

"The flock has deemed it needful," the female trilled. "For many reasons, the chiefest being that although this is not the primary reason for your journey, you are certain to find a place for a new Vale, and we wish to see if that place may be suitable for a new flock, split from the one here. But there is another reason, which is that the unknown may answer to us," she half-explained. It seemed to be a tervardi trait that to answer a question more fully, they made it more encompassing than direct, to add artistry to the simplest of exchanges. And vagary.

"You have my interest," he said, sitting back in his chair and folding his hands.

"Our senses are of a broad scope, and we can warm chilled souls with touch and song, somewhat like you may give your graces," the male replied. "Despite our vulnerabilities, or in a few cases because of them, we do not wish to merely *relay* the songs and stories of others."

The female chimed in, head beside the male's, "We do not wait upon death as spectators of life. And we are not entirely without abilities to thwart hostilities." The male bobbed his head encouragingly, then nuzzled into the female's neck-feathers as she continued. "What we give of ourselves in concert, we can give to the open air of the wild," which certainly qualified as continuing the I-swear-I'm-not-vague quirk of theirs. "We know tones of healing and calm, and for focus over distance. Little-known, as is wisest, we are our own defenders. Perhaps one in ten or twenty of us . . . can kill with song at a distance." The male snapped his "lips" together with an audible *click* and waited for Silverfox's response, staring at him.

"Why have you waited to tell anyone about this for so long?" he asked, finally. "Surely you could have confided in the Tayledras."

The female shrugged, and the male mirrored her. "Long ago, we did, and left it to your people to pass the knowledge along if you deemed it right. Over generations, it was seldom brought up again, and we did not make mention of it. We believe that your people think of the actions taken in our heroic tales as solely metaphorical," she summed up with a kind tone. The male picked up the story then. "Rising up singing, and destroying our captors with songs of freedom, was not thought of as literal, it seems, and as a whole we were content with you as our defenders. There was no reason to do more than hold our abilities in reserve. What your magic could not slay, your arrows could. What your weapons could not touch, your magic dispatched. Only those flocks who nest outside of Vales need to use this power, and it felt best that it not be well known that we host it. And this power is not an easy thing for us to use. It is perilous for the singers who must stand in the open, and it is somewhat perilous for everyone around them except the two singers."

"Wait—*two* singers?" he asked.

The male nodded, and the female did the same. "Those of us with the high notes can sing a tone that can cause great pain and distress, and sometimes rupture eardrums," the male said. "We can focus this song on a single target or spread it across a handful. But when two of us separate a distance of about two or three cart-lengths and focus on that single target . . . the head, specifically . . . our song can turn a brain to liquid. It is best no one is near but that target."

Silverfox bit his lip and contemplated that for a long, long moment. "And you think that since we are venturing into Pelagir lands, there may be something that neither sword nor arrow nor magic can harm."

"We have never yet found anything that can withstand the Death Song," the female said, with the artless simplicity that told him this was an equally simple fact to her.

"I am interested in the fact that you can rupture eardrums," he said, finally. "That might be more useful in both the short and long run. Non-lethal."

"Survivable. Everyone should be equipped with wax and silk-cotton earplugs." The male's tone was dry, but their posture told him that they understood he had tacitly accepted their offer, and they were relieved. "Otherwise many nearby will be temporarily deaf."

Silverfox reached for the list of "unusual things we need to make sure we take" and added the earplugs to that. *At least they won't take up much space.*

He had the sense that there was a lot more going on than the tervardi were willing to tell him about, at least right now. And normally, that would have caused him to reject their offer. But . . . their song-weapon was something he could not turn down. It was something apparently nobody but the tervardi knew about, and for that reason, it was unlikely that any potential foe, human or otherwise, would know about it either.

But the existence of such a weapon certainly explained how flocks of tervardi managed to live in the Pelagirs without a Vale to protect them. On a hunch, Silverfox bluntly asked, "Am I right that you have other—tones—for other things?"

The two of them touched beak to beak for a moment and the female replied, "So many things. We do not hunt so much as entice, and we can set up lasting resonance in bells that will ward off insects. Or draw them in, should you enjoy gnat sprinkles on your food." The male smiled wider. "As she does."

Silverfox was no stranger to insects as food, and of course hertasi farmed all sorts of juicy bugs. "That's good to know. Will you need any special sleeping arrangements?" he asked.

They both shook their heads. "On the top of a barge in good weather, inside in bad," said the female. "We have seen the bunks, and they will do. We will only need one."

That much, he had reckoned on. Mated pairs of tervardi slept entwined closely together in a way that humans would probably have considered uncomfortable, but their pair-bond, which surely had some components of Mind-magic to it, ensured that if one moved, even in the deepest sleep, the other would move seamlessly with them and neither would wake up.

He asked a few more questions and was about to stand up and see them out when the male dipped his head and spoke up. "The Bright Gryphon," he said. "We think he is a portent for us."

"Would you care to explain?" Silverfox asked curiously.

"We could share stories best kept private. We had rather not," the female said. "The Tayledras have their secrets, we have ours. He is not a *bad* portent," she added. "The opposite, rather. And that is all we wish to say."

He wished then that he knew what the tervardi meant by "portent." The word had shades of meaning from one culture to the next, and there was no way of telling at this point if they saw Kel himself as a being with mystical power, as the sign that something important was on the way, or—well, there were too many ways to interpret what they had said to make a meaningful conclusion. But as he saw them out and stood on the doorstep of the ekele watching them stride with their peculiar bobbing gait down the path to where their flock had made homes, he belatedly realized two things.

One—unique among the dwellers of the Vale, the tervardi

and the gryphons had been created by Urtho out of whole cloth, so to speak. Neither species had any doubt about that, and so, since they actually knew exactly who their Creator was, it gave them a rather—unique—view of gods and portents and prophecies. A fairly skeptical one. Tell a tervardi that you had come on an errand from a god, and the tervardi was very likely to look at you sideways and demand proof. But, once proven, it would be taken as fact.

And two—a portent for a tervardi might be just as likely to be something a Farseer had glimpsed or written as to be supernatural in nature.

Well, this is going to make for a very interesting conversation with Ayshen, he had decided, heading back to his office. *And without a doubt, Ayshen will already know about at least some of it.*

When Ayshen turned up at Silverfox's office to get the updated list of "unusual things we are going to need," Silverfox told him everything. The hertasi was a very good listener, and as Silverfox voiced his concerns that the tervardi were going to need special care on account of their fragility, Ayshen only laughed.

"They are not as frail as they appear and not as fragile as you think," he assured Silverfox, leaning back on his stool so that his tail took some of the weight. "They *bend.* When they need to, they can grow a down layer that is just as good as a goose's, so you needn't worry about cold. Their outer feathers are virtually waterproof. They may not be fliers, but they can run faster than a human. They swim, dive, and float. And . . ." Here he shook his head. "It amazes me that you humans have had tervardi in your midst for centuries now, and it doesn't seem to have occurred to you to *look at their feet.*"

"Urhm?" Silverfox said. But when Ayshen said nothing, he cast his mind back to all the times he'd seen tervardi.

"Oh. *Oh!*" he said finally. "The middle claw behind—"

Ayshen nodded. "That's a fighting claw. Meant to eviscerate with a kick."

"Like the maka'ar had!"

"Exactly. Urtho may have created the maka'ar to combat gryphons, but he probably used captured tervardi as his base."

Ayshen nodded wisely. "Don't underestimate them. Their wings might have been changed into arms, but they have *not* forgotten how to use that claw. I've seen them spar at dummies with a padded leather sheath over the claw. They're not helpless." Then he grinned, showing all his teeth. And there were a very great many of them.

"No more helpless," Ayshen continued, "than hertasi."

9

The trek from south of Deedun to k'Valdemar Vale was a long one. There was no urgent need for anyone to send messages, supplies, or people back and forth from the Guard encampment to the Vale, now that the Vale had Kelvren back, so no one made the effort to open energy-gulping Gates between the two.

So once Hallock had gotten the official word that yes, he was not just allowed, he was *ordered* to join Kelvren's expedition, he and Genni had loaded up a horse with their gear, added two horses to ride, and prepared to set off in the direction of Errold's Grove and k'Valdemar Vale. At least there was a road. *This is Valdemar. Of course there's a road. Anywhere in Valdemar without a road has a road under construction to where the next road will be built.*

And then came a twist.

Just as he was adjusting the baggage on the pack horse, Ammari, with Jefti trudging along by her side, approached him. It did not escape him that Jefti had a bag slung across his back.

"Don't tell me," he sighed. "You want me to take Jefti. You realize the dangers of—"

"Is't wuss than bein' on a battlefield?" Jefti asked, his chin raised in an unusual gesture of defiance. "'Cause I done that. I helped with the wounded while there was still shootin' goin' on."

"But—" Hallock turned to Ammari, but the woman just shook her head.

"This is Jefti's idea, not mine," she told him. "Jefti wants to help his gryphon."

"I know all kinda useful stuff," Jefti continued. "I ain't afeered of hard work. I'm mighty strong for my size. And—"

Hallock glanced at his wife, but Genni's expression was . . . oh dear gods . . . approving.

"You are still recovering from your wounds," she reminded him. "Another set of hands on the road won't come amiss. And when we get to k'Valdemar Vale, he can ask Kelvren himself if he can come along."

Hallock gritted his teeth and turned to the boy. "And if Kelvren says no?"

"Then I reckon I'll either come back here or stay there and work," Jefti said, wilting just a little. He obviously hadn't thought that far. "An' if they got work for me, they prolly got work for Ma, and I can send for her."

Hallock's head told him that this youngling was trying to punch *far* above his weight, and this was a terrible idea. But his heart reminded him of how Jefti took care of Kel when no one else would. And that perhaps a removal to k'Valdemar Vale would not be such a bad thing. After all, he'd have the Owlknight himself there as someone to emulate and look up to, and from what he knew of Darian Firkin k'Valdemar, who himself had been a despised orphan, the Owlknight would probably find some way to take him under his capacious wing.

And those marks on his face won't stand out so much when he's surrounded by Hawkbrothers and talking lizards, and the gods only know what else they have in there.

"Ammari—" he began, and Jefti stepped up in front of her by a pace.

"I raised my boy to *trust* my boy. He's tough as cadet soldiers, any day," she declared.

"All right," he said with resignation. "He can go to find work. But—"

Before he could say anything else, a giant shadow interposed itself between them and the sun. And a moment later, the gryphon Treyvan landed beside them, startling the horses so much that he and Genni had their work cut out to hold and calm them.

"Hurrr. Not usssed to grrryphonsss, I sssee," said Treyvan. "Mussst have come frrrom thossse mercsss. Sssorrry. Animalsss usssually have to sssmell me to trrrussst me, but I wasss not mindful, and ssstarrrtled them."

Hallock waved the apology off. It wasn't Treyvan's fault, after all; how was the gryphon to tell from above which horses would consider him a gigantic predator? Of course, he *was* a gigantic predator, and it was not unlikely he'd eaten horse in the past, but still. The great gryphon sat and sorted through one of his panniers, picking out bundles and scrolls. "If you would sssee thessse to theirrr rrrresscipientsss at k'Valdemarrr? Yesss. Good. I have come to inssspect the Worrrk left behind afterrr rrrejuvenating Kelvrrren forrr lassssting effectsss upon the land, and thought to sssee you off, Hallock Ssstaverrrn. And to thank you," Treyvan continued. "Alsssso, I am to give my offisscial blesssing for your unit to add a sssmall grrryphon outline to their Colorrrsss, to honorrr the ssstorrry. Tell Kelvrrren of the dissstinction."

Each of them shared their plans, and as expected, the horses calmed. Treyvan's facial feathers rippled backward when he gazed into the distance past the travelers, his large eyes seeming to focus on infinity for a handful of seconds. "Thrrree ssstorrrmsss gatherrr, to combine herrre by dusssk. Would you accssept a Gate to ssshorrrten yourrr jourrrney?" He paused. "If sssuch things trrrouble you, I will not be offended. Not all Valdemarrransss arrre comforrrtable with such thingsss. Therrre isss only a verrry sssmall chance that you will emerrrge on the otherrr side with two headsss, afterrr all."

Hallock started. Was the gryphon serious?

"I am not ssserrriousss," Treyvan added.

"A Gate would be much appreciated, Master Gryphon," Hallock told him, thinking about how good it would be to bypass indifferent inns and rough camping. "But . . ." He turned to Jefti. "Lad, will you abide by what Master Treyvan has to say about you coming with me and Genni?"

Jefti went a little pale and looked stricken, but nodded. "Him bein' Kelvren's lord an' all," the boy gulped. "Reckon I got to."

Treyvan sat back on his haunches and appeared to be deep in thought for a moment. "I think," he said finally, "that Jefti and Ammarrri ssshould both go to k'Valdemarrr Vale. Willing handsss arrre alwaysss welcome therrre. Opening a Gate for fourrr will not take longerrr than opening a Gate for two." He gazed at both of them with such intensity that they were both clearly uncomfortable with his regard. "You arrre not apprrreciated herrre asss you ssshould be. Ssso, you may go to k'Valdemarrr and ask Kelvrrren himssself if he requirrresss yourrr help." He tilted his head to the other side. "Boy Jefti . . . you arrre not too old to learrrn the crrraft of the trrrondi'irrrn. Whitebirrrd thinksss you have the touch and the ssstomach for the tasssk. Hallock Ssstaverrrn, as my rrranked witness, sssee it is ssso."

Jefti's eyes widened at that, as did his mother's.

"Ssso. Put the pack upon a horrrssse," Treyvan continued. "And let usss be about thisss quickly. I wisssh to open a Gate for myssself and rrreturn to my mate and children within the candlemarrrk. I hope the latterrr have not demolisssshed the Palassce yet."

Wordlessly, Hallock took the bag from Jefti's nerveless fingers and loaded it onto the pack horse. He mounted, as did Genni, and he gave a hand to Jefti, pulling him up to perch awkwardly on the horse's rump behind him, as Genni did the same for Ammari. It was quite clear that Jefti had never ridden a horse in his life, because he immediately fastened both hands into Hallock's belt with a grip not even death was likely to ease.

They followed Treyvan back to that now-familiar hill where Kel's transformation had taken place. Treyvan pointed out a place for them to wait, and after assigning someone to see to Ammari's affairs, sat comfortably on his haunches. From his nonchalant attitude, Hallock realized that this Gate business was so routine it was nearly as familiar as flying to Treyvan. So instead of watching the gryphon, he intently watched the spot where this Gate was supposed to appear, because Treyvan had made it very, very clear that it was not going to be open for long, and the faster they got across it, the better.

"Watch forrr the moment when therrre arrre treesss and a rrroad," he said shortly. "Then *gallop*."

This was only the second Gate Hallock had ever seen, and he didn't find the experience any less uncanny than the first time he had watched one—first the bloom of light in the shape of a disk, then a sort of rippling effect, then suddenly—the landscape that should have been on the other side of the Gate was gone, and in its place was, as Treyvan had said, a road and trees. He put spurs to his horse, who, startled, leapt across the intervening space and into the Gate, followed by Genni's horse and the pack horse.

He pulled up and moved to the side as soon as his horse's hooves touched the new road, to make sure that Genni and the pack horse got across all right. For a moment, as the latter dashed past him, he saw Treyvan, talons raised in some sort of gesturing motion—met his gaze for an instant—and then the Gate was gone, and in its place was just the road and trees.

There was no sign of any civilization. Even the air smelled different. Wilder, somehow.

I wonder how far he dropped us from this Vale.

And at least they were not handicapping the Guard by taking three good horses with them. The one thing that the camp had in abundance was horses; attrition had been high among the mounted fighters, plus they had all the horses from the mounted mercenaries they had captured. The captain knew everything about horses that Hallock didn't, so the three beasts he had selected for them were steady, sound, with high endurance, and not at all skittish. Just—wary of sudden gryphons.

The very last thing that the captain had done before they left on their way was to pass the title of First to the woman who was currently Hallock's Second, and to give Hallock a brand new title: Military Attaché. Give advice when asked, fight alongside the allies if needed, otherwise observe, don't be afraid to volunteer, and don't *command* anyone unless the leaders of the expedition put him in command.

Easy orders to obey, especially given this was exactly what Hallock would have done in the first place.

And that, essentially, was how the four of them, with Ammari up behind Genni and Jefti up behind Hallock, found themselves in the middle of nowhere on a "road" of sorts. More of a track, although it was wide enough for a cart to pass. Since they were under trees and he couldn't see the sun, and his navigation skills were average at best, that left him at an impasse.

Well, *now* where were they to go? The road went in two directions, after all . . . which was the way to the Vale, and which led away from it?

I don't bleeding know. I have to assume that Treyvan pointed us in the right direc—

That was his thought, which was interrupted rather rudely by half a dozen people stepping out of the thick undergrowth and onto the road to his left, bows bent, arrows nocked and pointed at them. Since the only Hawkbrother he had ever seen was Darkwind, and these people looked somewhat like Darkwind, and were dressed to blend in with the forest—

—and had various birds of prey flying in to roost in the branches overhead, within easy attack distance—

it was reasonable to assume that the Vale was in their direction.

Well, that seems definite.

Jefti gasped, and Genni let out a little squeak. Hallock eased his horse past Genni and Ammari. "Valdemaran Military Attaché Hallock Stavern, present and accounted for," he said, with a crisp salute. "Requested to appear at k'Valdemar Vale by Silver Gryphon Kelvren of k'Valdemar Vale, relocation facilitated by Silver Gryphon Adept Treyvan."

Two of the people with arrows pointing at him looked at each other, then lowered their bows. The rest did the same, more slowly.

"It would have been nice to get some warning," said the taller of the two, with evident irritation. Hallock had to admit that he lived up to the legends. His multi-colored, layered, and wrapped clothing in browns and greens was both unfamiliar to Hallock and instantly recognizable as camouflage, and his sharp features stood in notable contrast to the Valdemarans Hallock was most familiar with, farmers or Guards, who tended to be square-faced and bulked up with muscles. His hair had been braided and clubbed like a warhorse's tail, a practical adaptation Hallock approved of.

"Oh, Treyvan probably used his teleson to warn Firesong just before he put up the damned Gate," said the other, an older version of the first man. "And Firesong didn't realize how fast that one can work. From what I hear from the other gryphons, he can place a hole in the sky while flying toward it."

He bent his bow to unstring it and slung it behind his shoulder, then walked toward them, hand extended. "First Warden Leafblade k'Valdemar. I hadn't heard anything about a military attaché, but I *have* heard of you from Kelvren via the hertasi. Who's the rest of your party?"

Well, that blew over easily, without any perforations. "My wife Genni, who's a Healer's Hand, my . . ." *think quick, Hallock—* ". . . Guard apprentice Jefti, who has ambitions to be a trondi'irn after meeting with Kelvren and Whitebird, and his ma, Ammari." *Stretching the truth a bit, but not all that much.* "No gryphons with the Guard, so if the lad is going to study to be a trondi'irn, he needed to come with me. Master Treyvan personally charged me with seeing to Jefti not a candlemark ago."

"Well, you're lucky we all speak Valdemaran here," Leafblade said without any sign of anger. "Opening a Gate this close to a Vale is going to get the whole Vale roused. We'll walk you on in. Treyvan, eh? What's he like?" Jefti walked around to each of the Tayledras, and shook their hands, then let them all know what Treyvan was like, in enthusiastic detail, as they walked.

The walk wasn't remarkably quick-paced, but there was just so much of the *new* to take in that the newcomers kept going a few paces once their escort had stopped. A long-downed tree to the sunward side of the road gave its roots as the frame for the most remarkable pair Hallock had ever seen in his life. The human of the two paled in comparison to his bondbird, which was a *firebird*, and a huge male firebird at that, tail and crest streaming out behind him as he flapped his wings rapidly where he perched near his human's shoulder, false-sparks in a plume in the air behind him, the edges of his feathers all alight. Hallock was utterly mesmerized, and he wasn't the only one. Genni gave an actual squeal, Ammari gasped with her hands clasped under her chin, and a glance at Jefti showed the boy's eyes were like a pair of stars.

With the firebird to look at, the Hawkbrother, who otherwise would have stood out among these "Wardens" like a peacock among chickens, barely rated a glance.

Which was a shame, because he was worth looking at. He had long white hair twisted into many tight braids threaded with silver rings, and wore a mask that was apparently made of firebird body-feathers, probably from his own bondbird, the eyeholes and border rimmed in silver. His garments were a layered set of robes in silver, charcoal, and white, held closely to his body by a wide cloth charcoal-colored belt that featured a pair of embroidered firebirds on the front. Beside and behind him, a large gazelle-like creature with stacks of blankets on her back watched them patiently from where she lay on the greenery.

The masked man simply spread his hands, palm up. His firebird hopped to rest on his shoulder. "I'm sorry, Leafblade," the Hawkbrother said in Valdemaran. "Treyvan neglected to tell me he was going to open a Gate and send Hallock Stavern through, until he'd actually done it. He may as well have shouted 'Catch!'"

When Leafblade snorted and said, "Gryphons!" the masked stranger turned to Hallock's group.

"I am Adept Firesong k'Treva. You are obviously the Hallock Stavern that Kel wants on our journey, but who did you bring with you?"

That meant the same introductions all the way around, as the rest of the Hawkbrothers faded into the underbrush and were invisible within moments. Firesong looked extremely interested when Hallock mentioned that Jefti might be interested in learning the trade of the trondi'irn. "Is this so, youngling?" he asked Jefti directly.

Jefti blinked, and looked very shy, as if he had not been expecting to be addressed by such a glorious personage. "Well . . . I seed what Whitebird done, and I wished I coulda done that for Kelvren myself. But don't you got to be a Healer?"

"Well, as with most of life, it *helps* to be a Healer," Firesong replied. "But it's not strictly necessary, as long as you know your gryphons down to the last feather-vane. I'm sure Nightwind would be very happy for an extra set of hands, if you feel you can stand having a lot of learning stuffed into your head. And if it doesn't work out, you'll still have some useful knowledge. No learning is ever wasted."

Jefti raised his chin. "Ain't never backed down from a hard job yet," he declared. "Ain't about to start now."

Firesong chuckled slightly and clapped Jefti on the shoulder. "Nightwind is going to like you. Genni Stavern, I assume you plan to go on this quest as well? We can certainly use you. A Healer's Hand is welcome anywhere."

"Good," Genni said simply, and left it at that.

"I just want to be useful," Ammari finally mustered, shyly, as Firesong turned his mask toward her. "But if there's nothing I can do . . ."

"We'll see," Firesong replied, and in one motion, he sat sideways on the creature's blankets as it rose under him and stood. "But in the meantime, let's get along to see Kel. I think you'll be . . . surprised."

"Surprised" was not quite the right word to use when they walked their horses up the road to find a busy group measuring, building, rolling large swaths of shadecloth, and strange tools casting lines of light, with humans and hertasi laboring side-by-side, and many of the gazelle-like creatures being fitted to harness. The firebird darted to, backwinged, and perched atop a round tent on a platform, as if it was meant to be a crest for a pavilion. "Kel!" Firesong called. "Visitors!"

A glowing—*glowing!*—beak shoved the door-flap aside, and the glowing head emerged, swiveling toward them. This was no "glow" like light reflected from a bright spot onto a thing; no, Kelvren was the *source* of the light that gleamed from him, from the inside out, with the exception of his eyes. Hallock had thought that gryphons in general were imposing enough on their own, but to see one alight as if illuminated by the gods was enough to send an atavistic shiver up his spine. *If he's changed that much outwardly . . .* Despite having seen Kel's transmutation, and hearing that the glow had persisted at least all the way back to k'Valdemar Vale, it still came as a shock to see him lit up like a little sun.

But the next moment proved that, inwardly, Kel hadn't

changed at all. "Hallock!" he trumpeted, leaping down to the ground. "And *Jefti*!" Then he paused and added, "And Ammarrri! And you musssst be Genni!"

Jefti ran, top speed, to collide with his gryphon and embrace the little sun. A taloned hand the size of his entire back held him in return, snug against the gryphon's warmth.

"I came to make sure you were doing better," Jefti declared with his hands on Kelvren's beak.

"Oh, Jefti. I am now," Kelvren replied.

"You asked, I came," Hallock said truthfully after a respectful moment. "They gave me a fancy title that means you're important enough to get an official along, and dangerous enough they want it to be a military one." He shrugged. "My captain filled me in on the situation."

Kel snorted at that. "Sssituation! That'sss a nicsse way to put it. My rrreputation rrredussced to 'dangerrrousss monsssterrr' and—"

As he spoke, his glow increased; he cut himself off with an effort and shook his head so that his ear-tufts rattled. "Neverrr mind." And the glow ebbed.

Huh. I need to find out more about this.

"Never mind, exactly, Kel," Hallock felt moved to tell him. "What we're going to do is turn all this around. We'll show everyone that you're a good leader and a great explorer. When we're done, they'll realize that what you did to stop that revolt saved a lot of lives, and it was about the only way the fighting could have been stopped. Mercenaries hired by our supposed leaders to fight our own people! It's a disgrace!"

Firesong's nod, from his place atop the dyheli, told him that Firesong approved of what Hallock had just said.

"And I wanna see iffen I can be a whatcha-call, trondi'irn, like that Whitebird," Jefti said. "Treyvan said I might could do that."

Kel cocked his head to one side . . . and sighed, though his next words gave no clue as to why he was sighing. "Then you ssshould be ssspeaking to Nightwind, I think. If ssshe wantsss an apprrentissce, then you may ssstudy. But if not, therrre are otherrr trondi'irn herrre that will likely take you."

"I'll take them all to our ekele and get them settled," Firesong said. "We have the room, after all. Once I give them the Tayle-dras and Kaled'a'in tongues, we can meet with Ayshen and Silverfox and discuss all of this further."

Kel sighed again. "And I—will rrresssume my ssstudiesss. Even though they arrre drrry asss old bonesss."

He turned tail and nosed his way back into his tent, and Firesong led the little group past wagons and darting groups of hertasi, grazing dyheli, and a dozen assorted raptors further up the trail until it ended in a . . . shimmer in the air. It was almost like heat-haze. "This is the Veil that keeps the Vale at an even temperature year-round," Firesong explained. "It is also our first line of magical defenses, and it serves to keep things we don't want out."

"How?" Ammari blurted, then blushed.

"Magic," Firesong said in a teasing voice. "Oh, it's terribly complicated, and requires the constant attention of mages, but we've been doing this since long before your nation was founded."

That was probably about the most diplomatic way Firesong could have put it, and Ammari didn't look as if she'd felt slighted by the reply.

"Don't worry, you probably won't even notice passing through it," Firesong continued, and walked right into the shimmer. With a glance at Genni and a shrug, Hallock led his horse and the packhorse across the near-invisible border, and didn't feel anything worse than a slight tingle.

Inside, it was apparent that they weren't *exactly* in Valdemar anymore.

For one thing, the trees were *enormous*. And there were living spaces built into them, spiraling up their trunks and lodged in their branches. Lush underbrush flourished on either side of the path, there were at least a dozen different flowers in bloom, and colorful birds ranging from tiny to blackbird-sized flitted or perched everywhere.

This has only been here, what? A handful of years? How did those trees get that big that fast? Gates were one thing: totally incomprehensible. *This* impressed him.

There was really too much to look at, especially at the brisk pace that Firesong was setting. Hallock did see that there were dwellings—or rather, individual rooms in a row—spiraling up the trunks of many of those trees. There also seemed to be smaller dwellings nestled into the undergrowth at the foot of those trees. A harsh, wordless cry caused him to look up, and he spotted a gryphon landing on a platform in the top of the tree nearest him. The gryphon vanished into yet another sort of dwelling.

Jefti's head kept turning like it was on a swivel, and his mouth was wide open. Ammari and Genni's eyes were as wide as Jefti's mouth. Well, Hallock reckoned he didn't look any too different from them. This was—literally, evidently—a magical place!

"We don't have much of anything you don't already have," Firesong said, after he glanced back at them. "It just looks different on the outside. The things we do with magic, you all can mostly do with Mind-magic and good old hard work."

"Gates," Hallock pointed out. "And these giant trees."

Firesong laughed, and his shoulder-firebird bent its head and made a snickering sound.

"Them *birds!*" Jefti exclaimed, in tones that suggested he thought Firesong was telling less than the truth.

"Messengers. You have human messengers, we have birds. Our houses can't withstand the weather as yours can. And they are somewhat inconvenient if you have difficulty climbing stairs. Not to mention the fact that *everything* you want either has to be carried up or hauled up the side by ropes. Nothing about an ekele is terribly convenient. Most of us feel that the effort is worth it, but not everyone does, and they live on the ground. This is the ekele I share with Silverfox."

He stopped at a tree; there was a short, mossy path leading to a large structure built entirely around the trunk, but bulging far out to the right side. It seemed that the Hawkbrothers did not trouble themselves too much with doors; the doorway framed a curtain made of silvery-green beads rather than an actual solid door.

Before they could get close to the door, however, a quartet of hertasi swarmed the horses, stripping every bit of baggage off them before Hallock could say or do anything. Three of them vanished into that curtain laden with luggage; the fourth snatched the reins from Hallock and Genni's hands and led the horses off—somewhere. Hallock was left standing there with empty hands and a dropped jaw. He'd seen Ayshen, of course, and knew how fast the hertasi could move, but he didn't know they swarmed you in a pack!

Firesong held the beads aside so they could follow the hertasi. At this point, Jefti had been rendered utterly speechless again, Genni and Ammari didn't quite know where to look next, and Hallock had to admit he was pretty well dazzled, too.

The room they entered was like nothing he had ever seen before. Curved walls, a wooden floor sanded smooth, and the only furniture in it was a series of chests and tables around the walls. The walls seemed to be woven reed or willow—well, if you lived in a place where the weather was kept under control, there really was no need to hold in heat or keep it out—and were decorated with several masks, each more elaborate than the last, and other pieces of artwork, none of which were paintings. At the heart of it, of course, was the giant living tree trunk. The bulge he had seen from outside proved to be this single large room. Evidently they were supposed to sit on the oversized cushions piled everywhere.

Standing in the middle was another Tayledras, this one in a wrapped tunic and trews woven in shades of brown, and bearing ridiculously long black hair with gray and white streaks the whole length. There was no sign of this man's bondbird, but perhaps it was elsewhere in the ekele. "Welcome," the man said, his voice warm and practiced. "Firesong has told me about you, Hallock. I'm pleased you are honoring Kel's request and coming along. And I am sure Genni, the Healer's Hand, will be equally welcome." He paused a moment. "Whether or not Jefti comes will depend on what Nightwind says. He is of an age that causes concern, but our cultures are different." Come to think of it, Hallock hadn't heard or seen anything like children since they'd arrived, nor anything resembling toys. "As for Ammari—" He paused again. "What can you do, exactly?"

"Silverfox is the organizational head of this ever-expanding acrobat show," Firesong put in. "His work mostly seems to consist of telling me *no*." Hallock did notice that there was no acrimony and just a touch of ruefulness in Firesong's voice.

"I don't rightly know what I could do to be useful on your quest," Ammari admitted. "But I can garden and I know how to prepare herbs for every sort of purpose, so maybe I can earn my keep here?"

Silverfox started to say something, then stopped before he'd gotten a single sound out. He licked his lips thoughtfully, and started again. "You know, it just occurred to me. You can tell us a great deal about ordinary Valdemarans. That information will be worth more than silver. If we are going to interact with ordinary folk on a regular basis, we need to know what to expect." Then he chuckled. "And yes, another person preparing herbs and tending the garden will always be welcome."

Ammari lost some of that tenseness she'd had, as Silverfox smiled at her kindly. There was genuine warmth in that smile; Hallock decided that he liked the man.

But now Hallock wondered, looking at Silverfox, if all the Hawkbrothers looked as if they were from the same enormous family. Firesong was behind his mask, so there was no telling what he looked like, but the—Wardens, were they?—and Silverfox all had generally the same aquiline features. The ones who weren't white-haired were dark streaked with white, and they all had the same keen look to their eyes, like the eyes of their birds—the raptors anyway. They were all lean, whipcord rather than massively muscled.

Well, probably they are so closely related that they all look similar. I very much doubt they've been out raiding for brides and husbands from elsewhere all these centuries, or we would have heard about it! With what I've heard told about the Pelagirs, there can't be very many of them.

"We should get you settled before I start assigning you jobs!" the Hawkbrother continued. "Do any of you have a problem with heights?"

Jefti and Ammari both shrugged. Jefti spoke up first. "Dunno. Highest I ever been was on that Change-Circle hill."

"Well, I suppose we'll find out now." He beckoned and brought them around the tree trunk to a staircase that wound gently upward, with the rooms stacked one above the next. Silverfox did not stop at the first couple, tossing off that one was his office and the next was something Hallock didn't quite catch. But the third, which had partitions that screened the staircase from the room itself, he announced was the guest sleeping rooms.

Hallock had been bracing himself for this. He had literally no idea what kind of sleeping arrangements were common for Hawkbrothers. Were they all expected to sleep together in a pile of more cushions on the floor? Would there be cots in a row, like a barracks? Would they be expected to sleep in hammocks?

At least one fear was relieved when he saw that there were three smallish rooms sharing a close-stool. Each of the rooms had two comfortable-looking low beds, each able to hold two. So, no hammocks, and no having to go down sets of stairs in the middle of the night to take care of business.

"If you'd prefer hammocks—" Silverfox began.

"No," they all said at once.

Silverfox laughed. "They are an acquired taste," he admitted. "The hertasi decided who was to go in which room, but if you don't like the room the hertasi took your luggage to, you can sort things out as you prefer."

"Let's do that now," Firesong interjected. "I need to give them languages, and—"

"—and they will definitely want to lie down afterward, yes," Silverfox agreed.

Genni had already eased over to the rightmost room. "Our things are here," she called out. "It seems fine to me."

Jefti was faster than his mother was, looked in the middle room, and exclaimed in shock, "Wait! I gots a room all to *meself*?"

"Is that a problem?" Silverfox said immediately.

"No, I jest—I ain't never had a room all for me afore . . ." The lad looked a little dazed. "I *like* it," he blurted, then blushed.

Completely oblivious to the fact that for a tiny moment, his mother looked—pained. Hallock had seen that sort of look before, in the faces of the mothers of new recruits, who had only just realized that their baby wasn't *their baby* anymore, quite the way they had been minutes before.

"All right, you can unpack later," Firesong pronounced. "You aren't needed anywhere urgently, and you'll be tended to. I need you all to sit down on something, and I'm going to use magic to fill your heads with two new languages. Tayledras, and Kaled'a'in, which is what the gryphons speak. I need you sitting down, because having one language dumped into your head like vegetables into a stew-pot is quite disorientating enough. Having two is going to make you all sleep until sundown, and you'll *want* to."

Hallock was going to take his word for it. He joined Genni, perched on the side of the bed nearest the window. Firesong began muttering under his breath, and his hands started to glow. Then his right hand moved toward Hallock's forehead—

And the next thing Hallock knew, he was awakening from a set of very confused dreams in which people seemed to be reciting at him. He opened his eyes to see that someone had lit a mage-light beside the gauze-screened window; his mouth was dry, and he was hungry enough to have eaten even the miserable rations they'd first gotten when they came to Deedun.

Gingerly, he sat up. Genni sighed.

"I was waiting for you to wake up," she said. "My head feels stuffed, and I had the strangest dreams!"

Now that she'd said that, he noticed that his head felt just a little too small and a little too heavy. "It's probably just us *thinking* our heads should feel full, so they do," he reasoned out loud. "It's like having a cold made of lead." He took stock of his surroundings.

The bed had been supremely comfortable, so much so that if he hadn't been suffering from hunger and thirst, he would have lain right back down on it. Someone had covered him and Genni with a light blanket, but they really hadn't needed it. Balmy air scented with green growing things wafted in through the window, and there were distant murmurs of voices and other sounds coming in on that breeze.

"Be you awake?" came the not-quite whisper from Jefti's room.

"We are now," Genni laughed. "I think we should go back down to the ground floor and find out if—"

"Good evening, guests!" said a bright voice from the area

of the staircase. "I heard your voices! Please, come, come! I will take you where you can wash your hands and faces, and then there will be dinner!"

Hallock was the first to stand up and venture out into the stair, which was brightly lit, in contrast to their room. The owner of the voice was, as he had expected at this point, a hertasi. This one was dressed in what looked like leather: leather kilt, some straps wrapped around his torso and arms. *He—well, that's an assumption. Might be she, or something between.*

"I'm Deban," the hertasi said, which told Hallock that the hertasi was, in fact, a male, because the hertasi took gendered na— *How the hell do I know that?*

Evidently it wasn't just a language that Firesong had shoved into his skull, it was all the nuances and cultural implications! *All right. This's more impressive than trees* or *Gates!*

And that was when he realized he and Deban had been speaking Tayledras all this time.

"Hurry up, Ma, I'm starving!" Jefti said, in Valdemaran, as he burst out of his room. He stopped short at the sight of the hertasi. "Heyla, friend," he said, the "heyla" in Valdemaran but the "friend" in Tayledras. "Thank you for caring for us!"

The hertasi opened his mouth in a broad smile that showed an awful lot of teeth. "My pleasure, young Jefti! Please, come. Your likely hunger shall be appeased!"

That was when Ammari emerged from her room, nervously smoothing down her skirts. But before she could say anything or take a single step, Deban was scrambling down the stairs.

"Come *on*, Ma," Jefti urged and took her elbow. She had no choice but to take to the stairs, with Hallock and Genni following.

Hallock tried to figure just what sort of lights these were, for they seemed to be encased in frosted glass lanterns and did not waver. Finally, as he and Genni emerged into that large room they had passed through this morning, they found Jefti and Ammari at the "back" of the trunk, washing up at a pair of basins. While they dried themselves, Genni and Hallock did the same, then returned to that large room.

Firesong and his firebird—*Aya. How do I know that?*—were

sharing a plate of fruit. The tables had been pulled away from the walls and cushions piled next to them, and one long table held covered dishes, from which delicious aromas arose.

"Chow line!" crowed Jefti and headed straight for the pile of empty plates.

His mother turned to Firesong, blushing. "I swear, he has better manners than this," she said apologetically. "Truly he does."

But Firesong just laughed. "He is a boy, with a boy's appetite. At his age, I did the same. Still do, sometimes."

"Your new language should inform you what these foods are, and your own memories of what pleases you will tell you whether or not you will like them." That was Silverfox, accepting a berry from Deban and feeding it to the firebird. For some time, at least on the part of the Valdemarans, there was nothing but the sound of knives and forks and chewing, with murmurs of approval. Firesong turned and discreetly swapped the lower half of his mask for a beaded veil, to allow dining and drink. He seemed to be enjoying the same tea (amusingly, the Tayledras term for tea was "weed-water") that Hallock had chosen over wine. Hallock wasn't sure his head was up to wine after everything that had been stuffed into it, and there was no telling how potent Tayledras wine could be. Silverfox was attentive, doting on Firesong, but eventually seemed satisfied that his partner was all right. Finally, Hallock pushed his plate away, settled his knife and fork atop it, and looked straight at the two of them.

"I'm canny enough to know when someone is keeping me out of the way of senior officers," he said bluntly. "So why did you whisk us off here, then do something to make us unavailable for a while?"

"See?" Firesong told his mate. "I *told* you there's more to Hallock than a 'simple soldier.'"

"You win. The next time you do something stupid, I will refrain from telling you that I told you so," Silverfox muttered.

Firesong put down his cup. "I'll skim over all the nattering that's gone on about this expedition, because it's been addressed and dealt with. There was some resistance when Valdemar insisted that one of theirs come along; Kel quelled that by demanding you. But then you turn up this morning with three more outsiders in tow, *and*—and this is the important part—a military rank. Now the Elders all want to interrogate you to figure out whose side you are on."

"Kel's," Hallock said simply. "I owe him everything."

Firesong looked to his mate, who nodded. "Just hold to that, and don't waver, don't elaborate. They'll see you in the morning. Now as to the rest of you—Genni, they'd be fools to turn down a Healer's Hand. Jefti, Nightwind wants to see you tomorrow. Ammari, Nightwind wants you along. We have spoken about Jefti's travel with us as an assumed thing, mainly because Jefti makes Kelvren happy, but anyone could protest it. People his age are trusted, but inexperienced, and "danger" is too small a word for what we may encounter. I'm certain what she wants is to make sure that you are ready—as ready as any mother could be—to allow your son to be parted from you on a potentially dangerous quest."

Ammari bit her lip, but nodded.

"Be honest, both of you," Silverfox concluded. "After you speak with Nightwind, Springrain will test your abilities in the compounding shed."

Ammari nodded, but looked pleased. *Well, she did concoct that glow-dye out of Change-Circle dirt.* This was at least one area where she was probably comfortable.

Hertasi swarmed in, carried off all the detritus of dinner, and swarmed out again.

"Let's go see Kel, shall we?" Firesong suggested. "He's been having gathers of some of the people Silverfox already selected in the evenings."

"Lead on." Hallock said, levering himself up from his cushion and offering his hand to Genni. "I want to know how he's *really* doing."

"Remember you said that," Firesong replied.

Kelvren's shelter wasn't big enough for many guests, but that was no matter. The hertasi had created an entire outdoor space, carpeted in a moss that actually thrived when trodden upon, ringed with oil lamps for night-time meetings, and of course the ubiquitous cushions from inside scattered liberally about. Kel liked it. Lying out there was the closest he felt to being normal, and in a normal place, doing normal things. And as long as he ignored the fact that he was glowing . . .

On the other hand, he felt as if he was getting closer to the thing that Firesong wanted him to do. Create something like miniature ley-lines in himself, that would—if Firesong could pull this off—lead to something like a miniature Heartstone that he would wear. The big Heartstones that anchored Vales could hold an incalculable amount of energy; he wasn't sure how much this one could hold, but if this all worked, not only would he *not* be in any danger of bursting into flames, he'd be able to share the power he gathered by flying with all the other mages in the group.

He was getting to know the non-humans who were coming— he'd resigned himself to the fact that this was not going to be anything like a rapid trip, so he was trying now to make sure they all fit together and to get possible conflicts out of the way before they became a problem.

Of course, he mused, as he took his place off to the side of the clearing, *something will go wrong. But at least I can try to bring along those who will try to pull together rather than pulling apart.*

Hmm. Pulling apart, like that caramel and nut bread the hertasi make. I hope they bring some tonight.

The first to arrive, as usual, was the kyree pack: three young males and a neuter, Howellerr, Rruuss, Lerrirr, and Wirrell. As with the tervardi, part of the reason the kyree were coming was to look for good places to start one or more new packs. That was why Wirrell was along; as a kyree tale-teller and historian, he had a prodigious memory, and it was unlikely he would forget *anything.* Kel already liked all of them. They were eager, friendly, looked on this as a chance to make their mark on kyree history, and were prepared for just about anything, including great hardship.

"Rreetings, Elvren," said Wirrell, leading the four into the clearing. Kyree were notoriously bad at pronouncing hard consonants, but that was to be expected, given what they were working with. Mindspeech was much easier to understand, but out of courtesy, they had all agreed to speak aloud when they met, to get used to how the different species and individuals spoke.

"Greetings to the Pathfinder Pack, and good hunting," Kel replied with the traditional salutation. "You're early."

"Snacks," said Rruuss, with a snap of his jaws and a grin. "Rou rave rest snacks."

"Rruuss is rutting on rat for rourney," said Lerrirr with a flick of his tail. Rruuss play-snapped at him as they settled down nearest to Kel on his right. *Rutting on rat? Oh! Putting on fat.* While they were milling around, figuring out how they were going to arrange themselves, the two tervardi appeared. Kel couldn't sing their proper flock-names. Gryphon voices didn't work that way. And there were not very many humans who could either. So they went by Rililia and Lyreren. Kel thought they were a very handsome pair. The feathers that covered their bodies were tiny, with an iridescent quality to them, more pronounced on Lyreren than his mate. As usual, they raised their crests and sang their greeting. As usual, it was long. As usual, it was a lovely song, and well worth listening to. After that, they took places directly across the clearing from Kel, perching on a pair of stumps in a way that looked acutely painful, but which they had assured him was quite comfortable. Today, they had limited their body coverings to simple, light tunics that matched the subtle blues and greens of their feathers.

Then came the dyheli bachelor-herd, a couple of them pronking and prancing like kids. Ransem led them in and gave two of them a flick of his hind hooves to get them to settle down. They did obey their leader immediately, though, so Kel wasn't particularly concerned about herd discipline. Ayshen had a lot of good things to say about Ransem, and one of them was that while he was bidding to have as much mental power as Tyrsell, he was less ready to use it, either on his fellows or on other species. *Which is good. I don't want anyone else rummaging around in my head ever again!*

Last to come, and bearing the "snacks," were the hertasi, led by a hertasi Kelvren had not expected to see again, who was chattering away to one of the five others who were going to accompany the expedition. ". . . so once Treyvan found out Kelvren had reached here safely, he asked me if I wanted to leave him and join Kel," Pena said. "Of course I did! It's a chance for adventure I'd never get, keeping out of sight at the Valdemaran Palace! So Treyvan contacted Firesong by teleson and they opened a Gate between them, and I popped through while Kel was still being healed." Pena glanced over at Kel and saw he was watching and listening, and quickly changed the subject to the fact that Hallock Stavern had finally come, and brought with him more Valdemaran humans.

So that's how Pena got here. And he wanted *to be here with me.* Kel felt very touched, and a little abashed. Pena had been Treyvan and Hydona's right talon ever since they arrived at k'Sheyna Vale. That he had volunteered for this, to take care of Kel—that was something Kel had not known or expected. He felt his throat close for a moment. He coughed to clear it. *And Treyvan also subtly embeds a loyal agent on the expedition.* "Well, friends, knowing how gossip runs in the Vale, you probably already know that the Valdemarans are here, and at least two of them are coming with us. That would be the brave Hallock Stavern and his wife Genni, who is a Healer's Hand."

Rililia, the female tervardi, came alert at that. "A Healer's Hand!" she exclaimed. "Oh, this is very good. I have wanted to learn more of that craft."

"I don't see why you shouldn't be able to," Kel said, and made sure his sigh was entirely internal. "We'll likely be going slowly enough you should be able to gather herbs you know, and test those you don't."

:When are we to meet these humans?: asked Ransem.

"What about now?" said Hallock, in good Tayledras, as Firesong led him, Genni, Jefti, and Ammari into the clearing. He paused for a moment to take in the varied group, then gave an abbreviated salute to Kel.

"Now is good!" replied Kel, nodding. "In fact, now is excellent!"

Hallock smiled slightly and allowed Pena to usher them to seats at Kel's right.

"So!" Kel said. "What is the word from Valdemar?"

"In which language?" Hallock laughed, and mimed his head exploding. Everyone present had all likely gone through the linguistic ordeal at some point, and so the chuckles from so many species had a genuine note of sympathy. Everybody braving Lake Evendim—which by now felt like it would be hundreds of creatures, before the first barge embarked—would have the memory of entire ways of thinking and naming punched into their skulls.

May that be the last thing to give us all headaches!

The next morning, Deban turned up to wake Hallock just after dawn. Of course, Hallock was already awake; rising while the sky was still dark was so ingrained in him now that he doubted he could have broken the habit if he'd tried.

So he was not only awake, but washed, brushed, and in his dress uniform when Deban cautiously put his snout around the doorframe.

Genni was still asleep, and Hallock mimed "quiet." The hertasi nodded and pulled his nose back, with a faint rattling of beads.

Are the Hawkbrothers allergic to doors? But he had to shrug. They were living in a clearly magically manipulated giant tree, surrounded by creatures the average Valdemaran would gawk at open-mouthed, and he was focused on doors?

There were no signs of life from the other two rooms; Hallock saw no reason to disturb Jefti or his mother. This early-morning meeting with the k'Valdemar Vale Council was only for him. And not, he suspected, because the Council didn't see the other three as important, but because of that not-so-innocent rank he'd been given when he agreed to come here.

Military attaché.

If the Valdemarans were alarmed at the Tayledras and all their spooky magic settling down in the western wilds of their country, the Tayledras surely had reservations that had not been quelled in the years since k'Valdemar Vale had been founded. The Hawkbrothers, he had learned, took a very long view of things. A dozen years would not have been enough time to dampen initial doubts, and that was *without* Valdemar foisting a Guard officer on their exploratory jaunt even further west. And out to Lake Evendim, too—Valdemar didn't hold claim to anything much north of the fishing town of Zoe on the shores of the lake. So far as Valdemar was concerned, north of Zoe was one giant, sleeping bear, and everyone knew you didn't poke the bear.

Especially not now, not when those terrifying Mage Storms had passed over the country. There were probably more concerns about the scary, very foreign Darkwind, who with his even scarier *magic* had married into the royal family. And their own princess Elspeth a mage too! Things that had been safely left as hearth-tales and campfire yarns suddenly were *true,* and then a big, impersonal sort of magic had swept over what had been familiar, sometimes literally changing it into something strange. Small wonder people were rattled.

So now, the Hawkbrothers were going to wake the bear. That was what Valdemarans—at least, the ones who knew about this—were probably thinking.

And this's how I talk my way into the Council's good will, he reminded himself.

So while he sat and ate the excellent breakfast of fruit and bread that Deban had brought him, he tried to think just what else he needed to emphasize. *Make no mistake, Hallock Stavern, this is a fight. As real and as symbolic as the "fight" Kel engaged in when he flew over Deedun all ablaze. But I can't act on instinct like he did. I have to plan this.*

So he thought while he ate, and then, while he followed Deban down paths lit by mage-lights that were so inviting, greeted now and again by scents both sweet and savory, and listening to the murmur of the Vale awakening, he had to stop himself from going off wandering on his own. *Later. With Genni.*

At length, Deban brought him to an enclosure—you couldn't call it a building or a room, because it was open to the sky, although he could see clever arrangements of wires and canvas that he suspected would allow the entire space to be covered if it rained. The Veil wasn't there to keep weather *out*, it was there to keep weather pleasant.

It was a place never meant for deliberations in secret. The walls were of the same woven reeds as the walls of Firesong's ekele, and the doorframe didn't even hold a suggestion of a barrier, like a bead curtain. Once inside, he found himself at the bottom of a sort of "bowl" of tiers of bench seats rising around the room. Only a few of those were occupied right now, all on the bottom row. A dozen Hawkbrothers with snow-white hair, male and female, were conversing quietly while their bondbirds dozed on the benches at the highest level. The floor was a pleasing mosaic of thick carpet squares of woven grass.

There wasn't a seat in the middle of this tiny "arena," so Hallock took a standing position in the dead center and waited for the Hawkbrothers to say something.

They all looked up as he took his place, and the oldest-looking one gave him an inscrutable look and said, "You are Hallock Stavern of Valdemar."

He nodded.

The speaker didn't trouble to introduce himself or his fellow Tayledras. "You were the one whose injuries were so severe that Silver Gryphon Kelvren risked his own death Healing them . . . which brings us to the uncomfortable position where we are now."

There didn't seem to be any question there, nor anything he could respond to, so he just stood there quietly.

"Why do you think he did that?" asked an old woman with her white hair in hundreds of braids strung with crystal glass beads. Old, maybe, but undoubtedly strong, to hold all that weight up gracefully.

"He *says* it was because of my wife, Genni. He *says* it was because I somehow deserved not to die. I was just telling him about the most perfect day I ever had with her, and he *said* it was because 'no one should have only one perfect day.' As to what he was thinking, I can't answer that. I don't have Mindmagic. And even if I did, I'm given to understand it's bad manners to snoop on someone else's thoughts."

Stony faces, and more silence. *And I literally hear crickets.*

"Do you think you deserved that sort of sacrifice?" asked another, who was, uncharacteristically, garbed all in black. It made a fine contrast with his floor-length white hair.

"Do any of us deserve the good that comes to us? You'd have to ask the gods about that. I'm not one of those, either." He reminded himself that this was a test, and it was no time to get irritated with these questions. "I try to be a good man as well as a good soldier. I try to be a good husband and partner. I try to do good things in the world, but I am a soldier and my duties sometimes require me to kill people. I don't like doing it, but when someone is trying to kill *me,* I don't stop to ask them about their motives. Like I said, you'll have to ask the gods about whether or not I deserve saving."

He had the distinct impression that they were speaking wordlessly to each other. *I guess I prefer that to muttering to one another.*

"And why did you come here?" Back to the first speaker. How *did* they manage to maintain that expressionless look about them?

"Because Kelvren asked for me. I owe him a debt of gratitude, and my superiors in Valdemar approved of my coming." He tried to match their stone-faced expressions.

"Ah, yes. Your superiors in Valdemar. Who appointed you as a military attaché. An interesting title." Well, a blind man could have seen the challenge in that. *Are you here to spy on us? Are you here to recruit for Valdemar? Why* are *you here, Hallock?*

"They weren't going to demote me. They weren't going to release me. I was told this rank is equal to First of the Sixteenth, and I see no reason to think anyone was lying. I know why *I* am here: to help Kelvren. No one gave me any other orders, and I have no secret ways of sending back messages or information. The only other Valdemarans you'll have along are my wife Genni, and maybe young Jefti and his ma, Ammari. None of them are able to send back secret messages either." He shrugged. "Like I said. No Mind-magic. So if my superiors had an ulterior motive, they didn't give me orders about it, they didn't hint about it, they didn't imply anything, and only they and the gods know what they were thinking."

Silence, punctuated by distant sounds from the Vale. And the crickets again. *I hope this doesn't make me averse to crickets in the future.*

"What do you think you can do?" The question came from the first speaker.

"Fight. Work to instill some strategy into those Ghost Clan lads. If they are anything at all like what I've been told, their idea of 'strategy' is to run straight at danger, yelling at it and waving whatever weapons they have."

That got a hint of a smile.

"I know when to fight. More importantly, I am fairly good at telling when fighting is not the right solution. The situation at Deedun—fighting was not the right solution, but we were forced into it by the other side. Thankfully, Kel figured out a way to bring that nonsense to a screeching halt." He took a deep breath and let it out slowly. "Kel's good at strategy too. I figure between us, we can avoid as much fighting as is possible without getting ourselves into trouble."

"I would never have put *strategy* and *Kelvren* into the same sentence," the Hawkbrother said dryly.

"Then, you'll have to forgive me, but you don't know him *at all*." That last was said with perhaps too much force, but he was getting angry on Kelvren's behalf. "I'm sorry, that was harsh. Listen—"

He told them about what had happened in the tent for the seriously injured and recovering. He told them about what Kel had said about the fighting itself—how wrong it was, and how it was forcing everyone on both sides except the mercs into an intolerable position. How that was why Kel had done what he had done, and stopped the fighting cold, saved the day, and prevented any more useless death and pain. Kel's clever morale-booster of using his clipped feathers and Ammari's glowing paint. "And he did all that because he considered himself honor bound, as an *ally*, to come up with a solution to what looked like an insoluble problem. If that's not strategy, I don't know what is."

More silence. *I just bet they have some form of Truth Spell going. Not the sort I'd recognize, and not coercive, I don't think, but at least they know I'm telling the truth as I know it.*

"You speak strongly in his defense," said the one in black.

"He's one of the finest creatures I have ever met, and I'd say that even if he hadn't risked his life to save mine." Hallock forced himself to cool down. "I mean . . . he does have a different outlook than me. He's a gryphon. I've noticed that they tend to think of things in more black-and-white terms than we do. Maybe I can help him learn a little—nuance."

That actually surprised a real laugh out of some of them.

"A nuanced gryphon. That would be a prodigy I would like to see," said the one in black. So far he, the woman in braids, and the first man were the only ones speaking aloud, but at this point Hallock was absolutely certain they were Mindspeaking volumes to each other. Well, that was probably why they were silent; it was probably hard to Mindspeak and talk out loud at the same time.

"Is Valdemar intending to use this expedition as an excuse to push westward?" That blunt and unexpected question came from one of the silent ones, a woman whose hair was uncharacteristically covered by a wrapped cloth, and whose clothing was uncharacteristically austere. And she surprised a startled laugh out of *him.*

"Lady, I respect you all, but you've all grown up with centuries of magic as an everyday part of your lives. We're not primitives, we're just different. Valdemar is coping with the discovery that the magic we thought was nothing but legend and wonder-tales is a very real and present force in *our* world. We've got Change-Circles all over the bloody kingdom that are frightening not just the children and horses, but people who *never* saw the like before. We're *afraid* of what may be out there, but there's more to life than fear, and we've been blindsided before. We've got to have a look, all of you willing, beside friends.

We've only just ended a war with Hardorn, only just made allies out of Karse and Duke Tremayne, and we've got ambitious bastards inside Valdemar trying to stir up trouble and elevate themselves. Every Herald in the Kingdom is scattered around the land trying to quell fear and greed and insurrection. Which is why you didn't get a Herald for this, who might have been a more reasonable choice than me. We're juggling screaming cats already, and we're not going to add a couple of flaming axes to what we've already got in the air."

Evidently they had enough acrobats and the like in their own ranks to understand his analogy, which got a genuine laugh out of all of them.

"*We* don't, and never have, tried to expand by force," he continued. "When people join Valdemar, it's because they want to—they see what we are and want to share it, and that's how we like it. Some join us for protection, some because they are like-minded, some for opportunity. But they all join us because they *want* to, and it's vital to us that we explore, because the future is coming regardless. We need to learn. *There is no one true way,* after all."

"Well," the last woman said, allowing her face to relax into an expression of satisfaction. "The Valdemarans haven't changed since the Baron's day, it seems. And let me remind all of you that this attitude is why we helped them in the first place. I think we have nothing to fear and much to gain by adding at least this man and his mate to Kelvren's party."

The first man turned slightly, and bowed a little. "Even so, Willowheart. I believe we are all in agreement."

Expressions relaxed, nods all around. Hallock sighed, the tension draining out of him.

"We are pleased Valdemar has been willing to part with you, and are certain that you will be a valuable addition to this group," the man continued. "And if you can actually teach *nuance* to a gryphon, well, you will be nothing short of a miracle worker!" He patted the bench beside him. "Come, let us tell you our names, and discuss everything that *we* already know—which is precious little—and you can add your wisdom to ours."

Hallock accepted the invitation and joined them. *That went better than it had any right to,* he thought as they introduced themselves. *I wonder how Kel is getting on today? If I know him, he's eaten up with impatience to get on the move.*

"You look pleased with yourself," Kel observed, as Firesong arrived for his daily meeting—well, you couldn't call it a "lesson," when neither of them really knew what they were doing. At least, that was Kel's impression, although Firesong was so very good at presenting façade upon façade upon façade, like the layers in an onion, that he suspected even Silverfox had trouble seeing through to the real man.

"I've found your Heartstone," Firesong gloated. Yes! Gloated! There was nothing hidden behind a façade at this moment, mask or not. "Fool's gold was a very good choice, after all. Not suited to a *full-sized* Vale Heartstone, because the crystals won't grow bigger than the length of a hand, but perfect for what we want."

"Hurr, I hope that name is not somehow an omen," Kel told him, flopping down in his favorite spot in the tent, opening the book on gryphonic anatomy and its relationship to magic, and gesturing with his beak that Firesong should join him. "You place your faith in something you think is gold, which turns out to be worthless."

Firesong sniffed, and folded his legs up to sit beside Kel. "Hardly worthless. As it happens, the crystalline structure of fool's gold makes it much more suitable for harmonizing magic work than my first thought, sculpted ductile gold. Captured in hard glass to keep it from eroding, it can be added to or altered as we go, and it can be chained to substones for outside use, like 'flaring off' excess fuel," he continued, with hand gestures describing its internal structure akin to a flier describing their maneuvers. "High enough melting point to suit, which can only help."

Firesong's idea of reassurance is to tell me, "By the time it melts, you'll already be incinerated, so it's safe."

"Even in high flux, force should order itself in line with its crystal structures. Crystalline iron! Think of it, Kel! The strength of iron for stability, the structure of a crystal! It couldn't be more perfect for our purposes!"

Kel opened the book with a delicate talon hooked under the leather page-protector they were using as a bookmark. "I will feel happier when I can use the thing," he replied grumpily. *I am a creature of movement, yet I have scarcely moved for weeks. I am a creature of the sky, and it is still too dangerous for me to fly. So what am I now?* If not for the roughly two dozen beings fully invested in this expedition—and he was fairly certain not all of them would have been able to conceal if it was actually all a ruse on Firesong's part to keep his mind occupied and not brooding on how he should be regarded as a hero, and was instead regarded as a nuisance at best and a hazard at worst— he would have had *words* with Firesong shortly after they'd cracked this book.

Firesong straightened up. "Hertasi are setting it in a reference cage right now. It's used to make acid, it turns out, so they had plenty on hand in a refining outpost. Let's try something a little different," he said. "It occurred to me last night when I was trying to get to sleep. Have you ever tried the body-control technique of concentrating on one group of muscles until you get it to relax, then moving on to the next?"

"Well," Kel admitted, "no. A full belly usually is enough to get me to sleep."

That answer didn't discourage Firesong, it appeared. "Well, we have been trying to establish your own personal internal ley-lines as a single network, all at once. I think a more fruitful approach would be to start small. Very small. That's why I asked Nightwind and Jefti to join us here today."

That certainly got Kel's attention! "Why—" he began, when the trondi'irn and his little friend appeared in the doorway, and something arrested his attention so much that it drove everything else momentarily out of his mind.

All the patches on Jefti's face had been turned into painted artwork. Black curves and swirls enhanced the boundaries, and rather than separating the areas of dark and light skin, seemed to somehow unite and define them into a single coherent image. Jefti clearly read Kel's surprise and approval, and grinned.

"Do you like it, Kel?" he asked . . . in good, unaccented Kaled'a'in.

"Verrrrrrry much," Kel praised, drawing out the word "very" in order to emphasize how much he liked it. He nodded at Nightwind, who blushed. "Your art is, as always, amazing."

"Well," she temporized. "This is just temporary, and we are going to try more designs until Jefti fastens on one he really, really likes. I was thinking . . . if he *does* show ability at becoming a trondi'irn, we could try stylized feathers next. That would be very appropriate. And we can have Sharpthorn do the tattooing to make it permanent."

Jefti nodded with enthusiasm. "I like this, though. Makes me look tough!" For the first time in Kel's acquaintance with him, he was standing with a straight spine and a raised head. "Dunno what Ma'll think, but . . . it's *my* face, an' I'm old enough to figure what I want to do with it."

"You are fierce, Jefti. But what does this have to do with what you and I are doing?" Kel asked, turning his head to stare at Firesong.

"Well, the base mechanism for collecting free magical energy is in your feathers," Firesong explained to Jefti by talking to Kelvren, which was confusing. "When your feathers move, especially the wing-feathers, you collect magic as they sift it out of the air, which is why I've told you not to fly, because unless you can adequately convert what you can't personally hold into light, I'm afraid it will manifest as heat. So Nightwind is going to show Jefti how to care for your feathers, *which will move them,* but in a controlled manner. I want *you* to concentrate on the flow of that magic, one feather at a time. Isolate and observe. Continue doing that. Once you can See what is happening . . ." He paused. "I am very reluctant to ask you to try to cut that flow off. You're broken enough as it is."

Kel growled a little, involuntarily. *I do not like being referred to as "broken" all the time.*

Evidently he managed to keep the growl far enough down in his chest that no one heard it. Or at least, Firesong, who was nearest, politely pretended he hadn't.

Instead, Firesong gestured to Nightwind and Jefti, who took cushions for seats. Nightwind had her kit of trondi'irn supplies with her, and she gestured to Kel to spread out a wing. He obliged, and she started with the innermost primary, nearest his body. He put his head down, closed his eyes to concentrate better, and prepared to enjoy himself.

"First, we make sure all the vanes are aligned and locked together," she told Jefti, as she deftly smoothed the feather. "Feathers need to be a *whole*, both in order to fly, and in order to collect power without having it eddy around in the feather uselessly. Once all the vanes are smooth and locked, we take this particular oil—it's very light, and it's made from the seeds of a certain plant, and it is the closest thing to a gryphon's natural oil in his preen gland. We take a brush made from badger hair, and we brush it along the feather shaft, like this—"

As she moved the feathers, he concentrated his mage-sight on his own body, and carefully traced how the particles of magic were flowing, from the vanes of the feather, into the shaft, then into the—

—wait—

I thought it was going to flow into my veins. But it isn't. What is it flowing into?

At first, he couldn't figure it out. It was going *somewhere*, moving along a path that did not correspond *at all* to the veins and arteries in which his blood flowed.

But then, young Jefti, being new to this and clumsy, jarred one of the newly growing feathers, and while the physical sensation was merely uncomfortable for a moment, a bit like an insect-bite, what the *magic* did was make a brief and extremely tiny explosion, then rush to where the momentary pain was, and speed away along—

Nerves? It doesn't follow my nerves, but this channel parallels them. Personal ley-lines, was it? Fascinating!

Now that he knew what he was looking for, he could see it everywhere in his body when a feather moved. Merest motes of energy, like dust motes in sunlight, sped from vane to shaft, from shaft to nerve cluster at the base of the shaft, and from there to the physical organ that gathered his magic and stored it. And that organ was . . . well, it was rather full. Over-full, in fact, like his crop was now with breakfast.

He *knew* and understood what was happening within him

now. When Treyvan had flooded him with all of what he *now* knew was an essential Heartstone energy, restarting that entire system the way a skilled Healer could restart a heart with a burst of Healing energy, Kelvren had, as he had told Firesong, instinctively taken the power that threatened to incinerate him and turned it to harmless light, the simplest—and thus cleanest—spell he knew. As he was *still* doing now, and at this point, he could See that the process had become ingrained, a kind of muscle memory that worked without him thinking about it.

Or maybe it is just because I was desperate but it worked, so now my hindbrain needs to feel anxiety so I can live? Oh, that would be a cruel joke for someone who wants peace!

And he understood, both empirically and intuitively, that Firesong was going about this wrong. Firesong thought the proper way to go about this was to establish the channels for powering a miniature Heartstone first, then lock the Heartstone into those channels.

But that was not what needed to be done.

Kel needed the primed Heartstone, mounted in whatever fashion Firesong had intended, close to his skin. *Then* he could establish the channels to run through it to be tuned, and turn the light spell into a charging spell. In other words, he needed to have the cistern in place before he could install the pipes to carry the water, and only then could he—

Well, the analogy failed at that point.

But without the Heartstone, the channels simply wouldn't materialize.

He'd need Firesong's help for that, though. Most of his own manipulation of magic was strictly on the level of instinct. The light spell was one of the few he actually knew *as* a spell. That, and healing.

"Well?" Firesong asked, as Jefti's handling of his feather grew more confident, and his touch deft and delicate. "Did you learn anything?"

"I believe I need that trinket of yours in place first, and to 'grow' the channels from it, rather than establishing the channels first," he murmured, feeling free to now simply enjoy the ministrations of his trondi'irn and who was clearly going to be her apprentice. "Because if I try it your way, the channels are going to fill up, hit the end where I haven't done anything yet, and possibly bad things will happen." He clicked his beak a little. "Or not. I'm not sure. I'm not the mage that you and Treyvan are. But your way won't work. I need the Heartstone. I need to make the tracks for the power coming into it, then when everything is in place, I can open the connection between the Heartstone and the *virtutem*. Once I do that, you might have to teach me to turn the light spell into something else. Or maybe once the power has somewhere to go, I won't need to do anything. The reason neither of us have been able to figure out a way to connect the Heartstone and the *virtutem* is because we've been expecting the *indusvenarum* to do the work, and that's not what it was designed for. We need to build something entirely new that the system won't reject defensively from overpressure."

"Huh!" Firesong exclaimed. Then came the silence, broken only by the occasional murmured instruction from Nightwind, that told him Firesong was using his own mage-sight to examine what was going on in Kel's body.

"I think you're right," Firesong said finally. "I think this explains a lot!" he added with more confidence. "Well, my work for the day will be to go see Silversnow and get my little Heartstone mounted in something. Would you prefer a headpiece, breastplate, or a backplate between your wings?"

"Breastplate," Kel replied instantly. "A backplate would be irritating. A headpiece would be ridiculous *and* heavy. And how could I wear a teleson *and* a headpiece? I'd look absurd"

"Well, if I had been uncertain before that you are on the mend, the re-emergence of your vanity would tell me that my uncertainty was unfounded." Firesong laughed, and got up from his seat. "I'll just leave you to Nightwind's tender mercies."

"Yes, please, go away," said Kel, closing his eyes again. "This is the first time since Deedun I have actually enjoyed myself."

Firesong chortled, and Kel heard his footsteps leaving.

"Please continue, Nightwind," he murmured, relaxing into the now quite tender ministrations. "I'll give you and Jefti a hundred years to stop doing that. Take more time if you need it."

Silverfox was surprised to see Nightwind, Jefti in tow, turn up at his office doorway just before the noon meal. The boy had had someone paint his face in engaging imitations of facial tattoos, and the result was that the light and dark patches of his skin were no longer startling. The difference between the tones had been harnessed by the stark black outlines, and what had been disfigurement (at least in some people's eyes) had become the basis for personal art.

"Good afternoon, Silverfox," said Nightwind, one hand placed on Jefti's shoulder in a most proprietary manner.

Well, I know how the wind blows there. Treyvan was right. The lad has the talent, or Nightwind would not be here to tell me that she was claiming him as her apprentice, and on the brink of our expedition, no less.

He gestured to the padded bench, and they both took seats.

He waited while they settled, enjoying the soft chattering of the messenger birds—because they weren't *always* chattering peacefully, and he much preferred the chattering to the high-pitched shrieking and aggressive chirps that felt as if someone had driven a knitting needle into each ear.

"I see you have an apprentice," Silverfox responded with a gentle smile, once they looked comfortable. "Welcome to k'Valdemar as an inhabitant, Jefti. As a trondi'irn apprentice, you are now one of us, and by virtue of that, so is your mother, even if she had *not* proven that she has skills to contribute. If she wishes to stay, she is welcome on your behalf alone. If she wishes to make herself useful among us, as I am assured she certainly will, she will be even more welcome."

Nightwind smiled as Jefti's eyes lit up. "You always know the right things to say, Silverfox," she replied. "You know, of course, that he wants to come with me."

"I would have been surprised if he had not." Silverfox was not lying. Firstly, the bond between the boy and Kel was evident to anyone with eyes. Secondly, the boy was just about at that age when a boy craves change and adventure, and what could be more adventurous than this? "And how does Ammari feel about this?"

Nightwind smiled more deeply. "Before this morning, I think that she would have been more pained about the idea than she is now. As soon as the hertasi Jylan recognized that Jefti had the aptitude to become my apprentice, she must have told the entire hertasi clan. As Ammari finished breakfast, Yallist descended upon her and whisked her off to the sewing and design workshop—wherever that is. From there she was taken to Autumnleaf, the dyer. And by the time we finished with Kel, she was returned to us full of all the wonderful things she was going to do, starting this afternoon."

Bless them. What would we do without the hertasi?

"Ma's happy to stay," Jefti said, and there was absolutely a touch of relief in those words. "Real happy. I ain't seen her this happy in don't know when."

Well, and Autumnleaf is a handsome fellow. He is about her age, and without a permanent partner. That also might have played a part. The hertasi are such matchmakers . . .

At least this time the matchmaking would work in everyone's favor. Jefti knew he no longer had to look after his mother. Ammari knew that Jefti was an apprentice now, and apprentices had duties to perform and jobs to do, which she could not be involved in. That would have been true at Deedun, *if* she could have found someone to take Jefti without a fee. But here was someone offering to take Jefti not only without a fee, but in a highly valued profession. So Jefti could turn his eyes away toward the horizon without guilt. And Ammari . . . could, perhaps, make some tentative steps toward finding another partner without worrying about what Jefti thought.

"Well, then," Firesong said. "The hertasi have probably already picked out a spot for a home for her and have begun building it. By this time they know all her preferences. I would not be in the least surprised to see her moved from my guest rooms to her very own place before we leave, if her needs are simple." He said all this for Jefti's ears; Nightwind already knew how hertasi operated.

Jefti's expression changed after a moment. His jaw dropped. "Wait—" he said. "Y'mean she's gonna get her own *house*?"

"Of course. She won't want to stay here; my guest rooms are good for *guesting*, but not for actually living in. At least, not for very long. Of course, she is welcome to continue to stay here until her own home is ready." He contemplated that for a moment. "I'd like that, actually. It would be good to have someone staying here when we are gone."

Perhaps the hertasi could add a wing onto our home for her.

"But Jefti," he continued, "I want you to understand, this expedition is going to be dangerous. Nightwind has to come with us—she's Kel's trondi'irn. You don't have to. Nightwind will surely refer you to other trondi'irn if you want to stay." He put as much gravity into his tone as he could, so the boy understood this was a serious matter.

To be sure, I don't know how dangerous this is going to be—but danger has a habit of finding Kel. This would be *Silverfox's* first extended journey outside a Vale, and the first time he had gone where normally only scouts went. Firesong was a seasoned traveler, and more than that, had risked his life on several occasions. Silverfox hadn't. *And I've had second and third thoughts. But I still need to go, and for Firesong's sake as well as Kel's.*

The boy's heavy brows drew together. "I was working in a Guard camp, next to a battlefield. Dunno as there's anything much more dangerous than that."

"Well," Silverfox said after a pause. "There most definitely is. We have no idea what's out there, and the Pelagirs have a habit of creating nasty surprises."

"Still going," Jefti replied fiercely. "Kel needs me. And you promise to take care of Ma, right? No matter what happens? *Promise?*"

"Absolutely. She's one of us now, and we take care of our own." Silverfox looked up to gauge Nightwind's reaction to these statements and found her smiling, as if to say, *See? He's a born trondi'irn, blood and bone.*

"Then Ma'll be all right without me," Jefti added, although the slight lift at the end of the sentence suggested he was looking for reassurance.

"She will," Silverfox said. "She'll absolutely miss you, and she'll worry about you, but she'll have plenty to keep her busy and contributing here, and she won't have to worry about where the next meal is coming from. And she'll find friends, both here and in Errold's Grove. In fact, I will have a word with the hertasi to make sure they look after her."

Jefti beamed at him, and Nightwind put her hand on the boy's shoulder again. "I'm taking him off to meet the other trondi'irn," she said, cementing their bond as master and apprentice. "I'll send him back before supper."

With that, she took the lad out with her, leaving Silverfox to contemplate the rapidly diminishing list of things to do in front of him. There was really only one major thing left holding them all here.

Firesong had created his "portable Heartstone," but it and Kel had not been linked. And that was—

His thoughts were broken into by the exceedingly rare sound of hertasi claws scrambling up the steps at top speed. Ayshen burst into the room—breathless.

"News! I ran to tell you first!" the little lizard gasped. "Gryphons! Gryphons from *Iftel*! They're on the way here to join the expedition!"

"*What?* Oh, come on, are you serious?" he asked, his mind reeling as he stood.

"The message only just came by teleson. Poli ran to warn our wing of gryphons, and I ran to tell you!"

He was about to ask if Ayshen knew when they were expected to arrive, when the full-throated challenge of not one but several gryphons rang through the Vale, and was answered by another shriek from above.

———

Firesong had been measuring Kel's neck and chest more thoroughly than anyone ever had except when he'd been measured for armor back in Silver Gryphon. Normally this would have irritated him worse than mud on his feathers, but Jefti and Nightwind had done an excellent job of grooming him, and he hadn't felt this good since—

Well, since he'd been measured for that armor.

On Firesong's advice, he'd been invoking the healing spell whenever he got the chance, and it had an effect. Getting a *proper*, full grooming from a real trondi'irn had helped more.

If only there was something I was getting groomed for. He sighed. *I haven't exactly met anyone lately that I could—*

At just that moment, gryphon screams at full shrill filled the air from several directions, and shadows outside his shelter made Kel lurch to his feet and bolt to the entrance, Firesong beside him, to see what had caused them. Just as he reached the door and looked up, the full wing of k'Valdemar Vale screamed a challenge at the interlopers above.

And a shriek from the air, a shriek that would have translated in human speech as, *We declare ourselves, now we are here!* answered them.

Kel's mouth dropped open as he counted one . . . five . . . oh, more than five, many more than five! sizable gryphon shadows slowing overhead.

But what . . . but where . . . but how?

They banked out of sight, then before he could react to that, just above the track to his left, a gryphon broke through the canopy with a clattering of branches and a shower of twigs and leaves and landed on the track, backwinging frantically to stop and slow himself, and scattering hertasi in the process. When all four feet were on the ground, he charged up the track to Kel's aerie to get out of the way of the next . . . and the next . . . and the next. Leaves and the odd feather flew everywhere, and thundering wings made hearing Firesong yelling in his ear a bit hard to hear.

"What the Hell, Kel? Why are there gryphons from Iftel here?"

Gryphons from *Iftel*? *"I don't know!"* he bellowed back. But he was given no time to think. Within moments he was *surrounded* by gryphons, male and female by the sizes and markings. All of them were *huge*, and made Kel look like a dainty gyrfalcon. All of them were dark, with darker, black markings. They didn't mill about; they waited, eyes fixed on him, until he felt uncomfortably like a nice haunch of venison. But within a breath, one of them shouldered her way through the flock and stood before Kelvren, as a befuddled Firesong looked on.

And she was . . . beautiful.

Kelvren, wings up and blazing, lit the whole array of them.

She bowed her head briefly to him. "Do I speak to Kelvren Skothkar, Wingleader of k'Valdemar Vale?" she asked.

Her accent was strange. Perfectly understandable, but strange. It suggested that someone had given her Kaled'a'in magically, but the language had been filtered by something she already knew, like Kaled'a'in, but different.

He had never seen a gryphon so beautiful, so regal. The light coming from him surged, and for a moment he saw himself reflected sharply in her pinning eyes, like a gryphon made of sunlight, the light shining off the edges of her feathers, giving each of them a thin rim of gold. Leaves, pollen, and other light debris still drifted downward all around them.

"You speak to Kelvren Skothkar," he said. "But—" his light dimmed as, crestfallen, he admitted his demotion, "—Wingleader no longer. In my current condition, it is not safe for me to have that position." From bewilderment to euphoria to this . . . he felt as if he'd been caught in a downdraft and was tumbling through the air. But those words, and his obligation to say them, brought him to the ground. Not crashing, but in a bruising tumble, because it still hurt to say it, even though he knew it why it all was necessary. Why he was out here in partial exile.

The other gryphon snorted her scorn. "We were informed of the poor decision," she said. "It does not matter. We know what you did was mighty, gryphon-fierce and gryphon-bold. That it was *right*. That is what makes a Wingleader, not a badge or a title, much less an *appointment*. You are who we will follow."

For a moment, the praise distracted him. But heady as that praise was . . . "What?" he asked. "What do you mean by 'follow me'? Follow me how, exactly?"

They all straightened, raised their heads, and dropped their beaks, but the female, who surely must be *their* Wingleader, continued. "We are gryphons and gryphon-mages of Iftel. We have now joined with your exploration party."

She said it as an established fact, as if Kelvren had already accepted this. He blinked, feeling suddenly as if he could not get enough air. "That is unexpected to me. Why?" he asked. He didn't know a great deal about the gryphons of Iftel; he had never met Takisheth, the leader of the gryphon delegation that had come to Haven when Vykaendys, their name for the Sun God known by the Karsites as Vkandis, deemed it time for the magic barrier between Iftel and Valdemar to come down, and Iftel to join in alliance with Valdemar and Duke Tremayne of Hardorn.

"Because Vykaendys deems it needful," she replied, further shocking him. "He has told us that you dare the heart of our ancient enemy's former stronghold. There is great peril there, and the peril is growing. Had you not already determined to go there yourselves, the gods themselves would have sent us to tell you to do so—or so I have been told."

He actually reeled back a pace and sat down on his haunches sideways, heavily.

WHAT?

"So," Firesong said into the silence, sounding more than a little breathless himself. "We add Iftel gryphons and a Gods-Quest. Silverfox is going to love this."

The silence that followed that dramatic pronouncement was thick enough to choke on. Not even birds or insects broke it, which could have seemed dreadfully portentous—except, of course, half a dozen gryphons coming in at top speed and landing noisily had probably frightened everything witless.

"Hurrr," Kel said, feeling just about as witless as the wildlife.

"Indeed, and may our flights be true in your service," the female said, taking his stunned silence as a sign that he had taken her *seriously*. Which, of course he had, but words had fled him. *Gods? GODS? This was just an exploratory venture! Why would the gods mix themselves into it?* He didn't like this, no, not at all! Gods never spoke unless things were serious, and they never meddled unless things were critical. Weren't things complicated enough already? Inside, he felt his guts knot up. Outside, his feathers flattened against his body and he had to repress the urge to crouch down in a defensive posture.

"I think," Firesong said carefully, with a faint tremor to his voice that only someone who knew him would have noticed, "that we need to present all this to the k'Valdemar Council of Elders, right now. This way, you can explain everything just once, lady," he added, with a slight bow of his head, "rather than go over it a dozen times. I'll have a hertasi taking notes so we have a record of everything."

The female turned her piercing gaze on the Adept and contemplated him. Kel couldn't tell if she was contemplating him with an eye to snacking on him, or as a favorable reaction to his suggestion. Kel vibrated between alarm and admiration, because he had never seen an Iftel gryphon before. In the old stories, there had been several wings of gryphons based on eagles, like Skandranon, not hawks or falcons, but none of them had flown the skies of White Gryphon for centuries. They had been heavy-combat specialists, including dropping large and unpleasant things on enemy troops, and had been stationed with their support, not with the rest of Urtho's gryphons. And until Iftel opened its borders and Takisheth brought his delegation to Haven, no one had known what had become of them.

But oh, she is beautiful. And with my luck, already exclusively mated to one of those males.

His mind, which was inclined to wander off on its own at times like these, presented him, smugly, with the image of their height difference, and exactly what that would mean if she reciprocated his admiration.

Hurr, I'll stand on a rock.

He gave himself an internal shake. Now was *not* the time.

I should not let my mind wander. It is too small to be out alone.

"If I may escort you and your Wing to k'Valdemar Vale, Wingleader?" he managed to say, and somehow the words all came out clear and coherent. "I am sure Firesong has already summoned the Council of Elders."

"Hurrrrrr, Mindspeakers, then?" the female said with approval. "Good. Before we all leave on our trek to the Lake, you will give us all those . . . telebones? We need to practice with them. The ability to make them in Iftel has been lost to time."

"Telesons," Kel corrected gently. "It will be done." *Promising things you don't know if you can produce, Kelvren Skothkar?* his mind chided him. *Not an auspicious way to start.*

Hush, he told himself. *I'll make it happen, somehow. It's the least this Vale can do to make up for what they did to me when I arrived.*

The female's eyes gleamed with approval. "I am called Vindaria Lisson. Vindaria. Or Daria. I will make the others known to you when we speak with this Council."

"Yes, we shall do that," Kel agreed, hoping that didn't come out as submissive as it seemed to him. He didn't know if they expected the Proclamations of a Gods-Chosen Legendary Commander, but if they did, they weren't getting them from him. "Did you know, my great friend the Owlknight is called Darian?"

"Even so? That is a good omen for our friendship." There was nothing in her tone that suggested that she wanted things to begin and end with merely "friendship." *On the other hand, it is all too easy to read what I want to hear.* "But," she continued, "the situation is more urgent than any of us could have known before the gods spoke. So let us stand before you all, and we will explain."

Without any sign that he could see—which suggested that they were all Mindspeakers—the Iftel gryphons parted and paused, waiting for him to take the lead, escorting them into the Vale. So he did, flanked on either side by Vindaria and Firesong. His mind buzzed, but none of the thoughts were particularly coherent. Vindaria seemed disinclined toward conversation, but her silence didn't seem hostile or even annoyed. Perhaps she simply didn't see the need to speak unless speech was necessary.

Word had spread quickly, as it did in a Vale, and by the time they reached the Veil, the inhabitants were lined up on either side of the path. Weaponless, he was pleased to note.

But then he noticed that Tyrsell was the first in line to greet them.

It would beg the question of "can he control all of them at once," except I know the answer is "yes."

But Tyrsell gave no indication that he was there for any other reason except to greet the delegation from Iftel. Kel did note, however, that Vindaria's eyes pinned with surprise to see him, and she made a quick scan forward to see if there were any other creatures like this one.

:Greetings, Vindaria Lisson and Wingmates of Iftel.: Tyrsell's very powerful Mindvoice rang in all their heads, whether

or not the ones hearing him themselves were Mindspeakers, and made it very clear to all of the newcomers that dyheli were not . . . food . . . without saying it in so many words. It also made his powers very clear as well; you meddled with someone who could Mindspeak even to the headblind at your peril. *:I am Tyrsell, King Stag of the k'Valdemar dyheli.:*

"I thought your kind a myth," said Vindaria. "Or at best, lost in the past. I am pleased to see it is not so. Takisheth did not report about dyheli in the capital and Court."

Tyrsell just gave a nod. He'd made his point, and now it appeared he was going to keep his thoughts to himself. Meanwhile, Vindaria shifted her weight from foot to foot, and it was clear to Kel at least that she wanted to get to the Council Chamber as soon as possible and say her piece. He could also tell, now that the drama of their entrance was over, that she and her Wing were very tired, if not exhausted. He got the procession started again by moving on before Tyrsell's head came up from his nod.

They took the most direct way to the Council Chamber, which was also coincidentally the broadest path. As Kel had expected, all of the Elders, of every species, were gathered in the Chamber. Tyrsell, while king stag, was *not* the Elder of his herd; that honorific went to his mother, Tronia. There were two hertasi Elders, one kyree, and two tervardi. But no other gryphons but him.

Now, that is interesting. Are they tacitly saying that in this case, I am the "Elder," since Vindaria addressed me by name?

Kel stepped aside once they were in the Chamber, as did Firesong. Kelvren was on the edge of hyperventilating, controlling his effects upon local magic. More than a few attendees clearly wondered why Kelvren was even there, but none of them seemed inclined to step up to him to dispute it in such a gryphon-enriched environment. The Wing lined up in front of the half-circle of Elders seated on their benches, positioning themselves behind Vindaria. Once in place, they sat down, as did she—another sign, if he had needed one, that they were profoundly weary. *They must have flown well into the night every night to get here.*

"Elders of k'Valdemar Vale," Vindaria said into the silence. "We come at the behest of Higher Powers."

"Explain, please," said the hertasi Elder, Sayla, his snout quivering with interest.

"I will show you," she said simply, and made a gesture with her right claw that called up a misty sphere two man-heights tall which coalesced between her and the Elders, a sphere that soon cleared and showed the inside of what looked like a temple. At least, Kel presumed it was a temple, because what he could see of the structure was both more austere and more massive than he would have expected in any other sort of building. Not that he was terribly familiar with temples; the Vales didn't have them, and there were far more people in Silver Gryphon who worshiped at home or outdoors than there were those who gathered in Temples.

It looked like a perfectly ordinary day in a temple during a time when there was no worship being conducted. Someone was sweeping; someone else in austere garments was lighting incense sticks and taking away the ones that had burned out. There were mage-lights mounted up on the walls, and an altar. There was nothing to show which gods were being worshiped here, which was in keeping with the Kaled'a'in. While there were priests specific to the gods worshiped in Silver Gryphon, the temples there were nondenominational. In the early days of the city, temples had been of low priority, so all religions agreed to share, and that had turned into a habit. This had astonished the Haighlei, who had not been sure whether they should be offended, or admire such an economy of worship. It appeared that things were the same in Iftel. So there was incense, and lights, and an altar, but if you felt you needed to call on a specific deity, you brought what you needed, from priest to paraphernalia.

And then, with no warning, two glowing figures, male and female, each three times the height of a normal man, appeared floating above the altar. The female was garbed in shifting shadows, and herself appeared to be made of tiny motes of shadow. She was rimmed in silvery light, and only her eyes stood out clearly; they had neither whites nor pupils, and seemed to be composed of scraps of the night sky, full of stars. The male was similarly clothed in shifting, golden light, appeared to be made of motes of the same light, and his eyes blazed like the noonday sun.

The sweeper let out a shriek and fell to his knees, and then his face, on the floor. The priest who had been changing the incense wasn't quite *that* rattled, but it was clear that this was completely unexpected by the way that he took several steps back, then went immediately to his knees—involuntarily, as it looked like his knees just gave out under him.

"Rise," said the two together. *"Our people do not debase themselves before us."*

The priest struggled to his feet. The sweeper remained on the floor until the priest gave him a hand up.

"The gods request your help," they said, still together. *"The gryphon Kelvren Skothkar of the Vale in Valdemar means to journey into the lake called Evendim. The lake is the site of the Destruction of Ancient Ma'ar, but what was set in motion there has reverberated across the centuries, and now threatens even the gods ourselves. But the future is shrouded in shadow, the lake is a maelstrom of chaotic magic, and we cannot wisely pierce the shadows. We know that what is there has begun to affect even us. Kelvren and Adept Firesong will require more aid than has gathered. We have selected six gryphons of Iftel to Serve."*

Kelvren felt very much as if he had had all the air driven from his lungs. *What?* The Star-Eyed and the Sunlord *knew* of him? Well, of course they knew of him—they were gods, after all, and he had, on occasion, rendered a prayer or two to them— but here they were, with his name in their mouths!

He had to sit down. Hard. It felt as if all his joints had suddenly gone floppy and too weak to hold him.

"These are not champions of games; champions are not what is needed. What is needed are quick wits, deep knowledge, endurance, and will. They go into the unknown, and where they go, it is possible we may not be able to aid them." A piece of parchment or vellum appeared

on the altar, and the priest picked it up with a hand that was visibly shaking.

As soon as he had picked it up, the light around the two figures flared, too bright to look at, and then vanished. And there was nothing to show that anything had been there except the paper in the priest's hands.

Vindaria waved her claw again, and the sphere vanished. "This is all we know."

:Not true,: objected Tronia, her Mindvoice just as strong as Tyrsell's. *:We know that the Star-Eyed and the Sunlord rarely enter directly in the affairs of mortals, for we were given free will, and are meant to act on our own decisions, and repair our own mistakes. We know that for both of them to appear and say that the future is uncertain and potentially dire means that we must act on this information. And we know, for they told us, that the future is now so unsettled that we must tread with caution. Foreseeing can offer us even less guidance, knowing this.:*

"And we know that the gods themselves are bound by the rules they set themselves to allow our freedom and free will." That was Willowheart, one of the Tayledras Elders. "One of those precedents is . . . that for a miracle to occur, something equally miraculous often must be sacrificed. It may be a sacrifice you must make when you reach your goal, and their charge gives warning. Some of us felt that, as respected as Adept Firesong is, his concerns about the Evendim mystery stemmed simply from curiosity, and did not offer our full support. The gravity of this venture has changed."

Silence met that pronouncement. Not just silence in the Council Chamber, but outside of it as well. Because surely everyone here, except for the Iftel gryphons, knew that the last time such a bargain had been made, three leaders of what would become the Shin'a'in had knowingly sacrificed themselves to make the Dhorisha Plains Cleansed and blooming. It was a drastic solution, and the opposite of how their Tayledras cousins had Cleansed the Pelagirs, in the slow, steady way of creating Vales and Cleansing outward from them. But then, the Shin'a'in had had nowhere else to go, and faced with a barren, blasted crater, the sacrifice had probably seemed the only viable solution.

As for Kel—he felt he had to remain sitting for a while. He felt a little sick. His name in the gods' mouths! On the one talon, an incredible honor! On the other—did that make him a Chosen One?

Do I want to be a Chosen One? Did I make myself a Chosen One? No, no, no, did I set myself up for some kind of poetic, horrible Noble Sacrifice?

Vindaria continued, gravely. "We—both our mages and our priests—did our best to obtain more information. But the gods were not lying when they said it was impossible to obtain. Scryers see nothing but fog. Those with Foresight, and those whose spells can reach into the future, had no better luck. Energies, both magical and otherwise, are, well, a chaotic mess. Priests received only the message that 'This is all we know.' But we can deduce a little. We can deduce that somehow this state of being has worsened since the Mage Storms, requiring the gods to act."

"We can deduce other things," replied Stormtree, who besides being an Elder was an Adept. "We can deduce that this chaotic state is beginning to reach both above, to the realms where the gods live, and below, to those where demons dwell, and very likely across all the Elemental Planes. And that makes mortals uniquely suited to this task, for *we* are not as affected by the fluctuations and chaos of such energies."

"Well, that's comforting," said Firesong, his tone one of deep sarcasm. "As I know personally, *not as affected* does not mean *immune*."

Stormtree shot him a withering look. Firesong ignored it.

But Firesong wasn't done. "We can also deduce that the changes created during the Cataclysm have persisted into our time—certainly we Tayledras are still cleaning up after them— and now that the Storms have echoed back, they are interacting with things we have not Cleansed, and that is having some dire effects here, above, and below." He shook his head. "Master Levy and I didn't make any calculations based on that, because it never occurred to us to do so. To be blunt, we hoped we would all be lucky, because we could only thwart one of the two destructive centers. Then we found ourselves—those of us who survived—just happy to exist. Fixing the second problem was deprioritized, against my opinion."

While Firesong was talking, Kel was getting his thoughts in order, and it occurred to him that *no one* had said anything about him except that he was leading this expedition, and Firesong's name was *also* mentioned by the gods. So—hopefully!—he wasn't going to turn out to be the Chosen One.

Not that I don't want to be a hero! But I don't want to be a dead hero! And those who are Chosen Ones generally end up heroically dead! And Firesong, he'll be all right. He survives everything, then gets to explain it for years afterward.

But at this point, people's wits had returned to them, and the Elders had started talking among themselves, roping Firesong into the practical conversation and gradually drawing other mages in. Vindaria glanced over at Kel, who shrugged. "They'll probably be here for candlemarks," he opined. "And none of it will really make any difference to what *we* do. So let's go talk to Silverfox and Ayshen."

"Why?" the gryphon asked him. "Are they priests?"

"They're more important than that," he said, feeling a touch of his sense of humor sneaking back. "They're organizing the expedition."

The Vale was stirred up like a kicked beehive, and Silverfox saw no reason to add to the milling about by leaving his office. Apparently Ayshen felt the same, since the little hertasi came trotting up the stairs, Jylan in tow, shortly after Firesong informed him via Mindspeech who the new gryphons were, where they had come from, and what had brought them here. The three of them moved out of the office to the second set of guest rooms, which had a good view of the path the procession would take to the Council Chamber.

"Well," said Ayshen, as they came into sight. "They're certainly *big*, aren't they? The histories didn't mention how big the Heavy Wing gryphons were."

From here, roughly three stories above the path, they had

an excellent view, as nearly every other creature in the Vale crowded onto the verges to see the emissaries from Iftel. Even some of the messenger birds thronged the trees, and of course, the bondbirds were in the branches as close to their Hawkbrothers as possible. Most perched, but a hooligan of crows were playing "snatch the tailfeather" in the air above the path.

Silverfox raised an eyebrow, but Ayshen was not wrong. The Wingleader and Kel paced side by side in the front of the procession, followed by the rest, and trailed by Firesong. It was easy to see from here that the newcomers were just about twice as broad as Kel, and about half again as long. The Iftel gryphons dwarfed Kel, and Kel was not small. "Yes," he replied. "But I don't think size can compete with a glowing gryphon." And it was true, the eye tended to be drawn in by the radiant Kelvren, rather than to the somber black-on-charcoal Iftel gryphons.

:I am dyheli Ransem,: spoke a voice into Silverfox's head, stilted with formality. *:I will be your eyes and ears.:* By that, Silverfox knew that Tyrsell had assigned one of his herd to broadcast the proceedings to all the Vale. Ransem would not be doing anything except that for as long as the public parts lasted.

But of all the things that Silverfox had been anticipating, the appearance in Iftel of the Star-Eyed and Sunlord was not one of them.

In fact, the revelations at the Council Chamber left all three of them more than a little dazed when Ransem ceased broadcasting, and they stared at each other in silence, all three minds trying—and failing—to calculate all the implications.

"You're certain this isn't a trick?" little Jylan said at last, breaking the silence. "Maybe someone in Iftel . . ."

Her voice trailed off in uncertainty. "Not possible," Ayshen said authoritatively. "The Sunlord is more active in Iftel than the Star-Eyed is here. Anyone who attempted to impersonate him in His Own House would almost certainly end up a pile of ashes on the floor."

"But what if these new gryphons tried to trick us with an illusion of something that never happened?" Jylan persisted, her claws clasped together tightly.

"The Council Chamber has its own colony of *vrondi* that practically live there," Silverfox pointed out. "Untruths and half-truths are known immediately."

"But the gods haven't spoken to us in—" Jylan waved her stubby hands around in circles.

"It wasn't *that* long ago that Vykaendys spoke to the people of Iftel, telling them it was time to break their border," Ayshen pointed out. "And before that, Vkandis chose Solaris to be the Son of the Sun. It seems we have moved into strange times."

Jylan clasped both hands over her snout in patent distress. "I don't *want* to live in strange times!" she wailed. "I liked things the way they were!"

Silverfox immediately moved to comfort her, but he didn't blame her in the least. Truth to tell, he was as unsettled as she was. *I thought we had carved out a good space for the two of us. I thought Firesong's days of adventuring were over. He deserves peace and quiet! He shouldn't be forced to drag himself all over the wilderness again!*

But he had to admit to himself that it appeared that Firesong didn't particularly want peace and quiet. *Look at the way he assumed that he'd be going with Kel on the proposed expedition.* And not once had he indicated to Silverfox that he was anything but pleased about the prospect—once his lover had assured him of his comfort out there, that is.

Now had come this complication. And from the comments Firesong was Mindspeaking to him, in the middle of all the babble among the Elders, this hadn't deterred him in the least. If anything, it had increased his enthusiasm.

I know Kelvren is obsessed with Skandranon, and would do practically anything, however risky, to make himself into a hero like his idol—but I didn't think he'd infected Firesong with his obsession.

"What are we going to do?" Ayshen demanded, as if Silverfox had any say in this—as if Silverfox could march down there right now and countermand the will of the gods themselves.

No, he corrected himself. *It's not the will of the gods. It's the request of the gods.*

Somehow, this didn't make it any less frightening.

Get a grip, my lad, he told himself. *This doesn't change anything. Except that we now know in advance we are marching into a situation stranger and more perilous than we had imagined. That's not such a bad thing. We're forewarned.*

"Obviously, this has set the time-candles burning," he said aloud. "We need to adjust for six more gryphons, and get the rest of the provisioning and packing done quickly. Jylan, see about getting telesons for the newcomers, two apiece, three if possible. Ayshen or I will assign you to the next task once you have those."

It seemed that getting orders immediately poured balm on the hertasi's nerves. "Yes, Silverfox!" she replied, and turned and whisked out the door and down the stairs.

"I think we can assume that the gryphons can and will hunt for themselves," he said to Ayshen, to snap the hertasi out of his daze. "So we just need to reckon on a few days of emergency rations." He nudged Ayshen in the direction of his office. "I wonder if we shouldn't offer to house them in our gathering room?"

"What? Who?" Ayshen replied, then shook his head vigorously. "Oh, of course. Firesong will want to interrogate them anyway. We might as well keep them here so his bed is convenient to be stumbled into."

"Go to the Council Chamber and interject that invitation when there is a lull, please," Silverfox told him. They had just reached the level of the office, and he paused at the door. "They'll likely want you there as an expert anyway. I'll be here, making adjustments."

Ayshen ducked his head and dashed off. Silverfox took a seat at his desk and firmly resisted the impulse to bury his head in his hands. Instead, he took the steps he needed to compose himself. *I am a Hawkbrother,* he reminded himself. *And the Hawkbrothers are accustomed to dealing with the unknown.*

As if that thought had summoned him, with a whump of impact, Silverfox's bondbird, a startling-looking hertasi-sized lammergeier (also known as a bearded vulture) named Hesheth, landed on the windowsill and shook until his quills rattled like rain. He tilted his head to the side and looked at Silverfox. :*Spooked,*: he remarked.

Hesheth was a bird of few words.

"Very," he said aloud. "I'm inclined to read this in the most sinister way possible."

:Silverfox friend. Cup not half empty. Cup not half full. Cup has hole, and allll wine leaking out.: The bird made the hissing sound that passed for chortling.

"It's part of my job to prepare for the worst," he pointed out. But the bird was right. It could be a waste of time to compare the moment to anything in his experience. "Well, what do *you* think?" he asked Hesheth.

:Think, prepare, but prepare to trust. Who tries is who succeeds.:

Well . . . that made sense. After all, that was how the Star-Eyed operated, at least. Up until you had given your all, She was silent. But once your last pennyweight of anything had been spent, if need be, She stepped in.

Every Hawkbrother worshiped in their own way, so there were no "priests" as such to ask. Anyone could read the record of the Star-Eyed's few public appearances in the Heartstone, if they wished, and Silverfox had, several times. If she had ever appeared privately to anyone, they had kept the fact to themselves.

And his imagination was so afire that he actually *expected* for a moment that the thought itself would summon her.

But no. Just Hesheth, eyes narrowed to slits, head pulled down into his ruff, looking for all the world as if he was holding the answers to questions Silverfox didn't even know he had, and was not going to let go of them without a fight.

Humans do an awful lot of talking, Kel thought, and not for the first time that day. What was there to talk about? They knew what the gods had said. They might as well take it all at face value. The gods hadn't given them more information, because the gods themselves didn't have that information. They knew where they were supposed to be going, and now they had an entire wing of gryphon scouts who could fly ahead and plot out the best path for the floating barges. They would take every weapon possible; they would be ready to fight or to parlay. The only thing he was concerned with, now that he'd convinced himself that the gods were not personally interested in *him*, was that it sounded as if they needed to finish up these interminable "preparations" and get on the move.

Meanwhile he had more immediate concerns. Vindaria had effectively made him her superior. And that meant he needed to lead what was effectively now *his* Wing.

My Wing. All but grounded, sure, and I might explode, but I am a Wingleader again. Suck on that, doubters.

But yes, as Wingleader he needed to care for them. And right this moment, with every candlemark that passed, the Iftel gryphons drooped a little more, despite their efforts to look sharp and alert. Hertasi brought around honeywater, but there was only so much that honeywater could do.

Finally Kel decided he had had enough. If no one else was going to display common courtesy, he'd remind them of it. "Our guests are leaving now until they are rested," he said into a moment when no one was speaking. "And we need to find them a resting place. I do not think my 'ekele' outside the Vale can hold them all comfortably." In that same instant, Jylan was at his side.

"Silverfox and Firesong invite the gryphons of Iftel to rest in their ekele," Jylan said into the astonished silence. "They have space in the common room, or if they prefer higher vantages, on the sunning and night-viewing platforms at the top of their home. And Kelvren Skothkar is correct, they need to rest, for they have come a very long way." She turned to the Iftel gryphons. "If you would follow me, please."

The five—whose names he still did not know (since they never did get to the introductions before deliberations choked the air) and who had been almost entirely silent until now—immediately turned to follow Jylan. One of them was so very weary that he stumbled a little. "And this is where we part company," Kel said to Vindaria, with regret. "I am not safe to be this near the Heartstone for so long."

"Then I will come with *you*," she said, making him feel as if he was flying through lightning. "I will rejoin the others later. There are things you and I must discuss."

His ear-tufts perked, and he carefully reined his expectations in, not in the least because he sensed he was having to dump energy into more light. Well, he could not help but have *hopes,* but his more rational side knew very well that she probably had Very Serious Things to discuss and now was no time to be thinking about skydancing and—

Stop that right now, he told himself sternly. *Yes, you are infatuated. Why? Because she is near and you are a lecher. No, that isn't it. You think you* should *be a lecher but your heart isn't in it right now. You're infatuated by the idea of a possibility, of a chance, of maybe being lucky, if you had the strength. That doesn't mean she is.*

"I'll need to stay in the middle of the path," he temporized. "Right now I can be . . . hazardous to mage-lights. You can walk wherever you like, of course."

"That is part of what I wish to speak with you about, but I would prefer to do so with a half-full belly and more liquid than I've had," she confessed as they walked out of the Council Chamber, with the Elders still going on about just what they thought they should do about this new information. *Not* the situation; early on, they'd washed their hands of it and passed on the responsibility for what to do to Kel and Firesong. But they were more sensible than the Valdemarans, at least in Kel's estimation. Or perhaps they just had fewer *politics* than Valdemarans. Because what they were discussing was various means, arcane and mundane, of collecting more information. Of course, this did include the possibly risky ploy of contacting the gods, but—

Not my millpond. Not my otters.

If *they* wanted to do this, then they should, and Kel would thank them for it. For his part, he knew for a fact that things weren't dire enough to call on Them.

He had to lengthen his stride to keep up with Daria, and after a moment he sensed, as he never had before, the entire mechanism for how his feathers were sifting magic from all around him. And how that magic first tapped up his *virtutem,* then when that was full, needed to be released as light. He'd never been this acutely aware of what had always been instinctive, and it made him feel just a bit off balance. *Is this how*

Firesong always is? Probably not; he doesn't use the same systems I have. Mine were created, carefully plotted and mapped out and designed. His are . . . well . . . not designed at all.

But—*but!*—he noticed with hope that now that he was aware of these things, the mage-lights were not bending toward him. His feathers sifted out, for lack of a better term, *ambient* power, but he was not unconsciously reaching greedily for and absorbing everything else within his perimeter as he had been before. Or maybe it was more accurate to say that he was *consciously preventing* himself from doing so.

"I will be very glad to eat," Vindaria confessed as they drew near the Veil. "It was a long flight, and a hard one, but we had no notion of when you would leave, only that the gods felt we would reach k'Valdemar before you did. I will confess that there were three times we descended on some poor farmer, threw down gold to him, then ate his beasts. Not *all* of them!" she added hastily. "But we did noticeable damage to the size of the herds."

"Did you say gold?" Kel asked as they passed through the Veil, with himself feeling not unlike a sheepdog as he controlled his greedy feathers. "If you paid in gold, I very much doubt that you underpaid. You may have done the farmers a favor, allowing them to buy new, fresh bloodlines."

"We had permission from the Guard and Heralds at the Border to do this, after they saw the purses we brought with us," she said diffidently. "It was hard to estimate what the prices here would be, so we carry precisely measured gold rings, the same as we use with the traders we allow to enter Iftel. Gold is plentiful in Iftel; one of the reasons Vykaendys sealed our border was to prevent the greedy from swarming and overwhelming us before we were strong enough to defend ourselves."

New bit of information I am certain Darian will want to know and I will certainly pass on to Hallock. "Gold is plentiful there." For a moment he worried about thieves and bandits, or even a rebellious lord embarking on a wholesale invasion of the country to get at its riches, but then he remembered that it was Iftel. *The man who tries to make off with the wealth of a land full of Heavy Wing gryphons, and a country where the*

Sunlord is exceedingly interested *in the fate of the people, is worse than a fool.*

"Silver is plentiful also. Copper, brass, tin," she added. "But gold is worth more, per weight, so that is what we carried."

Kelvren's belly had already flipped a few dozen times, but it did so again as he realized Daria was being conversational. He had expected fanatical focus and military discipline, but here she was, being personable.

By this time they had reached his temporary home, and he could tell that—as he had expected—the hertasi had deliberately been listening as they walked through the Vale, had heard how hungry Vindaria was, and had prepared accordingly. He had no doubt whatsoever that her five companions were already stuffing their crops at Firesong's ekele.

She raised her head and sniffed appreciatively. "Fresh bread!" she exclaimed. "I have not had that since we left Iftel!"

"Fresh *sweet* bread," he told her. "If you have never had it before, I am sure you will love it."

As they shoved aside the curtain that closed out the insects, it was clear that the hertasi had indeed been listening very carefully to them as they walked, for the little lizards had laid out exactly the sort of meal that a gryphon who had made a long and arduous trip would need. First, pitchers of warm broth, to properly start digestion, followed by raw meat and fish, followed by the aforementioned sweet bread, a particular favorite of Kel's. Nothing but the bread was cooked, not for a hungry gryphon who had been traveling quickly. Cooking, while it did impart flavors, caused meat to be harder to digest for a gryphon. With a side glance at Kel, and an answering nod, Vindaria fell on the food and made short work of it, slowing down only when she came to the bread.

Kel just sat and let her eat. *He* wasn't hungry, thanks to the usual very good breakfast provided by Jylan, so he simply waited for her to be ready to talk.

Because she was so much larger than he, she ate a lot more quickly than he could have, wolfing down chunks of meat and bone that would have choked him. He didn't even have to pretend to be busy; it wasn't long before she took a huge sigh, and settled with a bowl-sized mug of cool water in one claw and a loaf of bread in the other. The bread was heavily laced with the fiber a gryphon needed to clear their crop. A gryphon hunting on their own would just eat the hide and fur or feathers, but one in an established aerie or a Vale where cooking was available would almost always choose this fiber-laced bread. It was much nicer to eat bread than mouthfuls of wool or fur.

"That . . . was needful," she sighed. "We pushed very hard this last leg; we began at false dawn. I think we will need a day or three to recover. Have you any notion of the land we are to cross to get to the Lake?"

"Only that it is at best partly Cleansed and at worst still displaying the effects of the Cataclysm and the Storms," he told her honestly. "And possibly laced with Change-Circles. You know what they are?"

She nodded. "Vykaendys protected us from the Storms and their effects, but we have all seen the Circles as we traveled, and the Herald at the border warned us about them."

"Iftel, I assume, has been tame for a very long time?" he responded.

"Much of it has. At Vykaendys's behest, we left certain parts wild. Not," she hastened to add, "that the Sunlord dictates everything we do! But especially in our early years, he would speak to us all, all at once, and make his preferences known, and give us reasons why. We were still free to make our own decisions, but according to our history, it very soon became obvious that it was better to follow his advice, unless someone devised a better solution."

"All of you?" He blinked. "At once?"

"Aye, this was his way of preventing a priestly class from gaining too much power by claiming they spoke for him. Possibly he was regretting what he had created in Karse, but that is my speculation and nothing else." She tore off a bite of bread, swallowed it down, and followed it with water. "But that is not what I need to speak with you about. It is the leadership of the Wing."

And before he could say something like "I'm perfectly happy to hand it back to you," she went on.

"It is yours," she said simply. "I come from a place where

there is little conflict, the land is safe, and we are tested only in games. I cannot possibly lead effectively here. My training is theoretical only, not sufficient for crossing truly wild lands, or for actual combat. I would be blindsided constantly, and I would not be prepared for surprises."

Well, I have certainly had my share of those. It was clear that she was parting with her authority reluctantly, though as a good leader, it was the only thing she could do. And he sympathized with how downcast she must be feeling. But part of him crowed like a happy rooster to have his title and position back.

"If you're sure—" he said.

She dipped her head. "I am sure, and so are my Wingmates. We talked about this last night before sleep. We might as well be green recruits out here, even though Vykaendys chose us for this. The Wing needs a leader with a lot of experience in unexpected developments."

You could certainly say I've had that. But if I *was unhappy about losing my rank, I don't imagine* she *is happy about it, even though she sees it as necessary.*

"If you are all in agreement, I accept," he said, then held up a claw as she began to speak. "But in matters of order and discipline in the Wing, you are still the Wingleader. And I have a compromise suggestion. I don't know your gryphons, and you do. The humans here—the Valdemaran ones—have a rank called 'captain.' I will be your captain, and you will retain your position as Wingleader."

Her eyes gleamed as she looked at him. It was clear that she was utterly delighted with this solution. He was very proud of himself for coming up with such a solution and offering it to her like a fresh-killed deer for her approval. *I wonder if she'll take it that way? She hasn't said anything about being mated—*

"Three of us are mages," she continued. "Once we are rested, we could both shorten the time it will take to get to this Lake, and bypass any potential danger spots by creating a two-mage Gate with one of your mages at the expedition and one of us at the advance point," she said, abruptly bringing him back to the present.

"Hurrr! It would! You could fly ahead with an anchor and find a good spot, and your mage and Firesong could send us through! We wouldn't even need to leave the beginning anchor behind, because a gryphon can fetch it and travel by air! And what Firesong and I are working on, I think, will power the entire thing!"

"Really?" Her ear-tufts came up. "What do you hope to create?"

"A small Heartstone. A portable one. Something I can safely store my excess power in." The more he considered this idea, the more excited he became about it. "In fact, this would be perfect for siphoning off some of it on a regular basis!"

"Even if you cannot make this 'Heartstone' work, we can still use Gates," she replied, with a dip of her beak. "We will just have to save them only for times when going *through* a spot is too perilous—getting past dangerous areas or difficult land to traverse."

"There isn't much the floating barges can't handle," he said—and then he had to explain the floating barges to her, where they had come from, that *any* barge could be made to float, but these were special because they could be moved by a single person when empty, which meant that the bulk of what the dyheli would be pulling would be provisions and other needful things. That opened up the question of "why don't the Valdemarans still make them?" which led to a slightly confused version of Valdemaran history as heard third-hand from Silverfox, who had heard it from Darian, who had heard it piecemeal from Heralds. And that, in turn, led to a lot more questions, most of which Kel was uncertain about. Which ended with, "And didn't the Tayledras know all about Baron Valdemar's people when they picked a place to settle?"

"Ah!" Kel replied, back on sure ground. "In fact, they did know a bit about them, enough to know that they could be trusted with the remains of a Vale. Silverfox says that the Tayledras have their own version of this story, but he hasn't given it to me. We could always ask him to tell us on the journey. It would make very good fireside storytelling material, and Silverfox is a very good storyteller."

"I expect there will be quite a few differences," she mused thoughtfully.

"Probably. Oh, and I can ask Hallock to do the same, if *he* knows the Valdemaran stories. Or his mate Genni could, if she does. They could take it in turn to tell us all about it!"

But her ears flattened. "What if they take offense at each other's stories, if they are so different?"

He snorted. "Not likely! Nothing rattles Silverfox, and Hallock is the same for different reasons." He caught her drooping after that question, though, and remembered how far she and her Wing had flown, and that she probably needed to rest.

And oh, the quandary! It would *definitely* be too eager to offer for her to sleep here, even if it was just to doze for a while. He hadn't even known she existed this morning! But a good *host* would give her the option, after all, and—

And he was still stuck in indecision when she yawned openly and stood up. "I should get back to my Wingmates," she said. "There is much I need to tell them, but that may have to wait until we have all slept off our meals."

Was there a hint of regret there?

"Of course! Do you—" he began, but Jylan appeared out of nowhere, as hertasi were inclined to do; and interrupted him.

"Wingleader Vindaria, I am here to show you to your guest quarters in Firesong's ekele," Jylan chirped.

"What of the Council?" Kel asked—figuring they were all still neck deep in discussing What This All Meant. And, just possibly, they were debating whether or not they needed to brace themselves and dare to petition the gods for a little clarification.

"Still talking," Jylan replied. "They've called Silverfox to determine if all these extra gryphons mean we need another barge."

"I think we need to leave as soon as we can, and not wait around for the loan of another barge!" Kel exclaimed. "The gods don't just appear and tell you to do something 'whenever you get around to it'! There is urgency here!" *Even if just a few moments ago I was talking about storytelling . . .*

But storytelling is important. People remember things better if they are in the form of a story. And she was pleasant to talk with.

"Don't worry, Firesong is arguing that very point," said Jylan, her tail swishing on the floor. "And since you and he were going to have to distance yourselves from the Vale to awaken that portable Heartstone he has been working on, he feels the sooner you get well on your way, the better!"

Finally he's on my side! That was unfair, of course, but not *entirely* unwarranted. Kel strongly suspected that Firesong and Silverfox had been stalling him. He wasn't entirely sure why they would have been doing that, but he couldn't shake the feeling.

"Yes," Vindaria said simply. "We feel that is the case as well." She got up and dipped her entire head to Kel. "Thank you, Kelvren. When we are rested, we will want to consult you on tactics, that we may prepare and practice. I am sure that the gryphons of Iftel and the gryphons of k'Valdemar have some significant differences in how we fight."

Was there a faint hint of pity in her voice? Was it because he was so small compared to her? Suddenly he was very self-conscious, and Jylan's little dance of impatience to show Vindaria the way was a welcome interruption. "Even so," he agreed. "May your dreams be full of—" he *almost* said "skydancing," but stopped himself just in time, "—good, peaceful rest."

"Thank you." Had she guessed what he was about to say? But she had already turned to follow Jylan back to the Vale.

As he watched her pace away—and there was genuine weariness in the way she walked—Ayshen somehow materialized beside him.

"You got on well," the hertasi observed. "That bodes well for the journey."

"Yes, it does," he replied, still gazing after Daria. And sighed. "I am not used to *pleasant* surprises."

Hallock and Genni only caught the tail end of the procession to the Council Chamber and initially were not invited inside it, having to stand outside with the rest of the residents and passively "listen" to Ransem's broadcast. So they all faced the woven wicker walls of the chamber, watched the birds flitting among the vines that covered the walls, and "heard" the voices from inside, but as if they were all coming from somewhere between their ears. It was . . . disconcerting. It was not the first time Hallock had been on the receiving end of Mindspeech, but the experience didn't get easier with repetition. And it was definitely a new experience for Genni, whose eyes grew very big and stayed that way the entire time that Ransem was relaying what was going on inside that chamber.

When Ransem stopped broadcasting, she shook her head to clear it, then looked around self-consciously, as the other denizens of the Vale began leaving to go back to whatever they had been doing before this surprise arrival. "What just happened?" she asked her husband in Valdemaran. "Was someone Mindspeaking to everyone at once? I didn't know that was possible!"

He didn't need to go into the obvious. "It was one of the deer-things—the dyheli. I didn't know that they could do that, either." He shook his head, but not to clear it. "*Gods* have gotten involved, Genni. That almost never happens. Worried gods, which is never a good thing. I think we're probably going to be pulling out on this journey a lot faster than Firesong intended."

She nodded soberly, and looked just as concerned as he felt. "I can see that. Is there anything I can do to help?"

"I expect, once these new gryphons have settled, that Ayshen will come look for us. You'll probably be wanted to help pack the barges. And Ayshen will probably want me to talk to the new gryphons and Kel and the Hawkbrothers and Ghost Cat fighters and work out how we're going to conduct ourselves. Or rather," he added, "we'll all be talking to the new gryphons to figure out how to work them into our tactics. They're bigger than Kel, which probably means they don't fight like he does." He rubbed the back of his head, as messenger birds started zinging past at top speed, showing that the rest of the Vale had already taken the urgency of the situation seriously. Someone had lit the time-candle now, and the wick was burning. "Right now, though, unless someone tells us differently, we go back to what we were doing before these gryphons turned up."

"Then I'll go back to Nightwind and Skysong," she said. "And we were actually loading the Healing and trondi'irn supplies into our barge, so that isn't going to change." She kissed him and gave him a brief embrace, which he returned, and then she vanished off down one of the side paths.

"I should go see to Uglik, Kandor, and Rina," he said aloud. The gods only knew what the Ghost Cat warriors were going to think of this business. They certainly would never have seen anything the size of the Iftel gryphons. *Hell, I haven't seen anything that size that can talk before. I haven't seen anything that size that wasn't a building!*

He devoutly hoped that the three Clansfolk hadn't been spooked by Ransem's broadcast. The three Ghost Cat Clansfolk coming with on the quest were housed in the Guest Lodge, although as long as the sun was shining, they were rarely in there, preferring to spend every waking moment practicing their fighting moves. Plenty of other Vale denizens were happy to practice alongside them. Silverfox had selected them: two brothers and a sister. The chief had confided to Hallock that this was partly because the three had always fought together as a unit, but also he had only suggested volunteers who were siblings to prevent any "foolishness." That could have had a multitude of meanings, and Hallock was disinclined to ask exactly what the chief meant. He had *no* idea what the Northern Clans did and thought about mating and marriage, and right now he wasn't all that keen on finding out.

As he had expected, he found the three Clansfolk at the practice field, although no one was practicing right now, since people were far more interested in the news than in what they'd been planning on doing today. All six of the Hawkbrothers who were coming on this journey were there as well, and the murmur of excited conversation met his ears long before he turned the corner that brought the field into view. The Vale could be very disorienting for the unprepared, because every possible effort had been taken to keep the place looking like a semi-tamed forest. Vegetation grew everywhere that wasn't a path, with plenty of buildings screened by vines that grew all over their walls, and paths had been deliberately constructed to twist and turn to cut line of sight to a minimum. This wasn't just for privacy; if a Vale was ever invaded, the invaders would have a hell of a time figuring out where they were and where they were going, while the inhabitants could fire on them from every possible angle and every sort of cover.

But the weapons-practice ground was one of the few large clearings. Unlike similar grounds at Guard posts, it did not have a fence around it, and rather than being sand or sawdust, the ground was covered with a tough moss that could take endless abuse, and which nothing seemed to find tasty. Otherwise, it looked like any other practice ground: extra weapons in a pile to one side, archery targets ranged along another, and a cluster of fighters talking excitedly in the middle.

"Hallock!" shouted Rina, who spotted him first. "When we leave, hey?"

"Aye!" crowed her elder brother Uglik. "When! Gods call, we must answer!"

Kandor just nodded, but it was clear he was of the same opinion. All three of the Ghost Cat fighters were right out of the same mold: strong, tall, very muscular, very blond, long-haired, and good-natured. They seldom wore their leathers and furs here, since they spent most of their time in the Vale where there was no "weather" to speak of, when they weren't out with a hunting party. But at the moment they were wearing the full sets of armor, a combination of leather and metal, that the Tayledras had made for them.

The six Hawkbrothers—Icestorm, Redlance, Sharpsight, Blackclaw, Swiftfoot, and Longsight—nodded in complete agreement. In appearance they were as varied as their names, ranging from the very tall (Redlance) to the very short (Longsight), and from deeply tanned to the color of brain-tanned buckskin, but all shared the Hawkbrother aquiline features and pale gray eyes. And shared the white-streaked or completely white hair of Hawkbrothers who worked at least partly with mage energies and did not trouble to dye their hair in patterns of brown and green to match the forest, nor back to its natural black. All of them were warrior-mages; their magic was limited to what was useful for combat and scouting, but their limited skills were as sharply honed as their combat abilities.

They were all holding or leaning on Hawkbrother climbing-sticks. It was obvious that, before the Iftel gryphons arrived, the Tyaledras had been cross-training the Ghost Cat fighters in the use of climbing-sticks as combat weapons. Hallock was not worried about the Clansfolk keeping up; the Ghost Cat folk had a version of stick combat based on their spears, and he figured they could hold their own with anyone.

"Don't know yet," he said, joining them in the center of the field. "But it'll be soon. Less than a sennight, I reckon, may be just days. Start making your goodbyes, and get any business wrapped up. It doesn't pay to fiddle-faddle around when gods are concerned. You don't want a god impatient with you."

"Noooooo," agreed Uglik. "Impatient become angry, even in God."

Redlance rubbed the back of his neck with one hand. "I

wish—" he began, when all three of the Ghost Clan members, Hallock, and two of his own folk interrupted him with a shouted *"Don't!"*

Dead silence surrounded that outburst. Even the birds stopped chirping.

"The gods have their eyes on us, you fool!" scolded Icestorm, her eyes flashing. "Don't *wish* when gods are watching. That's asking for trouble, and you're likely to get what you wish for in the worst way possible."

:Oh, I wouldn't go that far. They're not unreasonable tyrants, you know,: said a completely unfamiliar Mindvoice. And from the way all of them jumped—including Hallock—they had all heard it.

A dyheli? What else can speak to a lot of people at once? But why would a dyheli have said that with such utter confidence?

Hallock was the first to recover his wits and look around. "Who is that?" he demanded, suspecting one of the dyheli from the bachelor-herd led by Ransem, but seeing nothing like a set of horns anywhere. "Where are you?" Dyheli could hide themselves in undergrowth so thoroughly that only an expert could spot them, but he didn't see anything like even a horn-tip peeking up from the brushes around the grounds.

:Down,: said the Mindvoice.

"What?"

:Look down,: the Mindvoice repeated. *:I'm practically at your feet.:*

He did, and all he saw was a cat.

Now, there were cats in the Vale. Very, very well-behaved cats that knew better than to try to make a meal out of *any* of the many birds here. Most of them were the common tabby sort, some big and long-haired, some lean and sleek, with a scattering of black voids that blended with the shadows and had the habit of doing things to startle passersby. Hallock did not consider himself a cat fancier, although he admitted they were elegant and useful, so normally he couldn't have told one from the other. He'd found them napping on his bed from time to time, but he couldn't have told if it was the same one or a different one each time.

This cat, however, was different. Very different.

It had long white hair, except for its mask, paws, ears, and tail, which were a pleasant brick color. And it had very, very blue eyes. Blue eyes that reminded him disconcertingly of a Companion. There was the same intelligence there, and the same alert interest in everything going on around it.

As he stared at it, it sat down and curled its tail around its body. *:Thank you for the compliments. I'm Serenshey. I'm what's called a "Firecat." A bit like a Companion, but with a closer connection to the Sunlord than the Companions have with the Valdemaran gods.* Obviously *the constraints the gods placed on themselves prevent them from helping you directly, but Vykaendys sent me to assist indirectly.:*

Hallock's jaw sagged with astonishment.

Obviously? There's nothing obvious—

"*Spirit Cat!*" bellowed Uglik, interrupting his thoughts. The Ghost Cat warrior scooped Serenshey up and held the cat over his head like a trophy or a holy object. "Behold! Spirit Cat, my brothers and sisters! We shall be *mighty* and *blessed,* for we have Spirit Cat to guide us!"

Hallock held his breath, but the Firecat didn't seem the least upset. *:Thank you for that welcome, Uglik. Now, if you would, please put me down. I would greatly appreciate it.:*

Hastily, the warrior did as he'd been asked, patting the cat roughly on the head, then snatching his hand away as if he'd been burned. "No mean to offend, Spirit Cat," he said.

The cat purred. Loudly. And—was it smiling? *:No offense taken. Now, because I know that the Elders will monopolize me once they see me, I want you to ask me whatever questions you might have before they realize I am here and I need to join them.:*

They looked at each other. Then they all looked at Hallock, who scratched his head and slowly regained his composure. *Wait, isn't there one of these things at the Court at Haven?* That was right . . . it was with the Karsite ambassador, Karal. He had never personally seen it, because why would a lowly Second have seen such a thing? But he recalled now that cats like this one were accepted at face value by the Heralds. No reason not to trust it. "All right, the obvious. What do the gods know about this situation we're supposed to investigate?"

:Not much. Partly, that's because . . . well, the best way I can describe it is that there's a sort of roaring, out-of-control fire in the place where you are going. Middle of Lake Evendim, to be precise. And besides damaging things through all of the planes—you know about planes?:

Hallock and the Ghost Cats shook their heads; the Hawkbrothers nodded.

:All right, you Tayledras explain it to the others later. This magical "fire" has been burning ever since Ma'ar fell, but the damage was confined to your plane. It was confined entirely to just one physical place, and to be honest, even the gods were inclined to leave it alone and wait to see if it burned itself out. It should have, eventually.:

"Obviously it didn't," pointed out Redlance—who had a habit of pointing out the obvious.

But Serenshey seemed to be a particularly serene creature. Redlance's intrusion didn't bother him at all. *:Well, why meddle, when there were no mortal instruments nearby to work through, and when it wasn't actually threatening anything? It was just a dangerous anomaly, until the Mage Storms happened. And then . . . then things changed. It's begun expanding—slowly, but definitely expanding. It's now reached the Aetherial and Abyssal Planes.:*

Hallock glanced at the Hawkbrothers, who looked utterly appalled. Well, that answered the question of "just how bad can this be?" Very bad, evidently.

The Firecat gave him a little nod, as if he had read his thoughts.

Of course he read my thoughts. And avatars of gods don't operate by the rules of mental politeness that Heralds do. I guess I had better get used to this.

The Firecat certainly heard that, but was at least polite enough to pretend he hadn't. *:Mostly it is expanding into other planes, rather than on this one. And no one is there at its physical origin point to deal with it or even investigate it. It's causing disruptions and disjunctions, has gotten to the point where* *it actually threatens the gods themselves. It's not just Vy-kaendys and Kal'enal who are threatened, it's a lot of other gods as well, but the others all agreed that since it's nominally within the area where their devotees live, those two should be the ones to approach mortals about the problem.:*

"Why not scry it?" asked Uglik. "Shaman could scry—"

The Firecat shook his head. *:It's not possible. Not only is it too "bright" to see into, magically speaking, the entire area is also surrounded by a sort of magical fog or smoke. We can't even peer through it to look at the purely physical plane in that area. It's impossible to see what's going on there, even for gods, and that makes the gods disinclined to approach it. All anyone knows for sure is the closest analogy to what is going on is the worst thunderstorm you have ever seen, multiplied by hundreds of times, and reaching all the way from the ground to the stars.:* All of this was stated in a nonchalant tone that completely belied the sheer horror of what the cat was describing.

"How are *we* supposed to do anything about something like that?" Redlance demanded. "We're only hu—I mean, mortals!"

:And so was Ma'ar,: the cat pointed out primly. *:And you are free to act in any way you like on the mortal plane. The gods are not.:*

"Yes, but—" Blackclaw objected.

:It's complicated,: said the cat. *:Right now, you can go where they can't, and be their eyes and ears. And hands, if need be. But it's complicated by more than that. Obviously you know not all gods are . . . pleasant.:*

And here it comes, Hallock thought, grimly.

:Some of the not-pleasant ones are very likely to take advantage of this.:

"And there it is," groaned Longsight. "There it is. Are they—"

:No. The Abyssal gods are not yet aware of how badly the Aetherial Plane is being affected, because they can't see into it. Light can illuminate the darkness, but the darkness cannot peer into, or even bear, the light. But it's only a matter of time before they find out and try to take advantage.:

"Because they've got mortal minions of their own." Longsight shook his head.

:May I say it is a pleasure to work with people who don't have to be led on a leash,: remarked the cat. *:Exactly, and those minions are likely to try to get to the conflagration ahead of you and interfere with you.:*

"If they mortal, steel will cut, and arrows pierce," said Rina firmly. She grounded her climbing-stick with a *thud* to emphasize that. "And if they know not we come—" She paused. "*Do they know not?*"

:They do not know. Another reason for sending you instead of the gods going themselves. The gods would be seen if they descend to the mortal plane and begin acting. You will not be noticed.:

Rina nodded. "We be as the Cat: stealthy, silent, deadly."

:I can tell you that what you already have planned is, in fact, a good plan. But I can also tell you that the situation is . . . unpredictable, and you must be prepared to change your plans at an instant's warning. Is that all you needed to know?:

Hallock looked around. The rest all looked satisfied for now. He nodded.

:Good, I'll go present myself to the Elders. I'm among you as an advisor and I won't withhold anything from you. If there is something you should know, I'll tell you. If I don't know something, I'll tell you that, too. And I'll help you, not just talk to you. I can do quite a lot . . . : the cat bared his teeth, and unsheathed his claws, *: . . . including fight.:*

Kandor burst into a mighty guffaw. "He be little, but he be fierce!" he exclaimed.

:So I am. And now I will leave you, but I'm never more than a call away. Just picture me in your mind, and I'll come if I am able.:

And the cat did . . . something. It was as if he *folded* himself, and folded himself again and again, getting smaller each time, in the blink of an eye. And then he was gone.

:Ahem,: said a polite Mindvoice, just as Firesong was beginning to get bored with going over the same ground for the third—or

was it fourth?—time. Everyone's head came up at once—which is how Firesong knew that everyone had heard that Mindvoice, not just him.

This is turning into an . . . interesting day.

And before anyone could ask who had interrupted them, there was a kind of wiggle in the air in the open space in the middle of their circle—and a cat appeared.

Firesong was the only one who recognized immediately what he was looking at, and that, only because he was familiar with the Karsite ambassador and his . . . advisors? *"Firecat!"* he exclaimed in an involuntary shout, making everyone else jump out of their skins.

:Why, yes I am, thank you,: said the Firecat. *:Please call me Serenshey, and I am here to help.* Really *help. I am to come with you. The Star-Eyed and the Sunlord sent me to be their eyes, ears, paws, and your advisor and aide.:*

"So the Iftel gryphons know you are here?" Firesong asked, since the rest seemed to have lost their tongues. "Did they know you were coming?"

:No, they do not know yet, but they will be relieved. Firecats are far more common in Iftel than in Karse.: Serenshey didn't elaborate on that, but Firesong was well aware that for generations while the red- and black-robed priests ruled Karse, Firecats had been thought to be mythical. Even now, there weren't that many, but at least now the corrupt priests did not have a license to try to kill one if they saw it.

"What do you know that we don't?" asked Willowheart, coming straight to the point, as usual. Willowheart never beat around the bush.

That set the Elders off on a questioning session that at least had the benefit of covering newer ground than the earlier discussion had. Firesong held his peace and listened closely, but there didn't seem to be any of the usual opaqueness and double-talk there usually was when gods spoke.

Well, I can't speak from personal experience, he realized after a moment. *So that's probably not fair. But the last time the Star-Eyed spoke directly to a Hawkbrother was a long time before I was born, and that seemed to be couched in riddles.*

Then again, this time it appeared that the gods themselves

feared they were imperiled. So maybe that was the reason why their spokes-creature was being a lot more direct than usual.

But eventually, it got to the point where Serenshey had nothing more to say than, :*We don't know*.: And when he had repeated himself enough times, Firesong deemed it his job to intervene before the Firecat got annoyed.

"I'll take Serenshey to the Iftel gryphons," he said, breaking into oh-so-polite interrogation. "Since it doesn't seem as if we're going to get any more information without actually *going* where we are supposed to go. Meanwhile, my advice is that we get the expedition up and out of here with all speed." And with that, he got up and walked away. He didn't have to look back to see if Serenshey was following him; the Firecat's looming magical presence—roughly the size of one of those Iftel gryphons!—told him that Serenshey had taken his "suggestion" and acted on it.

:*Thank you*,: he Mindheard. :*I understand their anxiety. We're all anxious. But how many times and how many ways can I say "I don't know"?*:

"As many as you can take before you walk away," Firesong replied, only now looking back over his shoulder. "Do you want me to carry you, or something?"

:*That won't be necessary*,: the cat assured him, and stepped up his pace to a trot. Which looked so charming, Firesong had to smile.

"Does it bother you that you look like a cat?" he asked, finally. "It would me. I'd be annoyed. At least Companions are imposing."

:*We'd rather be overlooked. It's quite useful.*: The cat looked up at him and winked. :*Something your partner knows how to do, and you should learn.*:

He barked a laugh. "Never. But you knew that. Are you going to be at all useful when it comes to magic? We can always use mages on this journey. The more, the better off we'll be. Especially if you can call on the least little bit of divine help."

:*I don't know yet. If you think of magical energies as being notes on a scale, divine magic is not the same as the magic you use, or the kinds the Elementals use, either. I'm still learning about being on the mortal plane. It's hard to get used to being material, for one thing.:* Firesong was impressed by Serenshey's candor. He hadn't expected the Firecat to be anything but enigmatic. *:I don't think I can help with your Heartstone project, for instance, except that I can provide extra shielding when you finally decide to activate it.:*

"Well, do you eat?" he asked reasonably. "Do you sleep? Do you need rest at all?" All things not one of the Elders had thought to ask.

:I do, but I don't have to. If I call on those divine energies, I don't need to do any of those things, but that comes at the cost of being "visible" to things I'd rather didn't see me. I can be hurt and killed, which would be both painful and annoying. Everything extraordinary comes at a cost. So if I want to remain less visible, I do need to eat and sleep.:

"Well, that's magic in a nutshell," mused Firesong, and turned in to the little garden path that led to the ekele. "Let's see how my guests have made themselves at home."

On the lowest floor, in the big gathering room, there were no signs of the heavy feeding that Firesong knew had taken place. The hertasi had already cleaned up with their usual efficiency. Instead, the biggest pottery water-jars that the Vale produced had been set up along the side, with pottery mugs suitable for a gryphon's talons beside them, and three enormous, dark gryphons lay so heavily asleep on piles of cushions near the jars that Firesong suspected nothing would wake them.

:They'll sleep like that until sunset,: Serenshey observed. *:They pushed themselves hard to cover the last leg of the journey, and they know they are safe here. All their defenses are down, so they can sleep as heavily as they need to.:*

"The others are probably on the sky-terrace," Firesong guessed. "I can't imagine any of them in a guest room. They wouldn't fit on a bed. Let's go up."

Silverfox's office was empty, so either the kestra'chern was busy elsewhere in the Vale or he was on the sky-terrace with the rest of their guests. Firesong could have Mindcalled him, but why bother him?

They came up the last steps onto the terrace, which was little

more than a platform rimmed with a low railing, and loaded
with more of the ubiquitous cushions. There they found two
more gryphons asleep, and a third who was talking to Silverfox. At the sound of their footsteps she raised her head, and
pinned her eyes.

"A Firecat!" she exclaimed, and there was no doubt of the
relief in her voice. "So the gods have favored us!"

*:Nothing less than your due, Vindaria Lisson. But you should
rest.:* It looked as if the Firecat was about to say something
more, when suddenly *his* eyes pinned. *:Well. This will be interesting. It seems more than the Star-Eyed and the Sunlord have
decided to take an interest in your quest!:*

And before Firesong could ask what the Firecat meant, an
entirely *new* Mindvoice spoke.

*:Healing Adept Firesong, if you would be so kind, would you
come to the entrance of the Vale and assure the guards there
that we are not here to carry off any young Hawkbrothers?:*
the voice, which felt female, said in his head. And with that
Mindvoice came a flash of somewhat agitated Hawkbrothers
facing off against—

—two Companions.

He snapped off an oath and turned back down the stairs
to head for the entrance. Things had certainly gotten a lot more
interesting.

––––––––––

The Hawkbrothers called a halt to the weapons practice, largely
because no one could really keep their mind on practicing when
there was so much else everyone was aching to know about—
the new gryphons, the Firecat . . . Hallock sympathized, but
wondered if this meant that work loading the three barges had
just stalled as well. Practice could wait. Loading could not.
So as soon as they all broke up and went their separate ways,
he headed straight for where the barges were kept.

But when he got there, he found that he needn't have worried. Between Genni and Ammari, hertasi Jylan and a Tayledras
named Bluewater, no one was slacking off. Ammari had even

dragooned Jefti into helping, since he was small enough to get into places the adults couldn't, and stow away small objects that were going to be needed eventually, but not immediately.

". . . and they'll all still be there when we've got everything stowed," Ammari was saying to a chastened-looking Hawkbrother. "You won't miss anything. It isn't as if they all are going to vanish overnight. Besides, the new gryphons are probably sleeping, and do you really want to wake up a gryphon?"

Oh, dear. She's using the "mother voice."

She turned and spotted Hallock, and sighed with relief. "Oh good, here's the captain. He saw both the Iftel gryphons and the Firecat. He can tell you all about it." Then she turned and leveled a withering gaze on the Hawkbrother. "While you continue putting away those jars," she added sternly.

But at that moment, Hallock heard something he had not expected to hear again for as long as this journey took them. Something that was familiar in Haven, but rare in this Vale.

The sound of bell-like hoofbeats coming toward the clearing where the barges stood.

Genni knew what that was, too; she whirled in place and stared in the direction the sound was coming from. But before either of them could say anything, two Companions danced their way into the clearing. One was wearing full Search tack, complete with the barding.

Now, Hallock knew for a fact they weren't coming for *him*. In fact, there was only one likely person who could have brought them here—

Nightwind came to exactly the same conclusion and flew across the clearing to stand between the Companions and Jefti. There she stood, hands on hips, glaring, as her bondbird, a handsome kestrel, hovered above her head, matching her glare for glare.

"You are *not* taking my apprentice, horse!" she exclaimed, staring the Companions down. "Valdemar rejected him! I'm claiming him!"

One of the Companions started back. The other made a noise that sounded like snickering. *:Peace, lady. I'm not here for anyone. Sherris is here for someone other than your apprentice.:*

The smaller of the two Companions, the one who had shied

slightly in the face of Nightwind's accusation, flagged her ears and tail as she looked past the standoff to the second barge, where Ammari was bent over, back to them all, carefully packing up a box-shaped basket and oblivious to the drama going on behind her.

The female Companion somehow got herself across the clearing and behind Ammari without a sound—and put her very damp and probably cold muzzle right where Ammari's blouse had ridden up, showing her backbone.

Ammari shrieked, jumped, and whirled, her hand open to slap whoever or whatever had "assaulted" her, and then froze, looking deeply into the Companion's sapphire blue eyes.

"Bloody 'ell," said Jefti in Valdemaran, staring. "How's zat possible?"

Of course he recognizes a Choosing. What Valdemaran child wouldn't? Hallock thought bemusedly.

:Oh, well, Jefti, it's possible because until now, your mother wasn't free to become a Herald. Now she is.: Now the other Companion stepped gingerly around Nightwind—who was, herself, staring at Ammari and Sherris—and nuzzled Jefti's shoulder comfortingly. *:Now you can take care of yourself. You have a good place, friends, and people you can call family. You have an important job to learn, and you are going to be very good at it. We don't take people who have responsibilities they can't leave.:*

"But—what if them people *never* can leave?" Jefti asked, looking into the other Companion's eyes—and clearly not becoming as entranced as his mother was.

:Then we wait until things change or Choose another. Sherris has been waiting a long time for your mother.:

Hallock could almost *see* the wheels turning in Jefti's head. The boy was smart, and a quick thinker. Long before *he* had gotten over the shock of seeing two Companions in the Vale, Jefti had already come to several conclusions.

"So, she's a-gonna go to the Collegium." He made it a statement, not a question. "And she's gonna be there in Haven for *years*. Safe."

:Safest place in Valdemar. It will probably take her about three years before she gets her Whites.:

"So you're a-gonna take her there now, an' nobody's gonna be mean or nasty to her, an' she's gonna allus hev enough to eat an' a good place to sleep."

:And many new friends, and people she can call family. Just like you do, here. I know you were thinking that after she has cared for you for so long, it was time for you to start caring for her. I know you were worried that if you went on this quest with Nightwind, your mother would be alone again, perhaps unhappy, and perhaps these Hawkbrothers wouldn't care for her the way she deserves. You don't have to worry about any of that now. You're free, too.: The Companion nodded his head vigorously, and it was only at that moment that Hallock realized he did not have a scrap of tack on him, not even a halter—where Sherris was fully tacked up, complete with saddlebags and camping kit. As a Companion on Search always was.

Just like that, Hallock watched all the tension drain out of the boy, to be replaced by a huge, relieved grin. He didn't need to say anything; his posture said it for him.

:Can you spare a few moments from packing?: the male Companion said at last. *:I think we need to leave them alone for a bit. Your mother is still sorting through everything this means, and that's going to take some time.:*

"Why are *you* here?" Hallock asked bluntly.

:Oh, I was asked to come along and help,: the Companion said, casually. *:With Kelvren's expedition, that is. You see, Haven can't send a Herald, not even Shandi, without a lot of fuss and questions about why Valdemar is "wasting" a Herald on something outside our Borders.:* The Companion sighed gustily, blowing Hallock's hair. His breath smelled like honey and clover. *:You would think,:* he added, a little crossly, *:that people would have learned from the Mage Storms. But no. Politics!:* That last was said with the same vehemence and disgust that Hallock felt about the subject. *:But an unpaired Companion can go any damn place the Companion wants to go, and nobody can say anything about it. So. I'm here to help. Has Serenshey gotten here already?:*

:Serenshey beat you by candlemarks, hay-burner,: said the amused Mindvoice that Hallock now recognized. *:Serves you right for not Gating.:*

The Companion tossed his head and rolled his eyes. *:You know we don't do that.:*

:Not my problem,: Serenshey retorted. *:You could learn, if you wanted to. What are the Powers going to do to you? Take away your birthday?:*

The Companion dropped his nose and looked sharply at the Firecat. *:Huh. Do you think—:*

:I think interesting times require interesting solutions. But you should know that, given your past. How *many times did you bend the law until it looked like a fancy braid?:*

:Quite a lot,: the Companion admitted.

"This is all very well," Hallock interrupted them, "but am I given to understand that you are actually here to become part of Kel's expedition?"

:Didn't I just say that? Yes. And I *have the benefit of being able to communicate via Mindspeech directly to Haven. If you stir up something that's likely to have an impact on Haven, I can warn them. Among many other things.:*

Hallock's eyes narrowed. "How," he asked, slowly, "do you feel about pulling a barge?"

Ammari and Sherris were gone. The Elders, confronted by not just a wing of strange gryphons and a Firecat but an unpartnered Companion, had reached their saturation point. They had thrown up their hands and declared that there was nothing more the Vale could say or do as a Vale that would make any real difference in the success of the expedition. The Vale itself was buzzing. It had been quite a day.

But the day was not yet over. Not for Firesong, and not for Kel.

"It's about time!" Kel exclaimed, when Firesong turned up, accompanied by cat, Companion, and Vindaria. Kel would have been beside himself with curiosity about the first two, and all in a muddle over the third, except for what Firesong held in his hands.

A lightweight breastplate with a shining, gold-colored cube about the size of a fist mounted in the middle of it. The cube's sides had been polished flawlessly. And where Firesong had found what was an apparently flawless crystal of iron pyrite that large, only he knew.

"I know, I know," Firesong sighed. "I understand your impatience. But there is no reason to put this off any more. Especially not with three mages to help me, one of whom can bring some divine protection to bear."

The Firecat preened a little.

:What am I, chopped radish?: the Companion objected. But before Firesong could retort, he turned his blue eyes on Kel. *:Call me Jak, for Jackdaw.:*

"Which is not your real name," Kel speculated.

:It's good enough. Besides, it's easy to say, short, and no one else in your troupe has a name like it.: The Companion tossed his head and side-eyed Kel pertly.

"All right, Jak," Kel responded, not taking the bait. "*Can* you bring divine protection to bear?"

:I can do a lot of things, and that's one of them. Not a thing to do on a whim, but what you and Firesong are about to try is very new, and not even the gods can accurately predict what's going to happen. So Serenshey and I are here to tilt the odds in your favor.:

"And I am here to add my strength to yours," Vindaria said, modestly.

"Are we going to do this *here*?" Kel asked, looking around at the room. "It's very flammable."

"If things go wrong, *flammable* is going to be the least of our worries," Firesong muttered. Then said aloud, "Just let's get this breastplate on you. I'll do the preparation work. The rest of you . . . well, you know what you're doing better than I do."

Now it was obvious to Kel that Firesong was . . . annoyed. He had a good idea why. Here Firesong had planned out a very precise magical Working, all to be done by himself alone. He must have been calculating and charting and figuring ever since they let Kel become conscious again.

And now here were a bunch of creatures he didn't even know who had invited themselves into the Working without so much as a "may I."

No wonder he was irritated.

He was too good a mage and Adept to turn down help, however, especially help that came with a tinge of the Divine. Maybe more than a tinge. But that wasn't going to stop him from being annoyed that all his careful plans had been interfered with without anyone asking permission.

As for Kel himself . . . well, any help that was going to prevent him from self-immolation was greatly to be desired.

He stood patiently while Firesong and Vindaria strapped on the breastplate. He shrugged and wiggled a little, but the Hawkbrother smith who had made this thing had known what he was doing. The considerable weight of the iron pyrite crystal was distributed so evenly across the breastplate that the straps holding it in place were not in the least annoying. No rubbing, no chafing. Everything perfectly balanced.

And if this works—when *this works*—*I can fly again!*

That alone was enough to make him eager to get it over with.

"Lie down here," Firesong said, pointing at the center of the room. "And start growing those channels."

Obediently, he went to the center of the room, lay down, and closed his eyes, concentrating on the weight at the center of his keelbone, where the embryonic Heartstone lay against his skin.

Carefully, because this was going to be perilously close to his heart, he concentrated on the spot where the cool of the iron touched his skin and bone. The bone was the important part; he'd learned from the book on gryphonic anatomy that Urtho had planned for gryphon bones to conduct magical energies, rather than nerves as happened in humans. And what he needed to do was literally change his skin and bone at that point, to allow the connection with the Heartstone to be as solid as the connection of a Vale Heartstone with the earth.

He felt his flesh responding to his will, as he drew down power from his *virtutem* and sent it flowing away from the organ, rather than *to* it. *Like a nest,* he told himself. *A nest for a very strange bird.*

He could not have told how long it took, but eventually he was satisfied. The connection was firm and strong, and more than that, reliable. And now it was time to grow the channels that would take power, not only from the *virtutem*, but at need, from the entire *indusvenarum*, and channel it into the Heartstone at his keel.

He sensed the other four working around him; sensed energies swirling in patterns he couldn't follow, and changes happening in the stone itself. But he couldn't allow himself to be distracted; he had his job, and it was a job only he could do.

And as he inched the new channels closer and closer to their goals, he sensed more changes. First, Vindaria ended what she was doing, and joined her powers to his. Then first Jak, then Serenshey, encompassed him in protections, not unlike being cradled in enormous, gentle hands.

And then he waited, poised, for Firesong to energize the Stone and conclude the Work.

Anticipation filled him to the brim, leaving very little room for fear, though fear lurked in the background. It felt a little like it had when he was just a gryphlet, poised on the edge of the cliffside aerie in White Gryphon, wings spread, wind in his feathers, getting ready to make that first jump.

"Now!" Firesong shouted, clapping his hands together, and with an electric *crack* like lightning, he was galvanized.

The sensation was close to, but not exactly like, what had happened when Treyvan had concluded the Work in the Change-Circle. It felt as if every nerve and feather was on fire, but in a *good* way. As if he was full of life itself. As if he and this little Heartstone were one being, and they fit together like the bodies of lovers.

It was terrifying. And wonderful. His eyes snapped open. He saw the way clear to the door of his dwelling, with crackling energies still filling the room, and he stood up. Without another thought, he dashed for the door.

Out the door.

And leapt into the air, as he had on that day in Deedun.

But *this* time, this time was different. Energy filled him, energy coursed through him from every vane of every feather, but *now* it had somewhere to go. Into the Heartstone. Which took it in, arranged it all neatly, tamed it, and tamped it down, to make room for more energy. And more. And still more.

He sensed there were flaws in this new thing. He sensed there was a leak. But that was all right, he hadn't expected things to be perfect, and it looked to *him* as if the energy was leaking harmlessly away into a ley-line below him. But the important point was that that power no longer needed to be burned off as fast as it came in, lest it turn into a very real, very physical conflagration.

And once again, he could *fly!*

13

Kel soared above the rainclouds, soaking in the sun, very glad that he was *up here* and not down where the expedition was slogging its way through more rain than he'd ever seen in his life, including in Deedun. The pillars of thunderheads boiled up on either side, flashing lightning continuously from neck to anvil. Gryphons weren't lightning-attractors, but he *was* carrying a prototype Heartstone, and this was as much risk as he intended to take. There was disorganized magic in the lightning magnitudes beyond what he could survive a brush with. There was bravery, and then there was deserved disintegration.

They'd had no choice but to travel here, though, rain and all, because the distance at which any two Adepts could Gate these days was strictly limited to "about half as far as a gryphon can fly in a day." Even with Kel serving as a power source, thanks to the Storms, that was the best anyone could do. It was rain all the way to the Lake, according to the limited scrying they'd done. It wasn't "bad luck," either; according to Serenshey, this massive storm was due to all of the magical chaos in the area. Urtho must have planned for his gryphons to deal with such chaos, because none of them, not even Kel, were having any trouble sifting magical energies out of the air to keep themselves *in* the air.

But it was lovely up here: sun on his back, clouds rolling under him like a tightly packed flock of sheep, and after not being able to fly for far too long, he was taking immense pleasure just in being able to soar. *A gryphon belongs in the sky. I felt so . . . smothered on the ground.*

Daria—she'd had no objection to being called "Daria," even around the rest of the flight, and he couldn't help but hope this boded well for the future—flew on his left, and an Iftel gryphon called Hathorn Archist at his right. The three of them were overflying the route the expedition would have to take, scanning the ground, looking for Change-Circles or any other magic-based hazards to avoid. Jak and a kyree named Owerll were covering the same ground afoot, somewhere almost immediately below them. For ground-traveling creatures, they were able to move almost as fast as he and the other gryphons could move. The rest of the kyree had ranged out on either side of the expedition, sniffing for trouble, and the three Ghost Cats were covering the rear. *Hoping* for trouble, he expected. They were clearly hoping for some adventure. Evidently being established between Errold's Grove and k'Valdemar Vale was a bit too tame for their taste.

Not ideal, he mused. But the weather wasn't going to greatly bother Jak, the kyree had water-shedding fur, and the Ghost Cat fighters had proclaimed loudly this morning that "a little rain wasn't anything for a warrior to worry about."

I wonder if they still feel that way now. Then he considered how . . . *hearty* they were. *Actually they'll probably come into camp, announce that they enjoyed their "walk," then shake themselves like dogs, spray rain all over everyone, and laugh.*

Last night they'd had to camp nearer to a Change-Circle than Firesong liked; too near to establish a Gate. Not that a Gate was going to accomplish much in regard to the rain, other than to get them further along to the Lake. The rain was just *sitting* here, not moving. They were going to have to camp in the rain and sleep in the rain, and move out in the rain again, whether they walked or Gated.

The rest of the Iftel gryphons were hunting. One of the dyheli, Wendar, was helping by Mindhunting for large herbivores like deer or wild cattle, or even boar. If he found any, he'd freeze them in place, then put them to sleep for a gryphon to come and kill them painlessly. It astonished Kel that the dyheli would even do that; it felt almost like a kind of betrayal. But the dyheli did a lot of things he didn't understand, and perhaps they weren't willing to risk the gryphons growing hungry. A hungry gryphon, while they were obviously not going to actually eat a dyheli, would certainly be having thoughts distressing to dyheli when their stomach was growling. Six gryphons required about six deer's-worth of meat for their twice-daily feedings, and the only way to get that was to hunt.

At least if there was one thing that these wild lands weren't short of, it was game. Even though some of the game looked very strange indeed. Wild cattle with several pairs of twisting horns growing out of their heads, deer in astonishing colors and patterns, and creatures that the dyheli assured them were safe to eat that didn't look like anything he recognized. One herd had looked like nothing so much as oversized, overstuffed hassocks the size of a handcart. Their natural defense was Mind-magic not unlike a dyheli's to make predators look past them. Too bad for them that even an average dyheli buck was easily able to overpower them.

They did taste good, though. Very good, in fact, and he hoped that they'd find another herd of the creatures some time soon. Like a cross between pork and lamb. Lovely marrowbones. They almost seemed as if they had been designed specifically for eating.

I wonder if one of Urtho's under-mages did that? Hard to tell at this point.

He caught a bit of updraft and glided for a moment, wind ruffling his feathers, and the flow of magic smoothed out for just a little bit.

Flying was more work than it had been before Deedun. Not physical work, although he was still healing, even after all this time; mental and magical work. He had to be conscious of what the magic and his body were doing at every moment. Balancing all the inflows and outflows of the magic energies,

correcting the little glitches and hiccups of his Heartstone—
when he was flying, it all required constant attention, which
had caused Firesong no end of chagrin. Although you'd have to
know Firesong to know that this bothered him, because he
hadn't talked to anyone about it except Kel himself, not even
Daria or Snowfire. The Heartstone wasn't *perfect*. In Kel's mind,
this was a matter of "of course it's not perfect, no one ever tried
this before!" In Firesong's mind, though, it was "everything that
I lay my hands on has to be *exactly right, the first time, every
time*." And because this Heartstone wasn't absolutely perfect,
the imperfections were eating at him.

Because of that, when Kel was even the least tempted to be
hard on Firesong, he reminded himself that the Adept was far
harder on himself than Kel could ever be.

*Hurrr. We are both broken. And neither one of us likes to
admit it.*

He glanced over at Daria and caught her looking at him.
His skin warmed, his feathers prickled for a moment, and he
hastily had to burn off a slight surge of power as light. The
more he saw of her, the more infatuated he became. She was
magnificent! Strong, clever, wise, and beautiful. So very, very
beautiful! He longed for the chance to approach her on some
level other than "mission." They'd left the Vale so quickly, he
hadn't gotten any opportunity to begin overtures of that sort.
And now . . .

*I still don't get much time alone with her. The others are
always there.* It was irritating, but it wasn't as if he could ask
them to be somewhere else. By the time everyone stopped
for the day, they were all too tired to do more than eat and sleep.
The gryphons all slept in a knot under one of the rain shelters,
which was not what he was used to and didn't even allow for
whispered conversations.

*Be reasonable, Kelvren. This is not a pleasure trip. There are
serious matters afoot.*

As if to underscore that, Serenshey spoke into his mind,
interrupting his thoughts. :*Kelvren, have you detected any . . .
magical presences below you?*:

Just to be sure, he scanned below before he replied. :*No.
What are you seeing?*:

:We're not sure,: the Firecat replied hesitantly—"we" must mean that he was speaking for Jak as well as himself. *:But there seems to be something staying just out of sight on either side of us. And it's not a regular animal.:*

:Have the kyree scented or seen anything?: he asked. Then considered. *:They might be ranging too far out. I'll ask them to come in closer. We have enough meat for tonight and tomorrow morning.:*

:Wirrell,: he called by teleson. *:Range closer to the barge train. Serenshey thinks there is something shadowing it.:*

:Huh!: came the reply. *:I do not know how anything but rain could have gotten past us, but Serenshey is not likely to call false alarms. We will reposition.:*

That was all he could do from up here, and of all of the members of the expedition, the gryphons were the most handicapped by being on the ground. No reason to go down unless there was something more tangible than feelings.

He didn't like it, though. This rain was good cover for almost anything that wanted to sneak up on the expedition. They were setting a watch at night, of course, but it might be wise to double up on that watch. It wasn't as if anyone would be inconvenienced by anything but rain. Those on night watch could sleep in the barges by day, and did. The only creatures that couldn't do that were the gryphons and the dyheli, and the dyheli were fundamentally useless at night. Granted, the bulk of the night watching fell on the humans, but if they minded, they weren't complaining, and it wasn't as if the barges weren't comfortable to sleep in, whether they were moving or not.

And it is about time to recharge them.

Kel and Firesong—mostly Kel—were in charge of keeping the spells that made the barges float nicely topped up. Kel made it his personal duty to top them up whenever they dropped below a third. It wasn't as if—thanks to his *brokenness* and the Heartstone he wore—there was any hardship in his doing so. And although he would never say as much, he wanted to keep Firesong's personal stores as high as possible. If the Heartstone energy misfired, there was never any consequence that was dangerous, thanks to light-producing being practically a reflex now. Just a flash of light that blinded everyone for a while. But if they ran into something bad, and Firesong had just depleted himself by re-energizing the barge spells . . . the consequences could be dire. So it was much better that he be the one to "fill the jar." Just in case they encountered something that needed Firesong's considerable combat skills.

:I'm going down to recharge the barges!: he called over the teleson to Daria. She glanced his way again and nodded.

He did a wingover and powered his way back to the expedition, waiting until the very last minute to fold his wings and dive through the clouds. The wet air streamed past him, filling his nostrils with scent. He was by no means as good at smelling things as a kyree, but there was a lot of scent up here. Wet earth, wet leaves, crushed vegetation . . . not so much floral, but herbal notes, some of them strong. Definitely strong: wet fur and hair.

And now that he was in the wet, it was *cold*. Cold rain stripped all the warmth out of his body, and the cold air rushing past him only made it worse.

At least he wasn't actually wet. His feathers weren't waterproof, but they were, at least, water-resistant, especially slicked down close to his body as they were when he dove.

He broke out of the clouds into even more dismal rain. Not a thunderstorm, not a downpour, but heavier than a drizzle. His senses had not failed him; he came out almost on top of the caravan, which was visible through gaps in the trees. *:I am coming in to top up the barges,:* he said into the teleson on general broadcast. *:It's me, don't shoot me.:* No point in getting filled full of arrows. *I did that already, I don't want to repeat the experience.*

He picked a spot on their backtrail, found a gap in the canopy, and dove through it, pulling up at the last minute and backwinging furiously to avoid running into the three Ghost Cats acting as rearward scouts and guards. They were afoot, of course. No one was riding except Hallock, and then only when the Companion offered to let him. Nobody rode the dyheli and nobody asked to, by common agreement. And it wasn't as if riding would make the expedition move any faster—they were limited by the speed of the dyheli pulling the barges, which was just about a walking pace.

As he had expected, the three Ghost Cat fighters were ridiculously cheerful, given the conditions, and greeted him heartily as he trotted up to them.

"Is good, no?" said Uglik. "Rain. Rain is good. Keeps bad things close to dens. Washes away scent. Keeps bears away."

"You have a point," Kel agreed. "But I don't imagine the tervardi are very happy about this." Unlike the gryphons, the tervardi feathers were not water-resistant unless they were prepared with oils.

"Hoho!" crowed Uglik. "No! They stay in barge."

He actually felt sorry for the tervardi in this weather. Their feathers didn't do all that much to keep them warm, either. Last time he had looked in on them, they were huddled together like a couple of children, looking solemnly out from under the blanket they'd wrapped around themselves.

"I think we'll probably be stopping soon," he told the Ghost Cat warriors. "This kind of weather doesn't much agree with the dyheli either."

Earnest nods from all three of the warriors. "Good hunting, earlier, caught plenty of meat. Dark comes early in rain," added Rina. "You go talk to Firesong. May be good to stop early, get camp made while we can see."

"I will go and do just that," he agreed.

He loped to catch up with the three barges. They had been lucky so far; there had been enough room on the game trails they'd been following to allow the barges to squeeze through between tree trunks. He followed the area of trampled vegetation until he got to the stern of the rearmost barge, which was where Silverfox and Firesong rode. There was no sign of either of them outside—well, why would there be? There was no reason to make themselves miserable by riding in the rain. So he used the teleson to alert them to his presence.

A window popped open in the side nearest him, and he trotted up to it, to see Silverfox peering out at him. "I'm here to top up the barges," he said shortly. "But the Ghost Cats think we ought to stop early so we can set up the camp while we can see. They say we have enough meat." He spared a glance for the top of the barge, where boar carcasses were stacked like cordwood. "Looks like it to me, too."

"The hunters got lucky this morning and found an entire herd of swine lying up to avoid the rain. It didn't take long to ensure tonight and tomorrow's food supply." Silverfox craned his neck and looked up—not that he was going to see anything but wet trees, but Kel supposed it was a sort of reflex action. "I think the Ghost Cats are right. Tell everyone we're stopping as soon as we find a clearing."

:Silverfox says to stop when we reach a clearing,: he broadcast to everyone, then jumped up on the barge, causing it to dip and shift a little under his weight before it steadied. Once he found a place amid the boar carcasses, he sat down and concentrated on sending the energies he had stored in his Heartstone into the crystal that powered the floating spell, which was something of a complicated matter, since the spell was in force and working.

When he had re-energized the spell, he jumped down again, trotted past the dyheli pulling the barge with a friendly nod, and caught up with the second barge.

By the time he reached the third, there was a lighter patch ahead that probably signaled a clearing, and after he had completed his task, the dyheli did pull the barge into a cleared area— thankfully with no downed trees to have to work around.

:We have a place to camp,: he broadcast to everyone. *:If you haven't started back to the expedition, it's time to come in.:*

By this time, setting up camp, even in this rain, was an efficient routine. The dyheli pulled the barges into a rough half-circle, while the hertasi popped out of wherever they had been riding. They got the pullers out of their harness while Kel slowly damped the floating spell, bringing the barges softly down in place. The hertasi deployed the canvas shelters from the roofs of the barges. Anyone who had any magical ability at all used it to dry out the area beneath those sheltering canvas wings, and anyone who didn't went out to gather firewood or clear the undergrowth away from the ground, or gather fodder from undergrowth that the dyheli had identified as tasty. By the time the last of the Iftel gryphons came trotting into the clearing, and the last of the kyree stood off out of range to shake themselves semi-dry, the camp had been fundamentally set up. The barges were on the ground, and the floating spell damped so it would burn no power. The Iftel gryphons themselves hauled the dead boars off the top of the rearmost barge. Hallock, Jefti, Nightwind, and Genni started a cookfire under the canvas of the middle barge and set up the kitchen area, and Ayshen and another two hertasi had begun cooking.

Only then did Serenshey appear, and he did not get down off his barge. But Ayshen was prepared to cosset the Firecat, and brought him his own bowls of fresh water and diced meat, which the Firecat ate so daintily that he didn't drop so much as a crumb.

The dyheli were utterly indifferent to rain and proceeded to browse the vegetation in the clearing. They'd eat the growth of the clearing down about as much as cattle would but not as much as sheep; if they were still hungry after clearing the growth, they'd go to the stacks of potential fodder people had cleared from the forest around the camp while searching for deadfall. Jak joined them to eat, apparently as indifferent to the rain as they were—but then again, the Companion seemed to shrug off rain the way he shed dirt.

Rina had been right about how quickly twilight would come; darkness was closing in by the time the latrine area was set up and Ayshen began dishing out food.

For safety's sake, the cookfire was the only flame they used; no one knew how flammable the barges were, and no one was eager to find out, but the canvas for the shelter wings was certainly anything but fireproof. So the cookfire would be allowed to burn down to coals, and the morning's meal for the humans and tervardi would be cooked in several pots buried in the coals and ashes. For light at night, they used mage-lights. That was a risk, because things that were attracted to magic would certainly sense the mage-lights, but at least there was no risk of setting the canvas, the barges, or the woods on fire. And at least there was no more danger that Kel would drag the lights and their energy into himself by accident. Besides, wherever Kelvren was, he *was* the mage-light.

Kel dragged some of the smaller carcasses over to the kyree so they could eat under the canvas shelter of the end barge. The hunters really had taken out the entire herd of pigs; they ranged in size from half-grown piglets to a couple of monster boars. Ayshen had claimed some of the piglets tonight, and there had been enough pork and bones to contribute to a substantial breakfast. Out of the way of the shelters, the Iftel gryphons feasted. The Iftel gryphons were almost as indifferent to the rain as the dyheli were, at least when they were eating. *Maybe it's because the rain cleans them off while they're eating.* The gryphons of k'Valdemar were not what he would have called dainty eaters, but they also weren't as . . . raptorial as the Iftel gryphons were.

For his part, he dragged his share over to the shelter at the first barge, where he was joined by all of the Tayledras bondbirds, for the simple reason that he had taken it on himself to feed them. He carefully tore off the proper-sized chunks for each bird, always including some hide and hair, and gave each of them a chance at the innards before he took over. Before they were all done, he'd smash the bones into fragments so they each had some for the calcium, and Silverfox's lammergeier Hesheth couldn't be happier with the feast of bones. The Hawk-brothers all deeply appreciated this service, and he didn't mind doing it at all. In fact, he rather enjoyed it, truth to be told. The birds themselves were always on their best behavior with him. He liked Nightwind's bold little kestrel the best, but Red-lance's gyrfalcon had a surprisingly dry sense of humor, and Snowfire's magnificent eagle-owls Hweel and Huur always had a choice bit of gossip about the humans to share.

They ate very quickly; raptors were inclined to do that any-way, but they all sensed darkness was coming soon, and the diurnal birds wanted to get to their night perches. The rail-ings around the narrow decks running around the middle barge had been fitted out with padding so the birds could use them as perches—facing inward, of course. As long as it wasn't cold, Redlance even preferred to make up his bed on that walkway so he could be near his bird and away from the snoring of his fellow Hawkbrothers.

Once everyone had eaten, the diurnal birds had been lifted up or hopped up to their perches, and the three owls—two eagle-owls and one gray—had taken *their* perches under the canvas on the front and rear barges, vigilantly watching the forest, as their bondmates were. Those three Hawkbrothers were the night guard, and spent the entire day sleeping while the barges moved. It was a good arrangement. Everyone got a full sleep ration this way, as opposed to having their sleep interrupted to stand a watch.

With the leftovers and scraps added to the morning soup pots, people disposed themselves in the camp. The kyree shook themselves dry again, then came to Blackclaw to be completely dried off by magic, because no one really wanted to smell wet fur all night, not even the kyree. Then they curled up against the side of the middle barge, although they didn't go to sleep. Blackclaw was a particular favorite of theirs, and they were perfectly happy to let him use them as a backrest. The dyheli shook themselves dry-ish and took shelter under the canvas of the first barge. The gryphons took up the canvas of the last barge, and used their own magic to dry themselves. The tervardi settled nearest to the fire with the humans. Serenshey finally joined them.

And the rain continued to come down.

"Did any of you see anything unusual out there?" Hallock asked. He asked that every night, but tonight he seemed a bit anxious.

The rest of them noticed that immediately. "Did you?" asked Snowfire, his arm around his mate Nightwind, sitting up a bit straighter.

". . . not see, not precisely, but Jak and I thought we . . . we sensed something. Out past the rain. Whatever it was, it was fast and very stealthy. I don't know that it was soundless, though, we just couldn't hear anything over the rain." Hallock pulled at his ear, clearly troubled. "I don't have a bird with keen senses. I don't have magic. All I have is my instincts. And my instincts said something was paralleling us today."

:Mine too,: put in Jak. His Mindvoice sounded troubled. *: I do have some special senses, but I still can't tell you anything about what I thought I sensed. That bothers me. It bothers me a lot. I should be able to detect just about anything.:*

They all looked to Serenshey, who tilted his head to one side in a listening pose, then shook his head. *:There is something out there. But it's distant, and I can't tell what it is.:*

"But this is the Pelagirs," pointed out Nightwind. "Nothing is normal here. We should be on the alert precisely because nothing was normal to begin with, and then we had the Mage Storms and Change-Circles on top of that." She made a rueful little sound. "We should probably be grateful that trouble has taken so long to find us."

"If it *is* trouble," Silverfox cautioned. "We don't know that yet."

"But it's wiser to assume it is," Hallock countered. "I'm your military advisor and that's what I'm advising."

Uglik was sharpening his axe. It was just a hand-axe and mostly he used it for clearing brush, but he sharpened it at every opportunity. Kel thought he looked a bit sinister, in his leather and armor, half in shadow, and the *shing-shing* of the whetstone on the blade only added to that.

And I bet he knows that, and he does it on purpose.

"We did not see anything," Uglik said. "But that does not mean there was nothing there. If this is something clever, and not stupid like boar, or quick to anger like bear, it will stay out of sight while it studies us and decides what to do about us."

"And what if it's people?" asked Longsight, who was sharpening arrow heads—not nearly as noisy a task as sharpening an axe.

"People mostly stupid like boar or quick to anger like bear," said Rina sardonically.

"Impossible for a human to be that stealthy," Swiftfoot stated flatly. "And if a human was using a spell to disguise their appearance, Firesong would have detected *that*, without a shadow of a doubt."

"Well . . . probably," Firesong replied. But to Kel's eyes he didn't look that confident. In fact, from the expression on his face, he had already decided that he had better make a special effort at scrying the area before he went to sleep.

And of course, that was the moment when *something* out there decided to startle them all with one of the most uncanny cries that Kel had ever heard. It sounded like a cross between a woman having her throat cut and a wildcat snarl.

Everyone jumped. And the Hawkbrothers, except for Silver-fox and Firesong, all started to laugh, followed immediately by the Ghost Cats. Hallock, Genni, and Jefti were frozen and pale, when Uglik boomed, "Foxy making cubs. Ho ho ho!"

"What?" spluttered Hallock.

"Fox sex is very noisy," explained Redlance.

:Foxes have no decency,: grumbled Rruuss the kyree in their heads. *:Exhibitionists, every one of them!:*

That was enough to make even Hallock laugh, though Genni blushed, and Jefti looked puzzled.

"Well, if foxes are having sex close enough to us for us to hear them, I think we don't need to mount an extra guard tonight," Redlance pointed out.

By this time the food was making Kel sleepy. Since he was already comfortable and not in anyone's way, he decided he might as well just go to sleep where he was.

He missed his cushions, though.

And aside from being awakened twice more by amorous foxes, that was his last coherent thought for the night.

The rear of the last barge had been reserved for Silverfox and Firesong. It had many advantages: overhead storage in nets strung across the ceiling, a platform stretching across the breadth of the barge that lifted up for more storage, and a rear door in case they had to get out in a hurry. Silverfox had done his best to make sure that the area was basically one large, cozy nest of mattress and pillows, and had hidden the nets behind a drape of cloth. The space even had a door made of slats to give them some privacy, and Aya, Firesong's firebird, and Hesheth, Silverfox's lammergeier, were perched on the railing right outside their window. In fact, they could, and frequently did, poke their heads in through the window when it was open, just to be sure everything was all right.

And right now they were doing just that; Aya's feathers glowed enough that they didn't need any other light. Firesong sat cross-legged in the middle of the bed; Silverfox had bound his hair up and squeezed into as small a space as he could beside the window, giving Hesheth head and neck scratches. The lammergeier's eyes were closed in sheer bliss.

Firesong stared down, not at the usual scrying globe, nor a scrying plate, but a device of his own making, a board on which he could pin a blank piece of reed-paper. On it he had sketched— a drawing scarcely the size of a fingernail—the clearing, the barges, and even the canvas shelters. Now he stared at it, and slowly, as if being drawn by an invisible hand, other things began to appear on it.

He had taken off his mask completely and frowned fiercely at the paper in concentration. Ridiculously tiny writing appeared with each thing that the invisible hand drew. Silverfox, whose talents included being able to read things upside down, paid careful attention to that writing.

So far, there was nothing to be concerned about. Any animal that could potentially harm a member of the expedition had been noted, and Silverfox knew for a fact that the kyree scent would keep them away. The kyree had told Silverfox that they smelled enough like a wolf pack for potential predators to avoid them. There was a stream he already knew about, since they'd gotten the evening's water from it. There were a few game trails. But then—at almost the edge of Firesong's magical "reach," there was something else.

A series of blurred, short lines.

Firesong's frown grew fiercer.

"What is that?" Silverfox ventured.

"I don't know," Firesong growled. "And that's what bothers me. There's something there. Several somethings. Look, they're moving—" He pointed at his map, and sure enough, the little lines began moving across the page—not moving away from the caravan, but not moving toward it either. More little lines wiggled onto the page from the edge, joining the rest. "I don't like it. They have something to do with magic, and I can't tell what."

The lines flowed across the page, circling the camp, but at a distance. Whatever they were, it appeared they were well aware of the camp.

"Change-creatures?" Silverfox ventured.

"If they are, they're not like anything I've seen before. Or anything I've studied." He glared at the paper, and at this point, the lines chose to wiggle off the page and into the unknown.

"I don't like it," Firesong repeated, staring at the page accusingly.

Silverfox knew better than to offer any platitudes like "Maybe they were just curious" or "They probably aren't going to bother us." "You think this is what Hallock and Jak sensed?" he asked instead.

"Maybe. Possibly. I don't know!" Firesong rubbed his scars fretfully. "I'm glad we've got Icestorm, Longsight, and Sharpsight and their owls, though. I'm going to let them know what my scrying uncovered."

He closed his eyes to Mindspeak, and opened them after a little. "They're alerted. Longsight says Feeoor is uneasy too. He's the owl most sensitive to magic, so I'm not wrong, there *is* something out there."

"I never suggested there wasn't," Silverfox reminded him gently. "If anyone would know, you would. But you can't do anything now; if you do anything besides this sort of passive scrying, you *will* alert anything sensitive that you're looking. Our watchers are all experienced and warned. And we do have a Companion and a Firecat with us."

:*I am taking night watch, since Jak took day,*: Serenshey said, out of nowhere, making both of them jump. :*There is something. Magic-not-magic. Do you want me to . . . :*

:*No!:* they both Mindsent at the same time—then looked at each other and smiled wryly.

:*No,:* Firesong repeated alone. :*There's nothing really to ask Her or Him about, not yet. If we aren't in immediate danger, there is no reason to call on either of them for favors we might need later.:*

:*Well,:* Jak chimed in, :*that's probably wise. Especially since the gods themselves are worried about this place we're going to. All I can tell you is what Serenshey did—that there is something out there, and it has powers that neither of us can identify. And I can add one more thing. It's not troubling the wildlife. I cast my senses in the wake of those things, and there isn't even a ruffled bird.:*

"Nothing to be concluded from that," Firesong pointed out. "When predators aren't hunting, wild creatures often ignore them."

"But it seems interested in us," Silverfox reminded him.

Firesong took several deep breaths, then held his left hand up, palm up, and made several circling motions in his palm. Light flared briefly, and Firesong opened his eyes again. "I took a chance and strengthened the wards and shields," he explained, and glanced back down at the paper pinned to his scrying board.

The flock of little lines did not reappear.

"Time for sleep," Silverfox urged. "Icestorm is a strong mage, even if he isn't an Adept, Serenshey is a *Firecat,* and an avatar of Vkandis, and you just strengthened our defenses. Short of staying up all night and fretting, there is nothing you can do."

"I hate this rain," Firesong said, and Silverfox understood everything that he meant by those four words. He hated the rain because it made him ache. He hated it because it impeded their travel. He hated it because it made it impossible to count on the gryphons as reliable "eyes in the sky."

And he hated it because, in general, Firesong hated rain as much as Aya hated it, which was quite a bit. Firebirds loathed rain; instead of bathing like other birds, they cleaned themselves with fire. Aya was touchy and grumpy and his mood carried over to his bondmate. And it looked like there was nothing but rain in their immediate future.

Aya startled them both by suddenly squeezing in the window, hop-flounced across the bed and cushions to Firesong, and planted himself on Firesong's chest, shoving his head under Firesong's right ear and clinging to him with his claws. As Firesong managed to smile a little and began gently scratching the firebird's neck, Aya emitted a little crooning sound.

"Aya evidently agrees with you," Silverfox replied, as a gentle warmth spread from the bird all through the compartment, driving the dampness out. "So there it is, *sheyna,*" Silverfox told him, in a slightly stern tone of voice. "We have competent scouts, and kyree, and dyheli, who as you know are never exactly asleep, and a Firecat watching. I think you can afford to sleep."

"Very well," Firefox conceded, scooting round so he could lie with his head in Silverfox's lap, the firebird now flattened against his chest and still crooning. "Tell me a story?"

Silverfox smiled down at his love's closed eyes. "Once there was a young kestra'chern, and his name was Amberdrake . . ."

"It's as if the rain is just sitting in one place, not moving," Genni said mournfully, as she peeked out the window in their shared bunk into the dim gray light of dawn. "It's still coming down at the same rate it was yesterday. Shouldn't it have slowed down or stopped by now?"

Shoved up against the outside wall of their barge were the kyree, all of them curled up like snails, as far from the edge of the canvas as possible. Hallock could see them from the window.

Sharing the bunk under theirs were four hertasi. Hallock envied them their flexibility and their seeming imperviousness to damp. Right now they were all scurrying around, getting things ready to feed everyone breakfast. When he'd checked on them before climbing up into the top bunk with Genni, they'd all been curled up together like puppies, wrapped around a couple of rocks that Redlance had turned into bedwarmers, and so soundly asleep nothing had awakened them..

The rocks had been a stroke of sheer genius. It wasn't so cold that they needed the entire barges warmed, but the damp had gotten into everything, and climbing into a cold, damp bed was quite unpleasant. Everyone could have one or more of those rocks, actually, but only the humans, the hertasi, and the tervardi seemed to need them. Jak, the kyree, and the dyheli all declared that they were fine, even with the nonstop rain.

Of course, they're all still young, he reminded himself. *And I don't think any of them have any real injuries that hurt when the weather turns.* Aside from that gut wound, Hallock had also broken a wrist and an ankle in the past, as well as dislocating a knee and a shoulder. The cold and damp reminded him forcefully of those injuries.

"That's exactly what Firesong says is happening," he told her. "It can't just linger forever, though; eventually it's going to thin out and stop, because the clouds are going to run out of water." *I think. I mean, that makes sense, doesn't it?* Firesong hadn't said anything about it, but surely it would only take a few more days to get to the coast. Surely. Even at the slow pace they were going, relative to gryphon flight.

The hertasi were well on the way to getting everyone fed; outside, under the shelter of the canvas, they pulled the cook pots out of the coals, built the fire back up, and started warming water for washing and tea. The dyheli were moving too, getting to their feet and heading either for the woods to empty themselves, or for the fodder piles. Hallock couldn't see Jak, but he assumed that the Companion was doing the same.

:I am not. I took the time to drag some fodder to where I intended to bed down last night. I am literally having breakfast in bed, and not in the rain.:

He had to laugh at that, which made Genni look at him as if she wasn't sure what to think. "Jak just told me he made off with fodder last night so he could have 'breakfast in bed' this morning," he told her.

She smiled then, and combed some of her unruly hair behind her ears with her fingers. "I can't say that I blame him," she agreed. "I'd rather not go out there right now. But I will, because I'm the only one that knows where the willowbark is, and you aren't the only one who needs willowbark tea this morning."

True to her word, she unwound herself from the bedclothes, the warm rock, and her husband, and jumped down out of the bunk. Since there was only room for one person at a time to give themselves a sketchy bath with a cloth and get dressed, he stayed where he was. *I'll get a rain-bath later. But I'm going to want a warm rock waiting for me when I do.*

They shared the barge with eight hertasi in two bunks, Nightwind and Snowfire sharing one, the tervardi in one, and an empty bunk in case someone was too sick to be left alone and needed to be looked after. Putting a sick or injured person in the same barge as the trondi'irn and the Healer's Hand made the most sense.

The rest of the humans and hertasi were spread across the other two barges, and in theory there was some room to squeeze in the kyree at a pinch. If the weather really got miserable, the canvas wings could be made into one side of a tent by pegging them to the ground, and the dyheli and the Companion could have pretty good shelter under that. The "mated pairs" (except for Firesong and Silverfox) were in this barge because it was wider than the other two, and the bunks were just big enough for two—provided you weren't used to big, luxurious beds.

Big, luxurious beds . . . not that we've had those much. The only times Hallock and Genni had shared a big, luxurious bed had been when they stayed in Siverfox's guest rooms.

"Stay where you are until I can bring you your tea!" she said cheerfully, then made her way to the front entrance—quietly, since she'd been given a pair of Tayledras soft leather boots before they left on this quest. A moment later, and it was the turn of Nightwind and Snowfire to pry themselves out of bed, get dressed, and get to work. Nightwind went straight out after Genni, but Hallock caught Snowfire's shoulder before he got past.

"What do you make of these . . . whatever-they-ares that are lurking out there?" he asked the Hawkbrother. "You've been in the Pelagirs all your life. The first time *I* saw anything uncanny was during the Storms, and then not much. I wasn't even in a place where I saw the demons that Ancar conjured up to fight Valdemar."

Snowfire didn't look annoyed at being rudely grabbed, and leaned against the bunk to talk to him. "I'm not happy," he admitted, flicking a braid of hair over his shoulder. "The Pelagirs always have had a habit of throwing weirdling things at you, and the Mage Storms made it worse. *And,* if that's not bad enough, the closer we get to the Lake, the closer we are to what was actually in Ma'ar's territory. Not just the lands that he annexed, but the ones central to his power."

"And that's bad?" Hallock ventured, parking his chin on his arms draped on the edge of the bunk. "We don't know much about the Mage Wars in Valdemar, only that they happened and it was bad, and what we've learned from you Tayledras."

"Not just bad. They were *very* bad," Snowfire told him. "Remember, with Urtho and Ma'ar, you are talking about mages with a level of power that's not far removed from a god's. They could literally create living, breathing creatures. Urtho created the gryphons, the tervardi, and possibly the hertasi. And maybe more; we don't know, and if what he created had too small a population when he died, there wouldn't be any of them left now. But Urtho was careful with his creations. He kept them confined to his tower until he was sure of them, and only released them when he was certain they were stable in body and mind. Ma'ar wasn't. So if he lost interest in a project, or it didn't work out the way he wanted it to, he just booted the creatures out to fend for themselves. And there *were* enough breeders to keep some populations going. There's a kind of giant spider out here that doesn't need a male to fertilize it, and thank the gods it's friendly, because . . . well, giant poisonous spiders are not the sort of thing you want wandering into a town full of prey-sized people. There have been other nasty creatures, too, some of which we knew nothing about until we ran into them. So I would not be in the least surprised to learn that what's been chasing around our camp is something Ma'ar cooked up a thousand years ago, nor would I be the least surprised to learn the Storms or the Circles have played merry hell with them until they no longer resemble what Ma'ar set loose. They could be worse."

That was more out of Snowfire than Hallock had ever gotten before; clearly Snowfire knew his history, and seemed to be pretty passionate about it.

And that made *Hallock*, the "military advisor," more than a bit worried.

"I'm as eager to get to the Lake as any of us," he said, as Snowfire made no move to leave and in fact seemed to be interested in what he was about to say. "But I'm not altogether certain that moving on today is a good idea."

Snowfire nodded, which seemed encouraging. "Say on."

"What if these things follow us? What if they know the terrain becomes a channeling trap up ahead? I mean, I do understand we know nothing about them and they might be benign, but I'm your advisor, and my job is to assume the worst." He took a deep breath when Snowfire didn't appear to object to anything he'd said so far.

There was a long silence, punctuated by the sounds of hungry people getting bowls full of soup. The savory aroma made Hallock's stomach growl.

"Well . . . Nightwind will tell you that I have that same attitude," the Hawkbrother admitted, his white brows furrowed. "And I agree with you. We're not in a bad spot for spending a couple of days. This place isn't going to flood. We found that nice little spring-fed stream last night, there's browse for the hooved ones, and there seems to be plenty of game. We're in a good position if the rainstorms get worse, and what we have now is as defensible as you can get without having some stone at your back. So. If you're looking for advice, and it sounds like you are, then mine is that you need to go to Silverfox and suggest we stay here until we know more about these things."

"So I'm not seeing shadows where there aren't any—"

"Just because you see shadows, it doesn't follow that the shadows aren't there, and full of beasts with sharp teeth to bite you," Snowfire agreed, then raised his head. "And here comes your tea. I'll go chase down mine. If you like, we can both talk to Silverfox once we've eaten."

"I'd like that, very much," he said, relieved, because the truth of the matter was, he was no little intimidated by all the Tayledras. Their reputations had very much preceded them, and they were unnerving. Strong, skilled fighters, *and* magicians, *and* walked around with big, intimidating birds of prey as if they were no more dangerous than lapdogs. That last might have been their most alarming aspect . . .

"Here's your tea," said Genni, with a smile for Snowfire as he squeezed past her. "I'm glad you're finally making friends. What are you two going to go to Silverfox about?"

"Staying here a night or two, until we figure out what the things Jak and I didn't quite see actually are," he told her, taking the wooden mug of tea, blowing on it, and taking a cautious sip.

She made a face. "I'd really rather get out of this rain . . ."

"We're in for at least a couple days more of it," he reminded her. "Moving on isn't going to get us out from under it. Everyone who knows anything about it says it goes from here all the way to the Lake."

"And you can't see much in it." She nodded, pulled her braid to the front of her shoulder, and toyed with the end of it. "Maybe it would be a lot better to stay here and do whatever we can to make the camp more secure, since we know *something* is out there and we don't know what it is." She took his mug as soon as he had drained the last bitter drops. "I need to go help Ayshen. Let me know what happens."

By the time he got outside to collect his morning soup, it appeared that Snowfire had already had words with a lot of the others, because no one was hurrying, and no one was getting the dyheli into harness. He nodded at Snowfire from across the clearing, and received an answering nod and a jerk of the head toward Silverfox's barge. That was more than enough to get him to drink down the last of his soup, stuff the flatbread that went with it in his mouth, and join Snowfire.

He'd more than halfway expected Silverfox and Firesong to still be asleep, but both were up and dressed and perched on a couple of storage bags in the front of the barge when they got there. It appeared they had just finished their own breakfast, by the empty wooden mugs and bowls.

"Ah, Hallock," Firesong said, when they'd come inside. "Come to advise militarily?" He grinned a little at his own cleverness, but he also looked worried. "I hope you're as concerned about the—"

"The things that aren't there, but are," Hallock interrupted him. "Yes, I am very much concerned, particularly after what

Snowfire had to say about this part of the world. It sounds as if it's perfectly normal for these parts to spawn not just impossible things, but impossible *hostile* things."

"You're right," sighed Silverfox. "It is." He cast a slightly accusatory glance at Firesong. "*Some of us* spent all night fretting about it, in fact."

Hallock let out the breath he had been holding in. "Well, that's half my work done. The other half is convincing you to keep us camped here until we figure out if the Things Invisible are hostile or not."

Firesong tugged on his mask a little and Silverfox looked into his partner's eyes in a way that suggested they were probably Mindspeaking with each other.

"Two conditions," said Silverfox. "One, Hallock, that you spend as much time as you can reinforcing the camp defenses before dark. We'll put wards of many kinds on the camp, but frankly, we don't know as much about physically fortifying a camp as you do. When we leave our Vales to hunt or Cleanse something, we do so in small groups, and we camp up in the treetops, rather than on the ground. So that's the first condition. And second, we send Kel and—" He glanced at Snowfire. "Who in the Iftel Wing was the near-silent female that can anchor a Gate?"

"Torandi," supplied Snowfire.

"Right. Her. I want them to find a good spot to set up a Gate a half-day's flight ahead of us. You and Firesong can get this side up and linked, and the gryphons can come back here by going through it. That way we don't get too far behind our schedule." Silverfox scratched the back of his head. "It's not as if we make as much headway in this rain anyway, so the Gate will put us right where we would have been if we hadn't stopped."

"That's all sound planning," Hallock agreed. "All right. One more thing I want to do is order—advise—that no one leaves the camp alone. Always in pairs at least; three or four is better still. Silverfox, that's better coming from you than me."

"And it will come from me," Silverfox agreed. He and Firesong stood up. "I'll make the announcements."

Things must be more serious than I thought. Firesong is

dressed plainly. In fact, he had little more adornment than a headscarf and hat. Even his mask and neck drape were unmarked. *Maybe out here, his reputation would give no advantage, so he'd rather keep it secret from whoever we may encounter. Or may encounter us first.* Or, Hallock reasoned, he might simply be too somber right now for ornate clothing. Hallock knew Firesong was probably twice his age, and gathered that the Adept had been through enough emotionally to crush ten men. *No stranger to pain and loss, then, so the masks may be more than a courtesy to others. A masked face doesn't require conscious effort to hide feelings.*

When they all left the barge, it was pretty clear that everyone was expecting an announcement, because everyone, including the three Hawkbrothers who took night watch and would ordinarily be asleep by now, was gathered in under the canvas, watching for them to emerge.

Hallock reflected, as the group listened to Silverfox, that an observer who did not know Hawkbrothers would have been hard put to point a finger at any of the outsiders as not belonging—except for Jak, of course, who stood out like a white sheep in a herd of black. He, Genni, and Jefti had all adopted Tayledras field clothing: hard-wearing, practical outfits of long-sleeved tunics and breeches made of leather and soft linen canvas, with woolen pieces tucked away until needed, dyed in mottled "patterns" of greens and browns and flexible leather patches wherever wear—or likelihood of injury from a fall—would be highest. There were sorts of overcoats of dyed string and rags that made the wearer almost invisible among the vegetation or perched among the branches overhead, but they weren't practical for hard traveling, and no one had them on at the moment. And just before they had left, Jefti had decided on a facial tattoo—an abstract of curling lines and sharp points. Redlance and Swiftfoot both sported facial tattoos that were very similar.

Hallock paid very little attention to what Silverfox was saying; instead, he concentrated on the Hawkbrother's audience. Most kept eating while he spoke, but they were all listening carefully, and as far as he could tell, there were no objections. The Ghost Cat warriors were napping after being a partial night watch, and would serve as extra muscle when they were up. Ransem and a couple of the dyheli nodded along with the speech, and that was enough for the rest of the dyheli. They thought and acted as a herd, and if Ransem went along with this, the rest would follow. He couldn't read the tervardi at all, but their feathers weren't flattened to their bodies as would have been the case if they *disagreed* with Silverfox. The kyree were, as far as he could tell, perfectly happy to go along with anything they were presented with. And the hertasi all appeared to be in agreement.

Only the Iftel gryphons looked slightly dubious, and sure enough, Vindaria spoke up when Silverfox was finished.

"Wouldn't it be better to hunt these things down—if they exist, and we are not jumping at shadows?" she asked. The other gryphons, including Kel, who had grouped himself with them, all nodded.

"Actively trying to hunt for them has a lot of disadvantages, and no strategic advantage that either Hallock or I can see," Silverfox replied, in such a reasonable tone of voice that Hallock would have been inclined to agree with him even if this had not been his idea in the first place. Silverfox continued, ticking off the reasons on the fingers of his upheld hand. "This is their territory, not ours, and they know all the hiding places—and ambush spots—in it. If they think we are hunting them, that might spur them to attack us, when they would otherwise simply stay out of our way. We're going to need everyone to lend a hand with hunting, fodder-gathering, fortifying the camp, and putting up Gates. And lastly, it's been the Tayledras's long experience that we learn more about Pelagir weirdlings by pretending to ignore them. I don't mean *really* ignore them, and I *do* mean we should assume they are hostile and dangerous, but pretending we don't know they are there is likely to lure them close enough to study."

Vindaria turned her head to look at her Wing and Kel, and found them all nodding. She turned back to Silverfox. "Very well, then. Which of us do you want to fly off to create the other end of the Gate? I assume Kelvren, to power it?"

Silverfox nodded. "And Torandi to construct it with Kel's help. It would be very good if Kel learned Gate construction."

Kel laid his ear-tufts back, as if he didn't much like having another thing to learn piled on top of him when he was already coping with quite a bit, but nodded reluctantly.

"So, Torandi and Kelvren to fly as far as they can in a day and establish one end of a Gate," said Silverfox, as cheerfully as if Kel had been enthusiastic about this. "Firesong, Longsight, and Snowfire to establish this end. Hallock will tell off the work crews."

That startled Hallock a little, but he drew on his experience as a Second and a Captain, and named off groups of two and three. The five kyree all went with human hunters, though in two cases, "hunter" did not mean "meat-hunters," but rather gatherers and scroungers. The humans in those cases were Genni and Jefti, and Jefti visibly swelled with pride when he realized he was being sent out on his own like an adult, with Jak instead of a dyheli. With each hunter group went a dyheli to pack the results of the hunt back to the camp. The rest of the gryphons were sent out in pairs to look for really substantial prey.

Hallock organized the rest into two groups who would stay within earshot of the camp and each other. One group to bring in fodder for the dyheli and Jak, and one group to bring in as many thorn bushes as they could find. Those bushes would be the camp's first line of defense, outside the wards and shields Firesong would supply later.

When everyone had dispersed into the rain, he remained in the camp with a skeleton crew of hertasi, including Ayshen. He sighed. He was not looking forward to this.

At least it's not a cold rain. "Jylan?" he said, glancing around and trying to figure out which of the nearly identical hertasi, in their short, hooded rain-capes, was Jylan.

"Yes—what can I do to help?" chirped one, who stepped forward and looked up at him eagerly.

"We're going to make a barricade to keep things out physically," he told Jylan. "We need either small axes or very big brush-clearing knives." He glanced around at the others. "The rest of you can do whatever you think you need to do to help fortify the camp."

"Traps?" asked one, brightly. "We're very good at traps."

He shook his head. "Too easy for one of us to blunder into. But alarms, certainly. And barricades if you can build one."

"Defensive channeling traps into killboxes, then." The hertasi grinned.

Jylan trotted off and returned with both a hatchet and a brush-knife. Hallock took the hatchet and took Jylan with him to the perimeter of the camp. He picked out saplings about two thumbs broad, to cut and sharpen into long poles, which he drove into the ground around the perimeter using the hatchet as a hammer. Jylan couldn't reach the tops of the poles to pound them in, so she supplied him with poles while he hammered.

When the thorn bushes started coming in—cut exactly as he had specified, just above the ground—it took maneuvering by himself and three hertasi to get them "impaled" on the poles. But once they were there—and more importantly, once the branches started to mesh with each other—he reckoned this barrier would withstand at least a charge by a determined bull.

It was a long morning's work, but by the time he decided he could stop for a noon meal, half the perimeter had been set up with a thorn-bush barrier as tall as he was, and as thick as Vindaria was long.

It was absolutely dismal working in the rain, however, and he was very glad to stop and change into dry clothing. It wouldn't stay dry for long, of course, but at least he could take a brief rest and sit down in something that didn't squish.

Firesong finished creating the Gate inside the perimeter, and although Hallock couldn't read his expression behind his mask, his posture said he was as ready for a rest as the Valdemaran was. "We'd never have been able to do this so 'quietly' if it wasn't for Kel," the Adept said conversationally, as he sat down next to Hallock on a bit of tree trunk and accepted broiled meat and wild onions on flatbread from Ayshen. "He topped up the barge power stores last night from his Heartstone. Today I was able to tap them without exhausting myself or pulling local power, and he'll be able to top them up again once he's back."

Hallock wasn't sure why Firesong was telling him this, but he nodded anyway.

"Well," said Ayshen. "I just hope the hunters find another herd of wild pigs, or something equally bountiful. He and

Torandi will be ravenous when they return, if they haven't found anything on the way."

"Kel didn't seem any too pleased about what you sent him to do, Firesong," Hallock observed dispassionately. "Is he still afraid he's unstable?"

"Oh, he's unstable, but he has a *lot* of options now to mitigate that." Firesong rubbed the back of his neck fretfully. "I don't know why he didn't want to make the trip with Torandi. It's exactly the sort of thing his heroes would have done."

"Oh, *I* know why!" Ayshen chortled. "It's got nothing to do with the task, and everything to do with the company. He'd *much* rather have been sent out—alone!—with Vindaria!"

That made Firesong raise his head. "So the wind blows in that direction, does it?" He chuckled. "And what about the lady?"

"Keeping her mind on her job," Ayshen replied, with a disappointed sigh. "But if you cue us when things are safe enough—short-term, obviously—that they could be intimate, we can arrange things with Nightwind." Hallock was taken aback, but Firesong had no reaction at all.

Ayshen might have elaborated on that, but at that point the first of the foot-hunters came back with their small game, and the rest of the thorn-bush seekers arrived with their burdens. So Ayshen had to busy himself with the cooking and serving, and Hallock with building the defensive wall. Firesong was left beside the fire to stare into it and nurse his tea and his strength.

Just about dusk, as the last of every party but the Gate-builders returned, the Gate flared into activity for a moment, Torandi and Kel leapt through it, and the Gate shut down again. Firesong was there to see it, and jumped to his feet to join them.

"It's all like this as far as we went," Kel said, before Firesong could question him. "Trees, low hills, rain. So much rain! I was glad we could fly above it, mostly."

He flopped down under the canvas next to the fire and closed his eyes in concentration. Smoke began to rise from his feathers.

"Kel!" Hallock cried in alarm, and Kel cracked an eye.

"It's steam," he said shortly. "I am not setting myself on fire. I hope."

"Kel—" Firesong said, warningly. "That's almost not funny."

"Yes, it is funny," Kel retorted. The steam stopped rising from his feathers. "Funnier than rain and wet feathers."

"Did anyone see anything unusual today?" Firesong asked, ignoring him.

"Mebbe?" said Jefti, and Jak nodded his head. "It was . . . kinda like a plume of smoke, only stretched out sideways, 'stead of up and down. It didn't blow away, an' stayed together even with rain fallin' through it. I just saw it for a blink. Jak saw it twice."

:And Jak did not like it at all, thank you,: said the Companion. *:It felt as if it was sizing us up for dinner, and trying to decide if we would be worth the struggle.:*

"You're sure that wasn't your imagination?" Silverfox asked gently.

:Perhaps,: Jak admitted. *:Jefti didn't feel anything.:*

"To be sure, Jefti has never given us any indication that he has Gifts," Nightwind pointed out. "But—" She pinched the bridge of her nose between her fingers. "Jefti is small for his age, and hunger—I'm not blaming your mother, Jefti, but you spent most of your childhood hungry—hunger has led to delays in his growth. So he *could* come into Gifts on this trip."

"But he doesn't have them now," Hallock stated.

"No," she admitted. "Not that I can tell, at least."

"So we continue to be on our guard," Silverfox said, in a tone of voice that made it into a decree. "Let's—"

"Eat," Ayshen interrupted firmly. "You will be happy to know that the foot-hunters brought in more than enough to feed the birds for two days, and the winged hunters found enough in the way of a deer here and a boar there that everyone will go to bed stuffed and there will be plenty for breakfast."

Since the little hertasi was brandishing a very large carving knife and wore a bloodied apron, no one was inclined to argue with him. Firesong regained his depleted stores of energy thanks to Kelvren, food was shared out, and mage-lights under the canvas created a space that, while it was not cozy thanks to the pouring rain, was at least convivial. And the last thing that Firesong did before accepting a bowl of thick stew and flatbread was to put full shields and wards over the camp, just inside the ring of thorn bushes. Then he heard Genni and Hallock trying to stifle laughs.

"What?" he asked them, and Genni couldn't hold laughter back any longer.

Hallock adopted an expression of dark seriousness and replied as if his soul was being tortured, "It's Stew Day."

Before any explanation could be made, the tervardi began singing pleasantly, no louder than the rain was at its worst, and that was enough to warm everyone nearby in spirit.

Hallock felt exhausted. He'd been using some very different muscles than he did as a soldier. *And now I remember why I left the farm!* Genni had made a kind of back rest with some of the cut grass and a piece of canvas, and he leaned into it, drinking that gods-awful willowbark tea, with her leaning against his shoulder.

It was deceptively peaceful, with the rain coming down and pouring off the edge of the canvas wings in streams. Ayshen hadn't even needed to send anyone out for water; he'd done some tweaking of the edge of the canvas to direct most of the water into channels, and now their water barrels were full, the canvas troughs for the dyheli, kyree, and Jak were full, and he had water collected for kitchen cleanup. They would not just drink rainwater—every soldier knew that was disease waiting to happen—but they had ways of purifying it, and potable water was available in a white-striped barrel. Everyone was tired after a long day of hard work, and the only ones alert were the three night-watch Tayledras and their birds.

It should have been peaceful—as peaceful as last night had been. But it wasn't. Despite the fact that no one but Jefti and Jak had seen anything, people were on edge. The three of the night watch had put their birds up into the trees, equally spaced around the camp, and they themselves had donned rain-capes and stationed themselves where they could see past the fire. No one spoke much, and when they did, it was no more than a few words. Everyone ate quickly, and the hertasi cleaned up just as quickly, banking the pots of breakfast into the coals of the fire with heaped ashes.

The kyree made a heap plastered against the middle barge. The dyheli layered themselves about two deep on either side of their huddle. The gryphons bookended the dyheli, keeping their heads pointed toward the forest. About half the hertasi went to bed, along with about half the humans. Uglik stayed, sharpening his ax. Firesong dimmed the mage-lights with a wave of his hand, and the remaining humans and hertasi arranged themselves around and on top of the barges, weapons to hand. Hallock glanced over at Firesong, silently cursing the fact that with the mask, Firesong had no features to read. "Is—" he whispered.

"Shh," Firesong hushed him. "I'm trying to See through this blasted magical fog. And I can't see very far."

Hallock decided that now would be a good time to sharpen his sword.

Jefti crept in next to him, silent as a cautious rabbit. Hallock thought about ordering him into the barge, but if there *was* something out there, there was no telling which was safer, to be out here or in the barge.

The cursed rain made it impossible to hear anything out there. There could be an entire group of creatures sniffing around the thorn bushes and he wouldn't be able to hear them.

But that gave him an idea. He looked over at the huddle of kyree and picked a name at random. "Wirrell," he whispered, knowing that kyree ears were good enough to hear him over the rain. "Can you smell anything out there?"

All five heads came up. Three of the five got to their feet, split up, and trotted to the shield line, where they made a full circuit, sniffing the air. The remaining two jumped to the top of the barge and did the same up there.

:Nothing,: Wirrell said to all of them. *:At least, nothing that smells alive and active; just some faint, strange smells that could be almost anything.:*

They all came back to the banked fire, pausing just long enough and far enough away from the group to shake themselves vigorously.

"Our birds are not seeing anything, but they are hampered by the rain as well," came a voice from the top of the end barge.

"I do *not* want to use magic," Firesong growled.

"You're already using magic," Hallock pointed out reluctantly. "The wards and shield, the mage-lights . . . I'm guessing that Kel is basically one gryphon-shaped blob of magic."

"I heard that!" Kel hissed. "I am *not* a blob!"

One of the Iftel gryphons snickered.

"Hmm." Firesong pondered that a moment, then shook his head. "In for a grape, in for a bunch," he muttered. "At least if I do this and there's something out there, we'll be able to see it."

He got to his feet and made a couple of gestures with his hands. Kel got up and came to join him, standing right at his elbow, clearly illuminating the Adept. In the next moment, there wasn't any question about what Firesong was doing, because the thorn bushes all lit up as if someone had painted them with foxfire. Light—not bright enough to blind, but definitely bright enough to see—traced every single branch and twig.

They were encircled by what looked like an enchanted forest. Or, at least, an enchanted brushpile.

"There," said Firesong, sitting down rather heavily. "At least if anything is creeping around that barrier, we'll see it."

"Not if it's invisible!" Hallock protested.

But both Firesong and Kel barked a laugh. They sounded uncannily like each other. "Do you have any idea *how much power* it takes to become invisible?" Firesong demanded.

"Obviously not, or I wouldn't have said anything," Hallock muttered.

"If there was something out there invisible, anyone with Mage Gift, trained or untrained, would See it," Firesong went on. "The spell actually twists light, so it's got a signature that's bigger than what it's hiding. And even if someone was good enough to hide *that* signature, there would then be a hole to mage-sight where the invisible thing would be."

"Hurr," Kel nodded in agreement. "Especially with magic so diffuse now. There would be a sort of shadow in the magic-mist."

"Like that?" Jefti cried, jumping to his feet and pointing.

Hallock was *just* fast enough to see—something. But what he saw—well, he couldn't identify it.

It looked like a long plume of smoke, narrowing to a point at either end. It moved horizontally through the branches of the thorn bushes as if it was intangible, at about waist height. The smoke it was composed of seethed and churned as it moved. But at Jefti's cry, it froze for a moment, giving everyone who was looking in the right direction a good view of it, before it darted away into the darkness.

"I think that's what me and Jak saw," Jefti said, in a voice that trembled. "What *is* that thing?"

"I don't know," Firesong said, slowly and unhappily. "I've never seen nor heard of such a thing in my life."

Hallock spent the rest of the night awake. He didn't have to be, he supposed, but it felt like he *should* be. He wasn't the only one, of course; the gryphons, the dyheli, and the kyree all left sentries on guard, who lay among their fellows with their heads up and eyes and ears open. When the sentry yawned, he'd pick someone else to nudge awake, and the new sentry would take up the vigil.

Hallock didn't have anyone to relieve him, and neither did Firesong. So both of them stayed awake, much to Silverfox's disapproval, though he did bring them more hot tea to help them stay awake.

Of course Hallock had a hundred questions. *Is there more than one?* was one, and *Is it coming back?* was another, and a lot more after that.

But Firesong clearly did not know the answer, and asking questions like this was only going to frustrate him, possibly anger him, and certainly distract him. So Hallock sat on his questions as best he could.

But it was a very, very long night.

15

It was a very long night. Half of Kel's mind was going, *That thing, whatever it is, is probably all by itself, is just a kind of animal and we're overreacting.* The other half was going, *Hallock is right, this is the Pelagirs, we can't assume anything is innocent or alone.* Half of him just wanted to go to sleep. The other half of him wanted to go into protective overdrive.

The more time that passed, the more the second half won out.

The long night turned into morning, a morning that brought no relief. Kel was baffled and, frankly, furious. Gryphons tended to be very emotional creatures, and they tended to see things in terms of extremes. There was no proof that the thing was harmless, and therefore, in his mind, it must be dangerous. But he was also furious at himself, at his own senses, for letting him down. The thing, whatever it was, had been *right there* in front of him, but to magic senses, there had been nothing unusual at all. Not even a void where ambient magic should have been.

He was also furious because this thing violated all the rules! Gryphons *liked* rules, even when they violated them. Rules defined the world, and let you anticipate what you should do. Rules allowed the world to make sense. And this thing did not, in any way, make sense. It acted intelligent, at least as intelligent as a fox or a rabbit. But no one, not even Sharpsight, who had animal Mindspeech, had sensed thoughts of any kind. It was physically present. They could *see* it! And while he might have thought it was an illusion, there had been not a trace of someone or something that could cast an illusion. But there was another answer to that argument, that guaranteed it wasn't an illusion: there were enough mages here who could see right through even the strongest of illusions that it couldn't possibly have been any known kind of illusion.

But despite being something you could see, it had gone through the thorn branches as if they weren't there, or rather, the thorn branches had gone through *it* as if the creature was nothing more than the smoke it resembled. And there were no such things as living, corporeal creatures made of smoke, not in the records of the Tayledras, nor the records of White Gryphon. So it had to be magic. Didn't it? How could smoke be alive, unless it was a creature made mostly of magic, given form only by the smoke?

So it made sense that you'd be able to find it with mage-sight. But when anyone looked for it with mage-sight, there was nothing. The *vrondi* had been consulted, but they had nothing to say except a less-than-useless "It isn't from here." Aside from the ambient magic present everywhere, there was nothing, no magical creatures evident anywhere near the camp.

Even Serenshey and Jak said they had never seen or heard of anything like the creature, and even *they* couldn't detect it with anything other than their eyes. *This thing doesn't have a right to be here!* he fumed. *Everything about it is wrong!* And never mind that there were an awful lot of things in the Pelagirs that had no "right" to exist—at least they all followed the rules! If you could see them, they couldn't pass through things. If they were magic, they radiated that magic as an aura.

But underlying the anger—and the reason why he was

cultivating that anger—was a growing fear. He needed that anger to help squash the fear, and the growing realization that he had just encountered something for which he had absolutely no attack or defense. And they needed both! Just because it was intangible, that didn't mean it couldn't harm or kill them.

Were there more of them? He didn't know that, either, because there was no way of detecting them except to see them! He certainly wasn't going to go flying around out there in the rain—in which he was at a great disadvantage—and he wasn't going to let anyone send the Iftel gryphons, either.

By the time dawn arrived he was exhausted, angry, frightened, and confused. So confused. His head hurt. He felt all knotted up inside. This situation was intolerable! He wanted *answers*! But answers weren't forthcoming.

And it was worse that with the rain, everything out there was as dark as the inside of a cave, and no one wanted to put up any kind of light past the perimeter on the chance the light would attract the thing back, or worse, attract more of them. Firesong had made the shield glow slightly from the very top, so there was faint light being cast over the entire clearing. But that wasn't really helping, because the light glinted off the rain, making a kind of curtain that it was hard to see through.

Finally, the first light of dawn crept across the clearing. The entire group, both the exhausted who had been sleepless all night and the ones who had tried to rest and might or might not have gotten any sleep, all assembled under the canvas as that blasted rain continued to come down. As they attempted to revive themselves with food and tea, Silverfox recounted what had happened for those who had missed it.

"I'm baffled," Silverfox said flatly. "And so is everyone else who saw it."

"Treat it as hostile," Hallock advised bluntly, as Kel had known he would. "And assume there are more. I don't mean that you should attack it if it shows up again, but assume that *it* will attack *us*. Because from everything you all were talking about last night, right now we don't have a way to strike back at it. And frankly, I don't think even the tervardi song-weapon would touch it." He turned toward the two tervardi, who shook their heads. The male, Lyreren, spoke up. Even his speaking voice sounded like song. "Perhaps. Perhaps not. Perhaps we would only make it angry. Perhaps we would make it *stronger.* What if it thrives on sound?"

Hallock groaned at that, but Kel nodded. If they didn't know what the thing was, how could they guess what would make it stronger?

The hertasi had unearthed the kettles, distributed all of the soup, and quickly made flatbread. Once everyone had food, they began cleaning as they usually did. But instead of taking the cleaned kettles and griddles and starting the preparation for the next round of food, they stacked the implements next to the barges and moved all the consumables back into storage in the barges. To Kel's eyes, they looked uneasy at best and frightened at worst.

The leaden sky felt oppressive. People glumly drank soup from their bowls and ate flatbread as if it was wood and had no taste. No one spoke, not even in murmurs, once Silverfox had finished explaining last evening's incident. Only the rain drummed relentlessly down on the canvas and the barge tops. Not even birds sang.

Is that normal? Did that thing frighten them into silence? Do the birds know something we don't?

And beneath it all for *anyone* who knew their history was the unspoken question: What if this was some creature of Ma'ar's?

It wasn't impossible. After all, here they were, in the modern times, gryphons, hertasi, and tervardi, all creatures of Urtho's creation. Up until the most recent times, as far as the Valdemarans and the Tayledras had known, all three races had been lost in the mists of time. And no one in history or memory had been nearly as powerful as Ma'ar and Urtho, which meant any assumptions about them and their creations were subject to change at any moment.

True, it could be something a modern mage had created . . . but the problem with that idea was that, as far as anyone knew, you couldn't work such powerful magic without alerting other mages to the fact that you were doing it.

Maybe it was something left over from Falconsbane? Falconsbane had been the most powerful evil sorcerer anyone of this generation had encountered. The problem with that theory was that Mornelithe Falconsbane hadn't had the brains or the patience to make something like this smoke creature.

But Ma'ar? Definitely. And if these things didn't obey the rules of the natural world, there was no reason they couldn't be virtually immortal. If you are made of smoke, if you have no more physical presence than that, if you can't be harmed, why should you ever die?

And that just made things all the more perilous. Kel was cold, inside and out, a cold that had nothing to do with the temperature and everything to do with the uncertainty and the peril they'd stumbled into.

"I think we need to leave," Kel replied into the silence that followed Hallock's advice. "I know we are all tired, but I think we need to get the barges off the ground and get everybody and everything through that Gate and destroy it. No coming back for the anchor. I can feed an awful lot of power into the Gate when everyone is through, power that Firesong can turn in on the Gate itself to destroy it. I don't think we dare take the chance that this thing can follow us. We don't know what it wants, we don't know how it found us, and Hallock is right—we have to assume that it's hostile."

Sharpsight and Redlance, mages both, looked pained at that. So did Torandi and Daria. And Kel didn't blame them for being upset at his advice that they destroy the Gate; it was a tremendous waste of power and effort to just destroy a Gate anchor like that. He understood it, and he sympathized with it. If you weren't *him*, magic power was finite. It was hard to gather and hard to store, and if you didn't have a Heartstone attached to you the way he did, there was a hard limit as to how much you could sequester.

But that was dangerous thinking right now. It made you reluctant to destroy something that took a lot to make.

They can't let themselves fall for the sunk-cost fallacy. They can't! He clamped his beak shut and looked to Firesong; Firesong was the one they all looked to in matters of magic, just as they looked to Silverfox in matters of organization.

To Kel's brief relief, Firesong nodded wearily, big dark circles under his eyes visible despite the mask. "I don't like doing anything that wasteful, but I *also* do not think keeping an anchor intact is worth any lives. We Tayledras don't often come across something we haven't seen or don't understand, and this thing is both. What's worse, we're a small group, and very far away from the resources of a Vale. We don't have a choice here. Hallock is right, we *have* to treat this thing as hostile. That doesn't mean we should attack it; we absolutely should not do that. But we do have to get away from it, as far away and quickly as we can. This thing is potentially more dangerous than anything Falconsbane produced, and he very nearly destroyed an entire Vale."

Mostly people nodded, though the mages didn't look at all happy about this. The Ghost Cat fighters, however, looked baffled and rebellious. "But there's only one!" Rina shouted in frustration. "Why are you all so frightened of *one creature*?"

To Kel's surprise, Firesong didn't jump down her throat for being so obtuse. Maybe he was too tired. Or maybe he didn't have the energy to spare for anything but convincing people to pack up and go while they all still could. "Rina, we don't know what it is, we don't know what it can do—other than apparently it can move *through* things like the smoke it looks like, which is more than enough to frighten me. Weapons aren't going to have an effect on it. It hasn't attacked us yet, but what if it comes back and brings more like itself? I think Hallock is right, and I think Kelvren is right. We need to leave as soon as we can. Now, ideally. Before it's too late."

"Uh . . ." Hallock said in a strangled tone. Kel turned to look at Hallock, who had gone pale. "It's too late."

He turned to look behind himself, where Hallock was looking, and wished he could turn pale too. Right at the spot where the thing had been last night—it was back.

And it had brought friends.

A lot of friends.

He went not just cold all over, but icy, and his stomach

knotted. Every hackle on his neck rose involuntarily, and he felt his claws flexing into the dirt on their own. But not with the urge to attack. This time it was the urge to flee. Every instinct shrieked at him to get into the air and away, get up above the clouds and flee.

I think we can assume these things are hostile. Or at least hungry. Because they don't look intent on greeting strangers.

The things had arranged themselves in a group, flowing restlessly around and sometimes even through each other, like a bevy of otters did when they were confronting something on land. Or like *wyrsa*, evaluating possible prey. They slithered through the air, knotting and unraveling through each other, made all the more confusing by the rainfall. They stayed around hertasi-high from the ground without displacing a twig.

The things completely ignored the thorn branches, passing right through those as well. It appeared that they were uncertain what to do about the shields that Firesong had established around the camp. It was hard to tell how many of them there were—but more kept emerging from the forest, by ones and twos, to join the rest. Even though they flowed through each other, they kept their individual coherence: churning funnels of smoke, leading end rather pointed, trailing end fanned out a bit. They were a color something like the leaden underside of a thundercloud that is about to unleash a storm—and they looked a lot like stormcloud-stuff too. Roiling, tumbling in midair, thickening and thinning, but always keeping the pointed end toward the expedition. He didn't think it was his imagination that they seemed to exude an air of menace. They certainly kept their pointed ends "facing" the group huddled under the canvas wings, and as more of the creatures arrived, they increased their movement. Kel's mouth dried with fear, and his talons clenched again.

"How can we fight a thing made of smoke?" cried Parthan, one of the Iftel gryphons, a note of panic in his voice.

If you'd been a Silver Gryphon, you'd already know. You don't fight, you rescue!

"The shield seems to be keeping them out for now," Silverfox said loudly, his voice sounding firm and calm. Kel clung to that calm, even though he knew this was just Silverfox using his kestra'chern training to get everyone to listen to him and act rationally. As if you could be rational in the face of creatures that defied the laws of Nature! "But if they get through, if they attack . . . we can't face these things without knowing what they are and how to hold them off. They don't even present us with an obvious target or weakness. Firesong and Kelvren are right. We need to get out of here before they get tired of watching us and decide to do something." And when no one stirred, in a stern bark, he ordered, *"Now! Move!"*

That jolted everyone into action, and in the face of growing terror, thankfully they all reverted to their usual roles—except that those jobs were undertaken at speed.

The dyheli positioned themselves at their barges, waiting to be harnessed; the hertasi threw everything that had been set out—not much—back in the barges and rolled the canvas wings back into place. They didn't do a thorough job, but it would hold for a Gate-crossing. The bondbirds went to high perches near the Gate or on the tops of the barges, ready to fly through it the instant it opened; the kyree lined up at the Gate below them. The two tervardi joined the kyree at the Gate and the humans harnessed the dyheli in record time; every single dyheli was in harness, the better to get the barges moving as quickly as possible. Serenshey and Jak were the only two who didn't help pack up. Instead, they stationed themselves side by side between the expedition and the creatures, feet firmly planted, poses aggressive, saying with everything but words, *You'll have to get past us, and we are sent by gods.* And then, as if to prove that last, Jak glowed with an ethereal white light, and Serenshey literally lit up with flames—Kel didn't think they were illusory, either, since the rain hissed as it passed through them.

So that's why they're called "Firecats"—

"Kel!" Firesong shouted. "Gate power!"

Kel started, and shouted, "Gryphons! Through the Gate first, then help the dyheli pull!" The Iftel gryphons leapt to, bounding to the first barge and finding purchase to surge ahead when the shimmer was stable. Kelvren joined Firesong at the Gate, fanned his wings rapidly to collect magical energy, and uncorked his Heartstone for Firesong. Sharpsight, Redlance, and

Snowfire stepped to their respective barges and activated the floating spells in the barges.

And that was when the smoke creatures went wild.

They went into a complete frenzy, tangling around each other like hellish worms, smashing their front ends into the shield over and over and over again, and all in complete silence. Either their efforts at "pounding" on the shield were completely silent, or the hits were so quiet they couldn't be heard over the rain.

Kel *felt* those efforts, though; every hit on the shield vibrated all the ambient magical energy, which translated into something that he sensed in his *indusvenarum.* The result felt like fists pounding him all over, but from the inside. Or maybe like the pounding of great drums, or a bout of rolling thunder that shook everything, except without a single sound. That frightened him even more; that wasn't supposed to be possible! *Nothing* was supposed to affect the *indusvenarum* but magic!

The Gate opened with a visible shudder, the reflections in its surface pulsating instead of turning into a still, silvery pool, as if it, too, sensed those vibrations. Firesong cut corners, dropping the membrane between locations that equalized air pressure, so a mist of water droplets followed the stabilization through. *"GO!"* Firesong screamed, and the gryphons, kyree, and bondbirds all streamed through it. The gryphons turned once through and aided the dyheli in getting the barges in motion.

"Shield!" shouted Firesong, and those holding the line of protection turned as one, away from the Gate, to face down the creatures trying to break through.

The smoke creatures redoubled their efforts to get through the shield. The three Ghostcat warriors drew weapons and positioned themselves beside Jak and Serenshey, though what on earth they thought they were going to do, Kel couldn't imagine.

Then he got a surprise. And so did Uglik, Rina, and Tutack. Serenshey gathered himself, as if he was about to jump, and fire exploded out of him as he screamed a hellish feline battle-howl. That fire leapt from him to the Ghost Cat fighters' weapons—axe, sword, and sword—and engulfed the blades in flames. The blades glowed white hot, and flames danced across the surface, although the fighters didn't seem affected.

What—

"Ha!" Uglik shouted. "The gods are with us!"

And for a moment, Kel felt a surge of hope.

But it was short-lived.

Uglik might have felt that the gods were with them, but the smoke creatures didn't seem to care. If anything, they pounded harder against the shield, as the dyheli strained and heaved and got the first barge moving with the help of pushing humans.

It might have been "floating," but as had been explained in very great detail to everyone, that didn't make it weightless. All that weight was still there; it was just an arm's length off the ground and no longer subject to "drag" on the earth. In fact, these barges moved in the air exactly as they would have in the water, just with less inertia.

Kel closed his eyes, throttled down his fear, and poured more energy into Firesong, who had turned his attention to reinforcing the shields. It did occur to him to face the damned things directly while he was pumping his wings, to see if he could blow them away with the wind he was creating, but while the wind from his wingbeats plastered the thorn bushes against their posts, it didn't seem to touch the smoke creatures.

So they aren't really smoke. One more tactic that doesn't work. So he remained beside Firesong and trusted to the others to do their jobs and get themselves out of harm's way.

His feathers were soaked down to the skin. No flying away now, not while he was too sodden to get in the air. *At least I'm not in danger of catching on fire. For once.*

He took a quick look behind himself. The first barge was almost clear of the Gate, and Silverfox urged the dyheli and humans on guide-ropes to get the second one moving. The hertasi were of negligible weight, and they dashed around securing loose items and preventing losses atop the barges, rather than risk themselves on the ground. Firesong panted with the effort of holding the shield, hands thrust out in front of himself as if he was pushing something away.

The creatures were taking their toll on the shield, too. Now every time one of them hit the shield, there was a little explosion of what looked like cracks radiating out from the point of impact. The cracks vanished almost immediately, but Kel knew they were a sign the shield was weakening.

Snowfire left the barges and joined Firesong, adding his strength to the Adept's. Power coursed through Kelvren, not unlike it had when Treyvan had broken what he now knew had been a small, temporary Heartstone under him, restarting his *indusvenarum*. Then, he had transmuted power into light. Now he simply poured it into Firesong and hoped the Adept could take it.

Now the creatures started making a sound—a sort of high-pitched keening that sounded painfully like fingernails on a slate tile and made him clench his beak and flatten his ear-tufts and wish he had some wads of wax for his ears to shut the sound out. But of course, no one had anticipated the tervardi would have to sing—and the earplugs were all in the barges.

He glanced over his shoulder again. The second barge was halfway through, and the third had started moving. Silverfox had his shoulder up against the keel and was pushing along with Redlance and Icestorm. The other Hawkbrothers pushed the second barge into the Gate with every iota of their strength. Rina and Tutack looked where Kel was looking, glanced at their brother, and seemed to make up their minds about something. Rina handed Uglik her sword, so he now brandished two fiery weapons, Tutack sheathed his sword, and the two of them turned and ran to the last barge to add their strength to that of the Hawkbrothers.

Kel narrowed his focus to the power, his Heartstone, and how much energy he could get into Firesong without burning the mage up. He managed to compartmentalize everything but that—even though his terror screamed and whirled inside that mental compartment. His vision grayed around the edges, and every muscle and nerve seemed afire.

Uglik grinned and flourished the weapons, and opened his mouth—then clearly thought better of it and just glared at the creatures, as if his gaze alone could tear them to pieces.

Kel glanced back over his shoulder. The second barge was

through, and now as many people as could fit had their hands on the last, heaviest barge, and were straining to move it.

And then came the moment that Kel had been dreading and praying would not happen. But not all the prayers in the world could overcome the limits of poor, mortal flesh and bones.

Firesong made an odd little noise, his eyes rolled up into his head, and he collapsed.

Instantly, Kel transferred the energy he was building to Snowfire, before it could feed back on Firesong and hurt him. At the same time, Jak reared and pivoted on his hind legs and leapt toward Firesong, while Serenshey not only redoubled his flames, but . . . changed. Grew. Not quite horse-sized, but certainly the size of a mastiff. As Jak flung himself to his knees beside Firesong, Rina left the barge long enough to pull a limp Firesong over Jak's back, before running back to her place at the barge. Then the Companion lurched to his feet again and leapt through the Gate with Firesong's limp body.

The third barge was moving. But was it fast enough?

Fear tore through Kel, escaping his careful control, shaking him to his bones. Sweat and rain poured down Snowfire's face as he struggled to do what an Adept many times more powerful than he was had handled with difficulty. Kel considered for an instant that perhaps he should try to strengthen Firesong's shields directly himself—

But no. This was specialized magic, and on top of that, Firesong's personal variation on shield-making. Snowfire worked enough with Firesong to have learned how to handle Firesong's shields, but Kel certainly had not.

No, wait, I don't have to—I can just make my *shields and layer them behind Firesong's!*

Fanning his wings furiously to keep the power flowing, Kel left a channel open to Snowfire, then divided his attention— half on keeping the energy going, and the rest on doing what every mature mage he had ever known did as easily as breathing, because they had been practicing throwing up a shield from the time they began taking lessons. Shielding was always your first great Work, because shields not only kept you safe, they kept the world safe from you.

So Kel spun up his shields out of a single, tiny center of calm that never left him. Even though he was shaken *to* his core with fear, his core was unbreakable—it was the essence of what he thought of as himself, his identity and meaning. Kelvren was as terrified of losing control as he was of those monsters. Because there was no other option. Fail or—

He powered up his shield fully and expanded it until it just touched Firesong's. He poured energy into it. And just in time, as he *felt* Firesong's shield buckle, bulge inward, and then, miraculously, hold as his own shield came up to reinforce it.

"What's happening?" he gasped, tearing the ground with his talons, as if he was physically trying to hold the shield in place and push the shield with his forehead.

"The third barge is halfway through," said Snowfire through gritted teeth. "Kel, I can't hold this for much longer."

Kel tried to give him more power, but power wasn't the problem. Snowfire was exhausted—as tough as they all were, rain and cold sapped their durability, and his dear friend was very nearly about to pass out just as Firesong had.

Kelvren redoubled his efforts. *"Go!"* he urged. "Now! If my trondi'irn loses her mate, I might as well set myself on fire and have done with it."

Snowfire did not need to be told twice. "Good luck, Kel. See you soon." Kel heard him stumbling away.

"Kel! Uglik! Serenshey!" Hallock snapped, his voice making it an order. "Fighting retreat, back up! Closer to the Gate!"

For that, Kelvren had to open his eyes, but at least *now* he wasn't juggling keeping up his own shield with feeding another mage. Now he could concentrate every bit of power he had on holding his shield up against that relentless pounding. Still fanning his wings, sending sprays of water from the soaked feathers, he backed up one slow pace at a time, matching the rate at which Uglik and Serenshey were retreating. Serenshey uttered a snarl that sounded like the sky was tearing, but the smoke creatures didn't seem to notice. Uglik roared a wordless challenge, but they didn't seem to notice that, either.

Another glance backward showed the barge was three-quarters of the way through the Gate. But there was barely enough room for the barge, and none for the humans pushing it. There was going to be a crush in the Gate once the barge was through—

Kel paused until Serenshey was on his right and Uglik on his left. They matched each other, step by step, as Kel physically shuddered from the blows on the shield. It felt as if each of those hits was pummeling his heart.

Short of breath now, and lightheaded, he felt the shield start to give, as Hallock shouted just behind him. *"Now! Everyone! It's through! Go, go, go!"*

The barge was through!

Firesong's shield shattered. Kel's shield absorbed as much of the blow as it could, but it, too, split and peeled away like the skin of an overripe plum.

Kelvren staggered backward and almost fell. The smoke creatures surged across the clearing and stopped just short of Uglik, as if they weren't quite sure what to do now that they had breeched the barrier that had enraged them.

"Cat! Kel! *Go!*" Uglik bellowed, and laughed. "I hold! *GO!*"

Kel might have stayed anyway, but hands pulling at his wings could not be resisted, and he found himself stumbling across the Gate, backward, and finally falling under the rear of the last barge. From that vantage he watched as Serenshey whirled and leapt, soaring in a graceful arc over him and onto the barge.

Uglik turned to follow them.

And Kel saw the smoke creatures gather themselves like a giant wave to rear up over Uglik's head and crash down over him, silently obliterating him from view.

"Uglik!" Rina screamed.

The smoke creatures pulled their "heads" up again, boiling out by the dozen from the unmoving Uglik's nostrils and mouth. They reared up and began moving, slowly and deliberately, toward the Gate.

Kel lurched to his feet, fanned his wings furiously, and unleashed all the raw energy in his Heartstone straight into the Gate without any finesse at all, breaking its edges into warped eddies and overloading it.

With a crack like thunder, the Gate went down, cutting off one pointed tendril of "smoke," which hung in the air for a moment, then dissipated.

And Kel collapsed in the mud, Rina's howls of bereavement ringing in his ears.

16

Silverfox finally had a chance to sit down and breathe about a candlemark or two after Kelvren so dramatically put an end to the Gate, although the tasks before him were many, and all of them vital. Still. He knew that if he didn't take a moment now for himself, he would have nothing for others.

I feel like the man who fell into a privy and found exactly the tool he was looking for before he fell in, he thought, collapsing down onto the ground out of sight behind his barge, and dropping his weary head in his hands. The good—the "tool" he had needed before they all "fell into the privy"—was that the Gate anchor that Torandi and Kel had placed at their escape point was on an island in the middle of a swiftly flowing river, a salient little fact that neither of them had had mentioned. And yes, this meant they'd either have to build another pair of Gates to get off this island, or somehow cross a raging, swollen river with branches, bits of reedy bank, and entire trees careering by in it—but that was for tomorrow. Or the next day. Or a week from today. *If the gods need our help that quickly, they can send us a ferry boat.* He shook his head, took a deep breath, and steadied himself, taking a moment of comfort in the darkness behind his closed eyelids.

But this was important. Vitally important. The smoke creatures were leagues away now, so the only likely threats were purely physical beings. *Nothing material is going to get to us across that river. We're relatively safe. Maybe completely safe.* No one was going to count on that, of course, but it took some of the urgency out of the defensive preparations he'd set everyone to making as soon as they recovered from the Gate coming down.

And yes, he could have given everyone time to get over their shock and grief at losing a comrade. Could have, but didn't, because at the time no one had known they were on an island, and they had to be prepared for another attack.

Sometimes I am a heartless monster. Sometimes, that was what the job needed. Being a kestra'chern wasn't all comforting and counseling, pampering and inventive sex. *Sometimes you have to manipulate people in shock into doing things they don't think they can, because there's no other choice.*

He took stock of what he and Hallock had done since the Gate went down so spectacularly. Firesong was in bed, in their barge. Genni and Nightwind assured him that the Adept would recover; he was just exhausted and rather "bruised" internally from overexertion. For once, Firesong wasn't his primary concern; this wasn't Firesong's first time taking the brunt of an attack. *He'll recover. He won't bounce back immediately, but he'll recover.*

Kel, likewise, was resting. He had been set up in an improvised nest under the redeployed canvas wings of the first barge, and his heap of reeds and rugs had been thoroughly dried and warmed magically by Torandi and Daria before he fell into it. He was in the same shape as Firesong, physically. Mentally, well, he was in better shape than Firesong. A gryphon's pragmatism led him immediately to the mental state where he could mourn the loss of Uglik without blaming himself for it. He would rightfully put the blame where it belonged, on creatures that had attacked them for no obvious reason.

Firesong, well, he'd take all the blame on himself, without

saying a damned thing, and put on that half-amusing and half-arrogant attitude that covered virtually every iota of his real emotions. Silverfox would have to coax him through the whole process of coming to grips with the situation and realizing he was not personally at fault.

And that would be my job even if I hated him, rather than loving him. But because he loved Firesong, seeing him in emotional pain was hard to bear.

But I am a kestra'chern and this is what I do.

He let his mind go blank for a moment, going through an exercise of relaxing every muscle in his face, head, neck, and shoulders. A stolen moment of time he sorely needed right now.

Hallock has certainly taken as much on those broad shoulders as I could have asked. He had been the first to realize that since they were on an island, and it was going to take time to get back to the shore, they might as well take the rest that they had been planning to take before the smoke creatures moved in. And he was the first to realize that they were going to need food, and a lot of it, for the gryphons and the kyree. Potentially someone could use a spell to make the vegetation grow fast so the dyheli and Companion didn't overgraze this place, but gryphons couldn't eat leaves.

So at this moment, all the Iftel gryphons were now in the air, half of their attention on hunting, the other half scouring the landscape on both sides of the river for signs of any more of those smoke creatures. They didn't *like* flying below the clouds in the rain, but they were going to do it anyway, and he and Hallock could trust they would be thorough about it.

At Hallock's direction, the kyree had all stationed themselves in cover on the swollen banks to watch for trouble. The tervardi had climbed the tallest tree on the island and were standing lookout up there. The bondbirds were all out across the river hunting small game—except for his lammergeier, who was waiting on standby for a bondbird to take down something too big for it to carry.

The humans had more or less sorted themselves out into work groups without any orders from Silverfox or Hallock—Nightwind was with Rina and Tutack, and the rest were turning this abrupt landing spot into a properly fortified camp. Real defenses—no improvisation with thorn bushes this time, and every magical defense that the still-functioning mages could think of either had been put in place or would be completed soon. That included alarms, hertasi-rigged traps, and, of course, shields. Layered ones this time. Everyone who *could* make a shield had done so.

The hertasi were handling the living and comfort arrangements, and like the Hawkbrothers, had leapt into doing so without needing orders or directions.

The island itself was about the size of Errold's Grove, including all the gardens, and they were just about in the center of it, so there was plenty of cover in the way of trees and heavy brush along the rim to screen their presence from anything on the banks of the river. But just to make sure, Redlance had done something incredibly clever. *How,* Firesong had no idea, but the Hawkbrother mage had encircled the island with a ring of thick mist hanging in that brush and hovering just above the water, which managed to stay put despite the river rushing by under it. Maybe he'd done something with the endless rain. But between the rain and his mist, Firesong didn't think anything short of a bonfire would be visible from the riverbank. Which was a good thing, because they *needed* their fires right now, and at night, they would need the comforting presence of flame and mage-light. Once it got dark, hidden fears would come out to torment them all. Trauma did that.

Genni had made sure that there were no actual injuries to anyone from that mad dash through the Gate. Once she and Nightwind and Silverfox had made certain of that, both Genni and Nightwind went to be with Rina and Tutack. Nobody knew how they were handling things. Death and grief—how you dealt with those was as much a matter of culture as it was of emotion, and none of them knew enough of Ghost Cat culture to know what to expect.

I should be there too. But I need a moment.

The damn rain was just as bad here as it had been back at the ambush. He craved sun. He longed to lie flat on his back and soak up light and heat. He wanted, so desperately, to hear something besides the drumming of rain . . .

He wasn't even aware that he was cold until he realized he was shivering, and he hadn't done more than take his hands away from his eyes when Jylan whisked around the prow of the barge, draped a warmed blanket over his shoulders, and stood there with her hands clasped in front of her, waiting to hear if he needed anything.

He managed something like a smile. "It's all right, Jylan. I'll be fine. I just need a few moments more."

"Well, *Ayshen* says you need some of his hot tea with honey, and I'm not to leave you alone until you think you can go to Tutack and Rina." She jutted her chin aggressively, as a sign that she would not take no for an answer.

He nodded. *I suppose I should be grateful I didn't know Uglik all that well. I can do my job without my own feelings interfering.* There was no point in arguing with Jylan, anyway; hertasi could be terribly stubborn.

I wish Darian was here, he thought, as he got to his feet, blanket still draped over his shoulders. *He knows the Ghost Cat culture. I'm going to have to improvise.*

But hot tea first. *Set your mind to what only you can do. Everyone here is competent. Leave them alone until they show that they need your expertise, or have run out of ideas and need your guidance. Until then, let them handle things in their own way.*

A younger Silverfox would have been all over the place, asking if people were all right, and generally getting in the way. He wasn't that kestra'chern anymore, and that was all to the good.

Tea. Then sympathy. Then whatever else is needed. He pulled the blanket close and obediently followed Jylan to the cookfire.

Hallock supervised the defenses; not only would they have to serve against anything that came across the river, but he needed to improvise something against those smoke creatures. He'd had some ideas, once the initial shock wore off. The things were like air—well, what if harsh smells hurt them? It was a theory at least, and he put it into practice, working with Redlance to create magical "stink traps" that they planted just outside the shields. All Redlance had to do was trigger a trap, and the most noxious odor either of them could think of would be released. They'd both thought of poisonous gas, of course, but both had rejected the idea immediately. The problem with working with a gas was that it *wasn't* going to stay where you put it, and a breath of wind at the wrong moment could send it into their ranks.

And maybe fire would make them think twice, too—the creatures had seemed hesitant about going after Uglik until after Serenshey had left and Uglik had turned his back on them, so his flaming axe and sword were no longer in play. So Hallock had rounded up Serenshey, they'd had a consultation, and now there was a shallow moat around the camp, filled with dead plant material, material the Firecat had danced over and probably magicked. Serenshey swore he could fill it with flames higher than a man in the blink of an eye. *:They won't burn out or blow out, either,:* the Firecat had promised. If those things came again—and Hallock devoutly prayed that they would not—he liked to think they had better defenses now.

And there was no point in going down the fruitless road of *if only we'd had that when they showed up*, because no one had had time to think of such a thing, much less prepare it. Serenshey had made it very clear that he *needed* all that detritus in the moat to work his trick, so what were they supposed to have done, made all those preparations right under the "noses" of those smoke things? Probably the only thing Serenshey could have done in the heat of the moment was what he *had* done. Set himself on fire, set the weapons on fire.

So no second thoughts, and no recriminations, either. *We did our best, and lost Uglik anyway.*

He couldn't help the next thought that came—that compared to all of the fatally wounded Guardsmen back at Deedun, Uglik's death had been swift, and even unexpected. A soldier does think about death; it's part of the job, after all. *No one wants to die . . . but I have seen so much worse.*

He and the others had cut defensive stakes and buried them point-out toward the water. Hallock had also dug shallow pits and improvised quick man-traps with the help of a hertasi named Lervadis who was extremely adept at pits and snares, the two of them working at a speed he wouldn't have thought possible without that expert help. No point in stopping or trying to get dry; the rain in Deedun had been worse, and at least there wasn't much mud to deal with. By the time the bondbirds started coming back with kills of ducks, rabbits, and even geese, the entire perimeter of the new camp had been as fortified as possible without more people, more equipment, and the expertise of a military engineer. Serenshey and Jak trotted at his heels the entire time, very occasionally giving advice, but mostly just staying out of the way and lending a paw or hoof as needed.

Finally everything had been done that could be done. Especially in the rain. Which left Hallock wondering if he should go see to Rina and her brother or not. They'd left the work crew some time ago, and no one had objected. *Well, if they had, I'd have given the objector a piece of my mind.* But now, there was no excuse of "urgent work" to keep him from seeing to them. *I probably know them better than most of the Tayledras do . . . but I don't know them well. I wish the Owlknight was here.*

Nevertheless, he was the closest thing to a military leader that this group had; leaders saw to their underlings in all things, especially this. And he'd never shirked this terrible duty when he'd been in the Guard.

Dammit. I'd better go.

"Jak, where are the Ghost Cats?" he asked aloud.

The Companion pointed with his nose at the third barge. *:On the other side of that barge. The hertasi built them a kind of camp under the canvas. They don't seem to want to be inside the barges right now. But they had the hertasi bring all of Uglik's things out to them.:*

It's either some special rite or they're being pragmatic and splitting up their inheritance. "Pragmatic"— he could deal with that. A Ghost Cat rite—hopefully they wouldn't be offended if he had to ask what they wanted him to do for them. He nodded. "I'll go see if there is anything they need."

Jak and Serenshey stayed with him as he moved around the stern of the barge to see that the brother and sister had, indeed, set up a kind of camp under the canvas wing, their own little fire in a firepit, their bedrolls and belongings up against the side of the barge. They were both red-eyed, with faces blotchy from crying, although they were not weeping now. At the sound of foot- and hoof-falls, the two looked up.

"Your grief is mine," he said formally, stumbling a little over the unfamiliar syllables of the Ghost Cat tongue. "Your grief is shared by us all."

Rina gave him a watery smile. "Your accent is terrible," she replied in the same language. "But your words are true."

He squatted down on his heels beside her. Tutack remained silent, though his hands were busy. He and Rina seemed to be bundling up all of Uglik's possessions inside mats of woven reeds. "Is there anything I—or anyone else—can help you with?" he asked.

She hesitated, then a tear ran down her cheek, and she sniffed, struggling with her emotions.

"We send our brother on his way at sunset," said Tutack, hands still busy. "There will be a funeral bonfire; the hertasi are building it. Redlance has said he can hide it from view until it is no longer needed."

That must be that pyre-like thing they're making out of driftwood.

"We would like all to come," Tutack concluded simply. "He thought of all of you as good friends and comrades."

Hallock turned his head slightly and looked meaningfully at Jak and Serenshey.

:We'll see to it,: the Firecat promised. *:Everyone will be there.:*

"We would like you, god-cat, to light the fire, and give us the blessing of your god," added Tutack. He shrugged. "Our gods will know him, but it is fit that *your* god should give him honor too."

:I absolutely will do that.: Serenshey nodded his head vigorously.

Hallock was used to professional soldiers and how they handled a death among their comrades. But this was new to him. Uglik had been their brother, and yes, they were mournful and grieving, but this wasn't the utter emotional collapse he had anticipated. And he wasn't sure *why.* "Is there anything I can do to help?" he asked finally.

Tutack nodded at the crude reed mats. "Wrap for burning. When warrior dies, we burn his things, to set him free."

He nodded, although that seemed a bit wasteful. Still, it was a good bit better than having people squabbling over who was going to get what. He'd seen that a time or two in the Guard, and it was always ugly and depressing and demoralizing. Maybe this way was better.

So he picked up a couple of reed mats and some grass cord, and wrapped up an old leather belt-pouch, adding it to the pile. There was something inside, but he didn't bother to look to see what was in it. It was all to go in the fire, so what did it matter what was inside?

The work was curiously soothing. And after a moment of silence, the siblings resumed a conversation that his arrival had evidently interrupted.

"You remember when he made the sheath too tight on this knife?" Tutack said as he wrapped up a well-worn eating dagger.

"And he came to the cookfire and could not get it out?" Rina managed a thread of a chuckle. "And he danced around like a shaman with his cloak on fire trying to free it, while the rest of us were eating and watching him? Because he was too stubborn to cut the sinews he'd sewn so carefully?"

"Ah! Ah! Ah!" Tutack replied, bouncing in place a little, holding the knife over his head as if he was trying to free it. "That was all he could say. Ah! Ah! Ah!"

"Oh, and this shirt—what's left of it." Tenderly, she rolled a much-abused linen shirt into a mat. "I kept trying to tell him he looked like a crazy old man living in a cave because it had so many patches and worn spots, but he kept saying, 'There's plenty wear in it still!'"

There were more such stories, and gradually it dawned on Hallock that *this* was how they were mourning their dead. Remembering good, touching, or funny stories about him as they prepared his possessions for the fire. He didn't have anything to say, but they took care of that for him, starting a new story with every object he picked up to wrap. Funny stories only a sibling could have or tell.

And in the end, when the task was done, and they thanked

him for his help . . . somehow, he felt better too. He certainly felt that now he knew enough about Uglik to properly mourn him.

And that wasn't a bad thing.

What would you call this, I wonder, Kelvren thought as he joined everyone else around the pyre. It wasn't a funeral; there was no body. *A memorial, I suppose.* He was glad of it. He had not known Uglik well, but he *had* known the Ghost Cat warrior well enough to want to mourn him properly.

Dusk had fallen, but as yet the fire was unlit, and no one had put up any mage-lights. The siblings put a heap of mat-wrapped bundles on the unlit pyre, as the rest of the party straggled in to stand in the rain around the stack of wet wood. And that was when something occurred to Kel that made him blink in alarm.

"Isn't this fire going to show across the river?" he whispered to Hallock, who stood next to him. "Is that a good idea?"

"Actually, that was what I wanted a word with you about," said Redlance, on his other side. "I have a spell I would like you to power—if you can?"

Redlance proceeded to try to explain this variation on a shielding spell he had constructed, which would essentially turn a shield into a reflective surface, so that no light would escape. Kel's head was not up to the detailed explanations, so he just cut Redlance off and asked, "Does this need as much as a Gate?"

"No, no! It's trivial, really, not even as much as a real shield. You see—"

"Poke me with your elbow when you start, and I'll feed you power," Kel told him. "Otherwise . . . I think we should be quiet now."

Redlance is a fine fellow, but he turns "yes" and "no" into speeches. I don't want to hear speeches right now.

He tried to count heads in the gloom. It looked as if everyone was here. *I hope we're not going to be standing here all night in the rain . . . ugh, that sounds selfish and ungenerous, but . . . I really hope we're not.*

But then he felt a familiar tingle . . . a shield spell, yet another one, but he could tell from the taste and smell of the magic that it wasn't a defensive one. It was a barrier. Someone other than Redlance—

—oh, it's Daria! He made her out sitting up on her haunches, making passes in the air in front of her with her talons.

And a moment later—she had put up a different shield, one that was like a Vale shield, that at least for now kept the rain off. The muffled sighs of relief at that were matched by the murmurs of approval as Redlance put up his reflective shield. At that, Torandi sent several globes of mage-light to hover over the group.

That was when Tutack stepped forward. "Rina and me . . . we want you to know, there is no blame. And Uglik was so *happy* the shaman chose us for this! You cannot know. He thought sometimes his time of being a warrior was past, that it was too late for him to do great things. That there would be no chance for a song to be made about him. And then you say, come go on this journey! Nothing made him happier. He stood his ground and showed the gods he is a hero. Now, he will have songs made for him. In the lore of our people, he will live forever, his name always known. He is worthy to join the great heroes of Ghost Cat! There can be no better ending."

"'I do not want to die old and unremembered.' That was what he said to us, often," Rina added. "'I do not want to die a sad, withered stick in a bed! I want to die like a hero!' And he did."

Kel blinked in the mage-light. *I don't want to die a sad, withered stick, either! Actually I don't want to die at all . . . but I understand perfectly how he felt. All of us will die, and the stories of what could be will become stories of what was.*

The siblings stepped back and nodded to Serenshey. The Firecat leapt up onto the pyre and instantly set the whole thing ablaze, sizzling and steaming wet wood and all. Not just plain old flames, either; the flames leaping around Serenshey were every color, red, blue, green, yellow, purple—was this Serenshey's doing? Was it a peculiarity of the driftwood? Was it Uglik's belongings, or something his siblings had put in those bundles?

Was it even a sign that Uglik's own gods approved?

The tervardi began a wordless song, a curious mix of dirge and celebration; Rina and Tutack closed their eyes and clasped each other, swaying slightly to the music. Kel let it all wash over him: the smell of the fire, the crackle and hiss, the rain on the shield, the light reflected from the fire down on all of them from the shining shield above, making multiple shadows. *Should I be sad or happy?* He didn't know. So he just let whatever emotions he had rise to the surface, flood through him, and then fade. So many emotions . . . the only one he didn't let himself experience fully was rage. Rage at those unnatural creatures that had taken his friend. It wasn't fair. They'd done *nothing* to warrant being attacked like that! In fact, they'd gone out of their way to avoid a fight! If anything deserved the blame for Uglik's death, *they* did! Murderous bastards!

But this wasn't the time for rage, so he continued to feed Redlance's and Daria's spells and let the rage subside, submerging once again in that pool of *feelings* that at this point were almost as mixed as they had been when he'd returned to the Vale.

The Firecat remained coiled within the flames until every scrap that was burnable had been reduced to ashes. Only then did Serenshey allow the flames to die, and as he stepped out of the pyre, no longer on fire, the tervardi ended their song.

"Let his memory live forever," said Rina and Tutack together.

"Let his memory live forever," they all replied in a chorus.

Torandi dimmed her mage-lights down to just enough for people to see their way back to their beds. That was when Kel dropped the feed to Redlance and Daria's spells; the reflective surface faded away and the rain came down on them again.

Somehow, that seemed fitting too, that they all go their ways, thinking about Uglik, while the sky wept for them.

In the morning, the hertasi had already cleared the least hint of the pyre away; Kel had to assume that this was how the siblings wanted it, because they didn't seem surprised or upset. Breakfast was plentiful, hot, and hearty, but no one seemed inclined to talk. Rina and Tutack were the first to speak up, volunteering to stand watch on the riverbanks, and Hallock accepted without making the objections Kel thought he would—

But then, how do I know how other peoples do these things? He was familiar with the Tayledras way of death, of course, and it was not that dissimilar to that of the Kaled'a'in of White Gryphon. But he was just now beginning to understand how little he knew of the others on this journey.

I need to change that, he thought, collecting the stripped carcasses from beneath the bondbirds' perches, dropping them in a basket, and taking the basket to where Silverfox's lammergeier waited for him. The bird's eyes pinned in pleasure at the sight of the feast of bones. Lammergeiers mostly ate bone, not flesh—another thing Kel found fascinating and incomprehensible. How on earth did the bird get *any* food out of bone?

But he did, and thrived, apparently.

Kel found himself staggering a little after delivering his parcel, and decided that unless Silverfox or Hallock found something for him to do, he was going to go lie down in his nice dry nest again. He discovered when he got there that Ayshen—or Jylan—had lined the cup of bracken and grass with some old blankets, which made the nest look so inviting he just about fell into it.

And, of course, just when he started to doze off, Serenshey, Jak, Silverfox, Hallock, and Firesong came around the prow of the barge, obviously looking for him, because there was no one else back here.

"Hurrr," he said with resignation. "What is it you need to power?" The breastplate and the stone were practically a part of him now, except when Nightwind and Jefti took it off to groom him, or he slept. But even then, he kept one foot on it at all times. Just in case.

Because I am not a Firecat, and I do not wish to burst into flames, nor do I want to sleep in the rain to keep from bursting into flames.

"At the moment, nothing," sighed Firesong, and sat right down in the nest with him, putting his back up against Kel's belly and reaching under his neck-feathers to scratch him. Silverfox joined his mate; Hallock perched awkwardly on the edge of the nest, declining to join the pile; Serenshey perched velvet-pawed on Kel's rump and began soundlessly purring. Or he thought it was soundless, anyway. It was hard to tell over the rain. Jak was the only one standing, but he looked comfortable enough.

Actually, he looks the best-rested of us all.

It was rather nice, being here, saying nothing, listening to the rain while they were warm and dry.

It seemed as if the others wanted to say something, but were unsure of how to start. So before the silence grew too unbearable, Kel himself broke it.

"The others tell me that there is no sign of the smoke demons for as far as they have been able to fly," he said. "I was afraid that since one of them got a bit of itself across the Gate, they would be able to trace that bit here—but there is no sign of them. So *either* they can't move any faster than a human can walk, *or* they don't care about us now that we are gone from their territory. I think," he added. He shook his head. There were things that had occurred to him that he didn't want to talk about to just anyone. Nightwind, perhaps, Silverfox definitely, but . . . that "hostile" behavior from the smoke demons could very well have been simple territorial reactions from non-sapient animals that were top predators and had perceived them as different sorts of predators moving in on their territory. They were no more to "blame" for Uglik's death than a bear is "to blame" for killing a human. The bear is just obeying his instincts. That might have been the case with the smoke demons.

But Kel knew very well that such an explanation would not fare well with his comrades right now. They wanted an enemy; they wanted something to blame. *So I had better talk to Silverfox about this later, when we are alone.*

"The bondbirds haven't seen a thing, either," said Firesong. "But there is a concern. Have things worsened at our destination? Is there any indication that we *can't* rest a day or two?" He looked from Serenshey to Jak and back.

:*Well . . . gods don't talk to me. Not directly,:* Jak replied, and leveled his own gaze on Serenshey.

:*I am not* much *different from Jak, but . . . .* : Serenshey paused, and flattened his ears. :*They don't exactly "talk." I just know things. I know that conditions have not changed much at our ultimate destination. I know those conditions are deteriorating, but not rapidly. I know that we can probably afford to take some time for ourselves before we move on, especially if you elect to do so via a Gate.:*

"That's a start, at least," Silverfox observed. "When did you 'know' all this?"

Serenshey lifted his ears. *:I didn't know these things before those smoke demons appeared. I did just before they attacked us, but at that point, we were rather busy.:*

Hallock looked as if he wanted to say something—probably a demand about why the gods weren't more forthcoming. Silverfox forestalled that.

"We're fortunate they are giving us that much," the kestra'chern said, looking weary and melancholy. "This is very close to what we would be able to see for ourselves, if we had the best scryer in the Vales, *and* Kel could fully fill his Heartstone, *and* the scryer could take power from Kel. It's skating very near to violating free will."

"Hurrr. But you're right," Kel agreed. "And they aren't literally asking us to do anything, just giving us information." He swiveled his head to stare at the Firecat. "But I feel you have not told us everything yet."

The Firecat flattened his ears again. *:I was waiting to see if you would decide to rest. Yes, I know one more thing. There is a place, right on the coast, and on the way, that they want us to go to first. But I don't know why. I only know it doesn't have anything to do directly with our quest, but they seem to feel it's important.:*

Jak shook his head and neck. *:It might be an opportunity . . . . :*

"Sometimes they can be infuriating," Firesong muttered. "I was perfectly content before gods directly entered my life."

Serenshey flattened his ears again and looked miserable.

"No, you weren't," Silverfox chided. "You were restless and looking for a reason to enter the Valdemaran internal conflicts. I know. We discussed it often enough." Kel knew the look that Silverfox gave his partner. It wasn't an out-and-out accusation, but it certainly was a reminder that the kestra'chern had a remarkable memory.

"Well?" said Hallock. "Destrier in the room. Do we follow the gods' 'advice' and look into this location they want us to go to or not?"

Kelvren answered. "What I was taught about gods: the gods don't give solutions, they give mysteries to solve for rewards to be earned. The gods choose who they think will grow from the challenge. The names we revere are those who were enlightened by their journey. The journey is what teaches." Kel twitched his left ear. "We are on a journey."

:The place they want us to go is on the way,: Serenshey prompted. And then—Kel could scarcely believe his eyes when the Firecat did this—somehow Serenshey widened his eyes so that they seemed to take up half of his face, dilated his pupils, and made his eyes glisten as if he was about to shed tears. Kel knew that look. Gryphlet-begging.

I cannot believe you are doing that, he thought to the Firecat, knowing that Serenshey would pick it up.

:Hush.:

"It's bound to be something that will complicate our task," Firesong grumbled.

"But what if it leads to something we need?" asked Silverfox reasonably.

Serenshey's lower lip quivered.

You're shameless.

:I use the weapons I have.:

Firesong glanced at the Firecat and threw up his hands. "All right. We'll do it. Rest for a few days first, and then we'll do it. It's on the way, so we won't have to make some sort of excuse for a detour." But he glared through his mask at Serenshey. "This had better be worth it."

Shameless, Kel repeated—secretly envious. If only *he* could make his eyes big and tearful! There had been so many times that would have been useful!

:Effective,: the Firecat replied smugly. *:And don't hate me because I'm beautiful.:*

:There is another thing to mention,: Jak mindspoke to everyone there.

:I felt something that has stayed with me about the smoke creatures. I would like your thoughts on this,: he continued. *:I think we could not detect them because they were very weak,*

and not "all there," if that makes sense. As in, not entirely in . . . reality. What came to my mind was minnows on a streambank trying to stay hidden under leaves.:

"Why think they were weak?" Snowfire asked. "They hit hard at the shields."

:We looked at them as attacking the shield, but what if they were trying to escape it? If they were very weak, undetectability could have been a survival instinct, and as I recall, the Mage of Silence was called that because he left no excess energies to be detected.: Jak gazed at the mages in turn, and then the Companion just flatly dropped his opinion on them all.

:I believe they were, inasmuch as they were here at all, of demonic origin. It is possible they did not even intend to kill Uglik, but were attempting a possession.:

Firesong's eyes shone a little more wetly despite the simple mask he wore. "There's some merit to that. A lower other-planar could appear to be smoke, because in our world it might not even have what we would term a physical body. They saw the concern we all had for each other, so possessing someone would be a reasonable way to take refuge, since we wouldn't likely strike at their victim."

Snowfire said out loud, looking up and around the drizzling perimeter, what everybody there would have been just fine with not hearing at all. "Makes me wonder how much of this haze isn't actually rain."

Hisses and groans from more than one person snapped back, then there were more when Firesong added, "Weatherwork on this scale is not unknown to history. 'How do you hide a red fish,' the saying goes, 'except in a pond of red fish?'"

:They were the color of storm clouds. That's an unpleasant thought in pretty much every possible way, thanks,: Jak interjected. *:An invasion nobody sees coming because everyone wants to stay inside from the rain. But if the center of Evendim is what the Gods believe it may be, the normal layering of planes could be splintering and lower beings could reach higher. The inverse, too—there could be divine beings caught up in it.:*

Mercifully, the Companion did not say what a few of them immediately thought: *If extraplanar divine beings couldn't escape it, in theory, neither could gods.*

Kel could scarcely believe how much better he felt after a single candlemark up in the sky above the ever-present clouds, with the sunrise at his back and a beautiful blue sky overhead. He'd really gotten the hang of energy manipulation now, and it was immensely satisfying to feel every wingbeat feeding that hungry, depleted Heartstone on his breastplate. The last three days had been melancholy, to say the least. Between everyone mourning for Uglik, their lack of answers about the smoke creatures, and the damned rain, what should have been a good, solid rest had been marred by depression and gloom.

But *now*, with Nightwind's blessing, he was finally back in the sky where he belonged. And to his right flew the beauteous Daria . . .

Unfortunately, to his left flew the . . . well, Torandi was anything but homely, but Torandi was not the gryphon who made his heart beat faster, and he would certainly rather have been alone up here with Daria.

I might even manage to scrape up enough courage to say something to her.

Alas. Torandi knew how to make Gates. *He* did not. And the only reason why he was going along and not Daria and Torandi on their own was because of that faintly glowing rock set above his keel.

All three of them had teleson headsets, so at least they didn't have to shout at each other.

Hurrr. I can control who I speak to. This might not be so bad after all.

:*It's glorious up here,*: said Daria through the teleson, and with the words came her feelings—complicated, of course. She was a complex creature. Melancholy she was deliberately trying to cast out of her mind, relief, and the usual euphoria every gryphon felt in the air.

:*I think the rain was about to make me go mad,*: agreed Torandi. :*If it hadn't been for Jefti, I think I would be growing mold by now!*: She cast an anxious glance at her own back and tail. :*I'm not growing mold, am I?*:

:You're fine, Tiny,: Daria replied, with—finally!—a twinkle of good humor in her eyes. *:Jefti is very good and very thorough.:*

:Wait—: said Kel. *:Tiny?:*

Torandi groaned aloud, loud enough Kel heard her across the distance between them.

It was a perfectly logical nickname, seeing as Torandi was the biggest of the Iftel gryphons along on this journey, and probably bigger than most gryphons in all of Iftel.

:It's a perfectly nice nickname, Tiny,: Daria pointed out, her wingbeats strong and sure. *:No one means anything by it, except as a contrast to how strong and capable you are. You're the only one of us who's a district champion, you know.:*

:I keep feeling as if someone is teasing me,: came the surprisingly meek admission.

:No one is, Tiny,: Daria replied, and added fiercely, *:and if they ever do, I'll . . . I'll set Genni on them!:*

That was a potent threat. Sweet, even-tempered Genni turned out to have a sharp and fiery tongue when she chose to use it.

:I think it's a great pet name,: Kel decided to chime in. *:It's easy to shout, it's fun and funny, and anyone who doesn't know you will know immediately that you have a fine sense of humor when they hear it.:*

:Really?: Despite the wind, Torandi's ear-tufts pricked up. *:You really think so?:*

:I do,: he told her firmly. *:The Valdemarans have stories about a huge fighter named Tiny. They're all about how clever he was, how he could do practically anything, and how he always came to the aid of people in trouble. That's the first thing they'll think of when they hear the name.:* At Daria's grateful—and encouraging—look, he waxed eloquent on the subject, telling some of the shorter tales, and he felt very grateful that he'd paid attention when the Owlknight had shared those tales around the fire.

When he was done with the second story, he took a long, sideways look at Torandi and saw that she'd lost that slightly hunched look she so often had, as if she had been trying to hide her size. In fact, she was all stretched out in flight, not hiding anything.

:That was very kind,: Daria whispered into his mind.

:She's a good person. She must have been teased as a gryphlet.: That was the only conclusion he could come to.

:She doesn't open up about much,: Daria admitted. *:That's more than I have ever heard from her about herself before.:*

: I thought you all knew each other,: he said, surprised.

:We never met except in the games before we formed up to fly to k'Valdemar,: she confessed. *:I still don't know why I was made leader, but they all seem fine with it, so . . . . :* He sensed a mental shrug. *:At least I haven't led them into any disasters yet.:*

:We should include her in this conversation before she thinks we're leaving her out,: he cautioned, and won another approving glance from her. He felt positively euphoric—buoyed by far more than magic.

For the rest of the morning, they all discussed what life had been like in Iftel. Or, to be more on point, *he* listened, and *they* talked, and more than once Daria marveled privately to him how astonished she was that "Tiny" had suddenly begun talking about herself—and how clever he'd been to draw her out. The intoxicating praise—from *her!*—might have made him forget to listen to Torandi, except that he got the distinct impression that this was very important to her, and that she had never had anyone she could call a friend to open up to before.

He fairly quickly got the sense of why that was so. She had ambitious parents, and her size and power—which had manifested early, even before she fledged—made her a natural for the games. So they encouraged competitive thinking and discouraged friendships, and kept her so busy in practice and training that even when a potential friendship cropped up, it fell by the wayside under the relentless drive of training.

She only ran out of things to say when they were about to dive down below the clouds to hunt for something to eat. But by that time, he could tell that under that reserved, even shy exterior was a warm and caring creature who had genuinely blossomed into being over the course of the last few candlemarks.

They were lucky to find what looked like a sort of wild bull almost as soon as they broke through into the rain—although it had a twisted mass of what looked like distorted antlers or tree branches instead of horns. Without even thinking about it, they fell into line—Kel in front, Daria in the middle, Tiny bringing up the rear. Even a gryphon couldn't take down a beast of this size without a fight. And no raptor wants a fight. Wings are fragile things, and gryphon bones were all too prone to breakage. But, of course, gryphons had worked out how to compensate long ago, in Urtho's day.

They cast up as far as they could go and still be able to see. Then Kel did a wingover, pulled his wings in tight, and fell like a stone. The protective membrane closed over his eyes, and he thrust his fisted foreclaws out in front of him, adjusting his flight path with tiny movements of his wings. The air screamed past him and his vision narrowed to a single spot where the beast's shoulders met the spine. He'd have to time this so that he hit while the bull had his head down; those antlers could perforate him just as easily as arrows.

With a jolt that shuddered through every bone, he *hit* the beast, using the recoil of the strike to power back up into the sky and out of the way. As he headed back up, he heard the bull grunt and stumble, and then heard the hard *smack* as Daria hit its hindquarters, staggering it further. As he clawed his way back up into the leaden sky, he saw Tiny flash past him, a great, black thunderbolt hurtling out of the heavens, and heard the crunch of breaking bones as she scored her own hit in the middle of the spine. He gave her a heartbeat, still climbing, then did another wingover and hurtled back down again. The bull was down, its hindquarters splayed out behind it, bellowing. Red bloodlust flooded him, and he powered in for his second hit, this time aiming for the forequarters and coming in at an angle, to knock it over. Again, that satisfying impact, and the long climb up until he looked back and saw that Daria had the hindquarters in all four feet, with Tiny latched onto the face, wrestling it to the ground.

This time he came in with his forefeet unfisted and ready for the finishing strike. He hit for the third and final time, talons sinking deeply into the chest, notched beak striking at that spot where the neck joined the spine, which Tiny was so cooperatively exposing to his beak by backwinging with her foreclaws buried in the bull's face.

And that was all except for the eating.

"Good hunt!" he caroled, feeling his mouth full of fresh, hot, intoxicating blood, and his hackles rising with the excitement of the kill. "Good lunch," said Tiny, already picking out the tongue.

:Good job,: said Daria in his mind, warmth and approval washing over him like honeywater.

That was more intoxicating than the kill.

Under ordinary circumstances, they'd have eaten until their crops were full, then taken a nap. But they had a destination to reach, one Serenshey had planted as firmly into their minds as if they were compass needles and the destination was true north. The plan was to survey the spot, then if there was nothing obviously ominous going on, make a Gate, and bring in the rest.

Plans are nice to have. This plan went straight to the nine hells as they dropped down below the clouds just as that compass in their heads said, "We're here."

Because . . . no matter what any of them had anticipated, it wasn't *this*.

Below them were two human armies—small armies, but armies nevertheless—locked in a siege.

On the shore of the lake was what looked like part of a fort or castle. *Part* of one, because on the side where its feet were in the waters of the lake, there was a semicircular cut, as clean as if it had been done by a giant knife, that looked as if it had cleaved off about a quarter of the place. The cut edges were sharp, and the interior of the fort was exposed to the weather there. The inhabitants had made a token effort at covering the large holes, but given up.

:Change-Circle, it looks like. They could be from anywhere.:

Up on the intact walls were the besieged. Humans, wearing clothing and armor that Kel did not recognize. At all. The besieged all wore uniforms: charcoal surcoats with a wolf head outlined in red on them, uniform armor—but on closer examination, neither the uniforms nor the soldiers were in particularly good shape.

:They look like fighters who haven't been resupplied in a very long time,: Tiny observed.

:They do,: he agreed, and turned his attention to the besiegers. They did not seem to be particularly well armed—they certainly had no siege weapons—but were definitely not daunted by that fact.

:What the actual hell?: spluttered Tiny, as all three of them turned their flight into a hover, and climbed up just a bit so that the lowered cloud base's virga hid them somewhat.

:I . . . don't know,: said Kel, as baffled as she was. *:I didn't know there were even people out here, much less fortified soldiers.:*

The architecture was absolutely unfamiliar, but looked as if the fortress might have been constructed by magic. Partially, at least. And yet, no one inside the fortress was using magic at all. On the top of the highest tower was a flag with the snarling mask of a crowned wolf.

:Is that emblem anything you recognize?: he asked the other two. *:It's not Valdemaran.:*

:Does Valdemar even claim this part of Evendim?: asked Daria. *:Are these people allies?:*

They looked like nothing so much as a ragtag army of hunters, fishers, rangers, and farmers. Which was probably *exactly* what they were.

:Sketi!: swore Daria. *:The ones outside can't do the ones inside much harm—but they have them pinned down. The ones inside probably don't have anything to spare, so they aren't even bothering to shoot at them and waste weapons. They're probably hoping the ones outside will go away.:*

:They've got lake water and probably fish,: Kel observed. *:They aren't going to run out of food or water. But they don't dare get complacent, or someone could sneak inside and let the others in. We need height.:*

The three of them powered up through the clouds again, and hovered facing each other.

:The gods directed us here for a reason,: said Tiny into the silence.

"So they did," Kel said out loud, gazing downward. Faint and far below, he heard the sounds of shouting and sporadic, fruitless combat. "And I doubt it was to look at this, shrug, and be on our way. First, we'll quietly look for setups and traps from up high. Daria, you report in by teleson and brief the menagerie. Then, I think we should handle the situation diplomatically."

"Diplomatically?" asked Daria.

"Heavens yes, diplomatically," Kelvren gape-grinned. "—namely, I shine brighter, we dive upon them screaming, and we scatter them all."

"It should stop the fighting," Tiny agreed with a hint of a grin. "We follow you, Wingleader."

Gods, you can pick me as a Chosen One all you want, but if I'm going to die some heroic death on some miserable quest, I'm going to do it as myself, and I'm not known for solving problems unnoticed!

TO BE CONTINUED